Deep South

Nevada Barr

Deep South

WHEELER
PUBLISHING, INC.
ROCKLAND, MA

★ AN AMERICAN COMPANY ★

Published in Large Print by arrangement with G.P. Putnam's Sons,
a member of Penguin Putnam Inc. in the United States and Canada.

Wheeler Large Print Book Series.

Set in 16 pt Plantin.

Library of Congress Cataloging-in-Publication Data

Barr, Nevada.
    Deep South / Nevada Barr.
        p. (large print) cm.(Wheeler large print book series)
    ISBN 1-56895-867-6 (hardcover)
    1. Pigeon, Anna (Fictitious character)—Fiction. 2. Natchez Trace
Parkway—Fiction. 3. Women park rangers—Fiction. 4. Mississippi—
Fiction. 5. Large type books. I. Title. II. Series

[PS3552.A73184 D42   2000b]
813'.54—dc21
                                                              00-025381
                                                                  CIP

For
DOMINICK,
who has a genius
for taking care
of things

• • •

Because, as I was working on this book, they inspired me personally or professionally and took the time to answer all my questions, I am grateful to Hollis Morris, Terry Winschel, David Christianson, Steve Stilwell, James G. McGraw and the Mississippi Department of Fish and Wildlife.

1

The Rambler's headlights caught a scrap of paper nailed to a tree, a handwritten sign: REPENT. Darkness swallowed it, and Anna was left with the feeling she was surely on the road to perdition. God knew it was dark enough. Her high beams clawed the grass on the left side of the narrow lane, plowing a furrow so green it looked unnatural: neon green, acid green.

At least it's in color, she thought sourly. Everything she knew—or imagined she did—about Mississippi had been gleaned from grainy black-and-white television footage of the civil rights movement in the sixties.

Her worldly goods in a U-Haul, a shrieking Piedmont in a cat carrier, and an ever-faithful, if occasionally disgusting, hound drooling on her thigh, she'd driven straight through from Mesa Verde National Park in Colorado. Twenty-two hours. And she'd done it the old-fashioned way: without drugs. Caffeine didn't count, and six hours north of Dallas–Fort Worth it had quit having any appreciable effect. A marathon drive seemed the lesser of two evils if one was to be a night in a motel room with Piedmont.

Anna poked a finger through the wire door of the carrier buckled into the passenger side of the bench seat. Taco, the black lab she'd inherited after she'd killed her dear friend and Taco's mistress, insisted on squashing his seventy-five pounds between her and the cat. Wearily celebrating this sign of life from his mistress, he brushed his rubbery tail over her wrist where she reached across him. Piedmont wouldn't even bat at her finger. Eyes squeezed shut, he howled.

"We're almost there," she said plaintively. "Don't you want to rest your throat?" Taco's tail thumped. Piedmont yowled.

"Suit yourself." Anna rolled down the window in the hope that the wind would ameliorate the wailings. Her eyes burned. It was too early and too late. It was pitch dark. It was April 15. She hadn't paid her income taxes, and she was in Mississippi. Only a thin and cracking veneer of civilization kept her from taking up Piedmont's lament.

Another hand-printed sign, this one riddled with bullet holes, flashed out of the night: REPENT. FINAL WARNING. Ten miles back, Anna'd started having a bad feeling. Now it was worse. This was not at all what she'd expected the fast track to look like.

At forty-five, she'd finally heeded the ticking of her bureaucratic clock. The appeal of living out her dotage on a GS-9 field ranger's salary had begun to wane. Time had come to plan for the day she'd no longer want to sleep on the ground, swing a pulaski or argue with violent unsavory types. Promotions were not easily had in the National Park Service. First, one had to scour the pink sheets for a job opening one GS level above that currently held. Then one had to have, or fake, the KSAs—knowledge, skills and abilities—called for in the desired position. What made a good ranger at Kenai Fiords might be totally useless at Appomattox Courthouse.

That done, one sent in the application. The government then fiddled around in mysterious ways until half the hopefuls died of old age or went on to other jobs. With luck and timing, an offer eventually came.

Given the givens, it wasn't a good career move to turn a promotion down.

For Anna, the call had come from the Deep South; she had been offered a GS-11 district ranger position in the Port Gibson District of the Natchez Trace Parkway, the section that ran from Jackson to Natchez, Mississippi, ninety miles through the heart of one of the poorest counties in one of the poorest states in the union.

"You'll feel better when the sun rises," she promised herself. "Surely the sun rises even in Mississippi." Taco slathered reassurance on her kneecap.

The air through the window was cool but lacked bite. There'd been snow on the ground when she'd driven down off the mesa above Cortez. Heady scents she didn't recognize swept the cab free of the odor of stale McDonald's fries and cat vomit, but they could not clear the head as the scent of pine or rain on the desert did. Smell was primal. This stirred an image deep in Anna's subconscious. Hunched over the wheel, eyes on the writing black strip of asphalt, she waited as it struggled up through the layers of fatigue: Dorothy's poppy field, Toto, the lion, the girl, tumbling down in a narcotic dream on the outskirts of the Emerald City.

Flashes of green, unfurling black; the road had a mystic sameness that was stultifying. Maybe she should have stayed on Interstate 20 to Clinton, Mississippi, as the chief ranger had instructed, instead of following the tortuous directions for a shortcut she'd gotten when she called one of her soon-to-be field rangers in Port Gibson, a jovial fellow who called himself Randy.

She rolled the window up. With the sandman already in hot pursuit, the last thing she needed was a hypnotic. The road coiled around on itself in a hairpin turn. She was going too fast. The U-Haul bore down on the Rambler, then drifted, slewing the car to the right. She slammed on the brakes. Taco slid to the floor, clawing her leg in a last bid for stability.

The tail was wagging the dog both inside the Rambler and out. Anna stopped fighting the wheel and steered into the skid as if she was on black ice. In the hectic instant that followed, headlights slicing impossible colors from the night, animal caterwauling foretelling the end of the world, it crossed her mind that black ice was a thing of the past. What would replace it in the way of hazard and adventure, she had yet to find out.

Soundlessly, painlessly, the trailer left the road, dragging the rear wheels of the Rambler with it. The coupled vehicles came to a stop with nary a bump. The car tilted unpleasantly and the red-lighted trailer in the rearview mirror held a drunken pose.

"Everybody okay?" Anna's voice shook, and she was glad only furry and therefore sympathetic ears were there to hear. Taco scrabbled up onto the seat, his untrimmed nails doing the aging vinyl no favors. The engine had died. Anna rested her head on the steering wheel. Regardless of the situation, it was good to be still. Silence, after twenty hours of radio, trucks, tapes and the high-pitched whine of rubber on pavement, hit like the first drink on an empty stomach.

Something warm and wet and vile penetrated her ear, and she remembered she was a dog owner. "Two seconds," she begged.

The tongue insinuated itself into her armpit and Anna gave up. Having pulled the leash from under the cat carrier, she fought the usual battle to overcome the dog's joy at a potential walk long enough to clip it to his collar. "Me first," she insisted, and in a fit of good manners Taco waited till she'd slid clear and stood on shaky legs before bounding out the driver's door. The leash slipped from fingers numbed from too long clutching the wheel, and the black lab loped off toward the taillights of the U-Haul.

"Don't go chasing 'coons or whatever the hell dogs chase down here," she muttered. Outside the car, silence was shattered. Stunned by the sheer magnitude of sound, Anna leaned on the door and listened. A chorus, a choir, a nation of frogs sang from darkness curtained close by trees. Wide and deep, the sound chortled, chirped, tickled underfoot, overhead, from every direction. Basso profundo croaks, rough and guttural, were buoyed up by a cacophony of lesser notes.

Big croaks.

Big damn frogs, she thought. Or alligators. She'd seen live free-range alligators a few times when she'd been on assignment on Cumberland Island off the coast of Georgia, but they hadn't uttered a word in her presence. Without questioning it, she'd come away with the idea gators were dumb. Maybe that wasn't so. Mississippi had a whole new natural history she would have to learn.

Big frogs, she decided for the moment, and turned to follow in Taco's paw prints, to see what, if any, damage had been done. One step and she was on her butt, amazed and outraged but otherwise unhurt.

Wet grass lay over earth as liquid and slippery as warm Jell-O. A good surface to take a fall on. A foul surface to try and pull an overloaded trailer off of—or out of, as the case might be.

Using the door, she pulled herself upright. Slipping and grabbing in a parody of a vintage Jerry Lewis routine, she made it around the Rambler's hood and onto the asphalt. By the glare of the headlights she saw she was covered from the elbows down in caramel-colored

6

liquid. Taco padded up next to her, grinning in idiotic doggie bliss. "We're not in the desert anymore, Taco," she said, paraphrasing Dorothy's observation as she wrenched open the passenger door to fumble under the seat for a towel and a flashlight.

Piedmont had not stopped complaining. "You're getting on my very last nerve," she warned the cat. He remained unimpressed.

Flashlight and towel in hand, she closed the door on the vocalization of feline suffering. The towel smelled of things that had once been on the inside of the cat and the flashlight beam was only slightly less brown than the Mississippi mud, but it would suffice.

Taco danced like a puppy, though Anna figured him to be five or six at least, then dashed off to the rear of the little caravan, yipping and grumbling as if the news was not good for humans but extremely entertaining for dogs.

Anna followed, her moccasins squishing at each step. Frog music, velvet darkness, and perfumed air all closed around her, and the walk of twenty feet took on a bizarre timelessness. She'd been too long on the road.

At the back of the U-Haul she stopped and stared. Taco leapt about with glee. "This can't be right," she said stupidly.

Caught in the demon eyes of the taillights, a tree, a foot in diameter where it leaned against the bumper, lay over the trailer. Leafy boughs embraced the orange and white metal. Roots poked out of the ground, bent and angry as arthritic hands where the tree had been uprooted by the force of impact. Except there'd been no impact. Nothing but a gentle slide into this oblivion of sentient and predatory plant materials. Had she dozed off behind the wheel? She didn't think so, but it wasn't out of the realm of possibility.

Too dull with lack of sleep to do much else, she played her pathetic light over the rear of the trailer. No scrapes, no dents, therefore no impact. Unfortunately, logic had no effect on the tree. A locust, she guessed, twenty-five or thirty feet tall, had her vehicles in a death grip. If she pulled forward, the half-buried roots would act as an anchor and she'd dig herself into the slime. Back, and she'd ram the topmost branches down over the trailer and onto the roof of the car.

"Well, shit," she confided in the dog and stood a moment hoping things would be different. She could unhitch the trailer, drive off and return for it—or what was left of it—with the proper equipment. Assuming the Natchez Trace Parkway had the proper equipment.

Home was in that white and orange box, and a deep unsettling unease boiled up at the thought of leaving it on the side of a strange road in a strange land.

"Shit," she reiterated.

Headlights rounded the corner from the direction she'd come. In proper rabbit fashion, she stared into them. Engine noise and the metallic complaint of a derelict truck momentarily quieted the frogs. Fear, not even a thought before, sprang full-blown from some Yankee collective unconscious. James Dickey and Burt Reynolds, Ned Beatty and "squeal like a pig." *Mississippi Burning,* "I have a dream," and chain gangs in the cotton fields. Nothing personal, nothing even secondhand, yet Anna had been fed a nightmare of the rednecked heart of Dixie.

The truck clattered to a stop and was instantly enveloped by a toxic cloud of exhaust. A plaid-covered elbow hung out the window. Above it, thrust into the pale beam of Anna's flash, was a round face under a beat-up ball cap.

"Lady, you look to be in a whole heap of hurt." The voice was thick, its owner talking around a wad of chewing tobacco the size of a golf ball. Anna blinked, waiting to see if her leg was being pulled or if he really talked that way.

"A whole heap of hurt," he repeated.

"Looks like it," she said. Taco wandered back to resume guard dog duties. He leaned against her muddy thigh, beating a canine welcome on the bumper with his tail.

"Hunter?" the moon-pie face asked.

"Tourist," Anna said, too tired to explain about jobs and transfers.

The man's pale face split into a laugh, and Anna saw, or thought she saw, streaks of tobacco juice on his teeth. Her old Colt .357 wheel gun was in the glove box. The thought comforted her as she edged in that direction.

"What did she say, Baby?" a creaking voice cut through the one-sided hilarity.

"Tourist."

Ancient laughter crackled from the window, leaking around the man Anna could see.

"Not you," the driver managed, merriment abated. "Your dog. He a huntin' dog?"

"Tourist," Anna said again.

"What, Baby?"

"Tourist dog, Daddy." Much laughter. Anna found herself inclined to join in but was afraid it would turn to hysteria.

"Get on with it, Baby. I got work to do," came a querulous creaking from the invisible passenger.

The round face sobered, the wad of chaw was more securely stowed in the cheek and "Baby" got down to business. "Daddy wants to know if y'all need a hand."

By way of reply, Anna shined her failing light on the locust clutching her trailer. The verdant embrace struck her funny bone, comedy of the absurd, and she laughed. "You wouldn't happen to have a chainsaw on you, would you?"

Baby looked at her as if she was a half-wit, then said to the darkness beyond his shoulder: "Lady needs a chainsaw, Daddy."

Anna heard the unhappy notes of bent metal being forced as the passenger door of the truck opened and closed. Taco whined and wagged. Rummaging noises emanated from the pickup bed, then an old man—somewhere between sixty and biblical—came around the end of the truck, red brake lights lending his shrunken cheeks and spindly silhouette a devilish cast. In his left hand was a chainsaw with a twenty-four-inch blade.

"Whatcher need cut? That tree you backed on into?"

Anna was torn between efficiency and dignity. Efficiency lost. "I didn't back into it," she defended herself. "I slid ever so gently into the muck and, bingo, a tree was on me." Pretty lame, but it was the best she could do.

Daddy nodded. "Loess," he said, leaving her no wiser. "Melts like sugar. Back the truck up, Baby. You're just an accident waitin' to happen. Back on up now," he admonished sharply as the younger man started to pull ahead. "Git those headlights on the job. You know that."

Gears grated, meshed, and the truck lumbered back till the headlights threw the old man, the trailer and the tree into garish relief. Anna shaded her eyes from the glare and watched as, one-handed, Daddy drop-started the chainsaw and began cutting away the locust, smaller branches first. Baby, out of the truck so Anna could see the full effect, wore overalls over a plaid shirt and heavy boots. As his father cut, he swamped, hauling away the branches, some as big around as Anna's leg. Early on she offered to help but was warned she'd get herself "all over poison ivy" and so desisted. Pride was one thing, poison ivy quite another. She'd had it once and counted herself among the sadder but wiser girls.

The tree was quickly disposed of. A chain, appearing from the same rubble of necessities that had camouflaged the chainsaw, was hooked around the Rambler's bumper, and fifteen minutes start to finish, Baby and Daddy had Anna back on the road. Sensing an offer of money would be offensive, she thanked them by volunteering information about herself, an intellectual breaking of bread to indicate trust and a willingness to share as they had shared their time and strength with her.

"I got a job on the Natchez Trace," she told them after giving her name. "I'm working for the Park Service there in Port Gibson." She was careful not to mention she was in law enforcement. Either it made people feel as if they had to take a stand on the gender issue or it inspired them to relate every story they'd ever heard where a cop had done somebody dirt. Still, Baby and Daddy looked blank.

"The Trace there by Port Gibson?" Daddy said at last. The old man leaned on the front of the pickup, the single working headlight shining past his scrawny red-cotton-covered chest in a rural depiction of the sacred heart painting that hung in the hall of Mercy High, where Anna had attended boarding school. "Then what're you doing in these parts beside getting yourself stuck?"

It was Anna's turn to look blank. "Going to the Natchez Trace?" she asked hopefully.

"Nope," Daddy said.

"You're going nowhere," Baby added helpfully.

"That's pretty much it," Daddy confirmed.

"One of the rangers I talked to on the phone said this was a shortcut."

Daddy and Baby found that inordinately amusing. Gratitude was fading, but Anna hadn't the energy to replace it with anything but pathos so she maintained her good cheer. At least outwardly.

"What you want is Highway 27 out of Vicksburg," Baby told her, and aimed a stream of tobacco juice politely the other way. "Where you're at starts out as Old Black Road and ends up as nothing down on the river. It's where me and Daddy goes fishing. All's down there is moccasins and mosquitoes."

"I must have read the directions wrong," Anna said.

"Way wrong. Those old boys was having a joke and you were it," Daddy said succinctly. "You go on a couple miles'n you'll see a place to turn around. Then you go back the way you come twenty miles or so. You'll find 27. If you hit the interstate, you gone too far."

Anna thanked them again. They waited. She waited. Then she realized they weren't leaving till they saw her safe in her car and on her way. Having loaded Taco, she climbed in the Rambler and pulled back into the twisted night.

Daddy was right. She'd not misread the directions; she'd followed them to the letter. One of her rangers wasn't anxious to see her arrive: Randy Thigpen, a GS-9 field ranger she'd be supervising. Anna wished she could dredge up some surprise at the petty betrayal, but she was too old and too cynical. Nobody involved in the hiring process had come right

13

out and said anything, and in these days of rampant litigation and gender skirmishes, they
wouldn't dare. But she'd heard the subtext in
the pauses. There'd never been a female law
enforcement ranger on the far southern end
of the Trace, and there'd never been a female
district ranger in any of the nine districts and
four hundred fifty–odd miles of the parkway.
It had been unofficially deemed too conser-
vative, too old-fashioned for such an alarming
development. From the gossip she'd picked
up, she was hired because she was known to
have an "edge." She was an experiment. They
would find if she was to be a cat among the
pigeons or the other way around. The "old-
fashioned" people, Anna had thought, would
be the park visitors. Randy Thigpen evidently
wanted to carry the experiment into the office.

Jump off that bridge when you come to it, she
told herself.

When she finally found her way onto the
Trace, the sun was rising and, with it,
her spirits. The vague picture she'd formed
in her mind of a bleak and dusty place, over-
farmed by sharecroppers, dotted with shacks
and broken-down vehicles, was shattered in
a rainbow brilliance of flowers. "Wake up,
Taco," she said, nudging the beast with her
knee. "Hang your head out the window or something useful. The place looks like it's been decorated for a wedding."

The Natchez Trace Parkway, a two-lane

road slated, when finished, to run from Nashville, Tennessee, to Natchez, Mississippi, had been the brainchild of the Ladies' Garden Clubs in the south. Besides preserving a unique part of the nation's past, the federal government had believed, building the Trace would pump money, jobs and a paved road into what was then a depressed area. Unlike other scenic parkways, such as the Blue Ridge in Tennessee or the John D. Rockefeller Jr. National Parkway in Wyoming, the Trace would not be based on spectacular scenery but would conserve the natural and agricultural history of Mississippi. It would follow and, where possible, preserve the original trail made through the swamps and forest by Kentucks, entrepreneurs out of what would become Kentucky, walking back home after rafting goods down the Mississippi to be sold at the port in Natchez, and by the outlaws who preyed upon them, by Indians trading and warring and finally by soldiers of the Union Army bent on bringing the South to heel.

This morning no ghost of the violence remained. Mile after mile, the road dipped and turned gracefully through rich fields, grassy meadows, shoulders bright in red clover, daffodils, pink joe-pye weed and a water-blue flower Anna didn't recognize. Dogwood blossoms winked through the spring woods. Purple wisteria, vines covering trees fifty feet high, draped to the ground. Red bud trees added crimson patches. Carolina jasmine, yellow falls of blooms, draped over fences and downed timber. And there was no traffic. Not a single car coming or going. The dreamlike quality of the frog-song-filled night was carrying over into the light of day.

After twelve miles of garden beauty, the road widened briefly into four lanes and Anna saw the sign for Rocky Springs Campground.

"We're home," she told the animals. The words sounded mocking, though she'd not meant them that way. Mississippi was about as far from home as Anna had ever been, if not in miles, then in mind.

2

Anna had no trouble finding her house. Randy Thigpen hadn't been the only one to give directions. Those of the Chief Ranger John Brown Brown, based in Tupelo, Mississippi, one hundred sixty miles north of Anna's district, had provided her with a more accurate map: first left after the campground entrance, first house on the right. To Anna's tired mind, it sounded not unlike the directions to Never-Never Land.

As promised, on the right was the park employee housing, two identical brick structures. Long and low, built in the sixties with windowed fronts, they resembled dwarf school buildings with carports on one end. In the carport of house number one was a white patrol vehicle sporting a green stripe. According to John B. Brown, the keys to the car, the house and the ranger station would be atop the left front tire. Rangers the country over were so trusting it was touching. Anna hoped that would never change. That the members of the law enforcement agency boasting the highest average level of education also retained the highest level of faith in their fellows was an indication that things were not as bad as the media would like people to believe.

Anna parked, emancipated Taco, muttered unheeded promises of succor to the ever-shrieking Piedmont and went to retrieve the keys to her new kingdom.

Wooden beams, painted barn red, cramped the low-roofed carport. Every joist, junction, every crevice where wall met upright or upright met roof, was festooned in ragged gray-white. Spiderwebs, an immodest, immoderate, unseemly number of spiderwebs. Keeping her hands and arms close to her sides lest she inadvertently brush one of her neighbors onto her person, Anna peered into the web-fogged shadows. Seven of the nearer webs held visible arachnids. One of these was the size of a half dollar, bigger if one looked with the imagination and not the eyes. Anna had come to terms with tarantulas of the Southwest. She'd made every effort to refrain from annoying them. In turn, they stayed sedately on the ground. They did not drape one's corners and drop down one's collar.

Soon, in this carport, there would be serious

harassing of wildlife. Having looked carefully before thrusting her hand into the dark, she snatched the keys off the tire and fled back to the sunshine.

She was of two minds about the house. Compared with her tower in Mesa Verde, it was completely lacking in charm. Compared with much of the Park Service housing she'd inhabited, it was palatial. The floors were hardwood, the walls white. There was a bath and a half that appeared clean and serviceable, and three small bedrooms, only two of which she was allowed to use. Exhibiting true governmental logic, the NPS was willing to rent her the house at the slightly lower monthly rate of a two-bedroom if she promised she wouldn't use bedroom number three. "Not even for storage?" she'd asked. Not even for storage.

Those not employed by the parks might well ask: "Who would know?" Those with the Park Service for any length of time knew everybody knew everything all the time. Information traveled by gossip, innuendo and osmosis. Probably employees in the Port Gibson District—if not everybody from Natchez to Nashville—already knew more about her than a shrink or a priest would discover in a lifetime of revelations.

The kitchen was small, with white counters and a linoleum floor. Over the sink was a view of her backyard, a weedy mowed area divided by a broken clothesline and hemmed in on two sides by an apparently impenetrable wall of trees. Not the tidy spaced trees of the water-poor Four Corners area, forests where one could stroll and contemplate the serenity of nature, but a tangled, creeping wall of life. Trees tied to vines laced with Spanish moss formed a curtain of green that dropped to the ground. There shrubs took over. Her backyard looked not so much planted as carved from the forest and mightily defended by repeated mowing. Just such country had the original Trace been cut through with no tools but those a man could carry on his back.

Had Anna been rested, she might have been more appreciative of the feat. As it was, she just wondered why they hadn't stayed home.

On the counter by the refrigerator was a five-gallon plastic container of store-bought water with a Post-it note on it. She plucked the note off and held it to the light. Somewhere between forty-three and forty-five her eyesight had changed. That, or small print had grown insidiously smaller. "The water here won't kill you but that's all the good I can say of it. Welcome to the Trace. Steve Stilwell, DR, Ridgeland."

Stilwell. Anna remembered one of the many new names thrust upon her over the telephone during the past month. Stilwell was the district ranger in Ridgeland, the section of the Natchez Trace north of Jackson, about forty-five miles from Rocky Springs. He'd been doing double duty, his district and hers, till she came on board. Steve Stilwell, she was prepared to like. She had spent too many years in the desert not to feel kindly toward a man offering water.

A flicker of movement caught her eye, and she wandered into the dining area, the short leg of the L-shaped living room. On the wall near the windows overlooking the backyard were two shockingly green lizards, each about four inches long. For a moment she watched them doing push-ups as they gauged the distance between themselves and this intruder.

"If you eat spiders, I'll ask Piedmont to let you live," she told them. Saying the cat's name reminded her of her responsibilities.

Having rescued the orange tiger cat from the Rambler, she established him, a litter box, food and water in one of the back bedrooms, opened the door of his carrier and shut the door to the hall to let him acclimatize to one small piece of real estate at a time.

Back in the living room, she realized she had no idea where she was headed. The U-Haul had her goods locked up and, at the moment, she hadn't the energy for moving heavy objects. Food would help but she had none and no clear idea of where to get any. It was too early to call anybody and ask questions, too late to go to bed.

Taco bounded into the house, mud on his jaws where he'd tried to enjoy a little Mississippi cuisine. Anna decided to walk the dog. A tedious task but one that always made her feel appreciated. With Taco carefully leashed—she didn't want to be seen breaking the rules her first day on the job—she walked down the short spur where park housing was located. The day was already warm and promising to get warmer. Soft, damp air swaddled and embraced. She missed the light, indifferent caresses of the mountain breezes. To her right was the Trace. Just off of it, introducing the campground area, was a small brick building with public toilets and, she had been told, a tiny office for the Rocky Springs ranger. Because of budget cuts, two of the ranger positions in the Port Gibson District would go unfilled. The Rocky Springs office would stand empty. Anna's office at District Headquarters was twenty miles south in Port Gibson. Taco pulled left toward where the road forked. The campground was to her right. What lay straight ahead, she had no idea.

Too tired for adventures, she chose the known and allowed Taco to drag her toward the campground. Rocky Springs camp was laid out in a loop. A narrow asphalt road circled a wooded area several acres in size. Camps, cleared areas with grills and picnic tables, were located on both sides of the road. Two brick buildings housing toilets sufficed for the amenities. Though it was a medium-sized campground by NPS standards, the crush of trees made it seem intimate.

Incognito in civilian clothes, with Taco for cover, she wandered unimpeded past several RVs and a small silver Airstream with Michigan plates. Campers were quiet at this hour, sleeping or standing dully over wood fires, coffee cups clasped reverently to their bosoms. Birds, none of which Anna could see in the dense canopy of leaves, discussed the situation in hushed warblings.

Feeling mildly rebellious, she let Taco off his leash. The retriever loped off to a deserted campsite and stuck his nose into something she was sure she didn't want to know about. Enjoying not being in an automobile and not traveling any faster than the gods intended, she continued on without him.

Near the top of the loop, where the road curved to the left out of sight, a strange phenomenon brought her out of the meditative state. In the shallow ditch between the asphalt and the inner circle of camps, a stone the size of a large cantaloupe was moving, bobbing as if it rode atop bubbling waters.

Thinking again about the need to get her eyes examined, she left the road for the mowed grass on the shoulder. After she had walked a yard or two, the rock resolved itself into a more logical form. An armadillo was rooting through the grass in search of its breakfast. No stranger to these marvelous beasts, Anna had seen them in the Guadalupe Mountains, where she'd been a ranger once upon a time. On the Trans Pecos, they were fondly referred to as "Texas speed bumps." There was even a joke made for them: Why did the chicken cross the road? To show the armadillo it could be done. The animals were slow, nearsighted and not terribly bright. The armor they'd evolved to defend themselves was no match for speeding automobiles. This was the first one Anna could remember seeing alive.

An old alcoholic's tale said that, when sneaked up on and surprised, the compact little animals would jump straight up, sometimes as much as four feet. Having nothing she'd rather do, Anna decided to see if it was true.

Careful to stay directly behind the creature and to walk as quietly as she could—she'd never heard armadillos had keen hearing but this one had big ears and nature was usually a practical mother—she followed the animal in its single-minded grub seeking. Inch by inch she closed the gap between them. Her plan was simple, as befitted the gravity of the experiment and the fogged state of her intellect. When close enough, she would lunge, grab its tail, yell "Jump!" and see if it complied.

There is no Zen like the Zen of the predator. The world narrowed to the scope of the hunt. By the time the armadillo had nosed and waddled around the bend in the road, Anna was less than thirty-six inches from the gray and scaly hindquarters. She'd geared herself for the leap into scientific discovery when a voice blasted into her consciousness.

"Them's not very good eatin'."

The world shifted and Anna found herself back in the big picture. Finally wised-up, her armadillo scuttled ahead, winning back the ten yards Anna had so cunningly eaten up. Disappointment turned to irritation in the time it took her to turn her head toward the interrupter, and irritation vanished in amazement in the blink of an eye.

The man who had frightened away her beastie was a Confederate soldier: his crumpled gray cap looked as if it had seen more than one campaign, and his gray button-front trousers, worn and sweat-stained, were held up by suspenders, the trouser legs stuffed into battered black boots. The hallucination didn't stop with the soldier. Behind him, two tents, old and made of canvas, were pitched around a central fire, where a couple more soldiers, sleeves rolled to greet the coming heat, a day's growth of beard darkening their chins, drank coffee out of tin pannikins. One wore a saber at his belt. Three rifles, manufactured early in the nineteenth century but clean and oiled, leaned against an old wooden tucker box. Above the tents flew a Confederate flag, and a smaller flag, white with a red bar along one side, a blue canton with a white star and what looked like a magnolia tree.

"Whoa," Anna said.

"You wanting a little breakfast?" the soldier asked politely. He drawled. Not the tobacco-juice sort of drawl Anna'd heard when Daddy and Baby talked, but a genteel, Rhett Butler kind of a drawl that was in keeping with the captain's insignia on his cap.

"No," Anna managed. "I was..." Suddenly her experiment seemed too hard to explain to an army man of any stripe. Or era. "I was just watching him. I wasn't going to eat him."

The soldier looked at her long and hard. "You're not from around here, are you, girl?"

"Not really," Anna admitted. Taco appeared from the woods to slobber on her thigh.

"Hunter?"

24

This time Anna was prepared. "Just an overgrown lap dog."

"Let us give you a cup of coffee?"

Anna followed him into the Civil War and was treated to good coffee in a tin cup that burned her hands. Her costumed campers were re-enactors. She'd heard the term now and again but had never appreciated the scope or the enthusiasm with which the hobby was pursued. In fact the word "hobby" was met with polite outrage, as if she'd suggested to an Orthodox Jew that reading the Torah was a nice pastime.

The soldier who had ended her game with the armadillo was Jimmy Williams, a tax lawyer with a firm in Jackson. The other two referred to him as Captain Williams or "Cap." His lieutenants—this camp was conspicuously devoid of privates—were Ian McIntire, a Honda salesman from Pearl, and Leo Fullerton, a Baptist minister from Port Gibson.

Captain Williams suited the role of a soldier: lean and strong-looking with thick brown hair just beginning to show a salting of age. Though Anna put him at around fifty, his youthful body, married to a face creased with the kind of wrinkles only the sun can scour into flesh, gave him an ageless look. The Honda salesman was a different story. Ian McIntire would look more at home in a suit, preferably seersucker, and a tie. Probably of an age with Jimmy Williams, he had hair that was white, cut short and bristling like hoarfrost in the morning sun. Joviality oozed from him. His belly was round, his face oval and fleshy, his eyes bright St. Nick blue and his smile boyish. When he laughed, and that was often, the laughter was high-pitched yet pleasant. The kind of laugh actors love; one so infectious others must laugh along with it.

Reverend Leo Fullerton was the youngest, mid-thirties at a guess. Dark hair, low over deep-set eyes, and a wide mouth set above a long chin lent his face a crushed and cruel aspect. His left eye was crossed and it was hard to tell where he was looking. But for a bit of a paunch, he was a powerfully built man.

A ludicrous assortment for Civil War soldiers, Anna thought. Then it came home to her that soldiers in every civil war were just merchants and boys, thieves and laborers, husbands and bankers.

While Ian brought her a three-legged stool, the captain insisted she take a doughnut, fried that morning and liberally dusted with powdered sugar. Southern hospitality evidently was not a myth. The lieutenant reverend was the only member of the group who was standoffish, but it seemed due more to natural shyness than any malice.

With the unselfconscious delight of boys, they told her the history of the Jeff Davis Avengers, a ragtag company of rebels formed in Port Gibson near the end of the war, when Grant was wringing the last drop of resistance from a besieged Vicksburg. Begrudgingly, they admitted there were no records of the Avengers ever doing battle, but to a man, they were absolutely convinced those long-dead civilian soldiers of Port Gibson had been instrumental in the war.

"Covert Ops" popped into Anna's head, but she knew she couldn't say it with a straight face. Out of deference to this singular passion of her hosts, she kept her mouth shut.

Each item in camp was lovingly described: the iron skillets, the cooking tripod, the rifles. The good reverend must have had the strongest curatorial instincts of the three. When conversation moved to artifacts that they, as re-enactors, were breathing new life into, he became animated. It was a mildly alarming transformation. His slash mouth, too wide for his teeth, giving them a spiky feral aspect, might have come across as excited in another man but had a manic feel when manifest by the preacher.

"These things aren't just old stuff, junk," Leo said as he brought one of the rifles over to where Anna sat. "These are the actual weapons those boys carried. They were bought new by somebody's daddy or uncle." He pulled open the breach and looked to see if the rifle was loaded. "They were used for squirrel, deer, bear. Put food on the table. Then along comes the war and these boys stand to lose everything. I mean everything—not just a little blood and time like the North. A way of life, everything they stood for, believed, everything they owned. So out comes the squirrel gun and they go out knowing they'll be shooting boys like themselves."

27

He was standing too close, towering. The rifle was at eye level to Anna, deadly wood and metal bulk held in the blunt hands of an excited stranger. Anna's skull bones began to feel fragile. Evincing a sudden need to stretch, she stood and put some distance between herself and this son of the Confederacy.

As Leo Fullerton had been revving up, Ian and Jimmy had been growing twitchy. A strained look passed between them, and Captain Williams tossed half a cup of coffee he'd just poured for himself into the campfire as if trying to interrupt the preacher's flow. Maybe Fullerton was prone to psychotic breaks when faced with modern-day Yankees in his Civil War ideal. Anna'd heard somewhere that the South didn't lock up the insane, but integrated them into the fabric of everyday society.

"You'd think there'd be more pieces left," Leo said. "But not pristine, not like this. This came with its own history. This was a Union soldier's weapon till I got it. A fella from Connecticut fought right here. Right *here,*" he reiterated.

Williams had begun shifting his weight from foot to foot, like a man who wanted to pace, to stalk, but wasn't letting himself. Trained to watch hands when uncomfortable with her fellow men, Anna noted his fingers were flicking occasionally: aborted movements, as if he restrained himself from reaching out to grab somebody.

Reverend Fullerton aimed the rifle at an imaginary foe, and the captain laughed, loud and hollow, the stage laugh of a bad actor.

"Easy there, Leo. The lady doesn't want to watch you win back the South." Williams stepped around the campfire and clapped Fullerton on the back with a little too much force for mere conviviality.

"Are you interested in history?" Leo Fullerton asked Anna in the manner that lets one know a reply in the negative will be construed as proof of idiocy.

She was saved from answering by Ian. "What brings you to these parts?" He forced a change of subject. "Down for the pilgrimage?"

Other than Mecca, Anna wasn't aware of much in the pilgrim line. "I'm the new district ranger on this part of the Trace," she told them. Abruptly the weather changed, a cold wind blew down from the northward of their opinion. Like comic thieves caught suddenly when the lights are switched on, the three of them froze in tableau.

Anna got a whole lot wearier. "Taco," she hollered and the dog rose obligingly from where he'd flopped in front of one of the tents. "I'd better get to my unpacking. Thanks for the coffee."

The psychic equivalent of a nudge passed through the faux soldiers, and they came back to life. Anna departed in a flurry of "Sure you won't have another cuppa," "A lady ranger, huh?" and "Welcome to Mississippi." The tone was too cheery, covering up for bad manners. Or something else she was totally in the dark about.

She took the shortest route back to the road between two Dodge Ram pickup trucks. Plastered on the bumper of one of them was the familiar shape of the rebel flag. Across it was written: HERITAGE, NOT HATE.

As she and Taco walked across the apron of well-worn grass to the asphalt road, a small utility vehicle, a sort of glorified golf cart with the forest-green stripe of the National Park Service on its side, puttered around the bend.

"Frank, meet your new boss," Ian McIntire hollered, and trotted down the gentle incline to wave the machine and its pilot over. Normalcy had returned. The Civil War re-enactors were again at ease. Anna didn't know if they'd quickly acclimatized to the appalling phenomenon of a female district ranger or, and this grated on her overtaxed nerves, decided a lady cop was bound to be sufficiently inept that whatever had struck them dumb at the mention of her avocation was considered safe once again.

A wiry man pushing sixty, Frank had thick red hair devoid of so much as a spattering of gray. He climbed out of the car wearing the familiar relaxed green and gray of an NPS maintenance uniform. The inside of both arms from elbow to wrist were crosshatched with deep scars, as if he'd held onto a bobcat who did not wish to be held onto.

Anna introduced herself, and Frank shook hands gingerly.

"So you're it," he said as he pulled off his green ball cap and mopped sweat from his face and neck with a wad of paper towels he'd stashed in his hip pocket. "You sure got your work cut out for you. I'm not saying anything against anybody, but there hasn't been a whole heck of a lot done around here for a month of Sundays."

"You look like you're working hard," Anna said politely.

"Yeah, well, I ain't law enforcement," Frank countered. The rift that often existed between the two disciplines was evidently fairly pronounced on the Trace. "All I can tell you is I been trying to raise Randy and Barth for the past ten minutes. Either they got their radios off or they're playin' possum somewhere."

"What's the problem?" Anna asked because she had to. Being "the boss" put her in a double bind. As law enforcement, one didn't have the luxury of letting things slide, of looking the other way and letting someone else handle whatever it was needed handling. Now, as a supervisor, she had the added onus of being obliged to look as if she actually cared.

"Dispatch's had half a dozen calls about an obstruction on the road just this side of Big Bayou Pierre. Sounds like somebody's cows got loose. Nowadays everybody and his dog's got a cellular phone and is dialing 1-800-PARK every time a picnicker breaks a fingernail or somebody gets a flat tire. They don't stop

31

and help like they used to, they just poke them phone buttons and keep right on driving, feeling as pleased as punch thinking they done the Christian thing."

"I'll check it out," Anna said, not sorry to have something to do since sleeping or moving boxes seemed beyond her capabilities.

Frank headed back to his cart. Anna turned the other way, choosing the short side of the loop for the walk back to her quarters. "Frank," she called after she'd gone half a dozen steps.

"Yeah?"

"What's my number?"

"Five-eighty."

"What's dispatch?"

"Seven hundred."

Every park Anna had worked in had the same radio call number system. One hundred was the superintendent. Rangers were in the five hundreds. The numbers went by position, not personality. But after spending a surreal hour in the nineteenth century, she'd felt the need to check lest Mississippi did things differently from the rest of the world.

Fifteen minutes' digging through cartons freed up her uniform if not her hat. Leather gear, cuffs, badges, service weapon—the symbols of office—were provided by the park where one worked. Anna'd not yet been issued hers. Like most long-term employees, she managed to buy, borrow, and acquire through sins of omission her own gun belt, holster, Kevlar vest and handcuffs. Never had she had the *cojones*—or the stupidity—to accidentally-on-purpose retain a government-issue Sig-Sauer nine-millimeter handgun.

Enjoying a touch of the good old days before the NPS moved to semi-automatic weapons, she snapped her faithful .357 Colt into the holster.

Before departing to herd illegal bovines, she shut Taco in the back room with Piedmont. Not because Taco required incarceration, but because, to her surprise, Piedmont had taken a genuine if sarcastic liking to the big lab, and Anna knew it would comfort him to have his friend around to abuse during this time of trial.

Energized by the simple expedient of strapping on her gun—though strapping was no longer involved, it was all done with Velcro—Anna took possession of her new patrol car. It was clean and not more than a year old, a powerful Crown Victoria with a unit on the dash that flashed blue lights: an innovation that served several purposes. More compact than the traditional light bar, it wouldn't get damaged by low-flying birds and branches and, since it changed the expected police car profile, it made catching speeders easier. The only thing the car lacked was a cage. Mentally, Anna put installing one at the top of her list of things to do. She had no desire to have those she arrested sitting behind her with nothing between her scrawny neck and their hands but goodwill.

"Seven hundred, five-eight-zero, ten-seven," she called in service.

"Ten-four," a female voice returned from the dispatcher's office in Tupelo and: "Welcome to the Natchez Trace."

"Thanks," Anna said and cut to the heart of the matter. "Could you tell me where Big Bayou Pierre is located?" She'd forgotten to ask Frank for directions.

"Turn right and drive."

Getting lost was hard on a north-south road. If Anna stayed too long in Mississippi, her orienteering skills were bound to atrophy.

Until an automobile struck a cow and a litigious citizen filed a lawsuit, animals on the road did not constitute an emergency. Anna drove the specified fifty miles per hour, windows rolled down. Green and blooming, the Trace meandered through woods and open glades. Where red clover did not lay its carpets of crimson, the sides of the road were neatly mowed to tree line. At mile marker forty-nine the landscape opened into fields: a pasture with horses grazing, a cedar barn weathered to natural gray velvet and, behind it, the unnatural round hill of an Indian mound. This section of the Trace was known as the Valley of the Moon. Anna savored the romance of the words and the world.

More tree-canopied miles of dappled green and sun yellow, then the view opened out again and Anna saw a cluster of cars stopped in the road.

Three in the southbound lane, half a dozen scattered in the northbound, jockeying out from one another as drivers maneuvered for a look at the problem. A handful had done the unthinkable by actually getting out of their vehicles. A truck, once red, now rust, had tried to circumnavigate the obstruction and slid down the bank, where it remained, mired in the mud twenty feet above the bank of Big Bayou Pierre.

What was missing was any sign of livestock. Closer, and Anna saw what had caused the traffic tie-up. A log, maybe ten feet long and a foot or two in diameter, lay across the center line blocking both lanes. A small group of men stood around staring at it, waiting, no doubt, for the ranger to come move it. No trees grew near by. The log must have rolled off somebody's trailer.

Turning on her flashers in the faint hope it would keep the next car along from rear-ending her and knocking the collected automobiles into the bayou like so many dominoes, Anna pulled to the side of the road behind the last car in the line.

Out of her patrol car, walking toward the clot of people standing well back from the log, she called: "Go ahead and drag it off."

There was a moment of stunned silence, then a man in a suit and tie, who looked as if he'd spent most of his adult life eating fried food, laughed and shouted: "We're waiting for you to drag it off."

This annoying sally was met with a gust of laughter that Anna didn't understand till the impromptu crowd parted. The obstruction was not a log but, indeed, livestock of a sort.

Blocking the narrow road was the biggest alligator Anna had seen outside a PBS special.

"I see your point," she admitted, and joined the group staring at the prehistoric monster in their midst. Apparently enjoying the warm asphalt and the attention, the alligator seemed content to stay where he was. If it was a "he." Anna didn't know, and wasn't eager to learn, how one sexed the creatures. The gator had the unformed look of an animal slowly morphing back into elemental mud. The head was as wide as the body. Only the tail looked to be part of a living thing.

Fascinated, Anna moved toward this long leather portion. A black hand closed on her arm. "Stay back," he warned. "Big as this old fella is, he's fast. Gators are like lightning. I've seen 'em jump a dozen feet like they were shot out of a cannon."

More standing. More staring. "What're you going to do?" the deep-fried suit finally asked. "I got to get to work." This brought on a chorus of like complaints.

"I'm going to stay right here and make sure none of you harasses the wildlife." Another minute ticked by and Anna relented. "You can throw rocks at him, I guess, as long as they're small."

"Ain't no rocks in Mississippi," the man in the suit said. "All we got's mud."

A quarter of an hour passed and another four cars swelled the ranks before the alligator tired of the company and lumbered off to slide down the embankment and sink himself

36

in Big Bayou Pierre. Traffic cleared. Anna dedicated another half an hour to pulling the truck up the slope with a towline the former district ranger had kindly left in the trunk of the Crown Vic, then the festivities drew to a close.

Calling dispatch to clear herself from the scene, Anna realized she'd been thoroughly enjoying herself. The sun was warm, the alligator a rare treat, and it appeared that—if nothing else—a stint in Mississippi would give her stories enough for a lifetime.

Despite the fact that she wasn't officially on duty till the following day, she decided to continue south to the outskirts of the tiny town of Port Gibson, where the ranger station was reputed to be.

As in Mesa Verde, the road had markers at every mile, tasteful four-by-fours painted brown with white numbers and just high enough to rake hell out of a fender if one didn't watch for them when making traffic stops. The numbers grew lesser as she traveled, and Anna deduced the Trace was marked south to north with mile marker number one in Natchez, where the parkway began.

In Colorado, Anna had taken little notice of mile markers, only using them occasionally when she had to report the precise location of an accident. On the Trace, they were of significant interest. In the flatlands, down in the trees, there were no reliable landmarks. The endless, unchanging, bucolic splendor made one place very like the next. With familiarity would come differentiation, like moms learning to tell their twin offspring apart. Till then she'd have to do it by the numbers.

Several miles south of Big Bayou Pierre and its diminutive neighbor, Little Bayou Pierre, an NPS patrol car was parked on the grass up under the shade of the trees. Coming from the high desert, where even the dirt was fragile, she knew seeing people drive and park on the grass was going to take some getting used to. In this fertile bit of the world, vegetation was one of the sturdiest and most easily regenerated of the natural resources.

There were two possible occupants of the parked car: Randy Thigpen or Bartholomew Dinkin, Anna's two field rangers. The men with whom she would spend her days, whom she would rely on for assistance and, in a pinch, trust with her life. Thigpen had already made a successful attempt to lead her astray with bogus directions. Neither Thigpen nor Dinkin had garnered rave reviews from Frank, the Rocky Springs maintenance man, and both had failed to respond to their radios when dispatch needed an alligator wrangler.

The last thing Anna was in the mood for was to suck it up to make a managerial good first impression on either one of them. But to drive by the first day on the job seemed downright unneighborly—or cowardly—and instinct warned her that to appear either could prove disastrous in the long run.

Telling herself her new rangers were probably terrific guys and she was being unjust, condemning them on circumstance, hearsay and a misplaced practical joke, she pulled onto the grass and gunned the engine, enjoying a mild thrill as the powerful car whipped effortlessly up the bank. In classic law enforcement gossip formation, cars nose-to-tail, driver-side windows matched up, Anna put the Crown Vic in park.

Though she didn't consider the day particularly hot, the windows of the other car were closed and the engine idling—probably running the air conditioner. Five or six seconds elapsed before the window lowered. Long enough to trigger suspicions. The possibilities were many. He could have been dozing, hiding something, zipping his fly, being rude. Anna would never know. But she noted the delay.

"Good morning," she said. "I'm Anna Pigeon."

"I heard you were coming tomorrow. 'Bout damn time. Barth and I've been running ragged for eight months."

This, then, was Randy Thigpen. He didn't look like a man suffering from overwork. For one thing, he was immensely fat. Anna had nothing against fat; some of her best friends were fat. It was fat on people who were expected to run, jump, fight, defend and protect she found to be a dereliction of duty. Other than that, Thigpen was a decent-looking man: late forties or early fifties, thinning hair a sandy gold-brown color, dark hazel eyes and a spectacular mustache that obliterated his upper lip and the line of his mouth. His voice was easy to listen to: deep with no classic drawl but a slight elongation of vowel sounds.

"Met one of your locals," Anna said and told him of the alligator.

Thigpen heard her unasked question: *Where the hell were you when dispatch called?* Rather than looking sheepish or defensive, Anna thought, he looked ever so slightly smug. "I got tied up with a motorist assist down by Mount Locust," Thigpen said. "I was on my way when I heard you call clear, so I pulled over to run a little stationary radar."

Beyond him, on the seat, was a paperback novel laid facedown to mark his place and a paper boat filled with biscuit crumbs and squeezed-out honey packets. Anna had called clear six minutes earlier by her dashboard clock. Thigpen had been parked on this knoll considerably longer than that.

"No harm done," she said easily.

The man seemed displeased by her reaction. Whether he'd been hoping for a row or a piteous whine, she couldn't guess. Getting neither, he felt the need to gain some psychic ground.

"Alligators are pretty easy to move once you get the knack," he said.

"Sounds like a useful knack to have in these parts," Anna replied mildly. "How do you do it?"

"Oh. There's a number of ways. You learn 'em as you go."

Thigpen hadn't the foggiest idea. A good

40

person would have let him off the hook. Anna hadn't had enough sleep to qualify.

"What's your favorite?" she asked with genuine interest.

"Mine? Oh, I don't know…"

"Aw, come on, help a Yankee girl out," she cajoled.

She could see the gears grinding behind his high, unlined brow. "The best way's you find a dead chicken. They like chicken. Then you hold it a ways in front of them, and they'll follow you anywhere, like big old dogs."

"You do that? You lead them with dead chickens?"

Thigpen nodded.

"Now, that I'd like to see," Anna said honestly.

Adding a few banalities lest he realize she'd been leading him down the garden path, she took her leave. Time would tell whether or not Randy Thigpen was going to be a supervisor's nightmare. He clearly wasn't a dream come true.

The Port Gibson Ranger Station was a low white building set off the west side of the Trace. Asphalt and chain-link fence struggled against some truly fine old pin oaks and nearly succeeded in giving it a soulless governmental look.

The structure was H-shaped, with the hollow parts of the H as open porticos. To the left were garage doors, both open, where maintenance worked on the many machines needed to groom the ninety miles of roadway

41

in the district. To the right was a windowless block, the purpose of which Anna couldn't guess.

A patrol car was parked in front of the east-facing portico. By process of elimination, she deduced this heralded the presence of Bartholomew Dinkin. Dinkin was a complete blank, and Anna harbored a hope he would inspire more confidence than his compatriot.

Walking quietly from habit, she crossed the concrete and let herself into the ranger station. As she slipped through the door, a blast of cold stale air hit her. Though the day was fine, mid-seventies with a breeze, the air-conditioning was cranked up—or down—till the office hovered at sixty-eight. Cranked was an apt description. The building had not been designed for central air, and two aging window units, poked unattractively through either end of the tunnel-like office, clattered and clunked through their duties.

The staleness comprised two competing elements: grease and super-cooled cigarette smoke. To Anna's left was a small, untidy office, full of morning sunlight forced through dirty windows. In front of her, in the long dark core of this ungraceful suite, were two old wooden desks butted up against one another so they formed a single surface, chairs on opposite sides, a makeshift partners' desk.

At the nearer one sat the green and gray lump that had to be Field Ranger Bartholomew Dinkin. He wasn't as fat as Thigpen, but he was in the running. By the looks of what remained of his breakfast—three sausage biscuit wrappers and two of the cardboard packets used to serve up hash browns—he was competing for the heavyweight title. Dinkin carried the bulk of his weight "behind the counter," as a shopkeeper in New York had described the phenomenon to Anna. A lot of green polyester-wool blend had been procured to cover the posterior.

At his elbow was an ashtray half full of cold butts. A teensy-weensy ache began behind Anna's left ear.

Bull by the horns, she thought, and closing the door, moved into her new territory. "Hey," she warned him of the invasion. "You must be Bartholomew Dinkin. I just met up with Randy up the road a piece."

Dinkin stood, carefully wiping his mouth, then his fingers, free of sausage grease. That done, he stuck out a meaty paw for Anna to shake.

"I take it you're the new district ranger," he said amiably enough.

Dense black hair was sprinkled with wiry white. He wore it close to his skull, the part marked in by the barber's clippers. His face was lined more by the extra flesh than age. Beyond those drawbacks, Dinkin was an attractive man. His skin deep brown, the tone even and rich, his ears small and close to his head, his teeth crooked but not stained. His most striking feature was his eyes: whites clear and cool, the irises a startling gray-green. Against his dark skin they appeared luminescent, as though he saw things denied ordinary mortals.

Dinkin offered Anna coffee from a pot on top of a file cabinet behind the door. She accepted and wandered while he waited on her. The office was dirty. Not just old and cluttered, but dirty, as if maintenance had gone on strike. Or given up. The rangers' desks were elbow deep in flotsam: coffee cups, evidence, candy wrappers, phone messages. Two bulletin boards were completely covered with notes and notices, some yellowed and curling with age. Anna pinched up the corner of a notification of an electrical shutdown at the Mount Locust Historical Site. It was seven years old.

"We were going to get around to organizing those boards," Bartholomew told her as he set her coffee down on Thigpen's desk. "But we heard you were... well we thought that might be a good job for you."

Anna picked up her coffee. "Why's that?"

Dinkin sat, he squirmed a little. "You know. You being a woman and all."

"Ah," Anna said. She drank her coffee and watched Dinkin.

He began to look uncomfortable. He moistened a fingertip, blotted up biscuit crumbs and carried them to his mouth.

"What's with the cigarette butts?" she asked, to keep him off balance.

"Randy likes his weed. Way out here where nobody much comes, we sort of make our own rules," he said referring to smoking in a federal building. It had been a no-no for so long that the policy was no longer even controversial. At least not in most states of the union.

"That happens," Anna said. "But I expect we'd better move the smoking outside." Her first executive decision. She waited to see if it was going to cost her. Barth sat a moment, his face unreadable.

"You want to see your office?" he asked abruptly.

"Sure." Anna put down the coffee, having no idea whether she'd won or lost points in what was clearly going to be a tiresome course in power politics. As she followed him into the second office on the left, she tried without success to remember why she'd wanted to move up into management. She hated leading. She was damned if she was going to follow. As a field ranger in the West that individualism had stood her in good stead.

Now she was going to have to develop people skills.

Anna found herself wishing she was back on the road with the alligator.

3

Anna's office was small and dirty. Scraps of wisdom, trash, information and memorabilia from the last half dozen district rangers were crammed in drawers and file cabinets, thumbtacked to walls, taped to cupboards. A vintage computer, the likes of which any self-respecting grade school would turn its nose up at, sat dusty and forlorn in one corner. A deceased roach had turned up six feet worth of toes and lay in the dust beneath a counter built into the far wall and serving as a desk. An office chair, its once ergonomically correct back sprung out of alignment by weight or abuse, awaited her administrative behind. Still Anna was pleased. A real office, four walls and a door. She was moving on up in the world. The primitive, visceral, female need to clean, to impose order, rose within her. She shook it off. Once established, she could do as she saw fit. For the present, she sensed if either of these two guys saw her with a broom in her hand, it would put her ten steps back on a road that promised to be long and hard enough from the outset.

"I thought I heard voices. Either you're the new district ranger or the Girl Scouts have started wearing guns."

Anna left off her janitorial lusts and turned. In the door of her office stood a compact man in a class-A maintenance uniform. He was built of squares: jaw, shoulders, wide square hips, thick thighs. There might have been a bit of fat on him but it was spread thin as butter. Though not more than a few inches taller than Anna—maybe five-six or -eight—she guessed he was terrifically strong. And black. Not the golden chocolaty shade of Barth, but deep, dark, old-rotary-phone black. He smiled, a square smile, showing large square teeth, and stuck out his hand. "I'm George Wentworth, head of maintenance for the Port Gibson District. That other office is mine."

Anna liked him. There were no shadows about the man. Nothing felt hidden. She took his hand, and she liked him even more. It was warm and dry, dark on the backs of the fingers and a soft tan on the palm. The nails were clipped and clean, his grip neither too much nor too little for a big man shaking hands with a small woman.

"When did you get in?" Wentworth asked. Anna told him and he said, "Let me call a couple of my boys to give you a hand moving in."

"We're going to get along fine," Anna said and was treated to another beautiful smile, a study of warmth in black and white.

Anna'd taken George to be in his early thirties, but a few miles on the road with him and she upped it to mid-to-late forties. That or he'd married when he was eleven years old. George was a family man, and it didn't take long before he'd told Anna about Leda, his wife, who "put up with him just like he deserved it," and his three boys. The youngest was a student at Alcorn State and, George told her with great pride, on the way to being the next Air McNair. From the delivery, Anna guessed this was a good thing but had to admit she had no idea what he was talking about. Air McNair, he told her, was a football player from Alcorn who'd made the pros. Lockley—Lock— George's son, would put McNair to shame. A boy so fast, so handsome, so strong and smart and honest that girls whistled and coaches swooned wherever he went. The maintenance chief didn't say it in those words, that would have been sacrilege, but Anna got the message.

With the help of Frank, George and a scrawny, wiry little white guy—one of Wentworth's mower drivers—Anna's belongings were in her house within an hour and she had an invitation to lunch.

When next you see me, I shall be applying for the position of circus fat lady," Anna told her sister, Molly, on the phone that night. "I must have gained ten pounds."

"One swallow does not make a spring."

"It might if the swallow is deep-fried," Anna countered, and they both laughed, enjoying the nonsense codes of a lifetime together. "We ate in Port Gibson. This lovely movie-set little Southern town with a church— one of a *lot* of churches—on Main Street. Instead of a cross on top of the steeple, it's got a big gold finger pointed to heaven."

"You're kidding."

"Nope. Lots of God, little in the way of groceries. The culinary glories of the South don't seem to be represented in my district. George gave me a choice of the Piggly Wiggly plate lunch, a Sonic Burger or Gary's Shell Station."

"You chose Gary's?"

"How could I not? In the back of the gas station, there's a lunch counter. Doing a fine business, I might add, selling deep-fried everything. Everything deep-fried, I should say. I had deep-fried potatoes, onions and pickles. Want to know the creepy part?"

"I thought that *was* the creepy part."

"It was really good."

There was a faint groan from the New York end of the line and a lack of sound Anna was only just coming to get used to. No abrupt shushing as her sister exhaled smoke. Nine months before, Molly had been hospitalized for several weeks. She had very nearly died, and finally she'd been convinced that maybe, just maybe, she should quit smoking. Despite its homicidal bent, Molly loved her dear old drug and missed it terribly. During the first two weeks of the new regimen, Anna had been glad to live halfway across the country. The only report she'd gotten of the rigors of withdrawal were from Molly's fiancé. Being intensely loyal, as befitted his exalted position, all he would say was, "Thank God she's still got some Demerol left from the hospital."

Thinking of the fiancé, a man who had once been Anna's lover, thus providing evidence that life, if it doesn't mimic art, at least mimics the soaps, Anna asked: "How's Frederick? Any date set?"

There was a shivery intake of breath, and Anna had a sick feeling for a second that her sister had started smoking again, but it was just nervous exhilaration.

"A date is set," Molly said, giggled, then added, "I would say I hate feeling like a giddy teenager, being post-menopausal and all, but I don't. I'm getting a kick out of it. When it's not scaring me to death. September twenty-third."

"Any special reason the twenty-third?" Anna asked, because she knew Molly, like any giddy teenager, would want to talk but, unlike most teenagers, had been trained to listen instead.

Molly laughed. "Calendars. His, mine, and ours. We're both booked like single professionals. It was the first day we felt safe to pencil in a lifetime commitment."

Anna suffered a pang of envy. Or nostalgia. She wasn't sure. Her lifetime commitment had lasted seven years, then her husband was taken from her in a mindless, pointless accident. A while back she'd finally extinguished the torch she carried for Zach, but there'd been no new flame, at least not one that could hold a candle to the conflagration of the memory of that first and all-consuming love.

Anna shook off the loneliness, made sure none of it was left to taint her voice, and so her sister's joy, and asked: "Church? Courthouse? On horseback in the surf? I've got to know what sort of dress to buy."

"You wear a bona fide dress, and we'll get married wherever you say."

Anna was stung. She wore dresses. She'd worn one less than a year before.

"Just kidding," Molly said, and it annoyed Anna that her mind could be read so easily, even over the phone. "No place or plan yet.

Setting a date was trauma enough for us both."

Molly's and Frederick's was to be a thoroughly modern marriage. They lived in different cities—she in New York, he in Chicago. This was his third marriage, her first. There would be no children, and they would commute. The very things that might earmark a union for failure, but Anna knew this one would last.

Suddenly tired of romance and matrimony, she said: "Let me tell you about my alligator."

It had been many years since Anna had been stationed at a campground. The upside was a mildly pleasant proprietary feeling, one's own little fiefdom. The downside was long and steep. Campground rangers were never off duty. There were, of course, sixteen hours of the day for which they went unpaid but, if home, the campground ranger was fair game. Visitors routinely banged on the door to borrow sugar, report limping squirrels, complain about their neighbors or just have somebody to talk to. Traumas great and small were laid at the doorstep, noise disturbances called through the bedroom window.

Memories of those drawbacks had not been lost on Anna, but she'd forgotten the intensity of feeling that came with the loss of privacy.

Before bed, she dressed in civilian clothes

and took Taco for a walk through the camps. It was a coping mechanism. Occasionally, on an incognito round, a ranger could see a situation developing and nip it in the bud so it didn't flower later, requiring one to be dragged out of bed at an unseemly hour.

The night was sweet and warm and melodious with the symphony of frogs. Weariness from being up thirty-six hours weighed on Anna's shoulders and eyes. Taco, too, was uncharacteristically subdued and walked docilely at her side on his leash. Rocky was booked to capacity.

According to George Wentworth, spring and fall were the busy seasons on the Trace. Year-round there was traffic—local commuters and tourists—but it was February through May and September through November that the campgrounds overflowed. Not only was the weather at its most hospitable, but those were the months when the town of Natchez hosted its biannual pilgrimage. At her request, Anna was enlightened. In some ways it wasn't too different from Christians making the pilgrimage to the Holy Land. Here it was a pilgrimage to a glorious past still revered by many. Various clubs, mostly the colorful—and powerful—ladies' garden clubs, opened many of Natchez's antebellum homes to visitors. Dressed in petticoats and hoops, volunteers gave tours of the now air-conditioned homes. Operas were performed, balls held. Tourists came from all over the world. Pilgrims came from the South.

Rocky Springs was close and clean and free to campers. Trucks, cars and trailers lined the road on both sides. Through this semi-permeable membrane of Detroit iron, Anna could see the flare of fires, each surrounded by its own group of devotees staring fixedly into it. Outside these circles of worship was often a second tier: the followers of Bacchus, men and women in lawn chairs clutching the alcoholic beverage of their choice. Anna'd been in a lot of NPS campgrounds in many parts of the country. She had seen her share of imbibers, but she couldn't recall seeing quite this many gathered together. Or this many heavy people. It was as if Overeaters Anonymous had reserved the campground for an annual convention.

Deep-fried everything. She made a mental note to buy a vegetable steamer next time she found herself in the neighborhood of a Wal-Mart.

The third and outer ring was made up of kids. They eschewed the light and the tedious company of their elders to play in the safe darkness. The populated darkness: the wooded chunk of land encircled by the road was so crowded Anna was mystified as to what part of the wilderness people thought they were experiencing.

Boy Scouts had the large campground at the top of the loop outside the circle made by the road. They generated some noise but nothing to be concerned about. The Civil War soldiers were happily ensconced across from the scouts, their Confederate flags countering that of the Silver Beavers. Bourbon and poker kept Captain Williams and his boys occupied. That, Anna suspected, was something that hadn't changed much in Southern camps since the 1800s.

The site beyond the rebel camp was walled off from the road by three maroon vans with First Baptist Youth Group stenciled on the sides. Muscles along Anna's spine tightened and her right hand twitched involuntarily. Church groups were trouble, more often than not. The belief that God was on your side had a deleterious effect on the moral fiber.

Satisfied things were as peaceful as could be realistically hoped, she returned to her house. Her life was still in boxes. Her cat was still sulking and she was too tired for more than a couple of halfhearted cajoleries, both of which failed.

As campground rangers learn to do, Anna laid out pajamas ready to hand on top of a box marked "books" and her uniform and duty belt on another unmarked box she believed held pictures. This way, when the knocking came in the middle of the night because some hapless camper who wished to make s'mores had forgotten the marshmallows, she would not be answering the door in her birthday suit.

At two-forty-seven A.M. by the bedside clock, the emergency pj's were called into action. Knocking as rapid-fire and insistent as that of a woodpecker drilled through the black syrup of unconsciousness and was transformed into half a dozen images of varying weirdness before her tired mind made sense of the racket and dragged her body from bed.

Fortunately the hall to the living room was relatively long. By the time she reached the door she was oriented as to where she was and who she was expected to be. Rocky Springs's ranger abode had two luxuries: a porch light and a small window in the front door. Anna flipped the switch and took a look at her callers before greeting them in her night-clothes.

A stocky balding man in his fifties, his face naturally puffy and baggy, made less appealing by a look of self-righteous ill humor, stood with a flashlight pointed into the weeds by the step. At his elbow stood a tousled young man of fourteen or so who looked to be quite enjoying himself. Both wore burgundy T-shirts with the words "He Is Risen" emblazoned in an arc from nipple to nipple.

Anna opened the door. Her great security measures in turning on the porch light were made a mockery; she'd not bothered to set the locks before retiring.

"Can I help you?" was forming in her throat when the balding man said: "Beats me how you people can sleep through it. But maybe you've got used to it." He spoke with such emphasis that the half dozen strands of hair balanced across his pate quivered like a web with a fly ensnared.

"There's been a disturbance?" Anna asked politely.

"You bet there has. It's a wonder somebody hasn't got bad hurt. People come down here for peace and quiet and you got this going on half the night."

"Sounds like you have some serious concerns," Anna said. "Give me a minute to dress and I'll see what I can do."

His jowls ceased to quiver, and he was settling down to simmer as Anna closed the door. The warm-wall-of-mud defense, her old district ranger, Hills Dutton, had called it. Meeting hostility with a soft, meaningless acquiescence often took the starch out of the aggressor.

Anna was dressed in three minutes and took another half of that to put her duty belt in place and extra pounds of .38 hollow-point bullets in her pocket. Since the NPS had switched over from .357s to semi-autos, all she had on her duty belt were pouches for spare magazines. No place for stray bullets. She was expecting no more trouble than loud drunks and crabby insomniacs. The gun, the bullets, the pepper spray, the collapsible baton were donned from habit and by regulation.

Armored in the paraphernalia of her profession, she rejoined her nocturnal visitors on the porch.

Cars, the man said, had been "hot-rodding" through the campground. "Kids," he growled. Not good Baptist kids, Anna surmised from his tone. "Driving too fast and shouting obscenities."

"Not obscenities, Reverend," the boy interrupted. "Just hollering."

"Obscenities," the reverend insisted, determined not to let the hellions off on a technicality. "They could easily have run somebody over. Drunk's my guess."

His guess was probably right. Anna sighed inwardly.

"It's spring prom, everybody's out partying," the boy added wistfully.

With promises of immediate action and merciless retribution, Anna tried to extricate herself from the reverend. Not yet done being mad and wanting to tell her over again the misdeeds of the ungodly, he told his story a second time with even greater vehemence. After she got them headed back to camp, Anna climbed into her patrol car and called dispatch. No answer. Evidently the Natchez Trace didn't have twenty-four-hour dispatch. She wasn't surprised. Few parks did. Rangers got used to working without backup. That or they made unofficial arrangements with local law enforcement or the Department of Fisheries and Wildlife—anybody they could call for help in a pinch. Anna added finding out who, if anybody, that was in Mississippi to her growing list of priority "To Dos."

The campground was quiet but for the Baptist boys, stirred up by the reverend's ire. The hot-rodders had come and gone. An aspect of law enforcement Anna hated was the day-late and dollar-short realities. By the time a crime was reported, it was a done deed and, most likely, the perpetrators would never be caught. On the plus side, perpetrators were usually not bright. What they did once they'd keep right on doing, and eventually, they got nailed. Not tonight, though.

Because she was up and it was politic to at least appear to be doing her duty, she briefly questioned those campers who were awake. An older couple from Paris, Texas, traveling in a small Airstream with two dachshunds for family, verified the reverend's story. Two cars, one a late-model blue Mustang, had driven around the loop several times at a high rate of speed. Neither Texan could remember the make of the other car, but the wife thought it was yellow or tan. She said it looked as if the blue car was chasing the light-colored sedan but her husband thought they were just racing.

The rebel camp was dead quiet. Either the soldiers had grown so accustomed to the sound of battle they'd slept through the excitement, or they weren't as willing to face modern confrontations as they were to relive those of the past. Anna was surprised. Captain Williams seemed like a take-charge kind of guy.

The Boy Scout leader said the cars had awakened them. That the people in the cars were shouting, but he couldn't make out the words. Nonsense. Rebel yells.

"Those cars may've been headed up toward the old church," the scoutmaster called after her as she was leaving. "Kids like to mess around up there."

"I'll check it out," Anna promised. Her pride would not allow her to ask just where in the hell the "old church" was. There were maps and brochures; she could expose her ignorance in the sanctity of her patrol car.

Rocky Springs Church was on the easternmost edge of the parcel that included the main campground, picnic areas, the NPS shooting range and several chunks of the Old Trace. Loess, the stuff that had caused the locust to collapse on Anna's U-Haul, according to George Wentworth, was a type of soil prevalent in the area. Soft, very fine, it was easily eroded. A long spell of wet weather destabilized it to the point mature trees would topple of their own accord or, as in Anna's case, with very little provocation. Because of this, the Old Trace had worn deep in many places. Not the two- and ten-inch ruts of the trails out West but twenty- and thirty-feet-deep, wide ravines cut into the forests and swamps from the passage of horse, foot and, finally, wagon traffic.

As Anna drove the half mile from the campground to where the brochure had Rocky Springs Church marked on it, the road forked and she guessed she was passing through one such section of the original Trace.

Walls of golden-brown dirt rose on either side of what had suddenly become a one-lane road. Above the Crown Vic, roots poked out from the banks. Headlights caught their undersides, and in light and shadow they clawed fantastic patterns against the night. Above them, seen sketchily at the uppermost of the high beams, were the tops of the trees they supported. The sky was lost in the branches.

Anna emerged from this hobbit's-eye view of the world into a small paved parking lot. At one edge was the reassuringly mundane sight of an NPS notice board complete with empty brochure box and badly faded map behind a sheet of Plexiglas.

There was a flashlight in the car's glove box, but it didn't work. Another item for the list. Anna got out of the car, closed the door and listened. The frogs were still. A bird sang as sweetly as if the sun shone. Trees surrounded the parking lot, soaking up light from a waning moon. Beyond this black belt of vegetation, Anna could hear the unsettling sound of grunted laughter, the kind without joy. The grunting stopped. Still the frogs did not sing. Anna slipped into the shadow at the edge of the parking lot to listen. Nothing. At her feet, a path, paved for a yard or two in pale gray concrete, then lapsing into wood chips, led into the woods. According to the map, she was heading toward the old church and what remained of the original town of Rocky Springs.

Anna had no fear of the dark. She found comfort in its cloaking embrace. A catlike quality of the nocturnal hunter had been part of her makeup since she could remember. Even as an adult she took childlike pleasure in sneaking and creeping, being invisible to her fellow humans. But it was three in the morning and this dark was an inky, stub-a-toe, sprain-an-ankle kind of dark. The worst she had planned for the reverend's midnight marauders was a stiff talking-to and a couple of phone calls if nobody was sober enough to drive home. Hardly the stuff to lose the rest of a night's sleep over.

Had her prey remained quiet, she might have gone away. But they stirred and the hunting urge returned. From above and a ways away—how far, Anna couldn't tell, dense vegetation changed the quality of sound— came a thunk. Two solid objects colliding. Then the word "shit" and "let's get the fuck out of here."

Somebody wanted to get away. Instinctively Anna wanted to catch them. Moving into the woods, she trod noiselessly on a thick carpet of wood chips a kindly Park Service laid down for a path. Cypress or cedar, they gave off a faint pleasant smell. To her left was a split-rail fence. Touching the top rail, she used it to guide her footsteps into the lightless interior of the forest. A litigation-weary park service could be trusted not to leave anything sharp or dangerous on a marked trail, so she moved quickly.

The ground beneath her inclined. Cobwebs stuck and tickled on her face and arms. Faint sounds echoed her passage in the woods to either side. The skittering of small creatures foraging, the scuttle of a tiny night beast alarmed by her presence. Subtly the smell of the forest altered. An earthy odor permeated the air, and, almost imperceptibly, the nature of darkness changed. Wide-eyed to catch even the faintest hint of light, Anna stopped and looked up. The canopy of trees had opened. She was at the base of a steep bank, maybe fifty feet high. Roots thrust out from its face. Trees clung precariously to its upper edge. Above, black against a sky made light with stars and a sliver of moon, was the silhouette of a building with a tall central steeple. The old church.

Made of soft and crumbling soil, the embankment would be treacherous. Anna stayed on the path. With a memory of light to go by, she covered the last angle where the trail doubled back up the hill toward the church, Methodist according to a weathered sign. A road curved nearby along with a tiny paved lot for cars.

Because of the thick curtain of trees to either side, the Natchez Trace created an illusion of isolation, wilderness. In reality, civilization in the form of roads, houses and fields pressed close on both sides.

Seen by night, Rocky Springs Church loomed black and monolithic. Even so, Anna could tell it was a classic: simple and symmetrical in the way of many early American churches. Tomorrow—today—after sunup, she promised herself a trip back. Now she used the old building for its shadow. Keeping close to the brick walls, she moved quietly to the back of the church, nearer where she thought the voices had come from.

There she leaned against the still-warm brick and watched. Her reasons were twofold: to get an aural or ocular fix on her miscreants and to absorb the surreal scene that had unfolded as she rounded the corner. Behind the church, in a clearing beyond a decrepit fence with a wire gate, was an ancient graveyard. Stones lay broken on the ground. Those still standing had sunk into the earth, swallowed by the graves they marked. Moss, black in the weak light of the moon, erased names, dates, lives. On the far edge of the clearing, pushing into the night of trees, were monuments of marble, towers of once-white stone, ten and twelve feet high. Beyond them a walled area, overgrown with vines, was just visible: a family plot, exclusive even in death. In the strange warm embrace of the night, trees close on every side and Spanish moss hanging in dense veils silvered by the faint breath of moonlight, for a heartbeat Anna was afraid. Not of the dead, or of the undead for that matter, but of having wandered into Rod Serling country, a twilight zone in the nineteenth century from which there was no way out. Unpleasant tingling started at the nape of her neck and crept up the back of her head hair by hair. It was time to get some sleep. She was so tired she was scaring herself.

A sharp "fucking hell!" from the shadows beyond the clearing brought her back into the twentieth century. "Fuck" might be a good Anglo-Saxon word dating from the Middle Ages, but to Anna it rang with indifferent modern malice. She tucked more deeply into the shelter of the church and waited.

A moment passed, filled with the promising sound of stumbling feet, then Anna's patience was rewarded. Two high-school-age boys, emerged from the darkness on the far side of the graveyard.

Single file, unsteady on their feet, they threaded through the tombstones. It was too dark to make out their faces, but they were tallish—five-foot-ten to six feet. One had the wide shoulders and thick neck of an athlete. The other was the body type Anna remembered from her high school days: all neck and wrist and Adam's apple. Both wore tuxedos. The skinny boy had lost his jacket and his white shirt glowed in the moonlight. Neither wore a tie.

Quiet as the tomb, Anna waited till they'd come through the gate and walked within a yard or two of her lair.

"Good evening, gentlemen," she said pleasantly.

The geeky lad in the lead screamed, "Jesus Christ," and fell to his knees. The boy behind tripped over him in his stampede.

Anna laughed. A little low comedy almost made up for her interrupted sleep. She stepped out of the shadows where they could see her. Proving she was not an apparition but flesh and blood did not calm them as she'd expected it to.

The larger boy hauled his fallen comrade to his feet with an unsympathetic jerk on the latter's cummerbund. In the feeble light, she could see nothing but great dark holes where the eyes were and a black gash of mouth as they gaped at her.

"What brings you boys out so late?" she asked.

"Go, go, go," the bigger boy cried, and shoved the other before him. In an instant, they were sprinting down the path toward the road behind the church.

Anna had no intention of giving chase. They could outrun her without half trying. As she listened to their noisy retreat, she felt some genuine alarm for the first time that night. Over the years she'd interrupted a lot of kids in the midst of some sort of feral fun. Little kids ran. Teenagers seldom did. Unless they had really done something wrong.

"Damn," Anna muttered. Two choices: go back to the house and find a working flashlight or wait till morning to see what damage had been done.

She'd pretty much talked herself into the efficacy of waiting till sunrise when she heard the crying.

4

Thoughts of bed were banished. The crying subsided to a low moan followed by pitiful retching. Anna took the ghostly path through the cemetery, retracing the footsteps of the boys. The sound of the dry heaves remained constant, making her progress toward the source sure, but it tickled her gag reflex and she had to keep swallowing lest the vomiting prove contagious.

The rounded headstones of the moonlit clearing behind her, she reached the near-perfect darkness of the woods. A tapered stone marker disappeared into the trees above. At her feet was an unusual burial stone, a wide flat slab, large enough to sleep on comfortably and raised up on four sturdy blocks so it formed an elevated dais. Ahead was a walled enclosure, ramparts of brick roughly capped with concrete and about chest-high. This mortality exclosure was deep in the trees, shrouded in darkness and veiled with Spanish moss. Thin choking sounds emanated from within.

Picking her way over roots and an occasional shard of shattered stone, Anna eased toward the pale line of concrete topping the bricks. The puking came to a stop. By ones and twos and tens of thousands, frogs recovered their voices and began again to sing. Music swelled until the night grew close with it, and Anna felt a twinge of claustrophobia.

The bricks were high enough she couldn't see over. Hoping there was nothing unutterably vile on the far side, she hauled herself up and swung one leg over to straddle the wall. Secure on her perch, she surveyed the tangled interior.

The enclosure was about fifteen feet square. Without light, Anna could make out nothing but an uneven mass of midnight. From the rich, slightly spicy smell, she guessed it was rank with weeds. A fine place to hide a body, dead or alive.

Near the west-facing wall were two narrow pale marks in the undergrowth. Legs. Bare legs. Gingerly Anna lowered herself into the square. Plants crushed beneath her feet, and she smelled the scent of honey and licorice. Feathery tops reached to her armpits. High-stepping like a woman walking in deep mud, she moved through the vine-clogged morass of plants.

The South was thick with life, crowded with it. There was a feel of sentience to the soil, the night, the forest, and now this corral of graveyard grass, as if, by a will neither good nor evil but merely indifferent to human life, these things could swallow a woman up.

Closer did not mean clearer. The darkness was too absolute. Bending down Anna touched the white smudge. Warm skin. This was good. Her touch brought forth a moan. Another sign of life. The leg was smooth and shaved and coated with nylon. The stench of alcohol and the sour smell of vomit overlay the sweet

67

sweat of youth and cheap hairspray. A young girl, Anna guessed, and began to talk.

"My name's Anna. I'm a ranger here. Are you hurt?"

Moaning was the only reply. Then even that stopped. Anna knelt in the weeds, feeling them close overhead tickling her neck and arms. Tickling. Ticks. Ticks and the South were inseparable. The thought was fleeting, and she kept her attention on the girl under her hands. There was no need to check for breathing. The girl had subsided into a deep and stentorian rhythm.

"I'm going to touch you," Anna said, "to see if you're hurt, okay?" With the fleeing boys and the smell of booze, sexual assault was a real possibility. Quick and sure from practice, Anna palpated neck, skull and, finally, the face, legs, abdomen, back and arms. Though her patient was unresponsive, Anna kept talking, a soothing stream of information to let her know whose hands were all over her body and why.

The girl didn't seem to have sustained any serious wounds. Anna detected no deformities of bone or wetness of blood. Injury to the head was always a possibility, a blow that produced swelling inside the skull rather than out, but drunk was Anna's professional assessment. Dead, sick drunk.

The little inebriate was wearing a silly strappy little number that was barely long enough to cover her rear end if she didn't sit down. Pantyhose were intact, and she had on one shoe. Anna's mood lifted. Rapists of drunken children were not known for replacing undergarments.

Relief brought with it the luxury of irritation. "Oh for Christ's sake," Anna muttered. "What am I supposed to do with you?"

A hand punched her feebly in the stomach making her jump. In a voice raspy with vomiting and crying her patient croaked: "Danny. Running. Running." And something that sounded like: "Are you going to... you're nice..." The rest was a mumbled slur.

"That's right," Anna said. "I'm nice. And we're going to." Going to what? She couldn't leave the girl in the weeds and ticks and, had she been assaulted, alone with her fears or possibly her attacker.

Consumed with checking the child for injury, Anna hadn't given much thought to danger. Careless. Had the boys in tuxedos injured this girl, there was no reason they couldn't circle back and do further damage. For a moment Anna tried for fear, a spurt of adrenaline to give her a boost, but couldn't manage it. Anger was there, at the boys for leaving, at the girl for being young and stupid.

Anna felt for her patient's face and tapped the cheek lightly. "Come on. Wake up. Rise and shine."

Dead weight. Dead moaning weight.

Anna rocked back on her heels and looked around.

The girl was crumpled against one wall. Above her was a lighter patch a couple of feet off the ground. A family plot would have to have an entrance. Leaning over the patient—never recommended for a number of perfectly good reasons pertaining to the well-being of both parties—Anna felt for the lighter section. Her guess was right, it was concrete capping the brick but built low to allow people in and out. Why it wasn't open to the ground, she didn't care to speculate, but the comings and goings of snakes and alligators would certainly be curtailed by this configuration.

"Come on, honey, up you go. You've got to help me now. That's my girl." With tugging, badgering, pleading and, once, in desperation, pinching, Anna got the girl's fanny up on the low part of the wall and her feet to the outside of the square.

Fortunately the girl didn't weigh much more than a hundred pounds, a hundred and one if you included her clothes. From the half wall, Anna knelt with her back to the little drunk, drew the slender arms around her neck and stood up. By bending forward, she could get the girl's toes clear of the ground.

Doubled over, carrying a body, Anna crept through the tombstones like a grave robber. Only the feverish heat of the bare arms and the warm breath on the back of her neck reassured her the child was drunk and not dead.

A hundred pounds was just twenty pounds shy of Anna's own body weight. Even the short distance from the plot to the old church cost her dearly. She was breathing heavily, and the muscles of her shoulders and thighs burned.

Trudging one baby step at a time, noting only the changes in footing, the coming of light to the path, the path becoming the asphalt in front of the church, the sudden downward slope, Anna entertained half a dozen plans: leaving the girl in the church while she fetched around the car, presuming there was an easy way around. Driving back to Rocky Springs Campground and rallying the Confederate Army. Each plan she came up with that allowed her to dump her burden also required she leave it behind for a time. And one did not leave drunks, especially drunken children, alone. Wood chips came underfoot. Anna walked near enough to the rail fence that she could touch it with her elbow and so keep on the path. Several splinters shot home, but the pain was so minimal compared with that of her neck muscles that she scarcely noticed.

By the time she reached the parking lot, she was wringing wet with sweat. It poured in her eyes, stuck her shirt to her back and trickled between her breasts. In the West, sweat evaporated, thus performing its mission of cooling. In Mississippi, one merely contributed one's bodily fluids to the flow toward the nearest bayou.

After a bout of maneuvering, Anna got her charge dumped into the back seat of the patrol car and, at long last, got a look at the girl by the light of the overhead dome. She was young, sixteen or seventeen, and small-boned, with the charming unmarked face of a child. Anna felt old and stuffy as she realized she was

71

a bit shocked by the scarcity of fabric in the girl's party dress. It was a tiny spandex number with rhinestone-studded spaghetti straps and enough cut-outs on the sides to rattle the cage of any red-blooded male. Her hose had run, her dress and arms were muddied and she was missing one shoe. Other than that, she appeared undamaged. Around her neck was a gold cross. Anna snorted. A meager talisman to ward off the kind of evils a dress like this was likely to invite.

No hope of ID. If she'd had a purse it was lost in the weeds, and there was no place in her brief costume to secrete so much as a driver's license. Anna would have to wait until she regained consciousness to find out who she was.

Back at her house, Anna half dragged, half walked the inebriated child into the living room. Determined not to give up her own bed, she laid her out on the hard narrow cushion of her grandmother's couch, removed two ticks from the back of her patient's right knee, swabbed iodine on a scrape on her elbow and, having arranged her on her side so she wouldn't choke on her own vomit, threw a comforter over her.

Following a personal tick check, Anna went back to bed. Piedmont had come out of seclusion and lay on the rumpled sheets. As she wriggled in on the far side so as not to disturb him, Taco padded from the room. The retriever's instincts were in alignment with the law enforcement credo "to protect and serve." Anna didn't doubt that he would camp out next to the drunken prom queen and keep the bad guys at bay.

Excuse me, ma'am? Excuse me." Thin piping penetrated Anna's slumbers. Claws on her arm jerked her more rudely from her dreams as a still-skittish Piedmont launched himself off the bed and back to the imagined safety of the closet, his hiding place of choice when strangers intruded.

"Excuse me, ma'am. Do you have a phone I could use?"

Anna sat up. Foreseeing just such an awakening, she'd done the unthinkable—and the uncomfortable. She'd slept in her emergency backup pajamas.

Peeking timidly through the bedroom door was her little drunk. Mascara ringed the big brown eyes and the brown hair, done up to the nines and affixed with industrial-strength hair spray the night before, resembled a ruined cake. Around her shoulders she clutched the comforter against the cool of the morning—or the shame of the night. One small white hand was fiddling with the sable ear of her newly adopted protector, Taco.

"What time is it?" Anna asked.

"I don't know." The girl's voice faltered; then her face crumpled and fat tears rolled blackly through the makeup and down her cheeks. "I don't know where I am. I don't know what happened." Tears clogged the slender throat, making intelligible conversation impossible. She slumped to the floor, buried her mucky face in Taco's coat and bawled.

"Take it easy. Take it easy," Anna said and unwrapped herself from the sheets. "Dog-gone it, don't cry. You're okay." It annoyed her that she didn't have any tried-and-true soothing maternal phrases, and the annoyance made her voice sharper than she intended.

The girl cried harder.

Anna sat on the edge of the bed and tried to scrub some sense into her tired mind by scratching her scalp good and hard. "Okay," she tried again. "My name's Anna. I'm the ranger here, as of yesterday. I found you passed out drunk in the graveyard and brought you here to my house. That's where you are and what happened. Now how about you tell me who you are and we call somebody to take you home?"

The sobs changed tone. Anna could tell they were on the wane and sat quietly lest she trigger another storm.

Finally the girl lifted her head. Black tears glistened on Taco's coat but he stood his ground.

"Start with your name," Anna suggested.

"Heather," came in a whisper.

"Heather what?"

A long silence followed then the girl said, "Barnes. Heather Barnes. My father's going to kill me!" She dove wetly back into the dog's fur.

Anna stood and tugged on the corner of the

comforter. "Tell you what, Heather. Let's call your dad first. The sooner he finds out the less likely he'll be to kill you outright."

Heather clung to the dog.

"I'll talk to him if you like," Anna offered. "Give him some time to cool off. Tell me your number, and I'll call while you take a shower. You'll feel better. I'll feel better. Nothing wrong with that."

Heather let Anna get her up then and show her into the bathroom. As a gesture of good-will, Anna tossed in a pair of old sweats and a T-shirt so the girl wouldn't have to shimmy back into her handkerchief-sized dress.

At the joyous news her daughter was safe, Mrs. Barnes burst into tears. Then, proving Heather might not be oriented to time and place but her sense of family was intact, the woman added: "Her father's going to kill her."

The Barneses were from Clinton, a small town that butted up against the western edge of the state capitol of Jackson, a city of about 400,000. "We'll be there in half an hour," Mrs. Barnes told her. She stopped for a moment while someone hollered at her—presumably the killer dad—then amended her statement. "We'll be there in about an hour. I know the speed limit on the Trace is way low," she said virtuously.

Anna made coffee, then, remembering her first hangover, a pot of weak tea for Heather. Ten minutes later the girl emerged from the shower looking revived. And much younger. To Anna's jaundiced eye, Heather appeared to be all of twelve years old.

"Do you have any makeup?" the girl asked pitifully.

"Nope."

"A blow dryer?"

"Nope."

"You won't tell Daddy I was drunk, will you?"

"Yup."

"God, please don't."

Anna ignored the wailed request and sipped her coffee. "Sit down. I made you tea. After last night you'll be dehydrated. You need to drink something."

"Do you have a Coke?"

"Nope."

Heaving an exaggerated sigh, the girl slumped into a chair. She was on the way to full recovery.

"Tell me what brought you to my graveyard," Anna said.

Heather's gaze wandered around the room. Taco came over to sit beside her, lay his chin on her thigh and look dreamily into her face.

What a ham, Anna thought, but she said nothing.

"God," Heather said after a moment. "I can't remember a bunch. I mean, like, it's gone!"

"Alcohol will do that if you drink enough of it," Anna said. "Tell me what you do remember."

"The dance. I remember most of that. It was a real bore. The band was awful. Some of the boys had a bottle they were passing around. Then we all piled in some cars and left. That's about it." She looked at Anna in wide-eyed innocence. "That's all I can remember."

Anna didn't doubt much of the evening had been lost in a drug-induced blackout. She also knew the girl was hiding something. Not being her mother, Anna didn't much care what. Adolescent peccadilloes were not even mildly amusing at eight-thirty A.M. after a short night. "Ah, well," she said. "Maybe it'll come to you."

"I don't think so," Heather said with finality.

Mr. Barnes was not pleased but didn't look homicidal. Mrs. Barnes seemed a little more likely to commit murder. Without fear to temper her mood, anger had taken over. If her mother could be believed, Heather would not be dating, talking on the phone, watching television or any of a dozen other things until she was twenty-one.

Alone at last, Anna decided to take the day off—comp time for having been on duty the day before and half the night when she was not yet officially on the payroll. A second pot of coffee, and she was inspired to attack the boxes the maintenance men had helped her unload.

It took an effort of will not to dwell on the charm of the stone tower house she'd left behind in Mesa Verde, and the paucity of her belongings caused her to suffer a few twinges of rootlessness, but her Navajo rugs looked good on the gleaming hardwood floors and her grandmother's antiques lent interest to the boxy rooms.

She'd just reached that most satisfying of chores, the hanging of pictures, when a car pulled into her drive and parked in front of the carport. A Claiborne County sheriff's vehicle. Rocky Springs, she remembered, was in Claiborne County, one of the poorer counties in Mississippi and one having a high percentage of African-American households.

Automatically stepping away from the windows into the shadow of the front door, she watched her visitor approach: in his forties, a bit soft around the middle but well suited to the uniform. Thick shoulders were crisped up by ironed khaki, and his gun belt rode on narrow hips over muscled thighs that stretched the crease out of his trousers when he walked. As he neared the front door he took off his hat, a wide- brimmed Stetson in warm-colored felt, and exposed a shock of sandy hair in need of cutting. His eyebrows were so blond they were almost white, lending dark blue eyes an appearance of wisdom and acuity.

Judgment passed, Anna opened the door before he had a chance to knock.

He looked startled, then, to her surprise, embarrassed. "Good afternoon, ma'am," he said, not looking at her but at his boots. "I'm Sheriff Davidson. I'm looking for Phil Otis. He in?"

Sheriff Davidson had a nice voice. Enough drawl to soothe but not so much as to be annoying.

78

"Did he used to live here?" Anna asked.

"Yes, ma'am. He was the ranger down here."

"He's been replaced," Anna said. "Now it's me."

"Well then, it's you I need to talk to, so I guess I've come to the right place."

Anna invited him in, offering a glass of bottled water because it was all she had, but he declined.

"Much as I'd like to, I can't stay," he said. "We got a report from the Clinton police this morning of a missing girl. In cases like this— local kid, good reputation, probably not a runaway—we don't wait to look into it. Somebody said a bunch of the kids came down to the old graveyard here after a dance they had. I was just wondering if you could shed any light on the subject."

"She's home safe and sound by now." Anna told him an abridged version of the night's debauch.

A smile creased his face, and the skin at the corners of his eyes crinkled. Anna found herself smiling back, checking his left hand for a wedding band. There was none. The response was pure reflex, Anna guessed, brought on by Molly's impending nuptials. It had been so long since Anna'd had a serious relationship she feared she'd be like a dog chasing cars: she wouldn't know what to do if she caught one.

"Now, that's good news. I figured I was going to spend the day on a wild-goose chase. May I use your phone, let the Clinton PD know Danielle's been located?"

He was across the room and punching in numbers before the last bit of information sank in. "Hold it," Anna said abruptly. "Hang up. My little drunk's name was Heather."

"Drat," the sheriff said. He gave Anna a description of the missing Danielle. She was struck by the overwhelming likeness of the young. But for hair color, the child described could have been Heather, right down to the skimpy black dress. At sixteen, life has yet to leave many identifying marks stamped into the flesh.

Anna returned to hanging her pictures, but the sheriff's visit left her mind unsettled and she couldn't figure out why. Missing teenagers were a dime a dozen. A majority of them found their way home, maybe morally compromised, but physically in one piece.

Having put down her hammer and nail, she perched on the edge of her grandmother's unwelcoming Victorian settee and let her mind clear, so that she might see this thing lying under her thoughts like a cocklebur under a saddle blanket. Taco came over and began licking her ankles to assist the process. Despite the distraction, Anna found what was bothering her. Sheriff Davidson said the missing high school girl's name was Danielle Posey. When Anna first found Heather retching into the graveyard weeds she had mumbled, among other things, "Running. Danny running." Danny—or Danni—could be short for Danielle. Running from what? Just because the tuxedo-clad clowns had not assaulted Heather did not make them nice boys. Nice boys didn't abandon girls in graveyards, drunk or sober.

"Come on, Taco," Anna said. "It's time for a walk."

In the light of day, the old church and graveyard took on a different aspect. Anna could tell this would turn into one of her favorite haunts. A sense of history, undisturbed by the machinations of the modern world, hung over the place as palpably as the veils of Spanish moss hung over the old stones. Decay had set in above ground as well as below. Stones were broken, sinking, moss-covered, but even amid this slow reversion to the earth, an ongoing spark of the human heart showed in the bright flowers, mostly plastic but carefully arranged, that adorned the markers. People dead more than a hundred years and yet so dear to someone's heart that the graves were decorated.

The hum of insects—mostly bees—took the place of the night's frog concert, making it more sleepy by day than by night. Fitting for a graveyard.

There was little evidence of the previous night's activities, but Anna did find Heather's other sandal a couple of yards from the family plot where she'd ended her night's revels. Eyes on the ground, Anna began to backtrack from the thrown shoe. Maybe she looked for something, but mostly she tracked just for the hell of it, to see what differences in spoor and soil there would be in this Southern clime.

The floor of the graveyard was oddly barren, as if the ground had been sewn with salt by the wash of tears from those whom the dead had left behind. Even leaf litter, the inevitable carpet of any forest, was sparse, blown clear of stones and paths to collect in the exposed roots.

Having loosed Taco to free herself of sloppy kisses and unpredictable lunges, Anna concentrated on the earth. The high-heeled shoe was a tracker's dream. It had been bought new for the dance. Stitching was clearly etched into the toe, and the heel was of a sharp rectangular cut that dug deep at every step. Without much effort Anna was able to follow Heather's progress of the night before. As would be expected from a girl stupid with drink, the trail wandered. Eleven heel marks back, Anna noted with interest another set of tracks and marks of a minor skirmish. The print of a man's dress shoe, left foot, size ten or eleven, nearly obliterated the heel mark of the girl's sandal. Anna stopped and, blessing Taco's continued absence, studied this short symbolic history written in the soft earth. Maybe thirty inches away, too far for a natural stance, was the imprint of the man's right shoe. Most of the weight was on the inside of his foot, smashing leaves into the ground and forcing up a tiny mound of mulch.

Between these prints and a couple of feet in front of them, were two smooth oval indentations. Relaxing her eyes and mind, Anna continued to stare. Slowly the marks she knew had to be there emerged from the thin litter of leaves and sticks. Two partial handprints.

Heather had not been alone. A man—most probably one of the tuxedoed boys—had been with her. At this place, Heather had either stumbled and fallen to her hands and knees or she'd been forced down by her companion. Stumbling was the likelier scenario. She was drunk, it was dark, she was wearing silly, teetery shoes. And, too, there were no signs of struggling or scrambling. At an educated guess, the male companion had lifted Heather up after she'd fallen.

Stepping around the story, Anna continued on.

The edges of the cemetery were delineated by the resurgence of forest. The chemistry that kept the cemetery floor barren changed abruptly and foliage rebounded with a vengeance. Tracks disappeared into ground-creeping vines. Vines covered fallen branches and logs in various stages of decay, forming a floor designed to impede the progress of invading bipeds. On the fallen tree trunks, pushing through the tapestry of leaves, were saplings, shrubs, new trees half grown. These in turn were greening from the roots up, covered in vines.

Anna wracked her brain for the rhyme that warned children away from poison ivy. Leaves of three, let it be. Or maybe it was leaves of two, bad for you. No matter how many times she saw the stuff it never looked the same and bore little resemblance to the benevolent strains of ivy that routinely died from neglect on her kitchen windowsill.

In fiction and maybe somewhere in the world, there were trackers who could follow a trail through this kind of territory. Anna was not one of them. Perhaps, were she willing to crawl around with a pair of tweezers, inching up each vine to peek underneath, she might find another track or two, but she wasn't tempted. Mississippi was way too full of life: one-celled, two-celled, four-, six-, eight-legged, life that slithered, flapped, entwined. Anna had a sense that if she were to get down on the ground for any length of time she would be bound up in that fecund shroud like a fly wrapped up for the spider's larder.

From deeper in the woods Taco barked and, treading carefully, she pushed on another few yards. Beyond a crosshatch of fallen logs, the side of the cemetery hill dropped away in a miniature version of South Dakota's badlands, where the earth had fallen, melted or rotted. A bank thirty feet high and arcing away in both directions had formed. The wall of dirt was ragged with fissures. Root systems thrust out to scratch at insubstantial air. Trees hung precariously over the edge. A number had succumbed to weather and gravity and lay, heads down, tangled on the face of the embankment.

It was a climb Anna would choose to avoid: the dirt was unstable, the anchors untrustworthy, and there were many things upon which a body might impale itself. Taco, being a dog and, so, having a brain about the size of an apricot, would have few trepidations about scrambling up the bank. Anna stopped well back from the lip of the drop and whistled. A series of excited barks answered her, then she saw his black form bounding gracefully over a landscape that would cripple a human being. For a moment, she watched the animal and felt pure unadulterated joy. When he ran, dappled sunlight blue on his midnight coat, ears streamlined, Taco was transformed into a creature of beauty.

At the foot of the bank, he hesitated.

"You got down there," Anna reminded him unsympathetically.

Fascinated, she watched as he picked and clawed and scrabbled his way up the ruined cut. She was so fixated on his progress that she didn't notice he'd caught something until he was at her feet. Only its tail showed, trailing lifelessly from the corner of the dog's mouth.

"Oh, yuck!" Anna bent down in hopes of rescuing whoever belonged to the tail as Taco spun in gleeful circles. Anna'd thought, should she ever stoop to owning a dog, she would get a small frothy lady's lapdog, a Lhasa apso or a shih tzu—some animal that had at least the vestigial charm of a cat. Big dogs had big mouths and loved closing them around the hapless and helpless. At any given moment, Taco was capable of hiding an entire tennis ball in his jaws and once—and this was rare given the pointy nature of dog teeth—Anna had pried his mouth open and retrieved a baby bunny, soggy with dog spit but otherwise unhurt.

"Give it to me, doggone it. Down!" Looking deeply offended, Taco crouched on elbows and knees, his one trick. Anna gingerly took hold of the tail protruding from his doggy lips. Not fur, cloth. This was good. She had few qualms about putting injured socks out of their misery. "Open up," she commanded. Getting no response, she straddled his head and made him open his mouth. The wet disgusting item was a scrap of chiffon-like material with rhinestones sewn on. Taco had it half swallowed and Anna had to drag it gently up his throat while he wiggled and gagged.

"Serves you right," she said but scratched his ears so he wouldn't take it too personally.

Once it cleared the insides of the dog, Anna could see it was a scarf, the kind worn over the shoulders with evening dresses. Remembering what Heather had been wearing, it could very well belong to her. Still on her knees, Anna spread the fabric over the ground, sparkly side up, to assess the damage. The dog dropped his chin near one corner but knew better than to try and reclaim his prize.

The delicate fabric was in good shape, only punctured here and there where Taco's teeth had penetrated, but the rhinestones on one end were dulled, the glittering facets muddied. Anna touched one, the mud made liquid by the dog's saliva. Her finger came away stained with red. Half the scarf was drenched in blood.

"Open your mouth," she ordered the dog, then pried it open for him. Cheeks, tongue, roof and what she could see of his throat were all of a piece. There was too much blood on the scarf for it to be Taco's. Had the rhinestones cut him enough to bleed that badly he'd have been foaming from his mouth and probably his nose. Heather had been unharmed. There wasn't an inch of her Anna'd not checked. Therefore, the blood was not Heather's. Chances were the scarf was not Heather's either.

Danielle was missing, gone from the prom in her party dress.

Anna got a bad scared feeling. "If you were half the dog Lassie was, you'd lead me back to where you got this," she said.

Taco thumped his tail and looked at her with soft brown eyes.

5

Though Anna felt she dithered, no time was lost. While her mind crashed through the thorny problem of whether to return for help or begin the search for the owner of the bloodied scarf, her body was piling rubble to mark the place on the bank from where she'd seen Taco coming out of the woods, and her mind was making a note of the peculiarities of the trees at the place he'd first appeared.

She had yet to locate her handheld radio, another item for the ever-lengthening list. Her patrol car was in the church parking lot.

To increase her familiarity with its idiosyncrasies, she'd driven it, rather than taking her Rambler.

Ten minutes' fast walk brought her to the lot below the church. Randy Thigpen answered her third call. Barth Dinkin, Randy said, was on lunch break in Natchez, forty-five miles and nearly an hour to the south of Port Gibson, where Thigpen was in the ranger station. Fleetingly, Anna wondered why he wasn't out patrolling the road. She told him what the dog had dragged in; told him to call the Sheriff's Department, keep trying to contact Dinkin and meet her at the Rocky Springs Ranger Station with a spare radio in twenty minutes. There followed a silence long enough Anna wondered if they'd lost contact, then he drawled, "Ten-four." The drawl annoyed her. John Brown had filled her in on her staff. Randy Thigpen was from Smartswood, New Jersey. The drawl was pure affectation.

Anna had opted not to try and follow the trail of the scarf alone. If an all-out search was called for, she would have wasted valuable time, and she was unfamiliar with the territory.

Having returned home, she put on sturdy boots and her uniform, filled a backpack with an emergency first aid kit, compass and watch and, in just under nineteen minutes, was at the Rocky Springs Ranger Station at the entrance to the campground. Twenty minutes, twenty-five, passed and no Ranger Thigpen. At an even thirty, Anna radioed again and found he'd just left Port Gibson. Her sister, learned in things psychiatric and psychological, once told her tardiness was a form of covert hostility.

Thigpen rolled in twenty-five minutes late and pulled up beside Anna's car. He did not budge from his comfy seat behind the wheel, leaving her two choices: talk through car windows or get out and go to him. She'd intended to get out anyway and chose to split the difference. Putting down the electric window on the passenger side she said: "Hop on out and let me show you what I've got." He sighed. She made a point not to notice.

The ignition in his patrol car had been left on. A gust of cool air from the air conditioner followed him, and she could hear the strains of "The Shadow of Your Smile" from whatever easy-listening station he had his radio tuned to.

As Thigpen pried himself from his automobile at her behest, Anna realized it was the first time she'd seen his bottom half. The sight of it did not raise him in her estimation. Moving slowly, not because he was heavy but because it gave him the illusion of control, he closed the door and leaned one hip against the fender. Anna spread her map on the hood. Thigpen gave it a cursory glance.

What she had was a glossy brochure of the Rocky Springs area, the kind of pseudo map with dashes to represent trails and hand-drawn pictures of the various wonders to behold at the end of them. On this unexceptional bit of cartography, she had penned an

X where she estimated she'd been when Taco delivered the scarf.

"Looks like you were between the graveyard and the Old Trace this side of Little Sand Creek." He stated the obvious.

"That's my guess," Anna said. She traced the linear route Taco would have taken if dogs were linear beasts. "It's not exact," she admitted. "But it's a place to start." She glanced up to see if he followed her logic, to discover he was looking not at the brochure but at his fingernails, a parody of boredom.

Anna folded the map. "Sheriff Davidson. Did you get hold of him?"

Thigpen lost interest in his nails and became absorbed in a clatter of starlings in the treetop across the parking area. A few seconds ticked by and Anna's blood pressure rose a couple of points.

"I thought I'd better wait on it," Thigpen said, still studying the birds.

Anna said nothing. When one was new in town, waiting for explanations was good practice. Who knew what mysterious rules held true in the heart of Dixie? Thigpen wanted her to ask him why. Anna could almost smell his anticipation.

"Why's that?" she asked to get it over with. Had a child not been missing she might have played the game, silence for silence. She was better at it than most. Today other tasks took precedence.

"Well, I don't think we ought to go bothering Paul just because you dug up an old scarf you think might have blood on it. Could be anything. An old rag a hunter used to clean his knife."

Black chiffon seeded with rhinestones; hunting in Mississippi must be a whole lot more glamorous than it was in Colorado. "Call him now," Anna said in the even colorless tones she used shortly before she ripped someone's head off. "Tell him exactly what was found. Do you need me to write the description down?"

Randy Thigpen looked as if he was going to argue, then thought better of it. Leaving the car door open, he grunted down into the driver's side to radio the Sheriff's Department. When he'd finished and Anna had been exonerated by the sheriff of Claiborne County's immediate interest, she laid out her plan. It was rudimentary and she was understaffed, but though densely forested, the Natchez Trace was narrow. Fields bordered both sides of the green belt. If the search needed to be widened, farmers would be called and questioned. Anna had a sense that if Danielle had been with the other prom kids, she would be found near where Anna had seen them. At night, in dress clothes, even lunatics and teenagers tended not to wander too deeply into the woods. Anna would follow in the direction Taco had come from. Randy Thigpen would take the trail up through the sunken section of the original Trace that ran to the south of Little Sand Creek. According to the map, this segment was no more than half a mile long; then he'd turn west toward the cemetery. The wooded area was small enough she felt secure that neither of them could become lost. "I'll radio Sheriff Davidson in fifteen or twenty minutes and let him know where we are. If he thinks it's worthwhile, he can join us," she finished.

"There's a problem with that," Thigpen said. He'd stayed in his car. The left seat was a good two inches lower than the right where his faithful attendance had broken down the springs.

"That being?" Anna hurried him along.

"I couldn't find any batteries that were charged up. I got your radio, but it's deader than a doornail."

"That's okay," Anna said, needing to be in the woods. "I'll take yours. Frank—the maintenance guy—is around here somewhere. Ask him to lend you his for the duration."

Short of flat-out insubordination, Thigpen had little choice. With ill grace, he handed over his radio. Anna thought of taking his carrying case as well, but watching him take off his belt to unthread it was too gruesome to contemplate.

She collected Taco, not because he was a trained search-and-rescue animal but because he dearly loved treats. Since he'd considered the bloody scarf the most fabulous of finds, he just might remember and return to the source of the bounty. It was a long shot, but since the dog's services could be had for a pat on the head, there was nothing to lose.

The day had warmed rapidly and, down in

the trees, there was not a hope of a breeze. Leaves were as still as if painted on. Moisture breathed from the ground, from the dense greenery. Moving at an easy jog, Anna was drenched in sweat before she'd traversed the manicured trail between the parking lot and the church.

By the time she returned to her makeshift cairn at the top of the ragged embankment, the legs of her trousers were sticking to her thighs at every step. After one last meal at her expense, flying insects the size of pinheads were drowning in the sweat at her temples. She was careful not to think of the high desert, the open spaces and crisp dry winds.

Taco was leashed. Anna loosed him to let him make his own way down the treacherous bank, then followed, clinging to roots and keeping her fanny close to the dirt so any fall would be short-lived. Uncomfortable in the role of a female impersonator, the dog didn't run off Lassie-like to help in the search but seemed content to stay at Anna's heels. For a quarter of an hour, she picked her way through forest debris, down sudden gullies lined with soil that collapsed when she stepped on it. The whole state seemed to be rotting away, crumbling into whatever hell lay below the surface of the land.

The cycle of life was immediate in Mississippi. In the high deserts, dust-to-dust and ashes-to-ashes was the way of things. The fallen—plants, animals, people—became seared, desiccated, purified, reduced to fine arid molecules that were swept away, fed to the hills. With the rain's clear magic they became spring's new growth. Not so here. There was no phoenix-from-the-ashes mystery. Here the downed became fodder for new life before the body had grown cold.

Dead trees were rife with growth springing from the carcass before their own leaves had fallen. Older deadwood lay beneath a carpet of burgeoning life so thick the logs were merely a mound beneath. And everything was green; the living and the dead carpeted with moss. Last year's leaves were spiked through with this year's grasses growing toward vines that dropped from overhead. In turn, the vines were misted with Spanish moss.

The bones of the earth did not show through: no rocky ridges, no escarpments. And the land did not lie sensibly, mountains to foothills to plains with water cutting always downhill. The forested ground behind Rocky looked as if it had been crumpled by a giant hand and thrown down. Ravines, going nowhere, intersected then dead-ended. Ragged hillocks furred with growth pushed up without rhyme or reason. Water did not carve the land in gravity's rational manner as it did in the West, but sculpted at random as the winds of southern Utah sculpted the mountains.

Finally Taco began to bark and darted away from the narrow and fading deer trail they'd been following. Knowing he might be pursuing nothing more interesting than a panicked squirrel, Anna went after him. She found him in a vine-tangled clearing.

He'd located the source of his treat.

"Taco!" she yelled. "Get away from it."

Cowed by her tone, he backed off.

"Holy shit," Anna breathed and, shrugging out of her pack, she dug out the radio.

"Five-seven-nine, five-eight-zero," she said into the mike.

Thigpen answered immediately and for that she was grateful. "Where are you?" she demanded.

The radio clicked as if he fingered his mike button before answering. "Down by the creek," came the reply. Behind his words Anna could hear "The Girl from Ipanema" playing. The son of a bitch hadn't even left his car. He was still squatting in the parking lot outside the ranger station.

"Stand by," she said. Having changing frequencies, she put in a call to Sheriff Paul Davidson.

"Davidson," came back quickly followed by, "My twenty is about a mile north of Rocky Springs."

An efficient man. What his location was would have been her next question.

"I think I've found your missing girl," Anna said.

She told him to meet Thigpen at Rocky and gave him directions from the graveyard. There was probably a quicker way to get to where she was, but not knowing the lay of the land, she wasn't going to risk experimentation.

After tying Taco well away from the scene, ignoring his injured innocence at having been restrained through no fault of his own, she made three more calls: one to Randy Thigpen to bring an evidence collection kit, one to headquarters in Tupelo—chief rangers liked to know when dead bodies appeared in their parks—and the last to Steve Stilwell, the district ranger nearest her as the crow flies. She was going to need all the help she could get. This pathetic corpse had the earmarks of a political bomb. When it went off, she didn't want to be alone, the sacrificial maiden. The image was too apt, and she felt the weight of thirty years of the women's movement settle on her shoulders.

Sitting with her back to a tree trunk, Anna waited. But for the popliteal artery behind an exposed knee and the girl's wrist, Anna'd touched nothing. There'd been no pulse, the flesh cool with the unreal feel of death. Rigor had gone off. The child had been dead more than twelve hours.

Panic rummaged around Anna's insides. A stranger in a strange land, new to a job where she was not welcome. Reality—control—was trying to slip away. It alarmed her how anxious she was for Sheriff Davidson to show up and take command. Only that wouldn't do. Not now. Now she was a district ranger; she was in charge. How she handled this would set the tone for her entire stay on the Natchez Trace. *Lonely lies the head that wears the crown,* the words came unbidden to mind. The quote was wrong, she knew that, and she had no idea what it was from. Zach would have known. Loneliness swept over her in a wave that made her weak. Someone to share with. God. It had been a long time.

Zach was an actor. "Must have been Shakespeare," she said aloud to dispel the awfulness. Taco was unmoved.

Concurrent jurisdiction, she remembered. Law enforcement on the Natchez Trace was shared with the local constabulary. Some comfort in that.

"The timing sucks," she said.

To stay in her own skin, she began to do her job. Without moving, she took stock of what she could see. One thing at a time. She could handle that.

Anna'd seen dead bodies before. A baker's dozen or so who'd been taken out by automobiles, falls, fires and, once, a flash flood. She'd even seen corpses dispatched by human violence—not a lot, not like a "real" cop in a city. For the most part, parks were peaceful places, marauding raccoons and bad sunburns the staple of the crime-fighting units. Bodies didn't show up on every shift. But she'd crossed paths with a handful. Nothing like this, though. This made her sick and angry and scared. She wondered, without looking forward to it, what they'd find when the noose was untied and the sheet removed. There was no telling what the girl had died of but it was clear there'd been head injury. The cloth covering her face was drenched in blood, black now, like the flies that feasted on it.

"Sort it out," she told herself. "Sort it out." She began her notes, unaware that her left hand was clamped firmly in the familiar warmth of the dog's fur.

The body was in a wide space between the trees, not properly a clearing, but breathing space. Fallen logs interlocked with the living forest on two sides, forming a tiny natural amphitheater. The ground was green with vines and a low-growing plant thick with small, white, star-shaped blossoms. A delicate, sweet fragrance rose from somewhere, slightly masking the cloying smell of dead and fly-blown meat.

"Okay," she said to Taco just because talking to someone, even a dog, made her feel less like a neutron lost in the far reaches of space. "What's here? Two legs, encased in nylon—pantyhose—obviously belonging to a young girl. From what I can see, the hose is undamaged. Sandals." The shoes were so like those worn by Heather Barnes, Anna's fragmented mind flashed on innumerable phone calls she and Sylvia had exchanged in high school. *What are you going to wear?* Heaven forbid one should be so unique as to cause untoward comment. The teenage struggle to fit in yet be special at the same time. Maybe Heather and Danielle—Danni—had had like conversations. Times changed. People didn't.

Legs were exposed to the thigh. A border of black showed below the sheet. Probably

Danielle—if this was Danielle—wore a micro-mini dress like the one Heather had on when she drank herself insensible. Above the blackness was the creepiest part, if the murder of a child could be broken down into degrees of creepiness: a white sheet, with holes cut out where the eyes might be, had been draped over the corpse's head. The eyeholes, askew, showed only a nose and the flesh of one cheek. The sheet fell to just below the girl's crotch and the hem of her minidress. *Minidress,* Anna thought, relevant of nothing. Did kids call them that anymore?

"Focus, Taco," she admonished the unoffending hound. "Okay. A noose tied around the neck on the outside of the sheet. Heavy yellow line, nylon or plastic, like the kind used to moor boats." It was as if the killer had intended to hang the girl but had been interrupted in the process. Who had added the sheet? In the South—in all of America—a sheet with eyeholes was the symbol of the Ku Klux Klan. Had the girl been wearing it and thus was killed? Or had the killer put it on to make a point? The frail-looking legs, not broken but sprawled in the ungraceful attitude of death, belonged to a white girl, a Caucasian. Did the Klan hang its own? Was there still an active Klan in Mississippi?

Anna wished someone would come. Sheriff Paul Davidson, even the wretched Thigpen, would be a relief.

Davidson would know she'd found a body. Once he arrived, the machinery of investigation would follow: deputies, coroners, photographers. At least she assumed that's how it would go. She'd never worked with Mississippi law enforcement. Sheriffs were elected, not necessarily brought up through the ranks. Good, bad or indifferent, though, people would show up. Probably great heavy-footed sods. She'd called Thigpen herself. District Ranger Stilwell was on his way, and Chief Ranger Brown. Soon the place would be a zoo.

With a sense of duty and with time running out, Anna shook off her self-pity and stood, careful to keep her feet in one place lest she prove to be a heavy-footed sod herself.

Mississippi was good at covering her sins—and her scars. The weave of plant and insect life didn't provide a surface where the casual detective would easily find a clue, be it a button or a burned-out match. But given the crude violence of the girl's attack, perhaps Anna was not dealing with a murderer of great subtlety and stealth.

Focusing eyes and mind, she studied the miniature glade. It was slightly sunken, as if a giant had pressed his thumb into the earth. The sheet-covered girl lay in the middle of the depression. Her legs sprawled to the east and her head—Anna dearly hoped there was a head inside the noose-tied sheet—to the west. Weeds and vines gave nothing up. To the eastern edge of the sunken area, maybe a yard from the patent-leather shod feet, was a thigh-high fallen log, covered with plate-sized mushrooms that jutted out from the sides. A swath cut through them where someone had scraped a boot or dragged something over the log.

Staying to the edge of the scene and studying each step before she took it, Anna worked her way around to the far side of the rotting timber. Bark on the log's top, soft from decay, had been crushed.

Either the child had been found here or chased here and murdered, or she'd been carried here and dumped after she was dead. The sheet she was wearing, the noose tight around her neck, suggested an aborted hanging. Without more information, it was impossible to tell if the girl had dressed herself as KKK— or Casper the Friendly Ghost—and been killed for it, or if her killer had put the drape on her, attempted to hang her, when she ran and was clubbed down.

"Don't speculate," Anna told herself, aware of the danger of falling in love with a theory to the exclusion of the facts.

Standing with her back to the dead girl, she looked in the direction that she and her killer must have come from. The murdered girl wore square-heeled sandals, as easy to follow as Heather's. Despite the creeping river of life that covered the ground, if she'd come this way on her own two legs, Anna would soon know it.

Backtracking could wait.

She turned again to the green pocket holding the body. The feet looked so tiny and pathetic in their silly shoes. The patent leather of the sandals was specked with mud and the rhinestone-studded strap over the ankle of the left foot had been broken. Runs scarred the hose on both legs and smears of mud discolored the knees. This child had been chased, and not in fun. She had run hard enough and through rough enough country that she must have been terribly frightened. Considering the end she had met, the fear wasn't unfounded. One of her hands was hidden beneath the folds of the sheet that had become her shroud but the other lay palm up, sad and white on the rich drop-cloth of green. The nails were neatly painted, none broken or discolored. A few scratches crosshatched her forearms but they were thin, shallow; she'd probably gotten them from branches hitting her as she fled. From the looks of it, she had run, but she had not fought. Young ladies were not taught to fight. Not for the first time, Anna thought that was a crying shame. Especially in a world where young girls, like baby ducklings, were at the bottom of the food chain.

From where she stood, Anna could see the rest of the rope that formed the noose. Partially hidden in the grass and weeds, it snaked up from where it was tied around the neck to vanish into the undergrowth. Moving with care, she continued to circumnavigate the scene until she stood above the sheeted corpse, opposite the fungus-covered log. The rope was pulled this direction, pulled taut then dropped. The line of yellow nylon ran straight for about three yards, then the remainder lay all in a heap.

Had the girl been dragged, half blinded by the sheet, a rope around her neck like an animal? Tears and bile mixed in Anna's throat. Swearing softly, she turned away. She'd never given much thought to the hierarchies of murder, the good, the bad, the brutal. But this was the stuff of nightmares. This was why the NPS kept all those shrinks on tap to work with rangers after an ugly event. Anna'd always hated those sessions. Maybe this time it wouldn't be such a bad idea.

The sound of voices cut into her thoughts. She reminded herself she was a grown-up, a district ranger for Christ's sake, glad to see them but not *too* glad. Then she hollered, "Over here."

6

A county sheriff had never looked so good, but Anna congratulated herself on handling it well. The only slip was she did step forward to shake the man's hand just as if she'd not done the same thing when she met him several hours earlier.

Thigpen arrived in the sheriff's wake. He was wringing wet with sweat and huge with pompous proclamations about waiting for the arrival of the chief ranger, about his strong suspicion that the body would be found just precisely here. Other than to tell him not to smoke or in any other way risk contaminating the crime scene, Anna pretty much ignored him.

Davidson stood on the edge of the depression that held the girl, letting Ranger Thigpen's ongoing advice wash over him. Self-discipline or Southern manners kept him from demanding the silence the death of a child and the mind of a policeman required.

Under his breath, he whistled a tune Anna'd heard once before, a long time ago, but couldn't place. Comfortable in her skin again, she waited, letting him think. Finally he said, "You look around some?"

The question was an open-ended invitation. Anna accepted it and began listing the observations she had made while waiting. Thigpen stepped forward and in a loud voice began countering her observations with those of his own.

"The kid was hung. The rope must've broken. This is where she fell."

Rather than waste breath arguing the obvious, Anna made an executive decision she knew she'd pay for later but, hell, in for a penny...

"Randy," she cut him off. "I need you to go back to the ranger station. Get a measuring tape, 35mm camera, pens, paper, envelopes." She went on to list all the things in the evidence collection kit that he hadn't bothered to bring. Its absence didn't make her think worse of him. Murder in the parks, any crime that required intricate collection of trace evidence for that matter, was rare. Rangers were trained in it, but without cause to use those skills, most lost them. Anna had. She'd no more faith in herself to lift an important fingerprint or make casting of a boot print than she would to sing an aria. To do these things well required practice. What made her already low opinion of her erstwhile subordinate drop another notch was that he'd not had the respect—or the spine—to tell her he had no kit.

When she finished, Randy pursed his lips, nodded and said, "Barth can get 'em."

"I'd like you to," Anna said. "You've seen the situation firsthand. You might think of something I've forgotten. Also, I need you to be there when the district ranger from Ridgeland arrives. Show him where we are."

Thigpen spent a moment or two thinking. Anna guessed he was weighing how far he dared to openly flout her orders. Being in on something big in the parks gave a ranger status, bragging rights. Whether he wanted to work or not, Randy Thigpen didn't want to miss out.

A conclusion was reached, and he got in his parting shot. "Good point about Stilwell." He named the district ranger to the north. "A good man to have on the job. *He* knows what he's doing."

Anna let it pass. Many years had elapsed since her skin had been so thin a dart as meager as that could penetrate. Davidson was not so well-armored. He shot the big ranger a look that was equal parts anger and contempt. Anna allowed herself one small smile as she watched Randy struggle, knowing he couldn't apologize to the sheriff without committing himself to open warfare with his new boss.

He settled for telling Anna, "There is a better way than you had us come," and forged off through the woods at an oblique angle to the path they'd followed from the graveyard. According to Anna's brochure map, he was heading toward the fragment of sunken trace that ran just this side of Little Sand Creek.

"Where were we?" Davidson asked as the sound of Thigpen's progress faded. Anna finished her litany of suspected evils.

The sheriff had a camera in an olive-drab sack he carried. After taking photographs of the scene from various angles, he asked Anna to go through her list once more and meticulously photographed each item she mentioned—the shoes and feet, the fungus, the roping, the hands—three shots each to bracket the light.

That done, they stopped by mutual unspoken accord and stared at the sheeted body. "I guess it's time to unwrap her," Anna said at last.

"I guess." Neither moved to do it. "You do a lot of this?" he asked.

"No. You?"

"It seems like a lot to me but I guess it isn't. This is my first kid, believe it or not. You know—that wasn't a car accident or something."

"Mine too," Anna said, made free by his confession. "It changes it. And I don't even much like kids." She was wishing she hadn't added that last—it sounded so heartless given the circumstances—but Davidson laughed and she was, if not exonerated, then forgiven. "Let's get to it," she said.

Having donned latex gloves from her first aid kit, she carefully removed the noose from around the sheet-draped neck and slid it over the head. As she worked, the sheriff took photographs: the knot, the creases the rope left in the fabric of the sheet.

Anna'd forgotten how much a human head weighs. Slipping the noose free, she let the head fall a couple of inches and flinched when it thudded into the ground. Starting at the ragged hem, she folded the sheet up around the girl's thighs so any loose trace evidence there might be would be contained rather than shaken loose and lost.

The sheet was old, worn soft and thin. Guessing by the size, it came from a baby's crib or a cot. Faint dark lines ran across one corner and again up near the noose, stains that looked as if they'd been there through a number of launderings. All this Anna noted aloud, speaking into the tape recorder in the breast pocket of her uniform shirt. She preferred written notes but her hands were otherwise occupied.

The victim wore a little black dress, not quite so revealing as Heather's but nearly so, with a spider-web design in rhinestones across the chest. The girl was slight but full-breasted. The flimsy gown had fallen off her shoulders, exposing a black satin strapless Wonderbra with its carefully engineered upthrust. Times had changed. When Anna was in high school, girls had to make do with gym socks shoved into the Playtex. Not to mention what the nuns would have done had any girl at Mercy High showed up in such an abbreviated confection. "I'm getting old," Anna said to Davidson to make the image of this little girl, alive, excited, dressing up for her date, go away.

In a way, she thought, it must be harder for a man to see such a thing. Not only were they trained—at least the good ones—to protect women, but such a display of girlish flesh must cause, if not mixed signals from the body, at least the uncomfortable knowledge that such a thing was possible. "Baby women," Anna said, apropos of nothing.

"I see them all the time," he said. "Some friends of mine and I were down on the Gulf, and I saw this girl in a tiny bathing suit. I turned to my buddy and told him to take a look. The kid came closer. It was his daughter. I've known her since she was in diapers. I'd been telling my pal to leer at his own daughter. I'd been leering. I was half sick for a week."

Who was this guy, Anna wondered, telling her things like that. "Do you still leer?" she asked just to have something to say.

"On special occasions, but only if the leeree is clearly over forty."

"Not twenty-one?"

"Carding them prior to leering takes the fun out of it." Neither of them could carry the conversation further with the dead between them. Holding her breath though the body had yet to get really ripe, Anna began peeling the sheet off the girl's neck and face. Abrasions discolored the throat but there was no bruising, and no ligature marks. She'd not been hanged. Odds were the rope had been put around her neck after death.

The sheet came away from the left side of the face easily, exposing a girl in her early-to-mid-teens who had been pretty. Now the bugs had found her and she showed a nightmare countenance. Blood matting the hair, the skin and the cotton fibers of the makeshift hood stuck the sheet to the right side of her face.

"I don't want to jerk this off," Anna told Davidson. "I'm afraid I'll screw up any trace evidence in the wound or the hair."

Davidson took some close-ups of the girl's face while Anna finished her observations. Trace evidence would be sent to the Mississippi Crime Lab in Jackson.

"Looks like a severe blow to the right side of the head." That was it. A blunt and ugly truth. "Do you want to tell the parents or shall I?" Anna asked.

"I'll do it. If this is Danielle Posey—and we've got no reason to think otherwise at this point—I know her father to talk to. I worked a fender-bender on the Trace near I-20 there out of Clinton. A drunk hit him, an old black man in a pickup truck. Mr. Posey was not happy. He wanted that old man drawn and quartered, legally speaking. There wasn't much I could do. The old guy had no money, no insurance and taking away his driver's license was a moot point, since he'd never bothered to get one. When I asked him why he said, 'I never needed one till now.' "

Anna laughed. Davidson finished the photos, and she was grateful to let the sheet drop back over the child's face, hiding the fester of ants that marked where the eyes had been.

"Can't blame Posey a whole heck of a lot," the sheriff went on as they picked their way back to the side of what they'd deemed the crime scene area. "He's got an older boy that's nothing but trouble and Danielle, a farm that can't clear more than twenty or thirty grand a year, and a wife that's in and out of mental hospitals all the time. That'd be enough to fray anybody's nerves. Anyway, I'll get him down to ID the body. Poor guy. What could be worse? Asked to come see if a dead girl's your daughter and it is."

The deep and apparently genuine compassion in the sheriff's voice touched Anna. With that touch, the human tragedy of the situation came home and she felt sadness as a physical weight across the back of her neck. Paul Davidson began whistling again. This time Anna remembered the song. She'd heard it on Cumberland Island: "Jesus Met the Woman."

"You'll meet Posey," Davidson said. "I believe he leases some of his land from the Trace. Cotton or soybeans." There wasn't much else to say, and they stood side by side, Taco at their feet, staring at the ruined child.

The sound of voices approaching from the northeast, the direction of the sunken Trace,

110

Little Sand Creek and Rocky Springs campground brought the two of them out of whatever hole their thoughts were taking them down.

"Jesus Christ," Anna growled. "It sounds like a herd of elephants. If there was anything on Miss Posey's trail to find they'll have smashed it all to hell." The damage was done. It was too late to do anything but fume and Anna watched sourly as three men tramped out of the woods. Ranger Thigpen was in the lead, a cigarette in his hand that he only flicked away after making sure Anna had seen it. Behind him, trim and neat in NPS green and gray, was a ranger Anna'd not met. Trailing was a deputy in the crisp uniform of the Claiborne County Sheriff's Department. The deputy was first to speak. He was young and fit, the short walk not even causing him to break a sweat. He was a couple of shades darker than Anna's ranger, Barth Dinkin, and about forty pounds lighter. Showing his mama had raised him right, he took off his Stetson, nodded at Paul, then Anna.

"Sheriff. Ma'am." Amenities taken care of, he turned to his boss. "The coroner's waiting at Rocky. Says he'll take your word she's dead."

"He's not coming to the scene?" Anna was appalled.

"Dwight's getting on in years," Davidson explained.

"He's seventy-eight, ma'am, had a birthday day before yesterday," the deputy put in.

"He doesn't get around like he used to," Davidson added.

"And he keeps getting elected?" Anna asked.

"Without the money he makes as a coroner, he'd be pretty bad off," Davidson said, as if that explained everything.

Anna had a lot to learn about social welfare in Mississippi.

The deputy went into conference with the sheriff, and the natty ranger stepped up to Anna. He was compact and wiry, and his dark hair, shot with gray, fell over his forehead. A neatly trimmed, thoroughly grizzled beard covered his jaw. There was about him a puckish mischief that Anna suspected had allowed him to get away with murder most of his life. With a child's corpse at her feet, the hackneyed phrase jarred, and she said with more asperity than she'd intended, "Who are you?"

"Gunga Din at your service," he said, and clicked his heels together and bowed at the waist.

For a moment Anna was flummoxed and annoyed by the sensation, then she remembered. "The water boy. Steven Stilwell. Thank you. If the Rocky Springs water tastes as bad as it smells, I'm in your debt."

"Good. I like being owed."

Because one couldn't look or keep one's thoughts elsewhere else for any length of time, they turned toward the body.

"Not much of a welcome to Mississippi," Stilwell said.

"Not much," Anna admitted.

"John Brown's on his way. It's about a three-hour drive from Tupelo. I can do it in two and a half."

Anna nodded. One of the perks—or pitfalls—of being in law enforcement. It was easy to become a chronic speeder. Stilwell was in the next level of addiction: not only doing it but boasting of it. The only unacceptable level of the malady was boasting about it in the presence of civilians who were ticketed, and rightly so, when caught indulging.

"We can't just leave the body lying here being eaten by insects while the chief ranger drives down from Timbuktu," Anna said.

"Tupelo."

To Anna they were one in the same but she forbore comment. She wondered whether to talk with the sheriff about the next step, defer to Stilwell, radio the chief ranger and ask him what to do or just wade in and take charge. Much as she loathed it, given Thigpen and Dinkin's response to her arrival, the gender question was very much in the air. Davidson seemed okay and Stilwell had done nothing to set her radar off, but the situation had her second-guessing herself. She didn't like it.

Please yourself, she heard her mother's voice. *Then at least one person will be happy with your decision.*

"What's the usual protocol, Paul?" she asked.

"Tag her and bag her," Randy Thigpen said. Anna'd forgotten he was there. She chose to forget again.

"We'll get her covered up," Paul Davidson replied. "Get her out to the parking lot so Dwight can give his stamp of approval."

"How do you want to transport?" Anna asked. "Ambulance? Are the autopsies done in Jackson or where?"

"Steven Hayne at Mississippi Mortuary in Rankin," Davidson said and added, "Have 'em send an ambulance, I guess. All Dwight's got is an old pickup he uses to haul wood. We've used it in a pinch, but it doesn't seem right today."

Anna called dispatch for an ambulance, then radioed Chief Ranger Brown. He'd been instrumental in hiring her, but the call was more than just courtesy or toadying. Brown had talked to her half a dozen times during the interminable process of hiring and struck her as a fair-minded man who knew his job. From the scuttlebutt she'd picked up during phone chats with the secretary in personnel, he'd come up through the ranks from a GS-4 seasonal law enforcement ranger in Death Valley to the exalted position of chief, and not via the fast track with the Office of Personnel Management pulling the puppet strings.

John Brown was at mile marker 105 in Stilwell's district north of Jackson. Davidson suggested he meet up with them at the mortuary, but Brown wanted to see the crime scene. Anna put her radio away.

Sheriff Davidson, hat in hand, was standing over the sad little heap of rotting flesh that had so recently been a pretty girl going to her high school prom. Anna'd never seen a cop doing it before, but she could have sworn the sheriff was praying. For some reason it bothered her. To cover it, she said: "In the words of Ranger Thigpen, it's time to bag and tag."

Unruffled by her harshness, he finished whatever silent communion he was in the midst of, then restored his hat.

As Anna watched to see that nothing of importance was dislodged, the body was lifted into a black plastic body bag the deputy had brought. The rope, an ugly companion in death, was coiled into the bag with the child's remains. Everyone, Anna was sure, even Thigpen, was relieved when the zipper closed over her face.

Together the sheriff and his deputy lifted their burden. Davidson took it in his arms, cradling the body as carefully as if it were still able to feel human kindness. With Thigpen leading the way, the three of them left to meet the ambulance and the aging coroner at Rocky Springs.

"What's left to do?"

The question came from Steve Stilwell. Anna had forgotten about him. He leaned against a tree, hands in his pockets, a grass stem between his teeth. The sheaf of salt-and-pepper hair spilled over his forehead as if he'd recently been tumbled out of bed. He'd taken a tin camping cup from somewhere and filled it with water for Taco. Now the fickle beast lay with his great dripping jaws draped possessively over Stilwell's instep.

"Oh, God," Anna said, suddenly weary. "My answer of choice would be a drink but I guess we go over the back trail, or what's left of it. See if we can turn up anything."

"I've got a bottle of single malt whiskey in my car," Stilwell said unexpectedly. "Strictly for medicinal purposes, naturally. I'll buy you a drink when we're through."

"You're on." Though she didn't care much for whiskey, she was beginning to warm up to the Ridgeland district ranger.

"Trail" was a misnomer. The track back toward the campground that the others—and presumably the girl and her killer—had taken was just a way through woods as rugged and choked with decaying plant matter as the way Anna had traversed on her search for the body.

Rotten soil laid its booby traps. Stilwell called it "rotten" and that's how it appeared. The actual biological or geological phenomenon was unknown to Anna. Large patches of the ground could and did give way when weight was put on them. The sensation was like postholding: having one's foot break through the frozen crust on top of a snowfield. Except with rotten soil, it was never clear just how far the fall was going to be.

"Hell of a country for equestrians," Anna said as she extricated herself from such a place, scraping her shoe full of dirt in the process.

"They ride though. Horsey types can't help themselves. There's an active group out of

Vicksburg rides around here quite a bit," Stilwell told her.

To corroborate his point, they uncovered a bit of evidence in the form of dried road apples. They also found two of Thigpen's Marlboro Lights butts but very little else. Perhaps grasses were crushed, twigs snapped, leaves stomped into the ground—signs that would speak of recent passage—but only in books and in the eyes of the few existing trackers with a genius for it could the difference between today's pedestrians and those of the night before be told.

The lack of the unique mark the girl's rhinestone sandals would have left behind provided one scrap of information. Unless she'd come from another direction, she'd not walked but been carried to the place where she was found. Anna's best guess was that she was dead or unconscious during the trip. Otherwise there would surely have been some marks of a struggle on the body.

After thirty minutes of this largely fruitless search, Anna and Steve came to a trench. The sides were steep and twenty or thirty feet high, the bottom flat. It was six or seven yards bank to bank at the narrowest point and as much as twenty where the sides had been eroded back over the years. A foot path wandered down the center.

"This is it?" Anna asked.

"You've got about seven miles of it all told," Stilwell said. "In bits and pieces. But this is a section of the Old Trace. Hard to believe it was cut so deep with anything less than a bulldozer, isn't it?"

Considering the havoc the passing of Thigpen, the sheriff and the deputy had caused, Anna believed it. Where they'd first climbed, then, burdened with the corpse, descended, the bank was deeply scored and broken at the lip. Looking up and down this short stretch of history, Anna saw more evidence of horseback riders, great gouts of soil where destructive hooves had been forced up the inclines. She started a new list in her head: Things That Would Be Different from Now On.

Along the bottom of the banks more damage had been done, fresh digging.

"Armadillos," Stilwell informed her when she asked about it. "They have noses like army spoons. One of 'em can root up half an acre if the grub hunting is good."

"Ah," she said. The park being their home, the armadillos could stay. The horse riders would have to be rerouted onto less sensitive terrain.

Anna added to the damage by scrambling down the bank on fanny, heels and hands. She and Steve searched the floor of the Old Trace for forty yards in each direction. None of the skidding slides down the bank appeared to have been made recently. The edges of the tracks were rounded, dried and crumbling. Either the murderer entered precisely where Thigpen had obliterated all possibility of finding tracks or he had not entered the woods from the sunken

Trace. Anna figured it was the former. If the murder had occurred at or near the campground, or even on the new, paved Natchez Trace where it ran by Rocky, this would have been the most direct route to where the girl was found. At night, in the woods, carrying a hundred pounds of dead weight, one would tend not to take the scenic route.

The ruination of the back trail was a severe loss. Anna thought about that for a while.

Randy Thigpen had destroyed evidence, tried to contaminate the crime scene with ashes and butts, and attempted to lead Sheriff Davidson astray by misinterpreting the observations Anna was making.

"What do you know about Randy Thigpen?" she asked abruptly as they walked back to Rocky, still looking but no longer with any expectation of finding.

"Well..." Steve thought for a moment, then smiled, his small teeth glittering in his beard. "I know I'm really, really glad he's yours and not mine."

"How so?"

"In the four months I was acting district ranger down here—in addition, I might add, to my heavy load of responsibilities in Ridge-land—"

Anna smiled to show she was a fun kind of gal.

"—Randy went on disability for a soft tissue injury to the neck that can't be medically proved or disproved. Interfered with his ability to draw his weapon was the deal. Then sued on grounds of age discrimination to get back on patrol when it turned out John wasn't going to give him an indefinite vacation but merely a change of duties where the gun arm was not a factor. What else? Good with machinery. Lots of local contacts. Good at dealing with lessees. Fries catfish in some kind of batter that Chez Paul would die for. Married to a nice little woman from Crystal Springs who he's been philandering on with a gal in Bovina for years."

"Any connection with the Poseys?"

Walking just ahead of Anna through an infestation of kudzu that smelled disconcertingly like grape Nehi, Stilwell said: "He'd've had contact with the Poseys when renewing their lease, I guess. Other than that I can't say. Why? Hoping to pin a bit of homicide on him?"

Anna laughed. "It crossed my mind." She wasn't precisely compiling a list of suspects, but Thigpen was an irresistible target. Like a needle to True North, her suspicions turned to sexists and sloths. Wishful thinking. Most sexists and sloths lacked the intellectual acuity or energy to commit crimes of much intricacy.

Lost in thought, Anna hadn't realized she was no longer walking till Stilwell's voice cut through the fog.

"You don't want to stop here," he warned.

The possibility of danger brought her back into the three dimensional world. "Why not?" Automatically her eyes and ears probed for predators. Nothing but deep, fragrant, leafy vines in every direction, so thick she couldn't see the path at her feet and so aggressive they'd climbed a dozen trees, smothered them till dead and now cloaked the lifeless limbs with a parody of the original foliage. So dense six hundred fifty water moccasins could be lounging on their snaky little bellies within inches of her toes and she'd never know it till she waded into the middle of them.

"Why not?" she repeated with more urgency.

"You stand still too long in this stuff and it'll grow right up your leg. Who knows which of those green shapes were once trees and which were slow hikers. Kudzu grows up to eighteen inches a day in the summer." Stilwell combed his hair back off his face with his fingers. The movement was provocative but totally ingrained, as if twenty-five years ago he'd taken to doing it because it was sexy and somewhere along the line it had become habit.

Anna laughed and began moving. The idea of snakes didn't stray too far from mind. Most snakes, deadly or not, were beautiful animals. Not so the cottonmouth. Not to Anna's way of thinking. They were fat, like garden slugs, the color of mud and so nearsighted it made them mean.

Taco, piously leashed in honor of the chief ranger's impending arrival, minced along at her heels as if the same thing was on his mind.

Stepping where Stilwell stepped, Anna was haunted by the South. Things were out of whack. The land refused to show you its skeleton. Sheriffs prayed openly for the souls

121

of the departed. Children frolicked in ceme-
teries. Used-car salesmen captained armies of
ghosts.

In the South, it seemed, the dead, like the
poor, were always with you.

7

John Brown stayed through the time Anna had
hoped for a belt of Stilwell's single malt. The
verdict was clear: she was to dedicate all time
and resources to the murder case. In and of
itself, the murder would have taken some
precedence, though not too much. In areas of
shared jurisdiction, the parks were happy to
let local law enforcement or, because it was
on federal lands, the FBI—with their greater
expertise and connections in grisly matters—
handle things. But this corpse was draped in
a white sheet, a lynching rope tied around her
neck, items unpleasantly reminiscent of the
Ku Klux Klan and the volatile racial history
of the state of Mississippi.

Anna left the meeting, held knee-to-knee in
Rocky Springs' tiny office, with a list of phone
numbers and strict orders to report everything, every day, to Brown and to take no
action whatsoever before he was consulted. This
last was a codicil higher management dearly
loved to tack on the tail end of assignments.
Trouble was, often action was required in

such a manner that it was virtually impossible to say to the perpetrator "hold that thought. I've got to call my supervisor."

Still and all, Anna was satisfied. Brown was a good man and, unless the politics of the bureaucracy made it absolutely necessary for his survival, probably wouldn't hang her out to dry.

Davidson called in the afternoon to let her know Fred Posey had identified the body. It was his daughter, Danielle. She and Davidson split the chores. Anna would try and track down who was with Danni the night she died. The sheriff would see to the autopsy and coroner's reports and take care of sending the rope, the sheet and the child's clothes to forensics for possible trace evidence.

As district ranger, Anna needed to find a way to include Barth and Randy, if only peripherally. They had the local contacts and seniority on the Trace. To exclude them would be an obvious slap in the face that boded ill for what already promised to be a rocky relationship. To Randy she gave the task of interviewing everyone in the campground who had been there the night before, when the girl was killed. He made it clear the job was beneath him without saying so right out. With an attitude like that, he'd slough through it. Anna would do it again when he'd finished to preserve what scraps of information there might be.

She asked Barth Dinkin to talk with Danni's parents. During the impromptu meeting after the body had been taken away, she found he'd known Mr. and Mrs. Posey for seven years. Nothing warm and personal, but he and not Randy had handled the annual renewal of their lease. The Poseys farmed forty-three acres of Trace land up near the city of Clinton on the northernmost end of Anna's district. Posey grew corn and soybeans—part of the natural and agricultural look the Trace was dedicated to preserving. Familiarity went a long way. She hoped Barth would get more cooperation from the bereaved family than she might. Barth hadn't seemed excited at the prospect, but there'd been no undercurrent of rebellion or insurrection.

At the top of her own list was Heather Barnes. That worked well. Heather and her parents lived in Clinton, forty miles up the Trace. Anna had it on good authority that there were real grocery stores there. Her diet had consisted of granola bars and coffee with Cremora for the last day and a half. This morning a really serious issue had arisen; she was running low on cat food. The NPS frowned on rangers, in uniform, performing obviously personal chores on the taxpayers' time. Keenly aware the new girl would be watched like a hawk by all and sundry, Anna scrupulously cleared the planned foraging with Chief Ranger Brown.

The Trace between Rocky and I-20 was as beautiful as it had been the morning Anna arrived, but this morning she was better able to appreciate it. She played with the radar in her patrol car. Guadalupe, Isle Royale, Mesa

Verde—none of the other parks she'd worked were automobile oriented. There'd been no need for radar. Now she zapped oncoming motorists with a childlike glee. Sixty-six, sixty-two, seventy-one, fifty-eight: everybody was speeding. Because this was a park, fifty miles per hour was the posted limit. Judging by the fact that even the sight of her patrol car failed to slow the visitors, Anna surmised Randy and Barth weren't big on writing traffic citations. Cynicism pinched her thoughts as she noted her lack of surprise.

Today the speeders were safe from the rigors of the new regime. She was otherwise engaged. Still, she did look forward to catching some: the pleasures of the hunt.

Clinton was a pretty little town, with the main street paved in brick and a college that looked like a miniature version of Ivy League done in red brick instead of gray stone. The trees impressed Anna the most, great old oaks, feathery mimosa, stands of pine, elm, locust, crabapple in wild pink blossoms, Bradford pears in modest white. Their age and dignity reminded her that Mississippi had been settled long before most of the rest of the country.

The high school was a relatively new building set on the edge of town, essentially in the country by the standards of more populated states. What struck Anna most forcefully as she drove in the long entry road were the cars. The place had a parking lot to rival that of a small shopping mall, and it was full. Didn't anybody ride the bus down here?

Anna parked the Crown Vic next to a shiny red Honda Acura with plates reading SWT16. A good percentage of the students' cars were new models. There were a couple of Jags and one Corvette. Clinton had money.

The school—light, airy, modern, with white pillars lining a two-story foyer, high ceilings and wide clean halls—gave Anna the willies. On the rare occasions she had to enter high schools, there was always that ubiquitous adolescent sense that boys in groups were snickering at her. She found herself walking more quickly, hoping to reach the principal's office before the bell rang and the halls were flooded with teenagers.

The principal was in Atlanta on business. The vice principal, Adele Mack, showed Anna into her office. Vice Principal Mack was in her mid-thirties, neatly dressed in hose and heels. The only thing that marred what would have been a fine face was a heavy mask of expertly applied makeup. From ten feet away, Ms. Mack displayed a mannequin's beauty. Up close and personal, it was a little creepy.

"Can I help you?" Ms. Mack asked when Anna'd been politely seated. Actually, she said: "Kin aye help yew?" but Anna was already getting accustomed to the accent. It grew on a person. There was a gentleness to it that was reassuring.

Anna told her why she'd come and waited. In cases involving juveniles, she had learned to tread with utmost care. Though Heather was neither suspected nor accused of any crime, and Anna merely wanted to get what information she might have about Danielle, the night and the prom, she would go with the vice principal's recommendation on how this interview was to take place.

To Adele Mack's credit, Anna was thoroughly grilled. No student was going to be unnecessarily bothered on Ms. Mack's watch.

Anna sat up straight as Sister Mary Corine had taught her and answered clearly and quietly, to appear as unthreatening as possible. In the end, the vice principal agreed to call Heather out of class. Anna could talk with her in the teachers' conference room. Guessing that was where bad news, reprimands and other unpleasant exchanges between faculty and students took place, Anna asked if the gym was free. Kids tended to be more forthcoming with hardwood under their feet.

Heather was duly fetched, and she and Anna walked together to the gymnasium. The girl looked much improved from the last time Anna had seen her but infinitely less accessible. Her flawless little face was hidden behind a coat of paint nearly as thick as that worn by Adele Mack, and there was a sullenness about her that Anna hadn't noticed before.

The gymnasium was sunk partway into the ground, with high windows for light and two banks of bleacher seats like those one would expect on a professional basketball court. The shining wood floor was emblazoned with a white arrow inside a big red C. An odd school mascot, but Anna didn't dare ask about it for fear of appearing hopelessly out of it.

Heather plunked down on the highest bench of the bleachers, and Anna slid in beside her, uncomfortably aware of the nine-millimeter dragging at her hip.

"I can't tell you anything," Heather said, staring at manicured nails painted in pale blue glitter. "I was drunk, remember? The whole night's one big blank."

The remark wasn't a mere disclaimer. It was uttered with the finality of a closing door. And something else: fear. Anna'd been around enough frightened people in her life that she'd learned to sense the vibrations: a quivering of the breath, a skittering of the eyes, tension in the muscles of the face and neck. Not just a childish fear of authority. Heather was guarding something specific, hiding something from Anna.

Interesting. Anna's brain came into sharper focus. "I figured that," she said easily. "The higher-ups just want some background, I guess." Heather's hunched shoulders relaxed fractionally.

"Did you know Danielle Posey?" Anna asked.

Up went the shoulders.

"I guess." Heather tried for casual and missed. "I mean she goes to school here and all if that's what you mean."

"Were you friends?"

"I guess. I mean, you know, we weren't like enemies or anything."

Poor kid, Anna thought without a crumb of compassion. She was too young to know that evasion to a law enforcement officer is like scuttling to a cat. It made their metaphorical tails twitch, brought out the instinct to pounce.

"Were you with Danielle the night of the prom?"

"There were a bunch of us kind of hanging out."

Anna took that as a yes. "Were you drinking?"

"Not the ones driving," she said with well-rehearsed promptness.

Anna did not allow herself to smile. "Who was your date to the dance?" She tried another tack. Heather didn't answer immediately. Even through the layers of makeup, Anna could see a struggle taking place. Heather wanted to lie but was rapidly coming to the conclusion Anna'd already reached. Clinton was a small town, maybe twenty or thirty thousand people. Who one's date for the prom was would have been well advertised and easy to check.

Heather was sullen and scared and young but she wasn't a complete idiot. "Matt Dryer," she said.

"I saw two boys leaving the graveyard just before I found you. Was one of them Matt?"

"I don't remember. I don't remember anything. I was drunk, okay? Drunk?"

"Did you go out to Rocky Springs with Matt?"

"Why do you keep asking me stuff? I don't remember anything after leaving the dance.

You asking's not going to make me remember so quit asking... please."

Even under duress, the manners were holding. Anna was impressed. "Okay. You were drunk. A blackout. It happens. Who was Danielle's date?"

Heather stood up abruptly. "How would I know that? Look, I gotta go back to class. We've got a test."

Anna let her go. She would get nothing more out of her today. Staying in the bleachers, she watched until the door closed behind Heather. Of course she knew who Danni's date for the prom had been. She knew Anna could find out easily enough from a number of sources. Yet Heather hadn't wanted to be the one to tell her. It had been Anna's experience that people almost invariably wanted to be the one to tell. So much so it was common for them to make things up just so they could feel important, be part of the action. When they didn't want to, it could mean any number of things, usually that they had something to hide or something to fear. Heather showed symptoms of having both.

Anna sat a while longer. As a girl, she'd been strong and fast but never much of an athlete. Girls weren't athletes when she was growing up. The little ones were tomboys, the older ones misfits. Still, of all the places in a high school, the gym was the most comfortable for her. Perhaps it was because of Willy, Mrs. Williams, Anna's high school PE teacher. A woman Anna could have talked to about growing up when she couldn't talk to her own mother. She didn't talk to Willy—she bit those early bullets in silence—but she could have, and that made her memories good ones. Maybe it was simply because the genders were segregated in the gymnasium. There was a freedom in that, particularly at an age and in an age when sexuality confused, excited, shamed and glorified and all within a single heartbeat. As that thought coalesced, she realized that was why she'd brought Heather here, instinctively feeling she might have the same reaction.

As she was making her way back through the twists and turns of the halls toward the vice principal's office, the bell rang. Anna suffered momentary panic as the doors flew open and students poured out. Quelling the urge to flee, she calmed her mind and watched the colorful clacking mass, the hope of the future. Despite the noise and posturing that was part of the pack mentality, they looked to be good kids. On the whole a lot taller and prettier than when Anna'd been in high school. Acne treatments and early orthodonture accounted for part of it, but there was a worldliness to them that kids lacked once upon a time. Anna didn't think it was a bad thing. Just scary to parents who carried with them an anachronistic Model-T and milkman dream their own folks had worked so hard to leave behind.

The fashions didn't surprise her, except maybe by the lack of punk and piercing, but she did notice that in terms of how girls and women appeared, Adele Mack and Heather were not exceptions; they were the rule. Most of the girls wore heavy, beautifully applied makeup, the kind Anna would expect on a working model or an actress. No wonder Mississippi had won the Miss America Pageant more times than any other state in the union. They looked lovely in a glossy-magazine sort of way, but Anna had an almost overwhelming urge to catch them and scrub their faces.

Adele was on the phone but raised her eyebrows and grimaced to let Anna know her company was preferable to whomever she was currently speaking with.

"Ah. There. That's done for another month," Ms. Mack said after she put the phone down. "Did you have a nice talk with Heather?"

The vice principal had chosen to pretend that this visit was not promulgated by the murder of a child. In Ms. Mack's profession, little could be more heinous than the death of a student. Anna liked her for it.

"She's hiding something," Anna said, trusting Ms. Mack to understand. "I don't think it's about her, though. I get the feeling she's protecting or afraid of somebody."

The vice principal drummed the pads of her fingertips on the blotter, making a sound like a stampede of tiny pawed creatures. A habit developed, Anna guessed, to protect the porcelain nails. Customarily Anna waited out silences, finding it got more information in the long run. This time she didn't. It was probably a question of loyalties; Ms. Mack wanted to cooperate but the students were her primary concern.

"Do you know who Heather might be protecting?" Anna asked in a kindly but official tone.

"It's hard to say. Heather and Danielle were friends after a fashion. I think it was one of those friendships of convenience girls this age often form. Both of them had fallings-out with their own little cliques at about the same time. Sixteen-year-old girls are like ions—they seldom float around unattached for long. Even a best friend you don't really like is better than no best friend at all. I don't think they'd been palling around for long. Miss Wilson will know. She had both of them for homeroom and, if I'm not mistaken, geometry. Heather might could be protecting Danni, but I don't think so. Maybe Matt Dryer? He's the boyfriend. Or was before prom. They pair up about six weeks before the dance to guarantee they've got a date. The day after the crepe paper comes down, it's splitsville."

Splitsville. Adele Mack was older than Anna'd first thought. The paint job had fooled her.

"Matt's a terrific boy. There's never a dull moment when he's around. He does the usual things: shows up late, gets himself banged up, breaks girls' hearts and makes teachers earn their pay. But he's a real good boy. I can't imagine he'd get himself into any kind of serious trouble. He's smart. A smart, good boy."

"Can I talk to him?"

Adele Mack got the look of somebody who has inadvertently gotten their buddy in trouble.

"He was Heather's date. Since Heather was..." Anna was going to tell Mack of the girl's drunken state, then for some reason decided to cut Heather some slack. Maybe it was the fear she'd seen just under the girl's skin. "He might be able to remember things Heather can't. Fill in a few gaps," she concluded.

Vice Principal Mack procrastinated. She didn't want to give Matt up. She'd been much quicker to throw Heather to the wolves, assuming Anna was the wolves. If her reticence was because Matt was a good boy, did it follow that Heather was not a good girl? Suddenly Anna felt out of her league. She had no kids. Her sister Molly had no kids. Besides a brief and now long-distance relationship with fellow Park Ranger Patsy Silva's children, Anna knew no teenagers. What constituted "good" these days? In 1967, "good" had been synonymous with "virgin" for girls and "works hard" for boys. She doubted that was the case any longer.

"Matt's in band practice," Ms. Mack was saying. During Anna's momentary inattention, she'd called up Matt Dryer's class schedule on her computer screen. By the way she looked at it instead of Anna, it was clear she didn't want him disturbed.

This time Anna did wait, trusting Adele Mack suffered from a need to be fair to her charges. She did. "I'll see if he can be called out of practice," she said with a sigh and left to find whoever was in charge of calling out.

Anna decided against the gym. Good smart boys were too comfortable in general. She interviewed Matt in the front seat of her patrol car. Matt Dryer was thin, five-foot-eight or -nine, with light brown hair that looked as if it had been cut with lawn shears: coarse, very straight hair that no amount of gel or spray can tame. His mouth was wide and full-lipped, but instead of looking sensual or cruel, it lent an aspect of youthful innocence. Around his neck was a leather cord full of oddments—beads, rings, buttons—that probably meant something. He wore baggy paint-stained khakis, a white T-shirt and Birkenstocks. From the way he carried himself, Anna was willing to bet this mode of attire was on the cutting edge of cool.

"This has got to be about Danni, right?"

"How did you guess?"

"The Smokey Bear suit. Danni was killed on the Natchez Trace. It was in today's paper. Bad news."

Matt did seem like a "good" boy in the sense of a real boy, the kind Pinocchio wanted to be. He was open. He showed no flippant disrespect of the death of a fellow student nor did he seem to need to feign a personal grief he obviously did not feel.

"Did you know Danni?"

"Everybody knows everybody here, or didn't you notice? Yeah, I knew Danni. She was pretty obvious around school."

"How so obvious?"

Matt closed down slightly.

Anna took a stab at the cause. "Don't want to speak ill of the dead?"

He squinched his face up a bit and shook his hair into his eyes. Probably a hiding mechanism left over from his not-so-distant childhood. It undoubtedly drove the girls wild, the more so because it was done without self-consciousness.

"Tell me," Anna said. "It won't hurt Danni. Since I've only a professional interest in her, it won't hurt me, and it might help us catch her killer."

"I doubt it."

"Give it a shot."

"It's nothing that bad, really. It's not like Danielle was doing drugs or anything illegal."

"A slut?" Anna was intentionally jarring in hopes of shaking him out of his reticence.

"Not even that. She did this 'big woman on campus' thing mostly. In with the 'in crowd.' Nothing really. It just put me off. But hey, what do I know? Everybody else loved it. She was different this year, I thought. Since around Christmas. I was actually beginning to think she was turning into a real person. Maybe that's why I don't feel right about trashing her. Like that Princess Di thing. Somebody looks like maybe they're getting it together and, wham! Makes it worse somehow."

"What happened at Christmas?"

"What? Oh. I don't know. Maybe it wasn't

even Christmas. Just sort of last winter, you know."

"How did she change last winter?"

"It wasn't like a Jekyll and Hyde thing. It didn't happen all at once because she drank some kind of potion. It was just little things. Probably nobody else even noticed. Heck, maybe *I* didn't notice. I've got a very creative memory, you know." He grinned, and Anna couldn't help smiling back.

"Try," she said.

"Boy, you don't give up easy do you? Okay." He closed his eyes and leaned his head back on the seat. His fingers, balled into fists, pounded lightly on his thighs. "She was *nicer.* She'd smile at geeks like me in the hall once in a while—somebody who wasn't a jock. She stopped laughing all the time. Sometimes she actually looked like she was listening. She stopped trying to dress like she was some kind of socialite and wore regular clothes."

He sat a bit longer searching his self-imposed darkness for other salient observations. Anna expected him to start repeating himself, casting about for more, because that was the usual response when people ran out of first-hand observations, but he didn't. Anna hadn't been as self-possessed as Matt until she was about thirty-eight.

"Who was Danielle's date for the prom?" she asked.

Matt's eyes popped open. "Just the most popular guy in school. Brandon DeForest. Quarterback of the mighty Arrows. Face like James Van Der Beek, body like Kurt Russell, brain like Beavis. A major all-around most-valuable dork. Brandon's an anachronism. Or would be any place but here. Here he's a demi-god."

A chink in this good boy's armor? Jealousy of a geek for a demi-god? Anna didn't think so. Matt had referred to himself as a geek, but he'd done so with a perverse pride that suggested he not only did not believe it, but was confident no one else did either.

"Tell me about prom night," Anna said.

"You mean me and Heather? Not much to tell. We went out to dinner. Went to the dance. Heather kept going out to the parking lot with Danielle. She got sloppy drunk. I had better things to do than hang around till she got to the puking stage. Around ten or eleven I offered to take her home. She declined. I left her with her new *friends,* danced a few more dances and went home. End of story." He was quiet for a minute, not looking at Anna, not busying his eyes elsewhere. Then, meeting Anna's gaze with apparent frankness, he said, "Officer Pigeon, Heather's a good sort. I've known her most of my life. We were never a hot item, but we've been friends. She's just... just susceptible, if you know what I mean. Being Danni's friend was a big deal to her. She's not like a nerd or anything, but she's never been in what she calls 'the inner circle.' It's horse sh— It's silly, but her folks are Mormon and this is not Utah. Not like anybody came right out and said anything. Don't get me wrong. Heather's well liked. But she always felt it made her different. I don't think it was her being Mormon, but she did. So when Danni needed a new friend and picked up on Heather, she wanted to be like Danni. Drinking and what all."

"You didn't go with her to Rocky Springs."

"No, ma'am."

"You didn't abandon her passed out drunk in a crypt."

"Holy shit, no! I mean, no, ma'am, I did not."

Anna believed him. "Are you and Heather broken up?"

Matt seemed taken aback by that. For the first time he squirmed a little, shifting his narrow buttocks on the vinyl. "Heather and I were never together. Not like that. Like I said, we were just friends. Now that Danni's dead..."

He stopped there, just where Anna was beginning to get interested. "Now that Danni's dead what?"

"Nothing. Heather'll just have a lot to deal with for a while. Are we done? I should be getting back to band practice."

Anna'd never seen a bunch of kids so anxious to get back to class. Before she let Matt go, she described the boys she'd seen in the graveyard. Either Matt didn't recognize them from her description or he wasn't talking. Either way, the fruitful part of the interview was at an end.

Another pass through Adele Mack's office brought forth the information that Brandon

DeForest was on a bus headed for an "away game." Anna found herself more relieved than disappointed. This venture into the 90210 of Dixie had worn her out.

The refrigerator was stocked, Piedmont was fed, Taco had a new chew toy and Anna was in the District Office outside Port Gibson lunching on Doritos and RC Cola from Gary's Shell Station. Barth and Randy were telling her of their morning's adventures. As tragic as the murder was, Anna couldn't help but see a teensy-weensy silver lining. Randy and Barth were feeling important. That wonderful sense of importance would keep them invested, for a while, in their jobs. If she was very, very lucky and played whatever cards she had just right, some of that sense of their own importance would come to be associated with her. Never a bad thing. When men were sexist, they were scared. Tempting as it might be to slap them upside the head with a two-by-four, reassurance usually worked better. Marginally better, but better.

"The campers didn't have much to say," Randy told her. "I figured they wouldn't. The murder was way up the creek. I doubt who ever did it even came in that way. People down here aren't into hiking. Snakes."

"There are snakes in the Western parks," Anna said mildly.

"This isn't a *Western* park. What I'm telling you is people around here don't hike much."

Anna accepted the reproof without comment. It served her right in a way. "Go on," she said.

"So. Mostly it was a waste of my time." He was sitting backwards on a straight-backed chair that looked to have been stolen from a school teacher's desk in 1950. Folding his arms across his chest, he leaned his elbows on the chair's back. Anna had needled him. To prove himself right about the pointlessness of her choice to question campers, he wasn't going to share what he had found.

Anna ate more chips. "Mostly?" she pressed on doggedly.

Randy struggled but years of rangering overcame peevishness. "I got a pretty decent description of the cars that were haring around from the Boy Scout leader."

"Excellent," Anna said and meant it. "I got them the night of the disturbance. We'll see if they tally."

"If you'd told me you'd already gone and done it, I wouldn't have wasted my time."

Anna considered a lengthy explanation regarding the difference between on-scene questions and in-depth interviews, thought better of it and said: "Go on."

"As to who was or wasn't in the campground, I got nothing. Nobody knows who's next to them, what cars ought to be where, who's coming, who's going." Randy sulked.

"Follow up on the cars," Anna said. "Start with Clinton High School. It was their prom night. See if the kids need permits, anything that'll help you find the cars described and attach a kid to them. I'll give you any names I get. You can check to see if the parents have a car fitting any of your descriptions."

Randy nodded, either bored or lamenting the fact that doing his work had resulted in having more work to do.

"What'd you do with your time, Barth?"

Anna munched another Dorito. From the way Barth was eyeing them, she suspected Ranger Dinkin wanted some, but her need to win the guy over didn't extend that far.

"Lot of what you'd expect," Dinkin said, tearing his eyes away from the chips. "The Poseys are pretty broke up. I'd got there before Mr. Posey'd told his wife. The boy, Mike, knew—there's the two kids, or was, the girl and an older boy about nineteen, twenty. He's a piece of work."

"How so?"

"Just is."

By the firm set of Barth's mouth, he wasn't going to elaborate on that subject anytime soon.

"What else?"

"They weren't in a mood to talk much," Barth said casually. So casually Anna began to wonder if he was hiding the fact that he hadn't been out to the Poseys at all. She looked over at Randy to see how he was reacting. Both men were in her office, Barth in a second secretary's chair, his weight threatening to destroy its bowed spine, Randy straddling his. Randy rested his big head on hands locked across the chair's back. His mustache hid his upper lip

142

and his eyes were half closed. He wasn't looking at Barth and he wasn't looking at her. It was as if he watched a movie inside his own skull, and it wasn't *Pollyanna*.

"Randy. What are you thinking?" Anna asked abruptly.

The man's eyes refocused. "Let me go talk to them," he said. His voice was flat, the voice of a man rigidly in control of a violent emotion. Or the voice of a sociopath.

For a moment Anna watched him, trying to figure out what was going on behind those meaty features. Several more Doritos were eaten but they didn't do anything for her mind-reading skills. "I'll go," she said finally. "It's time I met some of the locals."

A nna gave the Poseys till the next morning. Two rangers, a sheriff and a dead child in one day would be enough to make anyone anti-social. A *child*. Anna winced involuntarily. Throughout her career she'd been told the death of a child would be harder to take than that of an adult. Till now she'd not believed it. *Not a child,* she told herself. *A teenager*. It didn't help.

As befitted the tenor of her day's activities, clouds settled low and dark, pressing into the trees, and a steady rain had been falling since before sunrise. Colors were muted, the sunshine of the Carolina jasmine and the glow of the red buds dulled as if the rain were tinged with gray paint. Seldom, if ever, did it rain like this in the high desert. Here water streamed and pooled, the grasses by the roadside wavering like rice paddies. Wood and mud and pavement were dark with water. Anna felt damp to her core. Though it wasn't warm, she had to run the car's air conditioner to keep fog from blanking her windshield.

Following the precise and neatly written directions Barth had provided, Anna found the Posey homestead without incident. From the Trace, she could see a house with worn white siding, dwarfed by old trees. A decrepit barn, with derelict automobiles nosed up to the weathered wood like piglets to a sow, stood to one side. Trusting Barth's descriptive powers, she guessed it was the Posey place, but she had another seven miles to drive before she could get to it. Part of the charm of the Natchez Trace—or the aggravation, depending on whether one was sightseeing or commuting—was that entrances and exits were severely limited.

A short gravel drive circled in from the surface road. A harrow rusted by the barn. A blue 1978 Chevrolet truck was parked in front of what was probably the kitchen door. Anna pulled around beside the Chevy and waited, the car idling, to let the inhabitants get used to the idea they had company. After a minute, the door opened behind the screen. Taking that as an invitation, Anna ducked out of the Crown Vic.

The figure behind the screen didn't offer anything in the way of welcome as Anna came up a concrete walk, buckled into disparate stones, weeds pushing boldly through ever-widening cracks.

When she was seven or eight yards from the door—and as far from her car—she heard the unmistakable sound of dogs growling, low and vicious. Watchdogs bark when an intruder arrives, a racket to alert the house. Attack dogs don't.

Anna stopped dead in her tracks. Slowly, she turned her head to find the source of the noise. Equally slowly, she put her hand on the butt of her pistol. A dozen feet away, the distance of a single lunge, were two white shepherds, big dogs, eighty to a hundred pounds each. The rain had flattened their fur, but along the hackles it was glued into spikes.

"Call off your dogs," Anna said quietly, never taking her eyes from them. The smaller of the two, but not by much, began inching toward her, stiff mincing steps. The second broke away, circling between her and the cars.

"Call off your dogs or I'll kill them," she said in the same even tone. This interview was off to a great start.

The shadow behind the screen neither moved nor spoke. Anna thumbed the snap free on the leather strap that secured her pistol in her holster.

"Bubba! Rocket! That's enough," came a sharp female voice from within the house. The hell hounds were transformed. Tails wagged. Tongues fell out in dopey grins.

Anna was unimpressed. Without taking her eyes from the animals or her hand from her nine-millimeter, she said: "May I come in?"

"Go on! Git!" came the same voice and Anna waited to see if the command was meant for her or the dogs.

Bubba and Rocket stopped wagging and grinning and slunk off toward the barn. They'd obviously been trained the old-fashioned way, with boot and stick.

The screen opened. "C'mon in. You're getting soaked. Don't mind them dogs. We don't get all that much company."

The speaker was the shadow behind the screen, visible now that she held the door open. A little woman, not as tall as Anna, maybe five-foot-two and skinny. The flat wide kind of skinny: broad pelvis spreading fleshless hips, wide rib cage with no muscles or breasts to give it depth. From head-on, she looked average; in profile, there was nothing to her. Adding to this peculiar now-you-see-it, now-you-don't physique was the ageless quality of an aging face. The blond hair was faded, not so much gray as colorless, the skin unlined but lacking the elasticity of youth. The woman could have been thirty-eight; she could have been fifty. She had a ghostlike quality of not being in real time. Anna found it hard to believe this wraith would set the dogs on her intentionally. Then again she found it hard to believe the woman would care one way or another if the beasts tore her to pieces on

146

the front step. Either way she seemed unof-
fended by Anna's threat to shoot them. That
was a plus. Anna was taking what she could
get this morning. "You are Mrs. Posey?"

"Mr. Posey says I am."

She stood aside to let Anna into a kitchen
that apparently served as dining room and entertainment center of the house. Shelves held the
usual paraphernalia of a kitchen. The floor was
covered in speckled linoleum gouged by a
bygone disaster of some sort. The walls had
once been papered, then peeled, but no new
paper had been hung. A Formica-topped
table with four matching chairs of chrome
and vinyl in cracked and fraying yellow took
up the center of the room. The air smelled of
coffee, cigarettes and an odor that took Anna
back to the sixties: hair spray. Aqua Net, if she
didn't miss her guess. From a rolling stand
between two doors leading to the rest of the
house, a television with a twenty-seven-inch
screen flashed the rude colors and noise of a
talk show. Beyond, it was dark, the blinds and
curtains closed, making shadowed caves where
too much furniture hunkered in the gloom.

"Can I get you a Coke?" the woman asked.

Anna started to decline, but the suspicious
look on Mrs. Posey's face changed her mind.
She said yes, and it lifted. Evidently Mrs.
Posey didn't trust people who wouldn't drink
a Coke at nine-thirty in the morning. Anna
watched as her hostess did the honors. The old
refrigerator was packed with Cokes, not Wal-

Mart cola but the familiar red and white cans. There must have been close to three cases, leaving little room for anything else.

A mental institution, the sheriff had said. Suddenly Anna was glad the beverage offered came in a hermetically sealed container.

Mrs. Posey set a Coke on the table for Anna and opened one for herself. "You sit down," she ordered. Anna did as she was told.

"Is Mr. Posey home?" Anna asked, mostly to make conversation.

"He's always somewhere or other. You're the lady ranger," Mrs. Posey said. "I heard about you."

"What did you hear?" Anna asked, genuinely curious.

"You found that girl that was killed." Mrs. Posey was looking past Anna at the television screen where an ample redhead was screaming and throwing her shoes at a little black girl who was doing a bad job of looking fierce while two television "bouncers" held her back.

"She stole the other girl's fiancé," Mrs. Posey said. "He was a white boy, too. It's him they oughta be talking about killing, messing around with a colored." Mrs. Posey seemed unaware that her pronouncement wasn't a universally accepted truth.

Anna said nothing. It wasn't her kitchen, and it wasn't what she was here for.

"I'd like to ask you some questions about your daughter, Mrs. Posey. Would it be better if I came back another time? When your husband's home?" Anna fought to be gentle over the contrived clamor of the TV.

"Fred doesn't know anything about Danni," Mrs. Posey said, still absorbed in the television. "Danni tells me everything." She stopped then, took a long pull on her soda and said, still without looking at Anna: "I know that girl you found was my Danni. I know she's dead." Her face didn't change expression and her voice lost none of its flat character, but tears began to run down her face and drip off her chin. If she was aware of them, she made no move to wipe them away.

"I'm terribly sorry," Anna said. She wanted to say more but every phrase that came to mind was so pathetically inadequate she couldn't bring herself to utter it.

Mrs. Posey watched her show, and Anna cast about for a good way to escape without being devoured by Bubba and Rocket.

The show cut to a commercial, and Mrs. Posey finally looked at her guest. "I'll talk about Danni being alive if that's all you want but I won't talk about her being dead. Not now. Not ever."

"Tell me about her friends," Anna said.

"Danni was the most popular girl at school. There wasn't nobody that wasn't her friend or leastways nobody who didn't want to be. But I'd tell her, Danni you *pick*; you don't be running with people not good as you. They'll drag you down. Danni always listened to me. She'd bring some girl home and I'd say that girl's just fixin' to be trash and that'd be the end of it. Danni always listened to me."

"Any special friends?" Anna asked.

"She had a hundred friends. Good friends."

Danni might have listened to her mother, but it didn't sound as if she talked to her much. Anna sat in silence and waited while Mrs. Posey cast about for a single name and failed to find one.

"Yesterday they sent that big nigger over here to talk to me about my girl. I'm not talking to no nigger man about my Danni."

Anna jerked in her chair as the words smacked into her. Barth Dinkin. This crazy rotten remnant of a woman was talking about one of her rangers. As anger flashed and she clamped her teeth against it, Anna had a sudden thought: was this why Randy had gotten so hostile? Because he knew the Poseys had treated Barth badly and he knew Barth was too ashamed to say anything? For the first time since meeting the man, Anna felt a wave of respect for Ranger Randy Thigpen.

"You can talk to me about Danni," Anna said evenly. "I'm white."

Mrs. Posey was oblivious to sarcasm. "They should've sent you first and not go insulting people like that."

Anna said nothing.

"Danni was going to be a model. Big, like Cheryl Tiegs. Did you know that?"

"I didn't."

"I knew. It was Danni and me's secret." The talk show came back on. Anna couldn't stomach any more of Mrs. Posey's personal brand of insanity. Largely unnoticed by the other woman, Anna thanked her for the Coke and let herself out the kitchen door.

The rain had not let up, and the overcast had not lifted, but after the Poseys' kitchen, Anna felt she stepped into glorious sunshine. Bubba and Rocket were nowhere to be seen. It was a straight shot to her patrol car and escape.

"Can I help you?" A man materialized from the gullet of the barn and was hollering at her. Two ghostly canine forms walked about in the gloom behind him. The voice was friendly enough, but Anna felt herself tensing; his voice sounded the death knell for her new-won freedom.

"Are you Mr. Posey?" Rain soaked through her shirt and grew cold against her skin. Somewhere in her new closet was her Gore-Tex rain gear. Today being a car-and-kitchen kind of day, she hadn't thought she'd need it.

"I'm Fred Posey. Don't stand out there in the rain." Anna hesitated and he added: "Don't mind the dogs. These old boys wouldn't hurt a flea."

Anna didn't believe him but trusted he wasn't fool enough to let them eat a federal law enforcement officer without a pretty good reason. Walking slowly, despite the rain, she crossed the gravel and joined him in the shelter of the barn.

Mr. Posey was considerably more substantial than his wife, but to Anna he looked to be in poor health. His skin was sallow, his hair thin and lusterless. For a man probably not yet fifty, his shoulders were rounded down and his neck

151

bowed. Too long carrying too much weight. Anna had seen it before. People expected farmers to be robust and hearty types, but it was a hard life. It killed and crippled people young. Those who were remembered were those who grew old at it. They were tough as leather and nails.

"Been talking to Cindy?" he asked. There was a guarded sadness in his face that Anna thought she understood.

"Mrs. Posey?"

"My wife." A challenge if Anna ever heard one. Fred would brook no disparagement, even in the form of sympathy, where his wife was concerned. Anna liked that in him and relaxed somewhat.

"We talked a little and had a Coke," Anna said.

"You come to talk about Danni?"

Anna nodded. "I didn't upset her, Mr. Posey."

"It's hard on a woman," he said. "You go ahead and ask me your questions." He sucked in cheeks grown loose over the years and craned his neck as if in pain, squeezing off the tears. Anna busied herself getting a notebook and pen out of her shirt pocket, giving him time to recover. Fred Posey struck her as the kind of man who might never forgive a woman for seeing him cry.

Out of the corner of her eye, she noted the whereabouts of Bubba and Rocket. The two of them had crawled under the hulk of some sort of many-bladed, wicked-looking piece of farm machinery. For the moment, they seemed content to let her live.

"I'm sorry to make you deal with this stuff," Anna said. "But the sooner we can get leads, the better off we'll be."

"I understand," Mr. Posey said. "Ask away." He wasn't doing anything. Not leaning on a rake or holding a tool. His hands weren't in his pockets. He didn't fidget or shuffle his feet. Pale, bent, he just stood in the watery light, arms hanging at his sides. For some inexplicable reason, Anna was put in mind of Boo Radley in *To Kill a Mockingbird*.

"Do you know who Danni's date was for the dance?" Heather's boyfriend Matt had given her a name, but she wanted to hear it again from another source.

"I think she was going to go with Brandon DeForest, Colonel DeForest's boy. Her mom says they've been kind of sweet on each other for a while. They been squabbling, so maybe she went with some other boy."

"The boy didn't come to the house to pick her up?"

"Yes, I believe he did."

"Were you out at the time?"

"I was looking at TV." A silence followed that Anna didn't want to break. When he spoke again, his voice rattled at the outset as he forced it through sorrow or shame or maybe regret. "Her mom said Danni looked real pretty. I guess she'd gotten a special dress for the party."

"Can you tell me about her friends?" Anna asked.

Mr. Posey looked out into the rain, his eyes

as colorless as the day. "She was always running around with some little gal or other. Her mom would know."

Fred Posey knew little about his only daughter, not even what year she was in school. Her birthday was the twelfth or the fourteenth of June. Her mom said she was a good enough student. He guessed she was happy enough.

Anna thanked him and left him to his barn and his dogs and his rusting equipment. On the drive back to Airport Road, where she could get back on the Trace, Anna found herself feeling sorry for the murdered girl. Her father had abdicated and her mother had gone crazy. Danni Posey must have been very lonely.

Ten miles south on the Trace, past the turnoff for the town of Raymond, just as she was beginning to dry out, Anna clocked an oncoming car at seventy-nine miles per hour. Too much over the speed limit to let go. Being damp and in a racist's kitchen had made her crabby. There'd be no kindly warning today. *They make an officer get out of a warm patrol car and stand in the rain; they by God get a ticket.* Anna flipped on the blue lights and was startled when blue lights flashed in return.

No traffic but for two law enforcement officers, both exceeding the posted speed limit. Anna slowed to a stop and let the sheriff's car pull up beside her. Davidson rolled down his window and smiled. Suddenly Anna felt the Poseys' farm had been an alien planet and now she was back on Earth.

"Hey," she said, lacking anything better with which to express her pleasure at seeing his officially rational countenance.

"Hey, your ownself," he replied. "I'm glad I ran into you. Save one of us a trip. I got the autopsy report back on Danielle Posey. If you want, we can pull off somewhere and go over it. I'll get you copies of whatever you need, but it won't be till tomorrow probably."

"I'd like a look at them now if you're not in a big hurry."

"No hurry. At least not at the present."

"I'll pull off," Anna said.

"Better not. Too much rain. One of us is bound to get stuck and nothing looks sillier than America's finest digging around trying to pry their cars out of the muck. I'll turn around and follow you on down to Dean's Stand. It's not more than a mile or two."

Vaguely, Anna remembered passing a tasteful brown NPS arrowhead sign with words to that effect. She led the way then turned left on a narrow tree-shrouded road. A quarter mile or less and it ended in a loop with a garbage can and a picnic table. Davidson parked next to her and leaned over to unlock the passenger door so she could slide in with only minimal exposure to the elements.

"Dean's Stand," Anna said. "I've got to do my homework. There's nothing here."

"There's history," the sheriff returned.

"There's history everywhere," Anna said, her humor not yet fully recovered. "That's the nature of the beast."

"Yes, but in the South we take note."

She had no answer to that. "So. What've we got?" she asked.

Davidson pulled a pair of half glasses from the pocket of his uniform shirt and slipped them on, adjusting them partway down his nose. That done, he leaned toward her to pluck a manila file folder from a battered brown leather briefcase. When he moved, Anna was aware of the warmth of his body and a faint pleasant odor of cologne. What kind, she couldn't hazard a guess. She'd not bought a man cologne or aftershave for ten years. Maybe not all grown-ups wore Old Spice anymore.

Normally she would have found it mildly annoying to sit passively by while someone spoon-fed her information she could absorb faster reading herself. Today she was content to wait. It was more than just enjoying the warmth of a dry car and the scent of manly perfume, it was the essence of sharing Davidson exuded. He prepared not to give, edit, spoonfeed, but to share information.

That's how women tended to work. Women and very clever men.

"Death due to blunt trauma to the back of the neck. The fourth cervical vertebra was broken and the spinal cord severed. No cuts or abrasions in that area. The trauma caused by a flat smooth object. Shape suggests a boot heel, worn smooth."

"The blow to the forehead didn't kill her?"

"Apparently not. She may have fallen backward when struck and hit something else that killed her."

"What? That forest is soft as oatmeal. Jesus. She was stomped. Like a snake."

"I'm guessing the killer struck her twice to make sure."

"Ish," Anna said, using her sister's fiancé's favorite expletive. Her own choice of words would have been too caustic for so small a space.

"Okay. Where was I? Blow to the right frontal lobe of the brain causing external hemorrhaging. That blow was from an edged weapon." He looked over the top of his glasses at Anna. "Not a knife or an axe. The medical examiner's thinking a shovel, a gas can, a tool box—something heavy and probably made of metal. There weren't any bits of anything she'd expect to find if a wooden implement was used, or a brick, or something along those lines. Just something with a hard straight edge."

"Scalp was cut?"

"And the bone cracked."

He went back to his folder. "Looks like you were right about the rope. The marks on the neck occurred after death. The killer had to be making some kind of point."

"The kind of mind that would stomp a young girl might be the kind of mind that would have a 'point' that makes no sense to anyone else," Anna said.

"True," the sheriff agreed. "But it's a start—KKK angle—the start of what, I don't even like

157

to think about. Cuts and contusions to hands and arms and the legs, consistent with running through the brush. No defensive injuries. No sign of collateral damage during the assault. Miss Posey had had sexual intercourse prior to her death but no signs of forcible rape. Her blood alcohol level was point two three. Her blood didn't test positive for any other drugs."

"Two three is awfully high. Unless she was already a seasoned alcoholic, she must have been blind, stumbling drunk," Anna said.

"Knee-walking drunk," Paul Davidson drawled. "Seventeen years old, drunk, dressed in a handkerchief, sexually active and out at two in the morning. Was that your idea of a Saturday night date when you were in high school?"

"The Sisters of Mercy would have frowned on that," Anna said. "When we were at the height of our wickedness, we'd smoke cigarettes out back of the dorm, and the nuns would pretend they didn't smell it on us."

"Catholic?"

"No. My folks sent me there because it was a good school. I'm nothing."

"That's too bad."

Anna let it pass. "Did you meet Danielle's parents?"

"Just when he ID'd the body. I didn't keep him too long. He said he needed to get back to his wife. Lonny's going to go by this afternoon."

"Your deputy?"

"Yes. Lonny Restin."

"The young black man?"

The sheriff took off his reading glasses, the better to read her face. "Why?"

Anna told him the story of Barth's lack of information and Cindy Posey's remarks. Talking of racism in the North was easy. Down here Anna felt awkward and uncomfortable and wondered why. Maybe because hypocrisy, though it existed everywhere, wasn't an agreed-upon thing in the South. People still spoke their minds even when those minds were small and nasty and scared. Respect for sixties Southern liberals flowered in Anna. In Minnesota it didn't cost much to be a bleeding heart. Down here it would have been a siege mentality. No wonder they were reputed to drink quantities of bourbon.

Paul Davidson sat quietly, mulling over Anna's revelations. "I'm of two minds," he said at length. "Lonny's well able to fend for himself and is an impressive young man. He's pried open more than one closed mind in the year we've worked together. On the other hand, I hate to make him go through it if there's nothing to be gained. You saw Mrs. Posey. Is it true she's a little off the beam?"

"She struck me as out of touch," Anna told him. "How deep her split with reality I couldn't say, but I doubt we'll get much use out of her. And I don't think she'll talk with Lonny." That she might set the dogs on the young deputy was a possibility, but Anna didn't like to tell of her own fear. *Officer Safety* sparked in her mind, and she swallowed her pride.

"She might set the dogs on him," she said.

"That bad?"

"Maybe."

Anna waited while the sheriff radioed his deputy and told him to talk only with Mr. Posey and to call before coming.

"Not going to tell him why?" Anna asked when he was done.

"Lonny'll know why. Mississippi has spent the last forty years trying to live down the Cindy Poseys. Educate them. Pray for them. Argue with them. One day they'll die out, but racism's got a half-life that's virtually nuclear. It persists from generation to generation, just in a less virulent form. You're a Yankee. Make sure racism's not all you look for. If it is, it's all you'll find. But it's nowhere near all there is." Sermon delivered, Davidson replaced his reading glasses on his nose and continued with the autopsy report. "Miss Posey died around one-thirty A.M. She'd had shrimp and lobster tails for dinner. Not pregnant. Healthy but for being dead."

"Legs scratched. We saw that," Anna added. "There should be tracks, but I couldn't find any. You guys don't have any dirt down here. Just plants."

"If there were tracks, they're gone now," the sheriff said, watching the rain sheet on the windshield.

"Maybe not." Anna was thinking of the square high heels. "She was carried. Chased,

160

hence the scratches, then killed or knocked unconscious—thus no defensive wounds, then carried—so no tracks from those heeled sandals. Then dumped and abandoned. Where was she carried from?"

"The Old Trace, there where the bank was tracked up?"

"Maybe, but we obliterated any sign there, and I didn't see the heel marks on the way to the campground."

"Other tracks?"

"Sure. Dozens."

"Right. It's a trail." He went back to the report. "The postmortem marks on the neck were minimal. Looks as though the noose wasn't tight and it was not used to drag her. Just window dressing."

For a bit they sat without speaking, listening to the hypnotic thrum of rain on the car's roof.

"Where would they have carried her from?" Anna wasn't so much asking again as still wondering.

"Kill her in the campground and carry her across the creek, through the kudzu, down the Old Trace, up over the bank and into the woods. That's a ways to carry a hundred and eight pounds of dead weight," Davidson said.

"The campground's about the most public area around. Doesn't make sense to choose it for the murder."

"Kill her on the road or bring her from wherever by car and carry the body in cross-country?" Davidson tried.

"Hard work," Anna said. "Why not just dump her in a river? There's plenty to choose from."

"Well, from what the kids told you, Rocky was the party place. We better figure Danielle was already there before she was killed."

"Why take her so far off the beaten path? To hide the body?" Anna said.

"Why hide it after going to all the trouble to make a costume that's steeped in racial fears and hatred?" Davidson countered.

"A white girl, dead, in a faux KKK outfit—black on white as in a taste of one's own poison?"

"White on white wanting it to look as if it's black on white?"

"White on white as in the Klan punishing one who betrays?" Anna took it one step farther.

"Not much Klan here anymore. Oh, there's isolated pockets of malcontents that drag out the sheets and pointy hoods once in a while, mostly to impress each other and feel powerful for an evening, but not an organization like it once was. I've been here most of my life and I've only seen it spark once. A cross burning just off I-55 down near Crystal Springs. Nobody ever did figure out what the point of the gesture was. Maybe Danni's shroud had nothing to do with KKK imagery. Maybe it was just a sheet with eyeholes meaning something else."

"Could they lift any prints off the girl's skin?" Anna asked.

"She'd been to a dance, there were dozens of partials and smears and overlays. During the chase, sweat obliterated most. There was one fairly clear print of a forefinger, but my guess is it'll turn out to be yours. It was checking the pulse point."

They weren't getting anywhere. The rain ran down the windshield, the water parting here and there to accommodate the pureed remains of hapless insects.

"Mrs. Cindy Posey," Sheriff Davidson said after a while. "Racist. Mentally unstable. Possibly violent if you're right about the dogs."

Anna thought about that for a while. "She's a farm wife; you can bet she's got sheets," she said.

"It wouldn't take much strength to hit somebody that hard—just a weapon with some heft."

"No struggle—someone Danni knew? Trusted?"

"She'd been chased, remember."

"Oh. Right." A question occurred to Anna, one that didn't fit with that sequence of events. "Read me the stuff about the blow. Could the medical examiner tell angle of delivery, that sort of thing?"

Davidson methodically went back through the pages, his blunt, square-tipped forefinger running down each sheet of paper. His nails were clean and clipped. Anna noted a raw place where he'd worried at the cuticle with his teeth.

"Here we go," he said. "The blow was most probably delivered from right to left and down. The weapon appears to have struck the girl above the right eye with the greatest force. The edge of the weapon is estimated at six to eight inches, or at least as much of it as impacted the skull area. The assailant was most likely right-handed."

"So." Anna tried to draw the picture out in her mind. "Danielle is hit on the right front quadrant of the skull with the trajectory of the blow coming from above her and to her left. Therefore, she was facing the killer, he did not strike her down from behind. They're face-to-face. He raises the weapon in his right hand and swings it down in an arc," she said.

"If she was running away, why wasn't she struck from behind?"

"Stopped and turned?" Anna guessed.

"Got cornered?" Every line of logic was falling apart. The rain was unceasing. Anna felt as if her brain was beginning to mildew. It was because Danielle was a child. A child of seventeen, but to the ways of the world, a child.

And there was no good reason to kill a child but pure stinking mindless evil, an evil so base it was hard for real people to fathom.

8

The day continued in its meteorological misery. Crying skies filled the two bayous between Anna's home at Rocky and the ranger station at Port Gibson. Water stood in the fields in the Valley of the Moon. Horses gathered beneath the trees and hung their heads.

Anna spent the afternoon working on her list, stocking her patrol car with flashlight, spare battery for her handheld radio and the numbers and radio frequencies of local law enforcement and Fisheries and Wildlife. By day's end, she was glad to retreat to Rocky Springs and Taco and Piedmont.

Rain had driven away most of the campers, and she looked forward to a peaceful night eating Marie Callender's frozen fettuccine and watching whatever came on either of the two channels her aging thirteen-inch portable television could pick up.

Three messages waited on her answering machine: Steve Stilwell asking how the investigation was going, Sheriff Davidson saying he had some interesting tidbits from the Poseys. And the last, from Anna's sister, Molly.

Business could wait till proper business hours. For half a minute she stood staring at the phone, thinking she should call her sister and wondering why she didn't want to.

She and Molly had been alone together for nearly twelve years. Alone in the sense that neither had husbands, children or family. They were family. Just the two of them. Professional women of middling years who knew they were not alone because there were two. They shared history and love.

And now there was Frederick, the fiancé. Anna's ex and Molly's love. Was that it? Jealousy? Sour grapes? Not only did Anna not want to believe that about herself, she was ninety-three percent sure it wasn't true. She reveled in Molly's happiness, enjoyed relief that her sister had someone to love and support her. But it was different now. The chemistry was changed. Whether for better or worse, Anna didn't know. Probably both. At the moment, though, calling Molly would add to the sense of isolation with which this country of deep-fried kindness and cottonmouthed hostilities imbued her. In another lifetime, Anna would have turned off the phones and unplugged the machine. That was a luxury rangers were not allowed.

Having opened the casement windows at the bottom near the floor on the living room's east side to better hear the hypnotic beat of the rain, she dimmed the lights. With a glass on the table next to her father's old Morris chair, she sat to await Piedmont's inevitable arrival.

Along with the groceries, Anna had purchased wine: Chardonnay, Sauvignon Blanc, and what promised to be a raw Beaujolais. Periodically, she swore off the stuff. Occasionally she admitted she might just possibly have a problem. Tonight she wanted a drink and a cat on her lap.

Dreams of cars, aborted laughter and stealthy voices abraded Anna's sleep. At forty-three minutes after one A.M. the ringing of the telephone ended it. Long practice had trained her out of that bemused state between waking and sleeping. Unpleasantly alert by the time she put the receiver to her ear, she answered: "Rocky Springs."

Crackling met her, the kind cheap cellular phones make. Behind it she could barely discern a murmur of hushed or distant voices, then a smothered laugh. "Hello?" she said sharply.

"I'd like to report an accident." Again the strangled sounds in the background. Either this was a crank call or there was interference on whatever waves transmitted cellular calls.

"Where?" Anna asked.

"Uh. Just outside of Rocky Springs campground." Another pause. "It looks real bad."

"North or south of Rocky?" Anna asked. Already she was pulling on her pants, the phone receiver clamped between shoulder and ear.

"Uh. North."

Before Anna could ask anymore, the connection was broken. Reports of accidents and incidents by cellular phone had become the rule instead of the exception over the past few years. The method of the call wasn't what bothered her; it was the mode. The strange tight voice, the laughter stopped abruptly, the muttering in the background smacked of a prank, kids calling asking, "Do you have Prince Albert in a can?" Except false report of a crime or accident was against the law.

Regardless of misgivings, the report could not be ignored.

Anna donned her wristwatch: quarter of two. Dispatch was shut down for the night. A common system for officer safety in parks without twenty-four-hour dispatch was to phone another ranger before leaving. They then stayed awake and monitored their radios in case backup was needed. If that wasn't the accepted protocol in the Port Gibson District, it soon would be.

Randy Thigpen lived closest, west of Port Gibson toward the Mississippi River. Anna dialed his number. On the eighth ring he answered.

"It's Anna," she said without preamble. "I got an accident report north of Rocky Springs. I need you to stay on the radio till I see what's up."

"Barth and I usually just cover those alone, but then we've been at it a lot longer. We've never bothered to keep somebody up on the radio. Sure, I can help you out if you're not comfortable on your own."

Son of a bitch lacks subtlety, Anna thought as sharp retorts racketed around in her brain. Pissing contests were for those penilely inclined. "I'll call if I need you," she said and hung up. Life on the Trace was going to be hell if she didn't either win those boys over or think of some way to kill them and get away with it.

The rain had let up but had not stopped. It was what the Navajo called a female rain: gentle and nurturing. Anna closed the front door on Taco's intended escape and clicked on her flashlight. If there was a switch that turned on a light in the carport, she had yet to find it. The walk was uneven. Puddles formed in the low spots. She hopscotched toward the drive in the vain hope of keeping her feet dry.

The inside of the carport was darker than even the rain-drenched woods. Anna closed her mind against the possibility of spiders dangling at collar level and plunged in.

She was reaching for the door handle when a blow smashed into her ankle with the force of a ball bat swung at close quarters. Pain and fear exploded, brain-numbing shocks coming one after the other: acute pain in her left ankle, a crack as she fell onto her side, elbow striking the concrete, skittering light as her flashlight rolled away, the gust of air knocked from her lungs. The Posey girl's skull crushed by a blunt instrument flashed behind the immediate images.

An instant, no more, of paralysis gripped Anna. Then she heard someone crawling beneath the Crown Vic.

"Stay back," she yelled. The Sig-Sauer was in her right hand. She pushed back to a sitting position against the rear wall of the three-sided carport. The heavy leather of her cowboy boot absorbed some of the impact, but her ankle throbbed and she wondered if it was broken. Spiders were forgotten. The flashlight had rolled to the far side of the car. Anna could see the spray of the beam rocking on the wall. "Come out slowly. Hands first. Let me see your hands."

From the darkness beneath the car she heard movement, a heavy drag across the concrete as if her assailant jockeyed for position on elbows and knees.

From inside the house came wild barking. Taco going ballistic. Anna realized she must have screamed when she fell.

"Out," she commanded. "Hands first." Her own hands were shaking. The crack to her elbow had robbed her arm of strength. Whoever was under the car said nothing, and she swallowed the desire to empty the magazine into the darkness.

A kid. Who but a kid would crawl under a parked patrol car? She could see the headlines now: "Lady Ranger Shoots Local Boy Thirteen Times." Bracing the Sig-Sauer with her knee, Anna freed her hand and wrestled the radio from her belt. Three calls, no answers. She hated handhelds. They only worked when they weren't needed. That or Randy Thigpen had rolled over and gone back to sleep.

"You under the car," Anna tried. "You're beginning to scare me. I get scared, I shoot. Neither of us wants that. Come on out now."

Nothing. Then a thrashing sound and the

disturbing note of nails scratching on cement. Fragmented pictures from a childhood filled with campfire stories about escaped lunatics with hooks for hands flickered through her mind.

Anna eased to her feet. Her left ankle hurt but it wasn't broken; it would hold. Taco was going mad. His barks had escalated into a frenzy, and she could hear thumping. He was hurling himself against the screen. She'd never known a pet dog to go after anyone like that. What triggered him, she didn't know, but it made the hairs on the nape of her neck stiffen.

The carport was narrow. With the Crown Victoria in it, there was just room on either side to open the doors. Anna didn't relish walking that close to whoever was underneath, but she couldn't stay trapped in the back in darkness. If the assailant was armed, he could easily move close to the wheels and kill her. Dying in a carport in Mississippi was not appealing. In a sudden leap, Anna made the hood of the Crown Vic and scrambled to the top of the cab.

A wrench of metal and a crash came from the house. Barking as if he was possessed by the ghost of Cujo, Taco came around the corner hackles raised, lips pulled back. He had lost any resemblance to the goofy house pet Anna inherited when Frieda died. Snarling, he rushed at the end of the car, his glossy coat shiny in the beam of the flashlight on the floor.

So fast Anna scarcely saw it, something shot from beneath the undercarriage and she heard a loud snap. Taco screamed, and Anna screamed. Gray-green scales rushed through the narrow beam of the flashlight. Taco cried, high and desperate, then was snatched beneath the car.

Anna could feel pounding up through the metal. The alligator—it had to be an alligator—was whipping the dog from side to side. The screaming continued.

"No," Anna yelled. "No." She slid from the cab to the floor at the rear of the car. The gun was useless. Firing, blind, into concrete she'd as likely kill her dog as the alligator. The tail that had knocked her feet from under her whipped out, an angular scaled muscle the size of a man's leg. Without stopping to think, Anna dropped the gun and grabbed the tail in both hands. Digging her heels in, she pulled. The alligator had claws, long and yellowed like a grizzly's. Over the cries of the dog, Anna could hear them scraping along the pavement.

Its back legs were out. Flecks of black, then red in the light, splattered onto the cement. Taco's blood.

"Let go of him, Goddamn you." Anna hauled back. Another two feet of ridged beast was dragged from under the bumper. The alligator turned, Taco clamped in jaws ragged with teeth and red with blood. Anna threw herself on the animal's back. It thrashed beneath her with a strength she could not have imagined. Behind her was the tail, in front of her the jaws. Both deadly to soft human—or canine—flesh. Holding tightly to one leathery foreleg, she ripped the pepper spray from her belt. Stopping her breath and turning her head away she sprayed it into the eyes of the gator.

A primeval roar came from its throat. It began to thrash with such violence Anna was thrown to one side. She kept rolling to get clear. Then she was on her feet. The alligator was wild. Roaring and snapping at the air, the tires of the Crown Vic, but it had let go of Taco. The dog lay in a pool of blood made shockingly red by the light of the flash. He whimpered and twitched the way dreaming dogs do. The way dying animals do.

Skirting the blind and flailing alligator, Anna scooped Taco into her arms. Hearing her footsteps, the beast turned and charged with lightning speed she'd never associated with the giant reptiles. She had the advantage of sight. Seventy-five pounds of dog clutched to her chest, she jumped clear. The gator continued his blind charge until he was halfway up the walk to the house.

Not waiting to see where he went next, Anna retrieved her gun and bundled herself and Taco into the driver's side of the patrol car. Jamming it in reverse, she stepped on the gas. If the alligator had come back and she ran over the damn thing, so be it.

A good thirty yards out of the drive, she stopped and caught up the mike to the car radio.

"Five-seven-eight, five-eight-zero. Five-seven-eight, five-eight-zero. Randy answer the damn radio."

He did and Anna blessed his worthless hide for being there. "Call Fisheries and Wildlife. I've got a crazy blind alligator in the yard. Tell them to get animal control here to kill it or capture it before it hurts somebody. Tell them it's got pepper spray in its eyes and is in a foul mood. You get up here and check out that report of an accident north of Rocky. And give me the name of a vet."

Silence followed. It seemed excessive to Anna but was probably only a few seconds.

"The name of a veteran?" Randy asked.

"A veterinarian."

"Hang on." More silence. Gentle rain. Taco laid his head on her thigh and licked fingers wet with his blood. The old poem of Rags licking his master and dying came to mind and Anna felt tears sting her eyes. She had let Frieda die. Killed her. Now she'd killed Frieda's dog. In the glare of the headlights, she could see the alligator. It was throwing its head from side to side trying to escape the burn of the pepper spray. Anna's own nose and eyes burned from the stuff. Aerosols were not a weapon of precision. "You'll live," she hissed to the gator. "Unless my dog dies." Even as she said it she knew she would wreak no vengeance on the alligator. It had merely been doing what alligators do, without conscience, without malice, without blame.

Was that how it was with Danielle's murderer? Was he a human animal, a broken person, a psychopath or a sociopath as blameless as the alligator?

"Five-eight-oh?"

"Five-eight-zero," Anna replied. Her hand was sticky with blood and the mike adhered to her palm.

"Fisheries is on the way. I'm on the way. Here's the name of a veterinarian. David Christianson. A guy the Fisheries works with. I'll call him. He'll meet you there."

Anna listened while Randy gave directions to Christianson's office. Randy was calm, efficient and didn't waste time with questions. And he didn't brook racism, at least not against fellow rangers. *Too bad he's such an asshole,* Anna thought uncharitably, and flicked on blue lights and siren.

Christianson was waiting when she arrived. She'd covered the twenty miles to Raymond in fourteen minutes. Enough adrenaline flowed through her veins that when she lifted Taco from the seat he seemed to weigh no more than a kitten.

The vet introduced himself as David. He could have been near forty but he was utterly boyish. And though it was the middle of the night, downright cheerful. Either because he loved them or, more likely, to calm Anna—she was shaking and trying to hide it by grabbing the exam table—he chatted on about his kids and his practice while he quickly sorted through the damage to Taco. Anna learned about his boys, his practice and his

175

wife's part-time job at the Episcopal church. Then he said: "It'll be touch and go. The gator got him by the right rear leg, maybe punctured his liver and his spleen. I can operate. It'll cost around six hundred bucks and Taco may not make it."

"Do it," Anna said.

On her way out, she stopped in the doorway of the examining room. "Your wife works at a church?"

"That's right."

"Does she pray for dogs?" Anna asked on impulse.

Christianson smiled his boyish smile. "Why do you think my recovery rate is so high?"

The surgery would be a long one, and though he told Anna she was welcome to wait, she would be doing no favors to anyone by hanging around.

Crusted with canine blood, depressed and aching from shoulder to hip, she limped to her patrol car. Rain had turned to mist. She breathed the fine droplets into lungs that felt burnt out. Too much screaming for one night. Too much breathing in pain and blind fear: hers, Taco's, the alligator's.

Sunup was still hours away. It occurred to her that since coming to the heart of Dixie she'd yet to sleep through the night.

Back on the Trace, heading south, she radioed Randy. He answered immediately. Instead of being impressed by his alertness, she suspected he was camped out in his vehicle letting somebody else do his work.

176

"No accident north of Rocky," he said. Anna knew that; she'd driven the Trace from Rocky to the turnoff for the tiny town of Raymond.

"It had all the earmarks of a crank call," she said. "Did the Fish and Wildlife guys get my gator?"

"They're just on him now. He'd gone around back of the house there and was flopping and snapping like mad. It took 'em a while to get him to come on down from the edge of the woods. You oughta be here about the time they get some lines on him to load him up."

"Good," Anna said. "I'm looking forward to saying good-bye."

"He's a little bitty fella," Randy drawled.

"Not when he's in your shirt pocket."

Illuminated by the headlights and flanked by large men, the alligator looked considerably smaller than Anna remembered, around six feet from snout to tail. The pepper spray had worn off or the alligator had worn down. The animal was relatively subdued. A rope on a long stick had been looped around its neck and its movements were being more or less controlled by a sizable black man in the forest green of the Mississippi Fisheries and Wildlife Service. A second man, also in green, was backing a half-ton pickup across Anna's sodden backyard to collect their catch.

She pulled on rain gear, not to evade the mist but to cover the blood on her shirt and pants.

Later she would talk about Frieda's dog—her dog. Under the glinting eye of her new employee, she didn't want to risk tears. Nobody had ever laid down their life for her before, not like Taco had.

"Are you the new ranger?" the man holding the alligator called as she walked into the high beams of Randy's car, pulled around behind her house to shed light on the reptile recovery.

"That's me."

"Your little buddy here put up quite a struggle. You sure you shot him with pepper spray and not methamphetamines?"

"Whatever's government issue is what he got," Anna said. She walked nearer, wanting to see the animal. Whipping its body suddenly, it lashed its tail.

"Easy, boy," the Fisheries man said, and, "I think he likes you."

"He sure liked my dog," Anna said. Then, before anyone could ask, she changed the subject. "They often come up and get in carports, under houses, things like that?"

"First time I've ever heard of it around here. You're a ways from any body of water big enough to support a guy this size. He's probably six or seven years old. But during mating season, they'll go a long ways across country sometimes."

"Is it mating season?"

"Nope. June and early July."

The truck stopped and the other Fisheries man got out. He was white, gone to fat around the middle the way once-muscular men tend to do in their fifties. Still, he looked powerful and had the deeply lined face and firm jaw that suggested years of facing problems head on.

"This is Pete. I'm William," the man with the alligator said.

"Anna," Anna completed the field introductions.

Leaving William to amuse the alligator, Pete leaned against the truck. He pulled off his ball cap and scratched through thinning hair. "What I'm wondering," he said with a drawl, "is how you came to be pepper-spraying a law-abiding alligator in the middle of the damn night?"

There was no malice in his words and Anna laughed. "It's a long story," she said.

"Well, I'm all ears, and William here's paid by the hour."

Anna told them. They laughed, gave her a bad time about wrasslin' gators for a new career, but they knew their alligators, and she could tell the men were genuinely pleased she was alive and unharmed. At least Pete and William were. When she'd finished, Ranger Thigpen lit a cigarette, blew out the smoke, and said with the slick sharp edge of a person who's not really kidding: "I can't believe you actually jumped right down on that alligator's back."

The Fisheries and Wildlife guys smelled a challenge. Pete went silent. William cast about for something to say but only managed introductory noises.

Anna looked at Thigpen and felt nothing. "Neither can I, Randy. Neither can I." The other men laughed. Thigpen joined in. A test had been passed, points scored, and Anna was sick of the game.

"I'll get his tail. You watch yourself, William." Pete dropped the tailgate. In a quick jerking movement, William hauled up on his pole, momentarily choking the gator as he lifted. Pete grasped the tail. In two seconds the alligator was in the truck bed, and the tailgate was closed.

"Here comes the fun part," Pete said. "We've got to get the noose off his neck."

"Hold up your hands, Pete," William teased. "Ten fingers. We'll count again after you've done it."

"Can I watch?" Anna asked suddenly.

"Sure. Climb up top the cab where you won't get et," William said.

Anna scrambled over the hood and lay on her belly across the cab so she could look directly down on the alligator. He was still young enough to be beautiful. His features were well cut, the ridges on his back sharp, the yellow stripes on his tail not yet faded.

William maneuvered the gator around till his nose was in the corner made by the tailgate and the side of the truck bed, then pushed the pole close to the creature's head and fed out a little rope. Pete pressed against the side of the truck behind the alligator. Balanced on the balls of his feet in case he needed to retreat in a hurry, he reached over the side to

180

pull the noose loose with deft precise plucks. "Hey, ho," he said with a spark of discovery. "Tighten your line up, William. We've got another little hitch in tonight's operation."

William tightened the rope as Pete left the back of the truck to retrieve something from the cab. He returned with a flashlight that he trained on the animal's neck. "This boy's already got a collar on. Lookit." Anna craned forward but Pete and William, bending over their captive, blocked her view.

"Looks like clothesline," Pete said.

"Probably is. It's cinched down plenty tight. No wonder he was so cantankerous. Hold him still."

William pulled the line tight and shoved the pole down on the alligator's throat.

Pete slid his glasses up on top of his head the better to see close up. "They got it knotted." Having dug a pocketknife from his trousers, he opened it to the smallest blade. "Hold him," he said again.

The alligator twitched his tail but was otherwise quiet in the occasional way of wild things that seem to realize they are being helped.

"Got it. Turn him loose."

William slipped the loosened noose from the alligator's neck. The beast whipped around with such speed Anna squawked and slid off the cab onto the hood. He wasn't attacking; he just wanted to hide his head under the metal toolbox that ran across the rear of the bed. Evidently he'd had enough of humankind for one night.

"Clothesline it is," Pete said, and held up what he'd cut from the gator's neck. "That answers why this boy was in your carport umpty-ump miles from any decent water."

"Clothesline?" Anna repeated stupidly.

"Here. A souvenir." Pete draped the line around her neck. It was the common cotton variety, white with a thin thread of blue; the sort of line that was bought by the yard at most hardware stores.

Anna was tired. Sliding from the cab to the hood had hurt her bruised elbow. Climbing from the hood to the ground stressed the ankle the alligator had whacked with his tail.

"Somebody's idea of a joke," William said. "About six months back me and Pete had to go get one out of the bathtub in the women's dorm there at Mississippi College."

"It's hard on the poor old gator," Pete said, sounding positively fond of the animal. He restored his glasses to the bridge of his nose and adjusted the earpieces. "Since we don't know where this boy's from and you've developed a personal relationship with him, you want him?"

"How do you mean?" Anna asked guardedly.

"We can turn him loose in Big Bayou Pierre. That's a good habitat for a fella this size."

"You can even name him," William said, and because he didn't sound like he was kidding, Anna laughed.

"We'll call him Will Peterson," she suggested.

"Unless he gets into trouble," Pete said. "Then we'll call him Boots."

They left with the alligator. Randy left to

sleep. His shift didn't start till noon. Anna walked back around to look in the now-empty carport. She'd left the Crown Vic parked behind her Rambler in the drive. It would be a while before she'd be willing to walk into the dark in that particular spot.

Taco's blood showed black in the hint of light fighting through the clouds to the east. There was a lot of it. Too much for a dog to lose.

An alligator placed under a car.

A ranger called out on a false alarm.

A dog mauled.

Not Anna's idea of a practical joke. Somebody wanted the lady ranger to go home. Or to the hospital. Trouble was, Anna didn't know if the enemy was "us" or "them."

9

Piedmont, who'd never had a good word to say about dogs in his entire nine lives, was unaccountably distraught. Maybe it was the smell of blood and vet that hung about Anna. Maybe the old pumpkin-colored cat just missed abusing his buddy. Whatever the cause, he sat on the side of the tub and complained as Anna tried to soak out the aches Will Peterson had pounded into her with his scaly tail. Rocky Springs's water was brown and gave off a faintly unpleasant odor.

"Smells like cottonmouths have been peeing

in it," she told Piedmont. He twitched his long banded tail, oblivious to the fact that he swished it through bath water.

"Turning swamp cat on me?" Anna asked. "Tail like our friend Mr. Peterson?" According to the Fisheries and Wildlife men, the alligator had been purposely put in her carport. A joke. A prank. The false accident report would be written off as a joke, a prank. It happened often to people who called attention to themselves or challenged the status quo: the first Asian ball player, the first black bomber pilot, the first female district ranger in southern Mississippi. Anna doubted it was anything so sinister as a plot to kill her—or her dog. Just put a scare into her. Or make a fool of her. Prove she wasn't man enough for the job.

Her own rangers could have masterminded it, but she didn't think so. Randy she pegged as too lazy to catch an alligator or set up a conspiracy so elaborate he could be safely at home when the false report was called in. Barth didn't seem the man for petty spite, or for midnight shenanigans.

Shenanigans. Despite its potential harm to her and its actual harm to Taco, this struck her as kid stuff. The snickering over the cell phone, the use of clothesline to snare the alligator. Kids, for all their posturing, were mostly apolitical. They might ape what their daddies said about women in law enforcement, but they were too wrapped up in their own world to care one way or another what adults did for a living.

If kids did put Will Peterson in her car-port as a prank, they would have stayed close—in the woods or parked out front—to watch the fun. Anna'd been pretty busy for a few min-utes there but she was fairly sure there wasn't a car nearby. The woods, she couldn't be sure of, but with the rain, it would have been off-putting to the average prankster and in the darkness she probably would have seen at least one flashlight during their retreat.

The third alternative was the most likely. Kids had put an alligator in her carport not as a prank but to frighten or disable her for their own rea-sons. Heather, Matt, the dead girl's boyfriend, Brandon DeForest, the two tuxedoed boys she'd seen fleeing the graveyard the night Danni died: these were the only kids she had any con-nection with in Mississippi.

"Stupid," she told the cat as she added more hot water to the bath, turning the knob with her toes. "Don't kids read anymore? An attack on the detective only serves to make her that much more determined."

At the first respectable hour after dawn, she decided she would call the sheriff and see if he had better luck than she at tracking down the boys who'd partied in the cemetery on prom night.

Paul Davidson. Anna let her mind float around his edges. A gentleness cloaked him that was unusual in a man and positively rare in a lawman. Years of sniffing out, chasing down and locking up wretched, unpleasant and dangerous people tended to smash one's rose-colored glasses all to hell. Cynicism was close under the surface of most law enforcement people. Some wore it on their sleeves. Even more boasted of it, as if it were their gain and not their loss. Those not in law enforcement became the enemy: perps, scumbags, bleeding hearts, whiners, junkies, whores. In the green and protected version of policing Anna'd dedicated herself to, the care of the national parks, much of that poison was avoided. But she'd swallowed some. She could feel it in her intolerance of intolerance.

Davidson, a white sheriff in a predominantly black county, one of the poorest counties in one of the poorest states in the richest country in the world, seemed untouched. It wasn't naïveté. In his position, to be naive would be deadly, not to mention nigh to impossible. His eyes had age in them that his face and body didn't lay claim to. Paul Davidson had seen the dark side of life, Anna guessed, and survived it, soul intact.

"Metaphysics," she said to the cat. "I must be farther gone than I think."

Her thoughts drifted, changing dimensions as her conscious mind turned its burdens over to the land of the Tooth Fairy and flying without wings.

The phone woke her. The water was cold. Piedmont was gone. Her skin was fish-belly white and shriveled.

Taco. The vet said he'd call. Naked and shivering, she slopped from the tub and squished down the hall. "Rocky Springs," she said into the receiver and knew video phones, where caller could see caller, were never going to be big sellers.

"Anna Pigeon?"

"Speaking."

"This is David Christianson. Taco made it. He's stable. I think you've still got yourself a dog."

"Good news," Anna said. Piedmont appeared from somewhere and was butting her shins with his head. Anna sat cross-legged on the floor and tugged his tail to let him know he was loved. "When can I come get him?"

"Not for a couple of days. I had to amputate his left rear leg. He'll get around just fine. You'll be amazed. But right now he's one sick puppy. I want to keep him here for a while. You can visit," he said kindly.

"I'll do that." Anna started to hang up then jerked the phone back. "Thank you," she said.

"My pleasure. Dogs are God's way of teaching us unconditional love."

Apparently God weaseled his way into everything in Mississippi. Anna hung up the phone. "Taco's going to be okay," she told the cat.

The crisis past, Piedmont feigned indifference.

Anna crawled into bed with her cat and managed two glorious hours of sleep brought to a heated close by a dream of the Southern sheriff so deliciously erotic she woke feeling warm and wanton and quite refreshed.

The investigation into the murder of Danielle Posey continued to weigh heavily, but the day-to-day housekeeping chores of her new position had to be attended to. Anna spent part of the morning at the Rocky Springs office on the phone with John Brown and the superintendent, and the rest wrestling with the archaic computer that had, to all intents and purposes, been gathering dust in the Port Gibson office since the NPS had acquired it. Near as she could tell, scheduling had been done by hand by the old district ranger and, if Steve Stilwell had done it differently during his tenure as acting district ranger, he'd used his own computer in Ridgeland.

When George Wentworth poked his head in her office at ten-thirty A.M., Anna was glad of the excuse to take a break. The rain had stopped but the damp continued, all-pervasive in a warm mist that kept sweat close to the body. Anna was impressed at how natty the maintenance head looked. Most NPS employees dragged their uniform shirts out of the dryer and hoped for the best. George—or more likely his wife—had ironed his. Creases from the pockets were crisp and sharp and the button-down shoulder tabs, vestigial epaulets, were starched to military precision.

Barth didn't come on till noon and Randy was scheduled for the four-to-midnight shift so they had the office to themselves. Having doctored their coffee with non-dairy creamer and, for George, with artificial sweetener, they plopped companionably down, one at each of the desks the field rangers had moved to face each other.

"How goes the murder investigation?" Wentworth asked. Anna'd tipped her chair back and rested her heels on Barth's desk, careful not to squash a half-eaten bag of Cheetos he had stashed there. The maintenance head was just being personable, Anna could tell, and she enjoyed telling someone who had no vested interest in their findings. Talking it through helped clarify things.

"I've had dealings with the Poseys," he said when she reached that part of the story. "When they leased that acreage, my boys had to bush-hog it. He's not a bad egg taken all around like a doughnut. These old farmers have a hard life, some of them. You can't really blame them for getting hard themselves. Mrs. Posey... Well let's just say I was ready to run her over with a bush-hog and swear on a stack of Bibles it was an accident till I found out she was mentally ill. I met the girl—Danni—once or twice. She turned out to be a pretty nice girl. Or seemed like one. But her brother's not somebody I'd want to meet in a dark alley."

Wentworth had a touch of a drawl, but the idioms he used reminded Anna of the cowboys she grew up with. "You're not from around here, are you?" She intentionally mimicked what seemed to be the sixty-four-dollar question in Claiborne County.

George laughed, showing his perfect teeth and, against the velvety brown of his lips, a startlingly pink tongue.

"I'm from San Diego," he said.

"Why did you—" Anna couldn't think of a comfortable way to finish the question. With the exception of commercialism and communism, talk of the "isms" had become socially unacceptable. Walls went up, defenses did likewise, people became cagey and hyperalert.

"Why did a black man move to Mississippi?" George rescued her easily. "Leda, my wife, is from Natchez, and once these girls get Mississippi mud between their toes there's no making them happy till you bring them home."

Curiosity overriding good manners Anna asked, "How has it been?"

"Maybe like a Jew returning to Israel. There's a downside, but there's a black culture here: black churches, businesses, social clubs. Not so much a sense of the silent majority blocking you with a smile."

The ease was gone, Anna had poked too close to the bone. She changed the subject to one she knew gave George pleasure, his sought-after football hero of a son. "Has your son"—Anna scraped around her brain for the boy's name—"Lock, decided to go join one of the professional football teams?"

The homely question didn't have the desired effect. George lost that edginess, but a new discomfort settled over his face. Worry, if Anna guessed right.

"Twenty's a tough age. It's hard to know what you want," Wentworth said guardedly.

Anna's coffee cup was empty and she was

striking out in the socializing department, but it seemed awkward to just jump up and go back to her office. She squirmed till she'd pretty much pulverized Barth's Cheetos before the two of them were rescued by the ringing of the phone.

"Time to get back to work," George said with a hint of relief in his voice and Anna picked up the receiver.

The call was from Sheriff Davidson. He dropped by the office around one o'clock. After the XXX-rated dream Anna'd had about him, she found herself embarrassed, as though he could read her mind. It made her gruffer than usual. To his credit, he was unperturbed and it was only a matter of minutes before the awkwardness passed. Still, she found herself looking at him with more interest than she had before he'd revealed himself in his incubus persona.

"Time to divvy up chores again," he said. He'd put his Stetson on the built-in counter that served as Anna's desk. Now he moved it in a circle, one half inch at a time, by pinching the rim. *Nice hands,* Anna found herself thinking. She rubbed her temples with the heels of her hands to force her brain to behave.

"The DeForest boy needs to be talked to. Chances are he'll have a good idea who the two boys you saw in the graveyard are. And one of us needs to track down those campers you mentioned, the Civil War re-enactors. They'll be locals. If they saw something, they might be able to make sense of it in the context of the personalities involved. Mississippi is a small town; everybody knows everybody else and about half the state is related."

"You choose," Anna said. "It's your turf."

Davidson thought for a minute. The hat made a quarter circuit. "Why don't you tackle DeForest. From what I hear, he's a brazen sort. Full of himself. Big man on campus at the high school. He may get his back up at me. If we're lucky, he'll want to brag if he gets a female audience. I'll talk to your campers."

Anna told him what she remembered: Jimmy Williams, a lawyer in Jackson; Ian McIntire; and a Baptist minister, Leo something.

"No sense starting with a lawyer," the sheriff said as he put on his hat. "I'll look up McIntire then try my luck with the minister. We speak the same language."

Davidson left a copy of the report he'd gotten back on the physical evidence. When he'd gone, Anna read it, glad to postpone for a few minutes another pilgrimage to the halls of Clinton High.

Danielle's dress was stained with mud and plant materials in accordance with where the body had been found. Fibers had been found on the dress that could have been from the seats of three different vehicles. Not surprising given the date motif. If necessary, the fibers could be matched to those of a suspect's vehicle. Except, at present, there were no suspects. The sheet she'd been draped in had trace evidence of grease, fibers, rust, mud, gasoline, paraffin, wool colored with vegetable dye in a process that hadn't been used in seventy years, and specks of rotted crumbling leather. The eyeholes had been cut recently and with a knife or scissors. The report was consistent with a piece of cloth that had probably been kept in the trunk of an automobile. In other words, a rag.

The dead girl's underpants had semen stains and stains from plant material.

Anna filed the report with the copy of the autopsy. The sheet had been a car rag. That suggested Danni had been killed near a vehicle, or had been transported by a vehicle after death, or her pursuer had carried the sheet with him for the express purpose for which it was used. Him. Anna thought about that for a moment. Not as opposed to "her," though Anna did think of this murderer as male. A whack on the head could have been delivered by a woman—or another girl—but few women had the physical strength to carry one hundred eight pounds dead weight very far, especially not in the dark and over rough country. Anna was thinking of "him" as opposed to "them." This was, or had been made to look like, a hate crime, with the amateur KKK overtones added after death. Lynchings were crimes committed by mobs. Danielle could have been put to death by a group. That was more chilling somehow: the mindless rage of the pack, humanity lost.

By the time Anna headed north, the mists had burned away and the sky was the deep blue she associated with autumn in the upper Midwest, cloudless and impossibly deep. After the wash of the rains, the green was so intense it looked unreal and everything sparkled with water droplets. As she drove the Trace, each curve revealing a scene rich with life and as picturesque as illustrations from a children's book, Anna was struck again by the beauty of the state. Over her years as a Yankee and a Westerner, she'd heard Mississippi described many ways. Beautiful had never been one of them. Maybe, like her, others had gleaned their impressions of the Deep South secondhand.

Adele Mack, the vice principal at Clinton High, was not overly pleased to see her, but she hid it well. Anna appreciated that. Business was business; good manners made it go more smoothly. Adele looked different from before, but Anna couldn't put her finger on it till Ms. Mack was talking into her telephone. The mask of cosmetics was exquisitely in place but the vice principal was experimenting with painting the lipstick just outside her lipline. From a distance it may have made her lips appear more full and luscious. Up close it gave her a disconcerting out-of-focus aspect.

When Anna told her she'd come to speak with

Brandon DeForest, Adele cheered up a bit. "He'll be in chemistry," Miss Mack said efficiently. "I'll get him myself. You'll want to talk to him in the office. Brandon is easily distracted." As she walked out, careful to close the door behind her, Anna got the sense that if any of Adele's little charges had to be given up, young Brandon would be at the top of her list of sacrifices.

Ms. Mack left Anna and the boy alone in her office. Brandon eschewed the second visitor's chair and sat in Ms. Mack's place behind the desk, then smiled at Anna as if he'd scored a point.

She smiled. Once one knew the games of intimidation, they served only to highlight the other's insecurities. DeForest was fighting for high ground before a single shot had been fired. Anna wanted to know why.

Theoretically he was a handsome lad: well-built, with the muscular upper body and thick neck of a young athlete made to do neck bridges and sprints. His hair was honey-blond, worn long on top and shaved close to the head on the sides. Anna knew that was the fashion of the moment, but when she was of high school age it was the earmark of a new and cheap haircut. Brandon's features were regular, his ears small and close to the head.

The qualifier "theoretically" came to mind because, though he'd photograph well and most people would see him as beautiful, in actuality there was something unappealing about him. A pimple in the corner of his mouth, an aggressiveness in his excessive eye contact, dishonesty in the pose he struck of exaggerated comfort. In the seconds it took her to make her appraisal, he tilted back in the vice principal's chair and put large sneakered feet on her desk, daring Anna to comment.

As she was dragged again into the realms of youth, an old taunt came to mind: Anybody who'll take a dare will suck eggs.

"Take your feet off the desk," Anna said pleasantly, risking the egg.

DeForest looked at her. His eyes were blue, the color of new denim. He was trying to read her, but he was a babe in the woods. She could read his thoughts the way an actor reads a TelePrompTer, word for word: "And if I don't? Want to make me? You've got no say here."

She waited. In the end he said nothing, just procrastinated long enough to prove insolence but not so long as to be insubordinate, then put his feet on the floor.

"Do you know why I'm here?" Anna asked.

"Ms. Mack said you had some questions."

Anna waited, an open, friendly look on her face. She'd already questioned two of his classmates. There were few secrets in high school. With the possible exception of the teachers, everyone in the building had a pretty good idea why a National Park Ranger was on campus asking to see the team quarterback.

Brandon tried to outwait her but lasted less than thirty seconds. "I guess you want to talk to me because I took Danni to the prom. I don't know what Matt told you, but you can't go believing what Matt Dryer says. Ask anybody. Matt's a waste."

Fifteen more seconds ticked by. Anna heard them faintly marked off by the wall clock.

"Look." Brandon leaned forward, put his elbows on the desk, full of boyish earnestness and the desire to please. "I cared about Danni, I really did, but she'd got wild. That's God's honest truth. She'd got to drinking and maybe into drugs, I don't know. After the prom, I was going to break it off with her."

DeForest considered his words then changed them. "I would've stuck with her. Got her some help, you know. D.A.R.E. or something."

Tick. Tick. Tick. Anna sat. Oddly enough, it seemed the longer one lived, the more time one had. At eighteen, DeForest couldn't stand it. "Danni got to drinking at the dance. I didn't like it, and I left. End of story. If you're fixin' to arrest me, I want a lawyer."

Anna wasn't fixing to do anything, so Miranda didn't come into play.

"After the dance," Anna said. "Who went out to Rocky with you?"

"Nobody. We... I didn't go out to the Trace. Me and some friends got some pizza, then went home. Maybe Danielle went out with somebody else."

"Who did you go out with after the dance?"

"Just some friends."

"Who?"

"I don't remember."

"You don't remember who you went out for pizza with?"

Brandon said nothing.

Anna came around in a new direction: "Mazzio's?"

"Huh?"

"Is that where you went for pizza?"

Nothing.

"Pizza Hut? Papa John's? Where?"

"It might have been Mazzio's."

"Might have been?"

"What difference does it make? Okay, it was Mazzio's. We went to Mazzio's. Happy now?"

"Easy enough to check," Anna said.

Brandon pushed back from the desk. He looked considerably younger than when he'd come into the office. Gone was the pose of being at ease. Anna thought for a second he was going to bolt from the room.

"Do you have a cellular phone?" she asked, purposely jumping subjects.

"A cell phone?" he said stupidly.

"A cell phone."

"Dad does."

"Do any of your friends have one?"

"Thad, I think. Why?"

"What's Thad's last name?"

Brandon didn't want to answer, but there was no real way out. "Meyerhoff. What's this about?"

"Describe Thad."

"How do you mean? Like what does he look like?"

"Tell me what he looks like."

"I don't know. He's thin. Maybe six feet tall.

I don't know. What do you want?" He was beginning to sound desperate. Anna liked that.

"Color of hair?"

"Brown, I guess."

"Long or short."

"Kind of short."

"Were you with Thad last night?"

The pieces fell together. "I was at an away game in Meridian. Ask the coach."

"What time did you get home?"

"I don't know."

"Before five? After midnight?"

"Ten, I guess."

"Then you were with Thad?"

"We might've hung out. I don't really remember. I mean it was just no big deal."

"Who went with you to Rocky Springs the night of the prom?" Anna asked.

"I didn't... we took..." His mouth closed tightly, his lips a thin line.

"Was one of the boys stocky, five-foot-ten or -eleven, dark hair, a football player and one a skinny guy, around six-foot, brown hair? Thad Meyerhoff maybe?" Anna described what she could remember of the boys she'd seen in the graveyard shortly before she'd found Heather.

"I want to talk to my dad," Brandon said.

"That's okay." Anna got up, reached across the desk and shook hands with a now bewildered boy. "You've been a terrific help. I'll let Ms. Mack know we're done. Thanks again." Anna smiled warmly and left quickly. She wanted to talk to Mr. DeForest before his son got to him.

A few inquiries led her to Brandon's father. He was the manager of the warehouse at the Sears in the Metro Center Mall on Highway 20 just inside the Jackson city limits. A helpful young man in khaki pants and shirt guided her through canyons of boxes to a small office with a picture window letting into the warehouse area.

Fred Posey had referred to Brandon's father as Colonel DeForest. Subconsciously, Anna had been expecting a much older man. Men her age, Vietnam vets mostly, didn't tend to hang on to the title of their military rank after they left the service. She'd thought that was reserved for lifers, or men who fought in WWII.

Mr. DeForest was probably Brandon's worst nightmare, if the boy was imaginative enough to be plagued by nightmares.

Once undoubtedly as good an athlete as his son and boasting as fine a physique, Mr. DeForest had seen his muscle turn to fat and congregate under his belt, all in front like a woman pregnant with twins, and yet Anna found him more attractive than his son. There was genuine concern in his voice when he expressed his shock over Danni's death. They'd known Danni Posey for three years, ever since she and Brandon had begun dating steadily. Danni spent a lot of time at the DeForest house. "Her mama had sick spells," Mr. DeForest explained delicately.

When he'd finished what he considered the necessary pleasantries to make Anna feel at home, he seated her in his claustrophobic office and said: "Now, what can I do for you, Mrs. Pigeon?"

Anna didn't correct him. In this part of the world she assumed "Mrs." was a title of respect, and this kindly man was giving her the benefit of the doubt.

"We are trying to talk with as many people as we can who might have been in or around Rocky Springs the night that Danni died in hopes somebody might have seen or heard anything that could help us."

"We'll sure do anything we can. What happened to Danni, that was just awful."

Anna wondered who "we" was but didn't want to break his rhythm of helpful cooperation by asking. "I know some of the kids that were there," Anna said. "Heather Barnes and your son said Thad Meyerhoff was with them and another boy—oh what was his name? Stocky, dark hair, football player type?"

"That'd be Lyle Sanders," Mr. DeForest filled in helpfully. "Those boys are like the Three Musketeers."

"Did Brandon happen to mention to you or his mom anything he might have seen at Rocky the night of the prom?" Anna asked.

"No. Not that sticks in my mind. The kids like to go out there. Makes the girls scared and needing protection is what the draw is, I guess."

"Or makes them pretend to be to get the boys

to put their arms around them," Anna said, and Mr. DeForest laughed. They were just reminiscing about the motives of their own youth. Seniors in high school now had resolved the kiss-on-the-first-date controversy by the time they reached fifth grade.

"I know the kids went out that way after the dance because Brandon was telling his mom you all had cut a bunch of pines out of the campground there and it's not near as pretty as it used to be."

Anna'd seen the stumps and asked Barth about it. "A lot of the pines on the Trace are diseased," she said.

"Ah. Anyway, I guess he and Danni had a falling-out. He didn't seem to want to talk much."

"Had they been quarreling?"

For the first time it seemed to sink in that this call might not be quite as harmless as he'd thought. Mr. DeForest's face hardened. Anna saw the underlying toughness that had gotten him to the rank of colonel.

"These boy-girl things run hot and cold," he said carefully.

"Was it running cold?"

"I think they were growing apart. Senior year. Applying to colleges. That sort of thing."

"But they'd been together, what? Three years? That's a long time at that age."

Colonel DeForest looked down at his desk. His hair was thinning on top, a circle reminiscent of a monk's tonsure. When he looked up, the friendliness was gone. "I can see the direction you're going with this, Mrs. Pigeon, but it's the wrong direction. Kids don't kill each other because of girlfriend problems."

Into the silence that followed came the memories of the high school shootings in the last half of the 1990s that had left children and teachers dead. Kids killing kids because of girlfriend problems. One of the deadliest had taken place in Pearl, just over the river from the city of Jackson.

"Mrs. Pigeon, we all liked Danni. She was a sweet girl. But I've given you all the help I can, and it's time I was getting back to work."

When an interview's over, it's over. Once Colonel DeForest compared notes with his son, Anna doubted he'd do much in the way of cooperating with the law and certainly not with her.

It was four o'clock. School would be out by now, the Sanders boy and Thad Meyerhoff would have scattered. More important, Brandon would have had time to talk to them. She would be surprised if the next time she talked with them they hadn't synchronized their stories. Synchronized to hide what? At that age, troubles tended to seem the same size, unwanted pregnancy as terrifying as assault and battery, cheating on an exam on a par with driving under the influence. Because the boys were lying to hide something didn't prove that something was murder.

The alligator with the clothesline around its neck, a prank gone sour that nearly killed her dog and could have killed or crippled her. The yellow line around Danni's neck, the newly hacked eyeholes in a dirty sheet; they had the same half-thought-out, reckless disregard of the alligator prank.

More and more, it seemed, murder, brutality, was just kid stuff.

10

After five o'clock, when Anna got back to the Port Gibson Ranger Station, there were two messages from Sheriff Davidson on the answering machine. The first told her he had information to share from the day's interviews; the second invited her to go with him to talk with Leo Fullerton, the Civil War reenactor and Baptist minister, in Port Gibson.

Anna erased them and stood for a moment awash in thought. This was business. She was new and female and single and in a strange place, a place where she was unsure of the rules. This was also social. Unless her romantic instincts had atrophied from years of neglect, the second of the sheriff's messages was tinged with the odor of a date. The words had been too casual, too offhand, as if he too knew they'd slipped over some professional line and he was unsure of himself.

Truth was, Anna wanted to go. She was interested to hear what he'd learned, interested to find out what the minister had seen, if anything, but mostly she knew she'd rather spend the evening in a patrol car with Paul Davidson than in her pajamas with Piedmont. It had been a long time since she could say that about a man.

Feeling the unpleasant frisson of a woman with a hidden agenda, she dialed the number he left. It was different from that on the Rolodex she had inherited. Probably he was at home.

Because of her tortuous thoughts, Anna was businesslike to the point of brusque. It was quickly decided she would meet him at the Port Gibson Sheriff's Department, where he had a loose end from another case to tie off. They would go from there. She hung up wishing he'd been stereotypical: a fat redneck with mirrored sunglasses. Then there would be no danger of complications. She deeply resented the space in her brain that the machinations of interpersonal relationships required. Lady Macbeth crying "Unsex me!" suddenly didn't strike her as unsympathetic.

The door banged open and she started guiltily, caught in the act of thinking about a boy. A man in a suit and tie came in. It took her a second to recognize George Wentworth out of uniform. Behind him was a handsome youth in blue jeans and a sweatshirt.

"You're working late," Wentworth said. "I'd like you to meet my son, Lockley. I'll just be a second. I've got to pick up some paperwork I need to fax." The Port Gibson Ranger

Station had yet to stumble into the age of the fax machine. They still used the local drugstore. George disappeared into his office.

"Anna Pigeon," Anna said, proffering her hand. "Your dad has told me a lot about you."

Lockley took her fingertips and shook them gingerly. Lockley Wentworth, for all his bulk and youthful vitality, looked drawn and pale. Anna'd never seen an African-American look pale, but he did. The skin around his eyes and mouth was drawn and had a grayish cast under the dark pigmentation. "Are you okay?" she asked impulsively.

"Yes, ma'am," Lock replied politely. He didn't sound it, and he didn't meet her eye.

"Your dad says you're being courted by the big leagues," Anna tried.

"The pros. Yes, ma'am."

The fellow didn't want to talk. That was fine with Anna. "I'm off, George," she called. "Don't bother to close the gate. Nice to meet you, Lockley," and she escaped to the sanctity of her patrol car. Though she'd cleaned it, it still smelled of blood and urine where Taco had lain. Yet another reason to be glad the dog had survived. Living with a constant reminder of his demise would have been hard to take.

Port Gibson was the city the Civil War reenactors told her retained its historical aspect because General Ulysses S. Grant had declared it "too beautiful to burn." Its glory days were gone. There were still beautiful houses and gardens that had been cultivated for more than a century, but many of the old buildings were in sore need of paint and repair. The court-house, grand and domed, seemingly too large for the shrunken city, lorded it over a shabby Main Street with an air of genteel poverty.

Behind the courthouse was the uninspired low-roofed building that housed the Sheriff's Department. On her tour the first day with George Wentworth, they'd driven by, but Anna'd never been inside. Familiarizing herself with it was one of the many things on her list that had been preempted by the murder investigation. Because of the vagaries of law, jurisdiction and accreditation, any individuals arrested on the Natchez-to-Jackson stretch of the Trace had to be brought to Port Gibson for incarceration.

Davidson's car was out front. Anna parked beside it.

Inside, the Sheriff's Department was even more depressing than most. A waiting room steeped in pain neglected was watched over by a glassed-in kiosk where a black woman buzzed the unfortunates and their keepers through a double-door setup, a sort of crime airlock. The only cheery note was the department's uniform. The woman in the kiosk wore a nifty burgundy number.

Anna introduced herself.

"I'm Cameron. We been hearin' about y'all," the policewoman said. "It's this big deal. Like there haven't been policewomen down here forever. Glad to finally meet you."

After stowing her weapon in a lockbox outside the jail area, Anna was ushered into the inner sanctum, where Cameron showed her the location of the Breathalyzer and the grim double row of locked doors. Prisoners, bored, hungover, angry, shouted questions in hopes of getting a crumb of attention. Anna ignored them. Cameron knew them by name and was good-natured about the distraction.

Davidson was waiting when Anna reclaimed her weapon and her freedom. The sun had set and the velvet evening was upon them. In her mind, Anna heard the strains of the old song "Blue Velvet." Blue velvet was the night, the lyric went. The songwriter must have been from the South. The sky was a deep blue pricked with stars.

Murder proved a nice distraction and, as the sheriff told her of his day's findings, Anna relaxed into the familiar role with which work always provided her. A comfortable place where reason and not emotion was the most effective tool.

"The boys are going to stonewall," Davidson said as he backed his vehicle out of the lot. "My deputy got to the two you'd named, Thad Meyerhoff and Lyle Sanders, but the juice ain't worth the squeeze. They're saying they were drunk prom night and remember nothing. My guess is that'll be Brandon DeForest's story when next we talk to him."

"The Three Musketeers: one for all and all for one," Anna said, then explained, telling him of her interviews with Brandon and his father.

"Colonel DeForest and the Meyerhoffs are

good people," Davidson said. "They won't take kindly to their sons saying they were so drunk they blacked out. Whatever those boys are hiding, they've got to figure it'll get them in worse trouble than admitting to drunkenness."

"If I hadn't actually seen those two boys—probably Sanders and Meyerhoff—in the graveyard, the story they made up would probably have been less toxic," Anna said. "Maybe the three of them playing cards or night fishing together."

"No doubt."

"How about the Sanderses? Are they 'good people'?"

"Lyle's father is an abusive alcoholic. Hearing Lyle admit to the family failing, my guess is he'll beat that boy half to death."

They ruminated on that for a while, the silence in the car deepened by the crackling worries of the police radio. What would a kid take a beating to avoid? Jail? A murder rap?

"Do you think they killed Danni Posey?" Anna asked.

"I sure don't want to."

Neither did she. "What did you get from our used-car salesman, McIntire?"

"Not much. He said they'd had a little too much bourbon and went to bed early. He slept right through the cars and the shouting that the other campers complained of. Says he knew nothing about it till the next morning."

"It seems alcohol's the excuse *du jour* in these parts," Anna said.

"Everybody everywhere drinks too much. It's just in Mississippi most folks don't waste time going to AA meetings in between."

That was the first cynical remark Anna'd heard him make. She liked him better for it. Saints had a way of wearing on the nerves of the less exalted.

"McIntire made a point of asking me to tell you he doesn't think it was your fault," the sheriff said. "You being new and all, and that he and his buddies have no intention of deserting Rocky because of it."

"Big of him," Anna said dryly.

"He thought so."

"Talk to the lawyer?"

"Jimmy Williams? Tomorrow, he's at the top of my morning. I did have one interesting bit of information turn up."

Because he was pleased with himself and wanted her to ask what it was, Anna did.

"I dropped by the Posey farm and talked to Cindy. I'd forgotten I'd met her before four or five years ago when her son got on the wrong side of things. Just the pre-penitentiary warm-ups, I'm afraid. Anyway Cindy and I had a two-Coke chat. She's sick enough I think Fred should see if he can get her back into care, but that's not my field. Not with this hat on. She said she'd had two other children besides Danni and Mike. She told me they'd been still-born and they were penguins."

"Jesus," Anna said.

"It gets better. Or worse, depending on how you look at it. I asked her how they came to be penguins, and she admitted that they weren't really penguins. That a black nurse at the hospital had chewed them up. After he spit them out, they were black babies so she had to turn them loose."

"Turn them loose?"

"She said she let them go in the woods so they could return to the wild. I got hold of Fred. Cindy had a miscarriage between Danni and Mike. He said that's when she started 'slipping,' with a fixation on African-Americans. He swears there were no babies, black or otherwise, turned loose in the woods."

"That's a comfort, I guess. Did you believe him or do you think there's baby bones buried somewhere under the cotton crop?"

"I believed him. We'll need to check it out as best we can, but I think he was telling the truth.

"Then she told me Danni had been insured for forty thousand dollars. After the penguins, I wasn't taking anything on faith but I checked. The girl was insured by Mrs. Posey. According to Cindy, Fred Posey didn't know anything about it."

"Life insurance on a sixteen-year-old girl? That doesn't make a whole lot of sense unless you intend to kill her. They might fool you and me, but insurance companies mean business."

Davidson laughed and Anna was relieved. Too often one man's joke was another man's insult.

"Not life insurance. Mrs. Posey had her

daughter's face insured. She'd heard on some TV show that an actress had her legs insured for a million dollars through Lloyds of London, she thought. And she knew Danni's face had to be protected."

"She'd told me Danni was going to be a model," Anna remembered. "As big as Cheryl Tiegs."

"Cindy Posey's heard that her daughter was struck across the right side of her forehead over the corner of her eye, disfigured, and she wants that forty grand. She says she paid for it, it's hers, and she means to have it," the sheriff said.

"Since the girl's dead, I wonder if the policy is still valid."

"Who knows. The point is Cindy Posey thinks it is."

"And maybe Fred Posey," Anna added. Secrets were hard to keep, especially secrets requiring paperwork, records, canceled checks. There was a time that it wouldn't have crossed her mind that anyone could murder their own child for a measly forty grand. No more. Forty grand might be a fortune to the Poseys.

"If one of the Poseys did it, the sheet and hangman's rope don't make a whole lot of sense," Anna said.

"Making sense doesn't seem to be Cindy Posey's long suit. This is it." Davidson turned off the two-lane road they'd followed out of Port Gibson and into the whale-belly darkness of a wooded dirt lane.

A tidy brick house was tucked back in the

trees and surrounded by white azalea bushes in such glorious bloom that they glowed like the light of the moon shattered and brought to ground. A Dodge truck was parked in the drive and the porch light was on.

"Are we expected?" Anna asked as they got out of the car.

"I let Leo know I'd be by tonight. No sense wasting a trip if nobody's going to be home."

Anna followed Davidson up the walk. The door opened and a cacophony of barks commenced. When they reached the porch, Anna saw the perpetrators through the screen. The minister had half a dozen Boston terriers, all clicking their nails on the linoleum, whiffling through squashed noses and yapping. Not a pretty sight.

"Father Davidson, come on in," said a voice Anna recognized as that of the dark man under Captain Williams's command. "Ma'am," he said as Anna was ushered in first. She'd forgotten how striking Leo Fullerton was. The lowering brow with black eyebrows that extended far beyond the corners of deep-set eyes, the full mouth that she suspected could turn cruel, but mostly the stiff way he moved, as if he'd not yet grown accustomed to the human form.

Amid the canine crisis that raged unabated and unreprimanded below their knees, Fullerton led them into a tiny formal dining room. Seated in straight-backed cherrywood chairs, they stared at one another across a centerpiece of fake magnolias and bunched ribbon that suggested a craft-mad woman tended to at least some of the minister's domestic needs.

"Like I said on the phone, Paul, I can't tell you anything." The statement was flat, lifeless. Leo's hands, palms down on the table, the fingers splayed, looked flat and lifeless, robotic limbs not yet needed. The only part of the minister that was animated was his eyes, and they disturbed Anna. One did not track. The other moved so quickly at times she caught herself glancing around the room to see if he followed the progress of a moth or a fly.

Methodically, Sheriff Davidson led Leo through the evening Danni had been killed. The minister said he and the others had turned in early. They slept in one tent, army-barracks style, on folding wood and canvas cots. He didn't hear the cars. He was a sound sleeper. Answers were given in dull monotone, and Anna began to wonder if he suffered from severe depression or was on psychotropic drugs for other reasons, but his eyes—or his one tracking eye—was clear, the pupil size within normal parameters. Not that pupil size mattered with psychotropics. Anna knew very little about them. She'd ask Molly.

The only time he came to life was when Anna asked if he, like McIntire, had consumed a little too much bourbon.

"I'm a Baptist minister," he said, obviously affronted. "I don't drink spirits."

Anna suffered an evil temptation to ask him if he danced. Not because he was a Baptist but because he came across as an audio animatronic Disney creation from the 1960s. The picture of him cutting a jig tickled her.

Finally, the questions were over. In a clatter of claws, the dogs escorted them to the porch and the minister closed the door, politely leaving the porch lamp on to light them to their car.

When they were partway down the walk, the preacher called from within, where he'd remained protected by the screen.

"Paul?"

"Yeah, Leo?" The sheriff stopped and turned.

"There's something I'd like to say."

"I'm listening, Leo."

"This thing is ungodly for the girl, for whoever killed her, but it doesn't end there."

Anna and Paul waited. Anna was waiting for some sort of Christian revelation. What Paul waited for, she didn't know, but she could feel the tension in him.

"How so, Leo?" he asked.

"That sheet, draping the girl like that, that's stirring up racial hatred that we've fought so long and so hard. Pointing the finger at old prejudices, giving them new life. It's as much a horror, as unforgivable, as the... the other. Don't you let it happen, Paul. Don't let this be written in that book."

They waited a bit, but he was done talking.

"I'll do my best," the sheriff said finally. "Good night, Leo."

"Good night," Anna echoed.

"Beating a dead horse," Anna summed up

her take on the interview. "There's something strange about that guy. He was creepy
when I met him. Tonight did nothing to
change my first impression. He looked like a
man in shock. The kind that are going to
walk around for a while right as rain and then
suddenly fall over dead."

"Leo's got a brooding aspect to him, but
there's something bothering him. I haven't
talked much to him since his mom died.
Alzheimer's. Long and slow and ugly."

"That would do it," Anna said. "Has he got
any reason to lie about what he saw or heard
that night?"

"None that I can think of. I've known Leo
for twenty-three years, and far as I know he
has no connection with the Posey family. Or
the DeForests for that matter. He's always been
an odd duck but not to do harm. He's one of
those fellows who feels everything. Though he's
just an awful preacher, his flock thinks he
walks on water. He feels their pain and carries their guilt in a way that would land me in
Whitfield." He named the local lunatic asylum.

Words Paul Davidson had spoken earlier,
that hadn't made sense at the time, snapped
into focus. Davidson had said of charity work
that it wasn't his job "in this hat." Once he'd
said of Leo Fullerton, the minister, that they
spoke the same language.

"Fullerton called you Father Davidson,"
Anna said. It came out like an accusation.

"I'm a priest," the sheriff said simply. "I had
the congregation at St. James for nine years

before I ran for sheriff. I still pinch-hit now and then when Father Johnson's sick or on vacation."

"A priest." Anna was appalled. Mentally she was inventorying everything she'd said or thought about the man since they'd met. Probably she was going to hell.

"You'll get used to it," he said mildly and, in the faint glow of the dashboard lights, Anna thought he was laughing at her discomfort. "In these parts, ninety-five percent of everyone is, was, or is married to the son, daughter, or brother of a priest. The other five percent are clergy spouses."

"Every region has its pitfalls," Anna said, managing to be rude without even trying.

Davidson pulled up beside Anna's patrol car in front of the Sheriff's Department and shut his engine off. The night was mild and even in town smelled of exotic blooms and was rich with the song of frogs. "Can I take you out for coffee one of these days, go someplace where neither of us has to wear a gun?"

Too weird. Anna's mind flashed to *Bedazzled* starring Dudley Moore and Peter Cook. The devil granting wishes, then screwing them up. She'd been lusting after a fucking priest. "Probably not a good idea," she said and pulled too hard on the door handle. Her fingers slipped off the chrome and she cracked her crazy bone so hard against the butt of her pistol that for a moment her arm went numb and she was blind with the uniquely miserable buzzing of nerve pain.

"Goddammit," she hissed. Then: "Oh my God, sorry. Shit, I did it again."

Davidson laughed. "Not a lot of men of the cloth in your past?"

"I've never known a priest," Anna admitted. "With the exception of Father Todd in high school who ordered the nuns around and, when he bothered to talk to us girls, always put his hand on our thighs."

"Abusive?" Davidson's voice turned so uncharacteristically cold, Anna focused past her tingling arm to the man's face.

"Ridiculous is more like it."

"Ah," he didn't sound much mollified.

"Coffee'd be fine," Anna said.

Davidson smiled. It was truly a lovely smile, even with teeth green from the light on the speedometer. "It'll be easy," he said. "No confession. I'm an Episcopal priest."

Layers upon layers, nothing was just what it was—Anna was at a loss as to where her Yankee forebears got the impression that Southerners were simple folk.

It was just past eight, dark and fragrant and warm. Anna'd put in a twelve-hour day and was glad to be going home. The town of Port Gibson lay just west of the Natchez Trace. There were two ways to get back on the parkway, one a mile or so south of the ranger station at mile marker thirty-nine and the other a road that angled northeast out of town to join the Trace at mile marker forty-three, closer to Rocky Springs. Having had her fill of business for the day, Anna took the shortcut.

On the way home, to amuse herself, she played with her radar. As it locked on each oncoming car, their speed was registered digitally. The previous district ranger had it set at sixty-two, twelve miles per hour over the posted speed limits. When any car exceeded that, and this night most of them did, the unit beeped and the number was locked in place till Anna erased it. Sixty-five, sixty-three, sixty-seven, Anna just couldn't get inspired to write any tickets. Since the speed limits on the interstates had been raised to seventy it was hard to get excited over sixty-seven, even in a fifty.

Traffic was light and she slipped into a pleasant torpor, dreaming about the frozen fettuccine Alfredo dinner waiting for her. On the long straight stretch crosscut by Big and Little Bayous Pierre, the radar unit shrieked her back into the present.

One hundred seventeen.

Too high to ignore. The car was by her in a flash. Anna stepped on the brakes, flicked on lights and siren, executed a Y turn and was behind them, way behind them. At one hundred seventeen miles an hour, you could cover a lot of country. The Crown Vic was powerful, but Anna'd not had call to test it. She stepped on the accelerator and watched as the needle climbed smoothly to a hundred and twenty. Uncomfortably aware of the Trace's deer population, she lifted her mike. "Seven hundred, this is five-eight-zero headed south from Big Bayou Pierre in pursuit." Now if she crashed, they'd know where to start looking for the body. For four quick miles—time enough for her pulse to catch up with her speed—she gave chase. The driver of the car ahead was either too drunk or too distracted to notice the lights in his rearview mirror. Or he was deciding whether or not he could outrun her. Finally his brake lights pulsed.

"Thank you, dick-brain." Anna hissed. She'd spent too many years on foot and horse-back. High-speed car chases scared her half to death.

Another three-quarters of a mile and the car moved to the side of the road and stopped. Anna pulled in behind it, parking nose slightly out toward the road, where her high beams would light up the interior of the other car and, in theory, her car would provide her with some protection from the next brain-dead speeder to come down the pike.

For a count of ten she sat, letting her mind, wild on adrenaline, stop crackling. "Seven hundred, this is five-eight-zero," she called dispatch, before she realized she hadn't the foggiest idea where she was. Undoubtedly a number of tiny roadside mile markers had whipped by in her peripheral vision.

"Seven hundred," the dispatcher's voice was female, calm and deep.

"Vehicle stop approximately five miles south of Big Bayou Pierre. A red Thunderbird. Mississippi plates CCJ-395. Could you run those for me?"

"Stand by."

Three heads in the Thunderbird, two in the front seat, one in the back. As she watched, the head in the backseat disappeared. Someone ducking down to hide? Just sweeping corn chips up that got spilled during the chase? Anna didn't like it.

"Five-eight-zero, seven hundred."

"Go ahead."

"Nineteen-eighty-two Thunderbird registered to a Loretta Doolittle, Alcorn address. Do you want that?"

"Not right now. Thanks." Anna put the mike back on its holder, got the flashlight out of the door pocket, and stepped onto the pavement. Holding the flashlight high as she approached, she shined it into the rear window, checking the backseat. The third head reappeared. A good sign. She stopped a minute, working her light over what she could of the backseat and floor. The car was a mess of fast-food wrappers and laundry. The man in the rear seat was young, dark-haired, white, and looked so familiar that Anna had a sense of déjà vu.

No weapons that she could see.

The driver had his window up and his hands down. Anna positioned herself behind the door post and tapped on the glass. "Window down please," she said.

Seconds passed; then the smooth electric purr and the window came down.

"Hands on the steering wheel, please." "Please" was habit. When she spoke, she could hear the cold tight bark of anger held at bay in her voice. Anger was a distraction. She knew it was the godchild of the adrenaline rush and breathed it out to keep her mind alert, keep herself from getting tunnel vision.

A faint smell of marijuana smoke and gum came from inside. Anna could see the driver's jaw working, chewing vainly in hopes of disguising whatever was on his breath. He put both hands on the steering wheel.

"Passengers: hands where I can see them."

The passenger in the backseat started to say something. "Shut up," the driver hissed. "Yes, ma'am."

Anna stepped up by the driver's side and shined her light in their faces purposely. A little night blindness wouldn't kill them. White boys, early twenties, roughly dressed in heavy boots and dirty jeans. Working men, not college boys. "Give me the car keys." Anna pocketed them and said: "Everybody step out of the car, please."

"Jesus Christ, lady, give us a break—" this from the strangely familiar face in the backseat.

"Shut up, Mike." The front seat passenger spoke this time.

"Fuck you," Mike said and started to jerk open the car door. Anna was well clear of it but wondered if he'd known that.

"Slowly," she said to the man called Mike. "I don't want anybody having an accident. Move back to the right rear of the car and wait there."

Making a point to move at his own pace and stand near the center of the trunk to prove he wasn't taking orders, Mike did as he was asked.

"Sir, you on the passenger side, get out please. Go to the rear of the car."

"Look, Officer, what's this about?" the driver asked. "We're just going home. Have a—"

"I'll be with you in a moment, sir." Anna cut him off and watched till the others had stopped at the rear of the car. "You in the blue T-shirt," she said to the boy who was not Mike. "Put both hands on the trunk and push down hard."

"What for?"

"Just do it, please." He did and Anna was satisfied it was closed and latched. She had no desire to be shot by the roadside because somebody got a weapon out of the trunk.

They were complying. Anna's adrenaline level was returning to normal. It was settling into a routine traffic stop, and she let herself relax a little. She joined the driver at the front of the Thunderbird, putting him between her and the two by the back bumper so she could see all three of them.

"Could I see your driver's license?" she asked, managing to sound almost pleasant. He fished it out of his hip pocket and opened his wallet to show it to her. "Take it out of the plastic."

Anna read the number into the radio and asked the dispatcher to run it. Jackson Doolittle. Anna slipped the license into her shirt pocket.

"Look, I know I was speeding but please don't

give me a ticket." Doolittle was whining around his wad of Juicy Fruit.

"Have you got a lot of tickets?"

"A couple."

"Five-eight-zero, seven hundred," the radio interrupted.

"Go ahead," Anna said.

"No wants, no warrants. Seven prior speeding tickets. One DUI arrest when he was sixteen and another when he was nineteen. No record of a conviction."

"How much have you had to drink tonight?" Anna asked.

"Maybe a couple of beers a hour or two back."

"Smoking dope?"

"No, ma'am. I never touch that stuff."

"Can I look in your car?"

Horror flickered across his face, then he said: "Sure. You can look if you want to. You won't find anything."

Of course she would find something. Beer for starters, she'd smelled it and seen a dark liquid stain growing on the floorboards on the passenger side where it spilled when he stashed it. She'd find whatever "Mike" ducked down to hide when they first pulled over. It never ceased to amaze her that these bozos almost always said "yes" to a search. Maybe the idea was if they said an officer could search, that officer would think the car was clean and wouldn't bother. Not likely, given the givens. A firm "no" and she'd be stuck waiting for drug dogs—if there were any to be had around here—to sniff the car for a hit to give her probable cause. Chances are, before that she'd get tired of the game and let him off with a ticket. Now she could look to her heart's content.

"Who are your buddies?" she asked.

Thinking she'd decided not to search his car, Mr. Doolittle was anxious to make friends. "The guy in the blue shirt's my brother, Sean, and that's Mike Posey. We all work out at the lumberyard."

Mike Posey, Danni Posey's brother. No wonder he looked familiar. But for a five o'clock shadow and an ugly turn around the mouth, he had the same pretty face as his sister.

"Mr. Doolittle, could you join your brother and Mr. Posey at the rear of the car?"

"Why? What are you going to do?" He was alarmed that the search was back on.

"I just want to take a quick look. It'll just take a minute," Anna lied soothingly.

Apparently, unaware he could snatch back his permission and not even have to tell her the reason he'd changed his mind, he walked to where the others waited.

Anna started on the driver's side. A bottle of Bud had been shoved under the seat. That which hadn't spilled onto the floor was still cold. Another bottle, open and cold, was shoved into a pocket on the passenger-side door. Anna set them on the roof of the car. "Mr. Doolittle," she said cheerfully. "Do you mind if I look in the ashtray?" The ashtray was closed and could be a gray area in court if she opened it without permission.

Mike Posey started drifting out from the rear of the Thunderbird and into the road.

"Move back with the others," Anna said. The adrenaline level in her blood shot back up.

Posey kept drifting, hands at his sides, palms toward her in a non-menacing gesture. Half his face was stark in the headlamps from her patrol car, the other half in the shadow. He was smiling.

Anna took the radio from her belt. "Five-seven-eight, five-seven-nine, this is five-eight-zero requesting backup."

Posey hesitated. The smile faltered but did not fail. Seconds crawled by and Anna began to be afraid. Finally her radio came to life. "Five-eight-zero, Barth and I are at Mount Locust. We're headed your way."

Mount Locust was one of the historical sites on the Trace, a stand—the historical term for an inn—where for twenty-five cents travelers could get a bowl of cornmeal and sleep in relative safety from bandits. Mount Locust was thirty minutes south of where Anna'd pulled over the Thunderbird. She knew it. The boys knew it. Mike Posey's smile hardened into place.

"Fan out," he said to the other two.

"Mike—" Jackson Doolittle tried.

"Fan out," Posey ordered. Clearly he was the backbone of the group.

"Stay where you are," Anna said. The brothers stopped but Posey waved at them, and they began to move away from the car, spreading out on the grassy knoll to the west where they could flank Anna.

She unsnapped the keeper on her gun. In all her years as a park ranger, she had never so much as drawn her weapon in a routine interaction with a park visitor. The belief that it was overkill clacked through her mind, and as she pulled the semi-automatic from the leather holster, she felt somehow melodramatic. She didn't aim it but held it down by her thigh, muzzle toward the ground.

"I'm asking you to move back to the rear of your vehicle," she said quietly. "Sean, Jackson, do it now."

Posey countermanded her orders. "Keep moving. What's she going to do? Shoot us all?"

The Doolittle brothers didn't continue to circle, but they didn't go back to the Thunderbird either. Jackals, Anna thought. They would feed on the carcasses Posey left behind.

Anna raised the nine-millimeter, aligning the iridescent green dots on the night sight to either side of Mike Posey's nose. "I don't want to shoot you all," she said. "I only want to shoot you, Mike." At the moment she really did want to blow the man's brains out, and he heard it in the ice beneath the words. He stopped, took half a step back.

Anna's radio bleated to life. "Five-eighty, five-seventy, I'm on my way." Steve Stilwell. He was even farther away than her own rangers but had sense enough not to give his location over the radio.

"Get down on the ground," Anna said to Posey.

Posey weighed the impending arrival of backup, the abandonment of his fellows, and Anna's willingness to shoot him. Abruptly his manner changed. "Hey, lady, we were just having fun. No harm, no foul." He smiled charmingly. "You didn't have to pull a gun. Lord, what'd you think we were going to do?"

"On the ground."

"Fuck." Posey got on his hands and knees. "I'm not laying on the goddamn road. I could get run over."

Anna could live with that. "Down. Now."

A rushing in the bushes to her left let her know the Doolittle boys had rabbited. They'd be picked up easily enough. She had the car, the driver's license, their home address and where they worked.

"Your pals have deserted you," she said. "Put your hands in the small of your back."

While Anna cuffed and searched him, Mike Posey outlined his defense. They'd been confused. Anna'd gotten scared and drew down on them for no reason. The Doolittles had narrowly escaped. She'd endangered Posey's life a second time forcing him to lie in the road. She invaded his person when searching him, fondled his private parts. He would bring a lawsuit against her. He would get her fired.

Anna didn't respond. Engaging was always a mistake. When she could get a word in edgewise, she read him his rights.

During confrontations over the years, she'd

heard Posey's line of reasoning more than once. This time it just might work, she realized uneasily. She'd have to write a report justifying unholstering her weapon, justifying pointing it at an unarmed man. Neither Posey nor the two brothers had made verbal threats. "All" they had done was refuse to stay in the one place. If anybody wanted to hang her out to dry, buy into the scared-woman-overreacts story, Anna was going to spend a lot of time defending herself to the brass.

Lest the vile Posey have additional fuel for his fires, she was careful to cuff him just right, ease him into the patrol car and buckle his safety belt. There at least would be no bruises, should he move on to a police brutality charge.

"What are you charging me with?" he demanded as she slid behind the wheel. "I got a right to know. I don't know what you Yankees do, but it's still America around these parts."

Anna radioed dispatch, gave her beginning mileage, and told them she was en route to the Port Gibson Sheriff's Department with a prisoner. That done, she radioed Stilwell. He was almost to Rocky Springs. He must have broken half a dozen land speed records on his way down from Ridgeland. Anna appreciated it. Stilwell would stay by the Doolittles' car till she returned. Then she called Randy Thigpen. "Did you copy? I'm en route to Port Gibson."

"Ten-four," Thigpen returned. "I'm about

229

fifteen miles south at mile marker twenty-four. Barth's right behind me."

"I got a right to know what you're charging me with," Posey demanded belligerently.

That question had been nagging at Anna. In her search of his person she hadn't turned up much: a pocket knife, a pack of Dorals, a receipt from the Burlington Coat Factory for a pair of pants. Tucked in the cigarette pack was a joint of marijuana, half smoked. Barely a misdemeanor. Mentally she'd been sorting through some catchall charges that could be used when a citizen was being non-specifically alarming and wretched: drunk and disorderly, disturbing the peace, drunk in public, obstructing justice, failure to obey a lawful order. The one she thought she could make stick was the weakest.

"Refusing to obey a lawful order, interfering with Agency Functions and possession of a controlled substance."

In the fractured slide show manufactured by her high beams, the country looked suddenly unfamiliar. It was virtually impossible to get lost on the Trace, either one was headed north or one was headed south. Anna was sure she was headed south. She was looking for the turnoff at mile marker forty-three, the shortcut to the Port Gibson Sheriff's Department, and not finding it. A mile marker flashed into view and she realized what had happened. During the high-speed chase they had traveled considerably farther than she thought. The Thunderbird had pulled over less than three miles from the ranger station.

Just as she got her bearings, she was thrown for another loop. The ranger station came into view. Parked in front were two NPS patrol cars: Randy Thigpen and Barth Dinkin. Less than two minutes had elapsed since she'd radioed canceling her call for backup. There was no way short of teleportation that the two rangers could have gotten from mile marker twenty-four to mile marker thirty-nine and the ranger station in that amount of time.

They'd been there all along. Sitting it out, refusing to come to her assistance. Anger so sudden and hot that Anna was surprised her hair didn't catch on fire swept over her. When it had burned down, she was left with a lost feeling that threatened to dissolve into tears. What the hell had she gotten herself into?

11

So, Mike, you think the insurance company is going to pay up on that situation with your sister?" Anna asked to spread the rottenness around a bit.

"We paid for it. That money's ours."

If there was a deep and abiding grief over the loss of Danielle, it didn't show in his voice. Anna took note of that and of the use of "we."

"Danielle was a model?" Anna asked.

"Danni was going nowhere fast. I told Ma that when she took out the policy. Looks like I was right."

So Mike knew his sister's face was insured, and from the sound of it, there was no love lost between the siblings.

"You don't seem too broken up about it," Anna said to see what would happen.

"Maybe Danni had it coming," Mike snapped back.

Anna thought of Clint Eastwood in *Unforgiven: We've all got it coming, kid.* "How so 'had it coming'?" she asked.

"I never said that," he recanted. "You're the one found her, aren't you? You have it in for us Poseys. Don't think I ain't tellin' that to my lawyer. You're all blundering around with your heads up your butts. I know who killed Danni. Ma's not half so crazy as people think."

Anna sorted through the apparently unconnected statements. Was Mrs. Posey not crazy because she'd insured her daughter, then killed her for the money? Or was she not crazy because she knew who'd committed the murder? If she knew, why not tell? Because her own son did it? Because she hired it done? Because she—or he—wanted to wreak her own brand of vigilante justice?

"All right," Anna said equitably. "I'll bite. Who killed your sister?"

"You'd better ask me nice. You sure as hell ain't finding out by yourself, and if I find him first, I'm settin' the dogs on that boy. All you'll find are tiny pieces."

The rearview mirror was angled so Anna could keep an eye on her prisoner. She watched him now. Alcohol, fatigue or indifference had cloaked his features since he'd abandoned the angry bravado that had gotten him arrested. Talk of who'd killed his sister brought a spark of that anger back to his eyes. Anna could be wrong, but it seemed an anger born of ego, not grief.

"Suit yourself," she said, sensing that playing nice would get her nowhere with young Mr. Posey.

Posey turned out to be the kind who can't shut up. She drove and he berated her for not really wanting to know who killed his sister because they weren't rich, because she was a Yankee, because she was a Fed, because the Poseys were white and she was a bleeding heart. Before he got around to accusing her of dereliction of duty because she was Scotch-Irish and a Pisces, he wound down.

"I don't have a name yet," he finally admitted when he couldn't get a rise out of her. "But I'll get it."

Posey seemed oblivious to the fact that he could be considered a suspect in his own sister's murder. Whether it was innocence, arrogance or stupidity, Anna had no idea.

Three patrol cars, with lights aglitter, made a show on the roadside when Anna got back to Jackson Doolittle's automobile.

The doors of the Thunderbird were open and

one exceedingly large rump protruded from the driver's side. Barth Dinkin was studying a number of items lined up like trophies on the trunk lid. Stilwell leaned on the hood of his car, arms across his chest, watching the proceedings with a slightly amused air.

Anna parked on the opposite side of the road and crossed over to join Steve where he loitered. At her arrival, Randy extricated his bulk from the other vehicle and walked importantly over. Like many heavy men, he leaned back to compensate for the weight of his gut, digging the heels of his shoes into the soft grassy earth.

"Glad to see you made it," Anna said dryly.

"It's a problem on the Trace. Understaffed. Turns out you're always fifty miles from wherever you gotta be," Thigpen lied without a tremor.

Practiced, Anna thought and, in his own mind, for his own ends, justified. *So mad she was spitting tacks*, Anna'd never known precisely what that meant, but she did now. She could feel their pointy ends poking her tongue, a metallic taste in her mouth. She felt she could spit words like a pneumatic nail gun and nail Thigpen to the nearest tree. Instead she said: "Find anything?"

"A little of everything. Not enough of anything for a good case. These boys around here are a little wild, but most of them are harmless."

Anna let the dig pass unremarked and walked over to the rear of the Thunderbird.

Barth was mumbly and fidgety and wouldn't meet her eye. He, at least, had the decency to be ashamed of himself.

"I'm glad you're okay," he said, and sounded more or less sincere.

"Why, thank you, Barth." Anna clapped him on the shoulder just to watch him flinch. "I feel a whole lot safer knowing you're looking out for me." A creepy cold edge that was making even her twitchy had come into Anna's smile. She changed the subject. "What've you got?"

"A couple six-packs. Half a dozen empties, three unopened, three opened, partially consumed. There were a couple roaches in the ashtray. No stash. They weren't selling."

"Too bad," Anna said unsympathetically.

"This little bitty vial," Barth pointed to a clear glass screw-top container about the size of his thumb and half filled with white powder.

"Probably coke," Anna offered. "Did you field-test it?"

They hadn't. Barth was on the verge of admitting something—probably that it had been so long since they'd field-tested suspicious substances they'd forgotten how—when Randy jumped in with: "We figured you'd want to do that. You being the boss and all."

Anna stared at him long enough he began to shuffle his feet then said, "Nah. You go ahead. I'm off duty. I'll watch."

For a couple beats, Thigpen was nonplussed, then said: "Well, our kits are pretty out of date..."

"Ah. I didn't know those chemicals had expiration dates."

Some people might have hopped in with an offer to do the honors just to pour oil on the waters. Not Steve Stilwell. He appeared to be enjoying himself.

"Leave it on my desk," Anna said. Anger fading, the game lost its appeal. "What else?"

"Two guns," Barth said. "A thirty-eight under the driver's seat, a twenty-two squirrel gun in the trunk. That's about it."

It wasn't much. Not enough to hold anybody on. Anna'd probably use it as leverage to see if she could scare one of the Doolittle boys into telling her something interesting about Mike Posey. Whether she could prove it or not, he'd meant to hurt her and, with the exception of Stilwell, every single man mixed up with the traffic stop—Randy, Barth and the Doolittles—had been prepared to let him. Sometimes it was best if a girl went well-armed.

The Thunderbird would be towed to the impound lot, and the evidence would be placed in a locker at the ranger station. Anna left Thigpen and Dinkin to deal with it and turned to go. "Steve," she said. "If you've got a minute, stop by the house."

"Right behind you."

She didn't miss the knowing look Randy shot his cohort, but there was nothing she could do about it. Long ago she had accepted the fact that the park service not only attracted more college graduates than any other agency but was equally irresistible to gossips. There wasn't a coffee klatch in the country that could hold a candle to a gathering of the men in green and gray.

She meant to talk with Stilwell about Randy and Barth, his take on their refusal to provide backup, but she found herself unable to bring the subject up. So she drank a little of his Scotch, thanked him for driving down at breakneck speed, and resisted the urge to flirt.

Stilwell had a way of looking at her that made her feel valuable. Probably a trick that served him well. She didn't have to ask to know that he wasn't married. He dropped that bit of information into the conversation early on, referring to himself as "between divorces."

Anna smiled at the memory of him even as she was glad he'd left. The person she really needed to talk with about her management dilemma was Molly. Since her sister's engagement to Frederick Stanton, Molly could no longer be counted upon to be at home evenings and, childlike, Anna crossed her fingers as ringing sounded on the line.

"Hello?" Molly said breathlessly, answering on the third ring. Gone were the days when she answered with the perfunctory "Dr. Pigeon speaking," after the sixth or seventh hail.

"Hah!" Anna said. "You're expecting Frederick to call."

Molly laughed. "I'm always expecting Frederick to call, and bless his little federally employed heart, he always does. But you're just as good."

Anna accepted this as high praise indeed. Molly and Frederick's courtship had been whirlwind, but in the ten months of their engagement Anna had seen both of them settle deeply and comfortably into love.

"I have a question for you in your role as psychiatrist and administrator," Anna said and told her sister of the situation with Randy Thigpen and Barth Dinkin.

"Those slimy, cowardly sons of bitches," was Molly's diagnosis. Her prescription followed: "They ought to be strung up by their thumbs or made to walk the plank or whatever they do to national park rangers who have become a danger to society."

Vindication, in the form of anger on her behalf, warmed Anna and melted the tears that fear and pride had kept frozen for the past three hours. "Here's the weird part," she said, her voice ragged and pathetic. "I feel so *embarrassed* and *ashamed*. Like a kid who doesn't get picked or who has cooties."

"Like a rape victim," Molly said coldly, and Anna was brought up short. As good fortune would have it, Anna had never been raped, but over the years she had dealt with nearly a dozen women who had. Hearing her sister's words, she remembered the deep sense of guilt and shame the women carried. How hard it had been to turn that shame into anger, to make them see that it didn't matter where they were, what they said, how they dressed, who they trusted, a terrible crime had been committed against them. The crime was what mattered. The perpetrator was the one who was guilty.

"Holy smoke," Anna breathed. "You think?"

"Yes, I think, for Christ's sake. I wouldn't trivialize rape by suggesting this was the same thing. You did not suffer the invasion of your person that is so devastating. You did not suffer actual violence. And you managed to retain your power—you won. But most of the elements of rape are there: power, man over woman, violence—do you think they cared what happened to you? The desire to hurt, to degrade. Fear of you. Resentment of your power. It's not quite classic, but it is most assuredly comparable. You called for backup. They hid out. All else is irrelevant: whether those jackasses really would have killed you. Lord! You cannot let this pass."

"I won't," Anna said. "The park service does have a watered-down bureaucratic version of flogging. I can't remember the disciplinary procedures, but this being the government, it's in a manual somewhere." Chances were good she had it on one of her bookshelves, a relic of some long-forgotten management class she'd stumbled into before she'd even considered getting out of fieldwork.

"I hope the consequences for those individuals are dire," Molly said.

The formalized venom made Anna laugh. "They won't be. The NPS tends to make bold disciplinary statements along the lines of: 'If you ever do this again, we'll tell you never to do it again.' But you get enough of those in an employee's file and eventually they can be fired. Usually it takes years."

Feeling much better, Anna let the talk run on more pleasant subjects. The wedding date was set, September thirtieth. The hall was booked: an exquisite little B&B two hours north of New York City. The party would be small and formal: tuxes all around. Anna felt echoes of her wedding to Zach, twinges of envy and nostalgia, but mostly she felt joy and hope: joy for Molly, hope that she, too, might be inspired to cross over matrimony's state line in the next twenty or thirty years.

Sure enough, the standard operating procedures were rife with disciplinary guidelines. Anna had her choice of a formal discussion with a written report that would go into the personnel files, a verbal warning that would be from her lips to their ears, or something in between: a verbal warning with a written chaser, a report that went into her personal management files so, should the situation be repeated, she would have documentation that the employees had been warned and counseled. This was to include a description of what had transpired and what the corrected behavior would consist of, and a warning as to what consequences could be expected if the undesirable behavior should be repeated.

Much as she was tempted to pull out the big

guns and wreak as much havoc in her rangers' lives as was humanly possible, Anna opted for choice number three.

This was her first management challenge. If there was any hope of making a working team out of the rangers in her district, she wanted to salvage it. Should the gods be in a mood to be fair, Randy and Barth would feel gratitude that she was choosing not to give them a permanent black mark. Should the gods be feeling generous, Thigpen and Dinkin would respect her for facing their gross dereliction of duty head-on and dealing with it in an open manner.

"Not bloody likely," she told Piedmont as she switched off the light.

Schedules in many parks were worked on a rotating basis. A ranger worked an early shift on his "Friday" and a late shift on his "Monday." The upside was the weekend was thus maximized. The downside was one tended to work a different shift every day. At this juncture it worked to Anna's advantage. Barth was on early, Randy at four P.M. She wanted to talk with Barth first and get his reactions before his partner in crime had a chance to work on him. At a guess, she didn't figure Dinkin for a stand-alone guy. Without Thigpen involved, she suspected he'd be more receptive.

She had no intention of seeing or speaking to either of them till afternoon. The rain and clouds were gone. Sun shone with a new fierceness, as if burning away the last vestiges of the kindly weather of spring and getting down to the serious business of a Mississippi summer. Feeling like a kid playing hooky, Anna left gun, cuffs, pepper spray and long trousers behind. Clad in uniform shorts, with hiking boots so old they resembled cordovan-colored lumps on her feet, she went around the loop of the campground. Walking purposefully lest she be sucked into conversation, she quickly reached the hillock at the west end and went down to the beginning of the Old Trace.

Partly she was just goofing off—the rain would have obliterated any sign Thigpen and the others hadn't pulverized with their elephantine tread—but still it was worth another look. Sad snapshots of Danielle Posey in death haunted Anna. Symptomatic of post-traumatic stress, so she knew it would pass. Most of it would pass. After each incident she carried away one or two pictures that became hardwired into her brain. At odd times they would flash behind her eyes, bringing with them emotion so strong it was as if they had happened again, in that moment. The image of the Posey murder that triggered the deepest compassion was that of Danielle's feet. Little feet, soft and rounded, the prettiness of childhood not yet callused, clothed in their grown-up shoes. Strappy, sequined, high-heeled sandals—shoes Anna's generation in crass moments would have called "fuck-me pumps."

On the feet of a sixteen-year-old girl they had spoken such innocence, a playing at the seamy side, posing as a woman of the world. The harmless charade of the very young, when aping evil is just a thrilling game and sophistication is achieved with paste jewelry and phony accents.

Those feet, those shoes, had plucked at Anna's heartstrings. Then they'd lodged in her mind. Like Heather's, the sandals had three-inch heels, cut square. The ground was soft. If Danni had fled her attacker, she would have made holes in the ground deep enough the rain might not have washed them away.

On the day Anna'd found the body, she'd not been able to pick up Danni's trail. Today, like a search dog ordered to track, she intended to circle wider, try and pick up the trail farther out.

Retracing her steps to the hollow where Danielle had been dumped wasn't as easy as she thought it would be. Unlike the desert, Mississippi healed itself with astonishing rapidity. Moving slowly, examining leaves and mold and twigs to acclimatize herself to the kind of surfaces she must learn, Anna noticed small branches, broken off by the traffic of policemen and rangers, had already sprouted new shoots. Crushed leaves had bounced back, regained their original strength, and near as she could tell, a redoubled robustness.

After an hour she took a break from her crash course in Southern tracking and sat on a log. Sweat soaked her shirt and the waistband of her shorts. According to the locals, it wasn't hot yet: eighty-five degrees and seventy-two percent humidity. Anna poured half a quart of tepid water down her throat to even up the moisture content between body and air.

The log was soft. The ground was soft. The air was soft. She was sinking into the geography. Moving was becoming more and more of an effort.

"No wonder they used dogs in all those old prison movies," she said to a box turtle trying to pass himself off as part of the forest floor. "Nobody can track in this stuff. It'd be easier to track a duck across a pond." A praying mantis joined them, sitting wisely on a fungus ruffled and tinted into a sculpture of poisonous beauty. Had she not found a tick crawling on the back of her knee, Anna might have stayed to be sociable.

She circled as well as she could the hollow where Danni'd been found. It was crumpled and cluttered, with no view of the sky, no landmarks, uphill and downhill as meaningless as that in a crunched-up ball of tinfoil, and she found it hard to keep her bearings. Each and every part of the whole steaming forest dripped, slapped, drooled, tickled or poked her. And, apparently overnight, a phenomenon of worms had descended. From every branch and twig little green worms hung down on long sticky fibers like spiders' webs. They numbered in the zillions, dangling like hung paratroopers, till Anna waded through them and carried them away in her hair and on her clothes.

And it was hot. Wet hot. Clothing itched and bound. Spiderwebs stuck. Mosquitoes filtered up from stagnant water. Anna discovered patience in Mississippi was an entirely different discipline from what it was in the Southwest. Here, with the sliming and sweating and tickling, it was nigh on impossible.

After the better part of three hours, dehydrated and disgruntled, she gave up the hunt as a lost cause and walked back in the direction of the Old Trace. There at least she could move without having to break trail through suspended invertebrates.

In acreage—if not in living matter—the area in which she'd attempted to find tracks was mercifully small. Ten minutes' walk brought her to the top of the bank marking the perimeter of the ancient road. There she stopped to let the heat of her body and mind boil off before scrambling back down into the path of park visitors. Her circuitous ramblings had brought her back just fifteen feet to the west of where she—and half a dozen other people—had tracked up the bank on the body retrieval. A great tree, roots exposed, doomed to topple in the next good windstorm, stood between her and the new-made trail to Danni's penultimate resting place. Anna stepped from sight behind this venerable pin oak and unzipped her shorts to do a quick tick check. The vile creatures seemed to have lost their taste for her. The parts of her anatomy she could see were free of blood-sucking intruders. Zipping up her fly, she noted the ground between the toes of her boots.

"Happiness is in your own backyard," she

muttered, quoting Dorothy in *The Wizard of Oz*. Neatly between her lug soles was a puncture in the earth's soft brown skin. Beneath the sheltering oak, the ground was less overgrown and much of the rain had been deflected. Though the edges of the hole were not squared, melted as they had been by moisture, it was not a mark that came naturally. Anna sat on her heels and studied it. If there'd been a corresponding toe print, the shallower mark had washed away, but next to it, close to the trunk of the tree, was another hole. This one, even more protected by the elements, had one clear edge. Danielle Posey had stood here, leaning against this tree, much as Anna had done.

For the next hour, Anna inspected each leaf and blade of grass in a fifteen-foot radius of her tree. One other mark that might have been made by the heel of the dead girl's sandal turned up two yards from the trail they'd carved during the body recovery. There was no way to tell if Danni had been traveling east or west, but she had been here and she'd been alive.

Having found all she was going to, Anna slid down the bank onto the bed of the Trace and sat in the soft earth to think. The claustrophobic embrace of the woods clogged her brain. Here there was a semblance of air and space. Idly playing dirt through her hands, she let pictures form. Danni was on the rim of the Trace, up where the going was hard, when down below was a gentle trail. Either she was lost, she was hiding, or she had come from some other direction, as Anna had, and happened upon the old road. The places a high-heeled girl in total darkness could logically have come from were limited. The Natchez Trace itself—even without a light, she could have found her way here from the campground. The trail was well marked and there might have been a moon on prom night. Anna couldn't remember, but it was easy enough to find out. Danni could have parted company with her pursuers at the campground and fled in this direction; maybe she escaped from one of the cars full of revelers the campers had complained of. Or the party could have moved up here and then turned ugly.

Another possibility was that they had come down the Old Trace from where it ended near the church. Anna tended to discount this: too far for drunks in bad shoes, and had Danni traveled the Old Trace in either direction, Anna was pretty sure, she would have seen the girl's tracks. The paved road up to Rocky Springs Church ran roughly parallel to the Old Trace, with about half a mile separating them. It was conceivable that Danni had escaped a vehicle there, tried to run and hide in the woods, and been hunted down and killed. From the number of scrapes and scratches she'd sustained, that seemed the likelier scenario. But if she'd come cross-country from the paved road, why had her body, in its grotesque impromptu costume, been found back in that same direction? Caught her here. Killed her.

Decided to carry her back to the car and hang her somewhere to make whatever twisted point the killer had in mind? Then tired, bored, or scared, dumped the body and cleared out?

That would have meant the killer had carried with him whatever he'd used to whack her, the dirty sheet, a knife or scissors to hack eyeholes in it and twenty-two feet six inches of yellow nylon rope. A bit cumbersome when crashing around in the inky night belly of the forest, chasing a girl.

If the plan had been to carry the body back to the car for the final robing and roping, then why cart the stuff along on the chase?

None of the stories hung together. Still, the morning hadn't been wasted. If Danni had been here, at the Old Trace, alive, then dead a ways back in the woods toward the main road, it made sense she'd been killed between here and there. Or killed here, right where Anna sat playing in the dirt. That thought was good for an unpleasant shiver and a quick look over her shoulder.

Time to go home and shower, Anna told herself, not liking to think she believed in ghosts.

Dusting the dirt from her hands, she noted a dull gleam in the embankment. Her mindless digging had uncovered a treasure. Thinking of the re-enactors' tales of General Grant, a faint dream of Union gold skittered through her skull. The South was a battlefield. War artifacts were found as commonly as arrowheads out West: buttons, musket balls, rusted wagon parts and weapons. Anna blew the loose dirt off her discovery. Not gold, brass: a tarnished belt buckle with an insignia engraved on the back of it, a circle, like a seal stamped on important documents. Maybe Civil War vintage, maybe Boy Scouts.

Park etiquette required the finder of indigenous treasures to leave them to be found and enjoyed by each visitor with sharp enough eyes and interest who happened along. Trouble was the next guy along was bound to steal it. The tragedy of the commons.

Rationalizations in place, Anna decided to keep it.

The campground was awake, cars and dogs and people fiddling about, tents being erected and fires burning—not because it was cold or anyone was cooking but because campfires hooked so deeply into the human psyche that all the environmental preaching the park service could muster did little to stomp them out.

The Civil War camp had reappeared Brigadoonlike in the same place it had been previously. Captain Williams, shirtsleeves rolled up over nicely muscled forearms, was rigging a cast-iron tripod over a neatly constructed fire ring. As before, he was decked out in work clothes in a fashion more than a hundred years old. Ian, his stalwart frame draped over a tiny camp stool, was watching intently, the apprentice at the feet of the master.

"Morning," Anna called, and left the pavement to enter their camp. Both men looked up, startled, as if she'd caught them doing something they oughtn't.

"Morning." Captain Williams recovered first.

"Morning," McIntire echoed. The joviality Anna'd noted at their first meeting clicked on belatedly as she was treated to his V-shaped smile. Neither seemed particularly glad to see her but good manners, or some other impetus she couldn't quite identify, forbade them from letting it show.

"Your squadron has shrunk," she said pleasantly. "Where's Mr. Fullerton?"

An awkward silence was born. Before it was ten seconds old, Ian slew it with a sudden gust of verbal energy.

"Leo's got to tend that flock of his. Visiting a hospital or hauling groceries to a sick old lady. It's all we can do to pry him away for one weekend a month. Coffee?"

No coffee was in evidence, no fire, not even any hot water. Captain Williams shot his lieutenant a hard look.

"Wouldn't take any time at all to brew some up," Ian defended himself.

"No, thanks," Anna said, then remembered the buckle in her pocket. "Hey, this might interest you guys. Look what I found." She dug the buckle out and held it in her palm. "Do you think it's anything?"

Williams wiped his hands on the thighs of his woolen trousers, then lifted the buckle. Ian crowded near, and the two men studied it. According to Anna's limited interest in Civil War relics—if this was one—they studied it way too long.

"Where'd you come across it?" the captain asked. He sounded as if he accused Anna of something. Since she did technically remove it from park grounds, though not yet from the park itself, she felt a stab of guilt.

"Up on the Old Trace," she said, trying not to sound as if she was admitting to shady activities.

"These are pretty common," Williams said. "Not like they used to be, of course, what with people picking 'em up over the years. But this one's in pretty good shape. I'm a collector. And an honest one. I'll give you two thousand dollars for it."

"Yikes," Anna said, then added virtuously, "It's not mine to sell. I'll give it to the interpretive staff for the museum." She didn't even know if the Natchez Trace had a museum, but it sounded good.

Williams hung on to it a minute more, loath to relinquish it to the impersonal fate of becoming museum paraphernalia. "Sure," he said at last. "That's the place for it." He dropped it in Anna's outstretched palm.

"I hear you got in a fracas with a gator," Ian said, his elfin eyes twinkling.

"News travels fast," Anna replied.

Captain Williams took a smoke from his shirt pocket and lit it, not a cigarette but a thin black cheroot as befitted a man of the Civil War era.

"Those Mississippi gators can be mean old boys," he said and winked at Ian. "You hurt him any? I hear even varmints are protected on the Trace."

"He's been relocated," Anna said evenly.

"I'll bet. Relocated right into somebody's freezer. Alligator's good eating."

They seemed to take the whole thing as one terrific joke, and though Anna could see the appeal of that, this morning it grated on her nerves.

"He got my dog," she said.

Immediately all traces of humor evaporated from their faces.

"No kidding?" Ian said sympathetically. "Got your dog? That big old black dog with you the other day? That's a terrible thing."

Evidently killing a person's dog was a serious crime in this part of the country.

"He didn't kill him," Anna said, somewhat mollified. "But the vet said he's going to lose his leg."

"You said he wasn't a hunting dog?" the captain asked.

"Just a dog dog."

"He'll be able to get around good enough for that."

Heartened by their dog-friendliness, Anna hazarded a question. "Any idea who might've put the alligator in my carport?"

"Kids," Williams said succinctly, the word coming out on a cloud of fragrant tobacco smoke.

"They probably thought it was a good joke,

you being a Yankee and all," said Ian. "I bet they'd feel real bad knowing your dog got bit."

"That's probably it." Anna was inclined to believe him. Kids, in the way of kids, taking an action without much thought to what the consequences might be. Maybe it was enough that she was a Yankee and a woman and a ranger to boot. Maybe. And maybe this group of "kids" had a reason to want her scared or hurt enough to leave the death of Danni Posey alone.

"Well, I've got work to do. Have a good day," she said to announce her departure.

Ian stopped her with a question. "Have you found out who killed that little girl?" he asked. From the depth of emotion in his voice, Anna guessed the murder of Danni Posey was what had put such a damper on the camp of Jeff Davis's Avengers. It made sense. These men were locals, maybe fathers themselves. They'd been here when the girl died. They would feel it more keenly than campers just passing through.

"The sheriff was talking to us," Ian said as if his interest needed explaining.

"The investigation is continuing." Anna voiced the accepted code phrase meaning "Nope, we got nothing."

"The newspapers said it looked like some kind of colored thing," Williams said.

Anna had to quell a knee-jerk reaction. To what, it took her a second to discern. Then it came to her. A "colored thing" let everyone who wasn't of color off the hook. It ghettoized the crime. "Did they?" she said.

"Well, not *said* it." Williams sounded annoyed at her pretended naïveté. "But that sheet and so forth. Like a colored wanting to make it look like a Klan killing maybe."

This was what Leo Fullerton had been talking about, the added evil of ripping open old wounds with the incendiary choice of draping the dead girl in a dirty bedsheet.

"The Klan's not big around here anymore," Ian said. "They planned a big old march up in Canton and had to bus in boys from Indiana to fill the sheets." Williams shot him a look that forestalled anything else he might have been going to say. No dissension allowed in the troops.

Maybe the Klan was dead. But like so many things in Mississippi, its ghost was evidently not laid to rest.

12

Anna looked the part. Her class A's were pressed to a fare-thee-well and, since they were still in the month of transition where either summer or winter uniforms were acceptable, she'd opted for the long-sleeved shirt and mannish tie: tricks to gain the psychological edge. A knock came on the door. She waited for him to knock again. Instead,

Barth poked his head in. "You wanted to see me?"

"Yes. Please come in. Sit down." Anna was well rehearsed. She'd gone over the manuals on disciplinary action. She'd prepared the questions she wanted to ask, the points she wanted to make. Now that the moment had arrived, she found herself feeling an entirely unexpected emotion: pity. Both her rangers were older, close to retirement, but because the new regs on twenty-year retirement hadn't come through till the early nineties, both had another five or so years to serve. Too few years to go anywhere else. Too many to spend in a burnout job. Thigpen had only worked one other park. He'd begun his career in the Great Smokies. Barth had worked on the Trace his entire career. He'd actually started out twenty-three years before as that rarest of creatures, a male secretary, at headquarters in Tupelo. Randy and Barth between them had thirty-eight years in Port Gibson, driving the same ninety miles of road, eating at Gary's Shell Station. They'd grown fat, literally and figuratively. Anna could understand it. Years of writing the same people the same speeding tickets, scraping new generations of drunks off trees—it was bound to burn anybody out. Now her. She didn't know if either of them had applied for the post of district ranger but she'd gotten it; white, female and a Yankee, she'd gotten it.

Leaning forward, she rested her elbows on her knees and looked up at Ranger Dinkin. Paul Newman in *Cool Hand Luke,* saying to Strother

Martin, "What we've got here is a failure to communicate," shortly before he got a bullet in the brain flashed unpleasantly through her mind.

"Barth," she said. "We've got a problem."

He squirmed. "What problem is that?"

Anna lost her taste for gamesmanship. "Yesterday, I called you and Randy for backup. You never showed."

"We were at Mount Locust," he began.

Not wanting to let him hang himself with more lies, Anna cut him off. "No. You were here. Not more than five minutes away. You hung me out to dry. Why is that?"

Barth looked around her office, but there were no Cheetos handy to soothe his nerves. He fastened his gaze on his leg where his ankle crossed his knee.

"Randy said..." he began, stopped, then started again. "We thought, you being new and all, maybe it'd be good for you to get your own idea of what it's like working down here."

Anna said nothing to that. The remark was so patently made up of nine parts bullshit to one part hatefulness that she just let it sit in the air between them and stink.

She watched him and, rightly or wrongly, thought she saw him weigh and discard several lines of defense in favor of the truth. "I don't know why we didn't back you up," he said at last. "I've been feeling bad about it. I'm just as glad to get it out in the open."

"Fair enough," Anna said. "I don't know how long I'll be here. I may start throwing in applications for other parks next month or I may stay here till I retire. Either way, right now we're working together. We're new to each other. We've got reservations. That's fine. I don't plan on riding in here like Matt Dillon into Dodge City. I want to learn my way around, get the feel of the place. I can do that without you, but it'll take me longer and be considerably more painful, but if I have to, I will. What I will not tolerate is any conduct that endangers my safety or that of you or Randy. That means I must be able to count on you absolutely to do what you can to your best ability when I call for backup. You can count on the same from me. Anything else is negotiable."

Barth nodded slowly. "I'm sorry about last night."

Anna believed him.

"Will this go in my personnel file?"

"No, I'll document that you've been warned and counseled. That you have agreed to alter this behavior and that you have been told that any further breach of conduct in this matter will be written up and put in your permanent file and that, at that time, an inquiry into relieving you of your duties will be requested by me."

Again Barth nodded. "It won't happen again."

She believed that too, maybe against good sense, but Barth held himself like an honorable man; he took responsibility for what he'd done and accepted the consequences without whining. Anna wanted to like him.

"While I've got you here, let me catch you up on the Danni Posey investigation." She would have updated him and Randy at some point; that she did it now, and in detail, was her vote of confidence in him.

"I've known Pastor Fullerton for years," Barth said when she'd related the interview with him and the sheriff. "My wife and I belong to Southern Baptist. He's our pastor."

Mississippi was, indeed, a small town. Anna was beginning to glimpse how small.

"You not being from around here, you might think that's ordinary but it's not. Down here there's black churches and there's white churches. That's just the way it is. Oh, you can go to a white church and white folks can go to our churches. Nobody much minds. You'd be made welcome and all. Folks just don't much do it. Lots of churches—black and white—have been working to mix up the congregations, but people are set in their ways. People need comfort. You don't blame them for that. But Pastor Fullerton has done it. Southern Baptist in Port Gibson's about fifty-fifty. It's a big deal. And he makes it not a big deal, if you know what I mean."

Anna did. She told Barth of the pastor's parting words, of his concern that race not be dragged into the mix during this investigation.

"He'd care," Barth said.

Anna moved on to the car stop. Barth knew Mike Posey. He'd pulled him over one night for spotlighting deer on the Trace. There was no hunting on federal park lands. Spotlighting deer, paralyzing them momentarily with high-powered lights, was a practice of slob hunters. Posey had been meaning to poach and was guilty of harassing wildlife. Barth had let him off with a warning.

"Think you've got a rapport with him?" Anna asked. Mike Posey needed to answer some questions, but since she'd recently arrested him she wasn't the obvious candidate.

"Nobody's got rapport with Mike Posey."

Anna was afraid of that. "How about a Sean or Jackson Doolittle?" she named the brothers who'd run from her the night before. "You know either of them?"

Barth smiled for the first time since he'd come in. Maybe for the first time since Anna'd met him—she couldn't remember. It suited him. His smile had a raffishness that the rest of him had outgrown. "Better than that," he said. "I know their mama."

"Terrific," she said. "I know where they work. Stay close. When I'm finished here, we'll ride out there together."

Barth took that correctly as a dismissal. "Anna?" He stopped short of the doorway.

"Yeah?"

"Randy's pretty good people mostly. His wife up and left him a month back. I might oughtn't to be speaking out of turn, but he's been kind of down on women ever since."

"Thanks," Anna said.

He left, closing the door behind him. For a couple of minutes, she rocked gently in her chair and reviewed their meeting. It had gone well. Unless Thigpen started working on Barth again, she suspected he'd be a good ranger. They could work together.

Her radio crackled: Randy making a vehicle stop at mile marker thirty-four. He was on his way toward the ranger station working traffic. Rather than summon him into her presence via the radio, Anna decided to wait. However her meeting with Randy Thigpen went, she doubted it would go as well as the one with Barth. Barth seemed more of a get-along-go-along guy. Randy struck her as a hardcore malcontent.

Twenty minutes later, she heard the door slam and left her office. She didn't want Barth to talk with Randy before she did.

Thigpen had come in with a cigarette in his hand. When he saw her, he made a show of suddenly remembering it, opening the door, and tossing the smoking butt outside, adding littering to his list of crimes and misdemeanors.

"Randy," Anna said. "Could you come into my office? There are some things we need to go over." In one management book or another, Anna had read that publicly shaming an employee was a sure-fire morale breaker. Besides, capitalizing on the pack mentality went against the grain.

"Lemme get a cup of coffee," Thigpen said.

Anna nodded and returned to her chair. Thigpen was playing his own version of the game she'd abandoned with Barth: making her wait, showing his independence. It bothered Anna not at all. She busied herself picking out the odd bits of paraphernalia previous district rangers had allowed to congeal in the shallow center drawer of the built-in desk.

After about three times as long as it takes to pour and condiment a cup of coffee, Thigpen wandered in, smoothing his mustache as he came. He had a habit of stroking it down in such a way that it looked like he was smelling his fingers.

"Why don't you go ahead and close the door," Anna suggested.

"Ah. Fixin' to get serious? Over one lousy cigarette?"

Anna said nothing. Randy closed the door and took the chair Barth had recently vacated. Middle-aged, too much lard, most of it carried above the belt and in front, Randy was never going to be poster boy for the American Heart Association. He was a cardiac arrest waiting to happen. Dead-end job. Wife deserted him. New boss. Anna tried to let the ameliorating factors leaven her mood. She still didn't like the guy.

"How's your dog?" Randy asked.

"He's going to make it, but he lost the rear leg the alligator bit." Good start, asking about Taco. It was on the tip of her tongue to thank him for the help he'd given her that night, but she suspected that was what he was angling for, so she didn't.

"We got a problem," she said, echoing her opening with Barth.

Randy fought with filibuster, clogging the

room with words, cruising easily from one excuse to another. Finally, when Anna pinned him down to the facts: she'd called, he'd been close, he hadn't come, he painted a picture she could tell he liked. Using much in the way of implication and innuendo, he suggested that he knew Anna was in no real danger and in his infinite and benevolent wisdom he'd decided it would be good for her to learn to handle things by herself, help her gain confidence. Of course, had he known she was going to do a fool thing like draw down on those innocent lads, he'd have come right on out and taken over before she got herself in trouble.

Anna thought wistfully about that heart attack, wondered what in the hell was taking it so long. But then, should he collapse, she'd be duty-bound to give him CPR and the thought of mouth-to-mouth was so vile she decided it was better he should live.

"We'll keep this simple," she said, giving up hope of a meaningful conversation. "Another ranger calls for backup and you don't move heaven and earth to get there in a timely manner, you will be given a written reprimand. Do it again, and you'll be fired."

Randy sat back as if she'd slapped him—or woken him from a pleasant dream. "You can't do that!"

"I can," Anna assured him. She had him sign the memo she'd prepared saying he had been counseled and he left.

Maybe he'd shape up. Maybe not. No good-will to lose, she didn't care which way it went.

T he Bogachitta Lumber Company was situated four miles west of Port Gibson. It had once been on a navigable bayou, but over the years the Army Corps of Engineers had altered the course of the Mississippi, and now the mill sat near a swampy creek scarcely deep enough to drown a cottonmouth.

Anna'd grown up in a logging town in Northern California, and Bogachitta Mills had the rustic look she'd come to expect of the industry. Computers might have invaded the offices, but the yards were still places of saws, piled logs, evil-smelling ponds and men who worked hard for their wages.

Barth was driving, Anna riding shotgun. Most places she'd worked, at least the places with cars, the men had loved patrolling with her; she had no competitive need to drive. Left to her own devices, she preferred to look out the window, watch the world go by and think her own thoughts. Her ideal was never to patrol in an automobile at all. Cars cut rangers off from the natural world, blunted their senses and, Anna was convinced, over time, by some alchemy of metal and glass, turned them from rangers into cops.

The crunching of tires on gravel announced their arrival. Barth parked in front of a derelict flat-roofed building with faded blue letters proclaiming Bogachitta Mills. Inside was a single desk, a computer and a woman in her late fifties or early sixties with cotton candy blond curls high on her head. A pack of Virginia Slims lay next to an ashtray full of dead compatriots. The most recent sacrifice burned in a groove put in the glass for that purpose.

"Sean's out in the field today," she informed them, then coughed through a throat full of phlegm. If she wondered what they wanted with the Doolittles, she hid her curiosity remarkably well. So well, Anna wondered if the long arm of the law reaching out to Bogachitta Mills employees was a common occurrence. Recovered from her coughing fit, the woman said: "Jackie's out on the chipper. You can go ahead out, but ya'll gotta wear hard hats."

Anna and Barth each took a yellow plastic hard hat from the row she indicated with a red porcelain nail and left their Stetsons in their places.

Finding the chipper did not challenge the detecting skills. The machine, full-sized trees being stuffed into its maw by two men and a Caterpillar armed with a giant pincer claw, made a horrific racket. Envying the men their ear protection, Anna stood with her fingers in her ears watching once living plants reduced to mulch. Years before, she remembered, a man in the Northeast had murdered his wife, frozen her body and fed it through a wood chipper. Seeing one in action brought the old story home in a graphic way.

"Yuck," she said, her editorializing lost in the din.

Several shattering minutes passed before the heavy equipment operator saw them and signaled to someone out of sight behind the chipper, and the operation was shut down. The ensuing silence was a palpable balm that flowed into the yard in a sweet wash, loosening the muscles Anna had tightened in an attempt to keep the noise from rattling the core of her being.

Under hard hats and protective eyewear and earwear, the men were almost anonymous. Almost. Anna had recognized Jackson Doolittle as one of the two men high on the lip of the chipper guiding logs into its gullet. He saw them the instant the chipper shut down and started to jump off the back side out of sight.

"Jackie!" Barth called before Anna could speak. "Miss Loretta wants to know what you've gone and done with her car."

Doolittle stopped, catching on to the chipper for balance.

"Come on down," Barth said reasonably. "We'll get your mama's car back to her. But you need to talk to this lady here. Come on, now."

Jackson Doolittle hadn't struck Anna as being burdened by an excess of brain cells, but it seemed even he finally realized there wasn't much point in running off again unless he planned to run from his job, his home and probably the only life he'd ever known. He jumped heavily to the ground. "Takin' a smoke break, Billy," he said to the operator of the mechanized claw.

Doolittle led the way to a picnic table in the shade of a tree that had grown draggled and downcast from watching the fate of its fellows. The mill worker sat on the table, his feet on the bench. Anna braced one foot up on the bench and waited. She was curious to see what he'd say without the guidance of a question. Barth didn't jump into the silence, and she was impressed.

Fortified by a deep drag from a Marlboro he'd fished from the pack and lit, Doolittle said: "How much trouble am I in?"

"Quite a bit," Anna replied.

"Is Mama going to get her car back?"

"That depends."

"Ma'am, I'm sorry me and Sean run off like that." He looked up through his smoke, and Anna saw the startling green of his eyes, green as a cat's. All cats are gray in the dark—she'd not noticed them before. "Mike was starting to show his butt. When he gets like that there's no tellin' what he'll do. We got scared is all. I mean, I knew you could find me if you wanted to," he added, as if this made running away null and void.

"When Mike gets like what?" Anna asked.

Jackson looked at the tip of his cigarette. Finding no answer there, he searched the new leaves overhead, already weighed down with the ephemeral tragedies of life. "Oh, I don't know. Like *that*. You know."

"No. I don't know. Was he going to hurt me?"

A long silence followed. Jackson searched the places that had failed to provide answers before. They failed him again. In the harsh light of April, with the dirt of the day's work on his face, Jackson looked like what he was, little more than a boy. "I don't know," he repeated his mantra. "Maybe. Mike gets kind of crazy when he's been... when he's... you know..."

"Coked up?" Anna suggested.

"Liquored up?" Barth said at the same time.

"Yes, ma'am. Like that."

"And he was coked up and liquored up last night?" she pressed.

"Yes, ma'am. I guess he was."

"And you, do you guess you were?"

Another silence, another search through the leaves and smoke, another disappointment. "Not coke. Not me and Sean."

"Drunk, though."

"Look, ma'am. I've got me a DUI—"

"One?"

"Maybe more than one. I can't get no more. They'll be fixin' to take my license then, and how'd me and Sean get to work?"

"Tough break," Anna said unsympathetically. "You sure that's not why you ran? Because of the DUI and not because you were scared?"

"No, ma'am. We was scared, too."

The man who had been working with Jackie feeding trees into the chipper was sauntering toward them. Barth turned to stop him, but Anna said: "It's okay. We're nearly done here."

"They bothering you, Jackie boy?" he asked. He slung one hip on the table and pinched the Marlboros from Jackie's shirt pocket, helping himself to one. He was a black man, probably in his fifties, strong and beautifully fit, his hair cropped close and grizzled at the temples. With the sweat and dirt and sawdust, both men were a uniform tannish-gray.

"Nah. They just come to see about Mama's car like I was telling you," Jackie replied. The older man punched Doolittle gently in the arm and tucked the smokes back into the younger man's pocket. It struck Anna that he'd been taking care of Jackie for a long time.

"Jackie and his brother gotta have a car," he told Anna. "Their mama can't work; she's laid up. Their dad, he's been gone awhile."

"I hear that," Anna said, warmed by his straightforwardness, but making no promises. To Jackie she said: "Mike Posey was making noises that he knew who murdered his sister. What can you tell me about that?"

Jackie looked pained. He shot his buddy a glance that Anna couldn't fathom. Fear but what of or for whom was unclear. "Mike just talks. Likes to seem like he knows more'n he does," Jackie said.

Anna was unconvinced and fixed him with an open, interested stare. Without words for cover, Jackie began to wiggle as if he wanted to hide his nakedness. The hum of the chipper, shut down but not shut off, wove around them like the drone of a summer day.

"Mike doesn't know nothin'," Doolittle blurted. Again the look at his friend.

The older man flicked his cigarette butt away and said to Anna: "Posey said he was gonna find the *nigger* that killed his sister." He filched another cigarette from Jackie's pocket. "What, Jackie? You don't think he talks that way when I'm around? He don't to my face because I could snap him like a dry stick. He's that kind that talks around the edges, making sure you hear him and pretending he's not talking to you at all. You and Sean steer clear of Posey, you hear me?"

"I hear you," Jackie said.

"Posey's not right in the head. Bad blood. His mama's been sick in her mind her whole life. He takes after her. Maybe it's not his fault. I don't know. But you get a rabid skunk in your yard, you don't go trying to make a pet out of it."

Jackie Doolittle took the lecture with good grace.

"I've got to get back to work," the man said. "You people finish up here."

"Beau's foreman," Jackie explained. "I got to get back."

"In a minute. Why does Mike Posey think his sister was murdered by an African-American?"

"Because he thinks everything ugly is black and everything black is ugly. Like Beau said, he's not right in the head."

"Think," Anna ordered. "He's drinking

and talking. Did he say anything at all about it? The sheet his sister was draped in, KKK, anything?"

"No. None of that. I think maybe he said something about his sister seeing somebody."

"Somebody black?"

"Maybe. It's just a thing I'm thinking. I don't remember him saying so right out."

D riving back through the town of Port Gibson, Anna found herself looking for Sheriff Davidson's car with the interest of a schoolgirl dragging Main Street in hopes of accidentally meeting *him*.

Cursing herself for a fool, she grabbed the first subject that came to mind. "The city too beautiful to burn?" she said aloud.

"That's what the chamber of commerce says," Barth replied. Black Southerners didn't seem to have the interest in the Civil War their white brethren did. Perhaps the fantasies of who they were could not be so easily glamorized.

"Then again maybe Grant didn't burn it because the town militia turned up its toes and cried uncle," Barth said. "There's histories and there's histories. Mrs. Posey's not the only crazy white person in the South. Round about then they had an alderman here got himself hung for killing his wife. He dressed her up as a Yankee soldier and ran a Yankee sword through her half a dozen times.

"Same night he took a deer rifle to six

270

slaves. Shot 'em and left 'em for dead on the garbage dump at the back end of this plantation he had. No law against that. He was hung for killing his wife."

"Were they?" Anna asked.

"Were they what?"

"The slaves he left for dead, they all died?"

"All but one, a kid no more than fifteen. He'd been shot twice in the head and twice through the belly. An old white lady who used to scavenge from the garbage dump found him and dragged him a mile and a quarter to her shack. Since his health was never good again and he didn't talk anymore, the alderman's heirs let her keep him."

"White of them," Anna said and glimpsed a half-smile chipped out of a racial memory bitter as quinine.

"That kind of stuff never makes it into the brochures," Barth said.

Anna laughed. The South was growing on her. The extremes were more honest than the even veneer of trendy sanity that afflicted Northern and Western cities. To be human was to be melodramatic, to feel things acutely, love and hate and lust, to search for the Holy Grail, outrun the other kids in the fifty-yard dash and care mightily about it.

"So. What do you think about the Posey girl being killed by a black man—assuming our killer's male," Anna asked.

"It sounds real handy," Barth said curtly.

"But not impossible."

"You know how many murders we had

around here last year?" Barth asked. "Eighty-nine. Eighty-eight of them were black on black. One was white on black."

"No black on white?"

"Not one."

Anna pondered that for a bit. Surely it had a deep sociological meaning, but whatever it was escaped her. "You don't think Danni was involved with a black boy?"

"I didn't say that. It happens but not as often as you'd think. There's strong opposition from both sides. Mixed-race couples scare everybody. Everybody. What I'm saying is if Danni Posey was involved with a black boy it wouldn't've been him killed her. More likely that brother of hers would've killed her himself, seeing as how she'd tarnished the family name." Barth laughed but not without bitterness. Anna didn't hold it against him. She felt honored he was talking to her at all. Maybe experience taught Mississippians that outsiders not only did not understand the complex chemistry that made up their culture but drew their own conclusions to use for their own ends, usually at Mississippi's expense.

Mike Posey might murder his sister if he'd found her with a black boy. Anna reached back to her odious interlude with the man. There'd been little or no evidence that he grieved for Danielle. And he'd said something. Anna closed her eyes the better to reenter the past. *Maybe Danni had it coming.* Her brother had said that of her brutal murder.

272

If he was so cold as to think a sixteen-year-old girl deserved to have the life stomped out of her, he might be cold enough to deliver the blow. Especially with the added incentive of forty thousand dollars in insurance money if he ruined her face.

Then there was Cindy Posey, a card-carrying lunatic who had "set free" her black babies to live with the other animals of the forest. Even if the black babies were delusions, it spoke worlds about her attitude. What if she found her girl, her beautiful Danielle, the super-model and great white-trash hope, had been betraying the family in such a way? Anna put the picture together in her mind. Mrs. Posey suspects Danni of seeing a black boy. She follows them on prom night. Danni leaves Brandon DeForest as he said she did. She meets up with her illicit lover. They come to Rocky. Have sex. Mrs. Posey whacks her daughter with an edged instrument. Panicked, the boyfriend flees. The sheet, the rope, moving the body: efforts of a crazy woman to point the finger elsewhere.

Fine and dandy, except Anna doubted Cindy Posey could have carried Danni as far as the body was carried. And why would she have blunt instrument, rope and sheet with her deep in the woods? Where was she taking the body? If Cindy Posey was guilty of the murder of her daughter, she had to have had help. Back to Mike Posey. They could have done it together. Mother and son were racists. Mother was mentally ill and son was very possibly following in her erratic footsteps. Mike's talk of getting the "nigger" who killed his sister could be a smoke screen to cover their tracks and cast the blame on a group of humans he'd chosen to hate.

That still didn't explain the time, the place and the bizarre accoutrements of the death. Nor did it explain the chase. By the condition of Danni's shoes and hose and the superficial scratches on her arms and face, it was clear she had been pursued for quite some distance. Would she have run from her own mother and brother? From what Anna'd been able to glean, Danni was the apple of her mother's eye. There had been trust and love of a sort between them.

If Danni did have a black boyfriend, why might he kill her? Lovers' quarrel? That seemed a little extreme, but it happened. Maybe he caught her back in the arms of Brandon DeForest and in a rage struck her down. If Danni had threatened to go public, perhaps his family would have been angered. Though the autopsy proved she was not, she could have told him she was pregnant and the boy was not ready to make a commitment that would be a hard one to keep in America's racial climate.

Boy. Anna thought about that for a moment. There was nothing to indicate that, if Danni had an African-American lover, he had to be a boy. Perhaps she'd gotten involved with a married man, a man with a wife, a family, stature in the community, a life he valued greatly and that would be blasted all to hell if a little white girl, of statutory-rape age, started telling people of their liaison.

Danni makes threats. He follows her on prom night. Gets her alone. She runs. He catches and kills her, then dresses the body in a pseudo KKK costume to throw the blame back on the white population.

Chases her deep into the woods. Strikes her down. Leaves the body, hikes back to his car, gets sheet and rope, hikes back through the dark, drapes and nooses the corpse, carries it a hundred and fifty yards and abandons it.

Nothing hung together.

"I need to have another chat with Heather," Anna said. "Want to come along?"

Barth drove through the gates to the ranger station and parked next to Randy Thigpen's patrol car. For half a minute, he let the engine idle. Anna guessed he was making hard choices. After the disciplinary actions, battle lines were drawn. Thigpen remained unrepentant. Either he would be kept in line by Anna's threat or he wouldn't. Either way she expected she'd have to weather the backbiting and gossip and undermining that was the bane of the park service, a plague she felt had only grown worse as salaries and living conditions had improved. The spirit of the NPS, created by the natural and cultural treasures and the love of them by those dedicated to protect them, had sickened somewhere along the line. Not died, just sickened, and morale suffered. To

Anna's way of thinking, Thigpen was one of those not only ailing but spreading the disease.

Barth was having to decide whether to risk climbing out of the barrel with a white Yankee girl or let the other crab pull him back into the safe and familiar morass of discontent and self-pity.

"I've got a lot of paperwork to catch up on," Barth said uncertainly, and Anna felt a pang of disappointment that startled her in its intensity. A few seconds ticked by. She reached for the door handle, sorry that she had to go it alone.

"It'll keep," Dinkin said with a sigh. "Sure. When?"

Anna was thrilled out of proportion for this tiny victory. She looked at her watch. If they left soon, they'd get to Clinton between school and supper. "Now's good."

The Barneses lived in a well-kept home in a cul-de-sac between Highway 80 and I-20 in south Clinton. The development had been built in the sixties, but the homes were in good condition, with the exception of the occasional roofline or porch eave that looked to have been bent. "Do they have earthquakes here?" Anna asked as Barth turned onto Smoke Hill Drive. She was remembering homes in Santa Ana, California, having slightly surreal architecture from one too many shifts of the foundation.

"Yazoo clay," Barth said. "It's under a lot of the county. It kind of buckles and moves I guess. One-sixty-one?"

276

Anna checked the address she'd written down the morning Heather nursed a hangover at Rocky Springs. "One-sixty-one," she confirmed.

Mrs. Barnes recognized Anna, which made things go more smoothly. After she'd been reassured several times that Heather wasn't in any kind of trouble and she had informed Anna that the errant girl was being kept on a very short leash, Mrs. Barnes told her Heather was at the home of her best friend, Shandra Lea.

"New best friend?" Anna asked, thinking of Danni, slated to be buried the following day.

"Old best friend. Heather and Danielle Posey hadn't been friends all that long." Anna noted the use of Danni's first and last name, the distancing of oneself from the violently dead. Few were comfortable with the memory of the murdered. Some, to make themselves important, claimed to be closer to the deceased than they were. Others, those with something to lose, severed ties.

"Heather and Shandra Lea made the finals for the Mississippi Junior Miss Pageant," Mrs. Barnes said with obvious pride. "They're trying on makeup."

"Danni was in the finals," Anna said, remembering Cindy Posey's remarks.

"Working on the pageant's where she and Heather started being friendly," Mrs. Barnes conceded.

A case from the not too distant past fluttered through Anna's mind. It had been a news bonanza for a couple days. A woman had murdered a teenage girl because she was in competition with her daughter for a coveted cheerleading spot.

Anna shook off the thought. Already the case had her knee-deep in crazy people; she didn't need one more. Anna didn't include Cindy Posey in that list—Mrs. Posey was genuinely mentally ill. She was thinking garden-variety crazy: rangers whose wives left them, dark-browed preachers, psalm-singing sheriffs, grown men playing soldier and dog-eating alligators.

Shandra Lea lived less than half a mile away. Mrs. Barnes gave them directions and went inside, probably to call ahead and warn Shandra Lea's mother and the girls. Anna didn't care. There was no element of surprise here, just a few questions.

The days were getting longer but the late April sun, though full with the heat of the mountain midsummer, retained the thin yellows of winter, backlighting the fresh leaves of two weeping willows until they glowed fierce green and cast long shadows on the lawn.

A cracked and buckled sidewalk cut neatly between the trees, leading a straight and narrow path to Shandra Lea's front door. Low-roofed, rectangular, snuggled down in a riot of azaleas grown as high as the eaves and iridescent in crimson blooms, the house had a fairy-tale aspect that pleased Anna.

Heather and a girl, who Anna surmised

was the old/new best friend, sat shoulder to shoulder, hip to hip on the front steps waiting for them. The girls wore brightly colored clogs and shorts that were hidden beneath voluminous T-shirts.

The two of them were disconcertingly schizophrenic, their faces old with the sophisticated makeup they'd applied in anticipation of a Junior Miss sash, their bodies childlike under the cotton tees.

"Hey, Heather," Anna said as she preceded Barth up the walk. "Your mom said we'd find you here." She was careful not to say any nauseatingly grown-up thing that referenced the girl's recent intoxication. Nobody likes to be reminded they, in Jackie Doolittle's poetic parlance, "showed their butt."

Anna introduced Barth, and Heather, mindful of her manners, introduced her girlfriend. Shandra Lea was pageant-pretty like Danni and Heather and nearly every other pubescent female Anna'd seen in Mississippi. Her dark skin was even-toned—due either to Max Factor or to nature—her eyes melting and close to black under winged brows. A wide nose and full lips lent her an inviting air that, had Anna been her mom, might have gotten her clapped in a nunnery till she was thirty. Shandra Lea had eschewed the slavish attempt to re-create Caucasian hairstyles on Negroid hair and wore hers in a sleek, glossed-down cap with sharp spit-curls at ears and temples. Very French. Very twenties. Very charming.

It was obvious the girls had no intention of

inviting them inside. As there was no car in the carport, Anna made an educated guess that Shandra Lea's mother wasn't home and that Heather's mom was unaware the girls were unchaperoned. Content to let them keep that secret, Anna settled comfortably on the warm concrete walk. Barth remained standing. Big men didn't take easily to sitting tailor fashion on the ground.

Anna decided to pretend rumor was fact and see what she could scare up. "Danielle had a boyfriend of color," she said without pre-amble. "Who was he?"

Shandra Lea and Heather exchanged a mascara-laden glance. Alarm? Conspiracy? Anna wasn't sure. What she was sure of, given the age of the interviewees, was that they had few secrets from each other.

Shandra Lea spoke first. "We don't know that she did," she said carefully.

"But you guessed." Again the glance. Anna pegged it this time. They'd not foreseen this line of questioning and so hadn't discussed what to say and what to leave unsaid. Time to divide and conquer. "Heather, why don't you give Ranger Dinkin your statement. I'll talk with Shandra Lea." Knowing the legal pitfalls of leaving a male officer alone with a young female subject, Anna suggested they adjourn only as far as the patrol car, in plain sight of Anna and Heather's girlfriend.

Left with Shandra Lea, Anna resumed: "You know how serious this is. We're trying to find Danni's murderer."

"To pin it on a black boy, you mean," Shandra Lea said. At sixteen, she carried the well-justified fear of an entire people.

Anna thought awhile before replying. This was new territory. She had to wait till the spurt of anger at having her motives impugned drained away.

"That's not part of my plan," she said when a better answer refused to frame itself. "I don't have a plan, really. I'm just asking questions." She waited patiently while Shandra Lea decided whether or not she could be trusted. Behind her she heard the mellow purr of Barth's voice. From the south came the rumble of trucks on I-20.

Shandra Lea pressed her fingers to her temples. Her fingertips were sheathed in porcelain nails painted in a psychedelic swirl of colors. An expensive affectation for a girl her age. She must have saved for a while.

"That girl was trouble," Shandra Lea said at length. "Not bad bad, like in evil. She just couldn't help stirring things up. Making people say, "Hey, that's Danni Posey!" She never got it that they weren't always saying it because they were impressed."

Given time and silence, she'd say more. Anna adjusted her face to an open look and watched the play of light and shadow on the painted concrete steps.

"Me and Heather talked about it some," Shandra Lea admitted after a while. "My brother goes to Alcorn State. We went down there, me, Heather and Danni, to watch one of his games. There was a party after, and we went. We think maybe Danni met up with some-body there. She didn't ride home with us. We waited, but we couldn't find her, so finally we had to go. Next day she said she'd met up with a girlfriend she hadn't seen in a while. Give me a break! In this town you see everybody every day. There wasn't no girlfriend. Why would she lie if it wasn't a black boy?"

"Maybe because it was a college boy," Anna suggested. "I doubt her folks would want her dating a college boy. Could be white."

Shandra Lea laughed. "You're not from around here, are you? Alcorn's a *black* college. Maybe there's a white boy there somewhere, but I never seen him."

"How long ago was this party?"

"Maybe three months—February some-time."

Plenty of time for a high school romance to blossom. "Danni's longtime boyfriend, Brandon DeForest, did he know about this?"

Shandra Lea looked to where Heather stood talking with Barth. There was a secret close to the surface—Anna could see it in the liquid ink of the girl's eyes. "He did, didn't he?" Anna pressed. "Heather heard him talk about it."

The liquid went dull, shutters drawn on the windows of the soul. "I don't know what Heather hears."

It was Heather's secret, not Shandra Lea's.

"Is Brandon DeForest a friend of yours?" Anna asked.

"Brandon's a jerk," Shandra Lea said disdainfully.

"Then you're protecting a jerk; you're not protecting Heather," Anna said. "You're protecting Brandon DeForest. Why would you want to do that? Because he's a big man on campus? Homecoming king? You want to get in good with the white crowd?" Anna dragged up everything she could think of to piss Shandra Lea off. With the last, she hit pay dirt.

"I don't give a shit about that," Shandra Lea shot back. "Brandon could ruin Heather's chances. And he'd do it."

Foul language. Anna was winning. She smiled but only on the inside. Teenagers have a nose for mockery comparable only to that of a cat for tuna.

"Chances for what?" Anna asked mildly.

Shandra Lea knew she'd been had, and she wasn't relishing the feeling. "I'm not talking to you any more, ' less you come back with a warrant." She stood up and went inside, slamming the door behind her. Shandra Lea might not have much knowledge of the law, but she knew you didn't rat on a friend.

At sixteen the emotion was pure, unsullied by the decision of whether ratting on a friend wasn't sometimes in that friend's best interest and having to find the courage to do it anyway, knowing you'd be forever called Judas.

Anna got to her feet. She could still do it in one fluid motion without using her hands, but where it had once been thoughtless it was now showing off. The effect was somewhat marred by the cracking of knee and ankle joints.

Hands in her pockets, she ambled to the car. Spring in Mississippi was too hot for winter uniforms, and Anna felt hers sticking to her back. Heather and Barth had run out of things to say and looked relieved at her arrival.

"So," Anna said to Heather. "Brandon DeForest says if you don't keep quiet, he'll ruin your chances. What a jerk."

Anna's little bomb was rewarded by an explosion of red suffusing Heather's cheeks. Shame first, then anger. "Did Shandra Lea tell you that?" she demanded.

"Yup."

"She had no right." Heather started to cry, loud and ugly and leading to hiccups, like the crying of a little kid.

Barth drifted soundlessly away. The man had excellent instincts, but Anna rather wished he'd stayed. Barth, at least, had children. Presumably he'd learned to deal with them on an interpersonal level. Anna'd grown up on John Wayne movies. When women cried she wanted to spank them, yell at them or shoot the guy that hurt them. Frieda, Christine, Lynette—the women in Anna's life had taught her the rudiments. At their uncorporal urgings, it crossed her mind to summon up her courage, take the wet wailing girl into her arms and mutter, "There, there." The prospect was too alarming so she stood, leaning against the Crown Vic, arms crossed, watching the celebration of light on the azaleas till Heather subsided to the gasping, snorting stage.

"You about done?" Anna asked kindly.

"Yes, ma'am. Do you have a hankie?"

"I don't carry one. Hang on." Anna got a brand-new red oil rag from the trunk of the car. "It's clean," she promised.

Heather fixed that. Anna was amazed one small girl could have so much liquid in her.

Nose blown, Heather looked up with watery red eyes. "She had no right," she said, starting over.

"She had no choice. It's the law," Anna lied.

"What did she tell you?" Recovered somewhat, Heather was getting cagey.

Anna decided to go on the offensive before Heather called her bluff. "Brandon DeForest can ruin your chances. That's why you've been less than forthcoming, isn't it?"

Heather folded the oil rag into a smaller and smaller square and said nothing.

"Chances for what?"

Nothing.

"He said if you didn't keep quiet he'd do it. That's blackmail. Blackmail's illegal."

Nothing.

Exasperated, Anna went back to the shimmer of flowers beneath the eaves until her desire to shake Heather till her teeth rattled subsided.

"Can I go now?" Heather asked in the voice of a little girl.

"Nope." A fat gray squirrel ventured partway

across the lawn to study them. "Here it is," Anna said finally. "I have got to find out who killed Danni. I don't necessarily have to screw up your life in the process, but I don't mind much if I do. There's bits and pieces of information you're holding back. They may be of use to me. They may not. But I've got to have them."

"You can't make me talk. I want a lawyer. You can't ask any more questions after I ask for a lawyer." Heather'd seen plenty of cop shows on television.

"Sure I can," Anna said. "You're not under arrest. You're not a suspect. I want you to tell me about Brandon, Danni, prom night—anything you can remember. If you don't, I'll tell Brandon you told me everything. I'll let on you're working with me."

A veil of innocence fell from Heather's face, leaving it looking indefinably older. Anna was sorry she'd been the one to make it so. "Why, you're no better than he is!" Heather exclaimed.

Anna was in no position to argue that one. "No guarantees," she said. "But I can promise that I will do my utmost to keep your secret—unless it's dangerous or illegal—and to see to it that the DeForest kid does too."

"It's not dangerous or anything. He's just got—he's got this thing and if he shows it to somebody he can—I won't get something I want."

Eyes down, words vague, color up: Anna guessed Heather was awash with shame. Guilt, anger and resentment didn't drag down the corners of one's eyes, bow one's neck the way shame could.

Sixteen, not illegal, not dangerous—Brandon could have proof she'd cheated at school. That would cost her a grade or a reward, maybe even college. He could have proof of an indiscretion that would cause her parents to revoke some coveted privilege.

Anna studied her face, streaked now, tears rendering the pageant queen a sad-faced little clown.

That was it. "Brandon has something that could keep you out of the Junior Miss pageant, or make sure you don't win it."

"I wouldn't even have a chance." Heather's voice was rising to a wail. Waterworks threatened.

"Take it easy," Anna ordered. "That's my last clean rag. Tell me what he's got. I'll see what I can do."

"Can Shandra Lea come back out?"

"Sure. Barth!" Anna hollered.

"Here."

She was startled to hear his voice so close. The man had faded back, out of her line of sight, and had been standing stock-still in the shadow of a red-tipped fotina that edged the yard. Effectively gone, reassuringly near. "Hey," Anna said, smiling at him because she felt like it. "Could you get Shandra Lea?"

The other girl came outside before Barth was halfway up the walk. She'd been watching from one of the windows and noted a change in the action.

"You had no right—" Heather started the litany.

"Come on, Heather, this is real," Shandra Lea said dismissively. Heather quieted. It was easy to see who the leader was in this two-some. Anna expected it. Heather Barnes was one of those very biddable young women, the sort blown easily by the winds of fashion, popularity and trends.

Anna took over. "Heather's told us Brandon DeForest has been blackmailing her. Is that right?"

Shandra Lea looked at her friend for permission to rat, but Heather had her head down, acquiescent. "That's right," the black girl said. "He's got a picture he's been threatening to show around that would spoil Heather's chances at the Junior Miss title."

"Pornographic picture?" Anna asked.

"Yes," Heather mumbled, and her head drooped further.

"Oh, give it a rest," Shandra Lea snapped. "You don't know porn, girl. It's this silly-ass snapshot Brandon took at a swim party when Danni and Heather flashed him." She mimed pulling up her top and showing her breasts for Anna's edification.

"You're kidding," Anna said. "They'd throw you out of the Junior Miss for that?"

"Maybe not throw me out," Heather said, talking to the pavement between her feet.

"But they won't go giving you no rhinestone tiara if they got a picture of you flashing your

288

titties for the camera." Shandra Lea was a pragmatist.

"I'll see if I can get your picture back for you," Anna said. "Tell me about prom night."

After twenty minutes poking and prodding, Anna was able to piece together a better picture of what had happened. Heather had gone to the dance with Matt, Danni with Brandon DeForest. Both couples had been fighting. Danni was "in a mood" and dropping hints about her college boyfriend. Heather left the dance to join Danni, Brandon and his two cohorts, Lyle Sanders and Thad Meyerhoff, in the parking lot to drink. Matt followed, offered to take her home. When she refused, he left. Brandon got drunk and abusive, calling Danni a slut and threatening to kill her and her new boyfriend. Danni ran to the car and said she'd been with a "real man" before Brandon picked her up, and she was going to him, and she'd just used Brandon to get out of the house. Heather jumped in DeForest's car with Danni, and they left. Brandon, Lyle and Thad followed them in Thad's car. On the Trace, they kept trying to run Danni and Heather off the road. Heather found a fifth of some kind of booze under the seat, and she and Danni passed it back and forth.

That was where the story ended and the blackout began. No matter from which direction Anna came at it, Heather couldn't remember anything else.

At five-thirty, Anna let the girls go. She'd

seen Heather late on prom night, and believed that she had lost the end of the evening to alcohol.

"Do we go see the DeForest boy?" Barth asked when they were back in the Crown Vic, threading their way out of the neighborhood.

"Let's talk to Sheriff Davidson first," Anna said. "See what he wants to do with it." Bullying children had given her a headache. It felt good to lean back against vinyl cooled by air-conditioning and let Barth keep the car on the road.

"Sounds like DeForest to me," Barth said. "Drunk. Mad. Showing off for his buddies. Things got out of hand."

"Sounds like," Anna said absently. "I wonder who she was going to meet, where she was meeting him. Maybe she had a rendezvous set up at Rocky before she even left the dance with DeForest."

"Sounds more to me like she was running to boyfriend number two because she was scared of boyfriend number one," Barth said obstinately.

Boyfriend number two was black. Barth sincerely didn't want a black man to be the killer. Anna could understand that.

"She said she'd used DeForest to get out of the house. That suggests to me she might've had a plan to meet number two from the get-go."

"Steal number one's car and drag girlfriend Heather along?" Barth said. "Doesn't sound like much of a plan to me."

Danni could have stolen the car to meet her lover because she was drunk or angry, or wanted DeForest to meet the Other Man. Who knew? Maybe she wanted them to fight over her. And bringing Heather along—same story, wanting an audience to her popularity. Or maybe Heather was uninvited and just jumped into the getaway car. Still Anna conceded the point to him. Arguing suppositions was a waste of energy.

Barth steered smoothly off I-20 and up onto the Natchez Trace Parkway. To the north the road ended at a battered barricade, indicating a gap in the ambitious plan to run the Trace from Natchez to Nashville. This was a ten-mile stretch of road between where the Trace ended at Clinton and where it began again in the city of Ridgeland, a northern suburb of Jackson. At present the section was under construction. Secretly, Anna hoped to be gone from the Trace before it opened, bringing with it urban crime gathered as it passed through the capital city.

Barth turned south. Though the concept of wilderness was an illusion on the Trace, a narrow strip of well-manicured gardens crowded on both sides by homes and farming concerns, Anna felt relieved to be free of the towns, to rest her eyes not on the smeared faces of baby beauty queens, but upon the ten thousand shades of green that bedecked the woodlands. Green was a soothing color. Green was the color of the walls in sanitariums, the color of the NPS uniform. Far less authoritarian and menacing than the blacks and blues favored by the police.

Several hundred yards down the Trace from I-20 was a pullout. Near as Anna knew, it had no historical significance but was a rest area with a picnic table. Three cars were parked there and a pickup with the ubiquitous rebel flag on its bumper. A lone man sat behind the wheel of a late-model Oldsmobile. No one else was in evidence.

"What's with all the cars?" Anna asked, just to speak of a subject other than murder.

"Clinton pullout's kind of a problem area," Barth said with disgust. Peeling off the two-lane road, he cruised behind the cars.

"Hinds County plates. They're from around here. So why use a pullout?" The question was rhetorical and Anna waited obediently for the answer. It was not forthcoming.

Barth's demeanor was undergoing rapid changes. As Anna watched, she saw the disgust being tempered by confusion, which melted into alarm, then resolved itself into the pain of an innocent—a child discovering there is no Santa Claus.

"Joggers," he said abruptly. "Just folks leaving their cars here while they run."

Before Anna could speak, Barth pulled out of the turnout and put his foot on the accelerator. A quick glance at the speedometer: he'd nearly floored the Crown Vic. The needle was easing up on seventy-five.

Another time, Anna might have amused herself by trying to ferret out the reason for her companion's peculiarities. At the moment, she was content to let it be. Tonight, the vet had promised, she could retrieve Taco. A three-legged dog, a disgruntled cat and a bottle of good wine were all she wanted to think about.

T aco was ecstatic. So was David Christianson. Both were grinning widely when Anna arrived. Mrs. Christianson's prayers—and Anna's, had she admitted to being the praying kind—had been answered. The black lab, his left haunch swathed in bandages, was a great deal more healthy and exuberant than anyone had dared to hope.

When Taco saw her, he struggled to stand, fell on the legless hip and whined at the sudden pain. Anna's eyes stung as he dragged and scooted across the linoleum, willing to endure the unendurable for the privilege of washing her feet with doggie devotions.

Anna met him more than halfway and sat on the floor letting him lick her face and snort dog breath up her nose without recrimination. To the vet she said: "Every law enforcement officer should have a dog. That way you're guaranteed at least one somebody will be glad to see you." Christianson laughed long enough to let Anna rid herself of the lump in her throat. A good doctor for animals and people.

"He'll learn to get around," the vet promised. "In a month he'll be his old self. Till then you'll want to work on your upper body strength. He's a big boy." With that the vet easily lifted the mass of wriggling dog flesh and, at Anna's instruction, deposited Taco on the nest of blankets she'd prepared for him on the front seat of the Rambler.

Christianson had stayed late at his clinic so Anna could be reunited with her dog. Southern hospitality. Having thanked him with deplorable Yankee reserve, she drove into the long and gentle twilight of Mississippi's spring. Though the sun had been down more than half an hour, the temperature was still in the high sixties and the air soft and fragrant. Humidity held life close to the earth, retaining heat and scent, cloaking it close around the body. Anna loved the scouring air of the high desert, the arid winds that stripped the day from skin and soil, but ears full of frog music and senses alive to the richness of this new place, she began to suspect she would come to love this too. A vague sensation of being somehow traitorous to the Southwest plagued her for a moment. She banished it by telling Taco of the adventures he'd missed since his run-in with the alligator. Anna wasn't talking to him as though he could understand or give her good counsel—he wasn't a cat, after all—but because she wanted to talk and Taco wanted to listen.

In peaceful conversation, everybody happy with their role, Anna drove the three miles on Clinton Raymond Road to I-20 and then onto the Trace. As she coasted up the on ramp to the parkway, she reached the part in her narrative where Barth had gotten squirrelly and sped away from the Clinton pullout. As she told the tale to the dog, it occurred to her that it was more than Barth's sudden decision to head home that bothered her. Four empty cars, one man. Joggers, Barth said, and it made sense at the time. Except there hadn't been any joggers. The Trace, at least on the Clinton end, had no trails, no dirt lanes. The road was bordered by overgrown, weedy, boggy terrain and very little of that. Joggers would have to run along the one, the only road. Anna and Barth had driven it together for forty miles, and she'd not seen a single runner.

"Mind if we stop a sec, Taco?" He thumped his tail. Anna took that as a yes.

No cars were at the pullout. She parked crosswise, so she could watch oncoming traffic and reviewed what Barth had said: a problem area, the two cars she'd paid attention to had Hinds County plates. Barth had posed the question of why locals would come to a rest area off the beaten path when they could go home. He'd cruised slowly through the tiny parking lot, past the Olds with its single occupant, a couple of nondescript sedans and the pickup truck. In that brief span of time, he'd seen or thought something that spurred the sudden retreat.

"It's a drag trusting no one," Anna said peevishly.

Taco raised one eyebrow. Not trusting was alien to his nature.

"I'm going to look around." Not wanting to call attention to the fact he was a cripple and couldn't go, she added, "Guard the car."

Light lingered above the treetops and in the open spaces. Beneath the trees, night was already gathering for its assault on the sky. The mowed grassy knoll was unremarkable but for an abundance of litter Anna'd not found in pullouts farther south. The wooden picnic table was scarred with carved graffiti. In the waning light, she couldn't read it, but she suspected it was the usual mix of love and mathematics: Alice + Joe = defacement of government property. Better the picnic table than the trees; the table was already dead.

Beyond was the band of greenery that edged the Trace. Already the shadows had congealed, but the suffocating darkness of the woods at night had yet to solidify. In the growing gloom, Anna could see half a dozen paths—social trails, the parks called them, not officially maintained trails but trampled lanes visitors made, usually taking shortcuts. Nothing was at the Clinton pullout to take shortcuts between. People wandering into the trees to pee? Six trails: a lot of natural-world peeing for a place less than a mile from a truck stop with modern facilities.

Picking the path that showed the most traffic, Anna pushed into the gloom. Behind her, she heard Taco begin to bark.

Vegetation had grown up thick and wild as is the way with natural areas that have been deforested and allowed to come back. Natural selection had yet to cull the weaker species. Every weed, vine and shrub struggled desperately for light and space.

This was not a good place. Anna could sense it. It lacked the feel of earth and clean, living things. There was about it a tired carnival air, as if hard boot heels had ground lime snowcones into every scrap of ground. Weeds, spindly, clawing, head-high, plucked at her hair and clothes. A cotton ball brushed her shoulder and she stopped. Not cotton, Kleenex. Staring to catch what light remained, Anna realized the plethora of pale puffs she'd taken for feral cotton blossoms were toilet tissue.

Most of them were toilet tissue. A closer look and she realized condoms festooned the bushes. Used condoms. Ahead of her, on one of the few trees that had fought past the stringy starving phase, was a square of paper. She followed the path to it, contorting her person to avoid contact with the scatological flotsam.

Without a flashlight, the page looked to be a print of modern art ripped from a magazine, surreal shapes and forms meaning nothing.

Anna pulled it from the tree and, holding her breath, backed through the sewer, ran to her car, climbed in and slammed the door.

"Too gross even for a dog," she told Taco. "Don't lick me—I'm defiled." A past master at eating revolting forms of offal, Taco licked her anyway.

Anna switched on the overhead light and

looked at the picture she'd torn from the tree. The strange forms became comprehensible. It wasn't surrealistic art but graphic pornography so up close and personal that the body parts lacked humanity. At the bottom, written in black magic marker, were the words "Follow Me," and an arrow.

13

Night was in full-throated song by the time Anna and Taco returned to Rocky Springs. Invisible creatures, frog and cricket and nightingale, celebrated in dark festival. A half moon hung above the treetops, so bright its perfect light dappled the road surface with the shadows of leaves. Laden with perfumes intoxicating enough to sweeten the hand of Lady Macbeth, a breeze stirred the shadows and the asphalt appeared insubstantial.

Anna turned the Rambler into the campground entrance. "Almost home," she told Taco. The dog had worked his crippled hindquarters around till he could rest his chin on her thigh. His breathing sounded shallow and his nose was warm. Anna worried she'd brought him home too soon. The vet had argued for several more days in the hospital. The drawback was Christianson was a large-animal vet who spent his days making barn and sty calls and couldn't care for an inpatient. He'd argued for removal of Taco to another vet. Anna'd argued for home care and won. Now she wondered if she'd placed the restorative power of love too far above that of medical science.

"Here we are," she said and, "We've got company."

Parked in the driveway, neatly to one side so her patrol car was not blocked, was a battered and aging Toyota pickup. Arms folded across his chest, a man in khaki pants and pink polo shirt leaned against the rear fender.

Had she not the faithful and ailing Taco to consider, Anna would have thrown the Rambler into reverse and fled to a Motel 6 for the night. Each religion had its own version of hell: fire, ice, an eternity without the love of God, pointy-tailed vermin with pitchforks and unsavory appetites. Anna's was a place where she had to talk to and be talked at by people day after day. A place where there was no solitude, no silence, no sacred meadows, nowhere one didn't feel the scrape of others' eyes upon one's skin. A place where words fell in a constant assault upon the senses.

According to these lights, Anna had had a particularly hellish day. Words had battered down like hail. Threats, lies, excuses, hopes, dreams, packed into words and shoved from her and to her. Whoever had come up with the chant "Sticks and stones may break my bones but words will never hurt me" had been an idiot. Words could hurt worse than any stone, and the bruises lasted longer.

Harboring every intention of being rude, she cranked the wheel and turned into her driveway. Headlights, purposely left on high to be more offensive, raked across the intruder. He raised his hand to shield his eyes, and Anna realized it was Sheriff Davidson.

Her intention to be rude joined other paving stones to hell. It wasn't merely that her mood lightened, her heart leapt in accordance with the rules of paperback romances. To Taco she said: "Hey, look, we've got a helper." Her voice was so downright chipper it annoyed her. "Fucking Pollyanna," she muttered to maintain equilibrium.

Abreast of the defrocked lawman, Anna stopped and spoke through the window. "Are you up to carrying seventy pounds of man's best friend?"

"I can do that," Davidson agreed. "I take it you got your dog back."

"Most of him," Anna said. She had inherited wide shoulders and a strong back. Working outdoors kept her fit. In a pinch she could bench her body weight but genetics decreed she was to be female, five-foot-four and a hundred twenty pounds. History had tagged more than forty years onto that package. Though Anna knew she could lift and carry Taco, she liked the dog well enough to admit she couldn't do it smoothly and painlessly.

That was what she told herself even as a weasly little voice, muffled by layer upon layer of pride, reminded her it was a very old and very feminine form of flattery to ask a man to lift heavy objects.

Davidson had gone around the car and opened the passenger door. "Hey old buddy, old pal, old doggie, old thing," he was murmuring kindly to the damaged pooch. He leaned in, and Anna leaned over to help scoop Taco into his arms. The faint aroma of shampoo came off the sheriff's hair and, when she brushed his arm during the canine transfer, his skin was warm and dry. Desire passed through her in a wave that left her feeling vulnerable and exposed. Even the marginal glow of the cabin light seemed enough to illuminate her nakedness. Pulling back suddenly lest rampant pheromones give her away, she cracked her head on the door frame.

"Damn!"

"Are you all right?" This was said with such warmth and concern that Anna felt compelled to snap his head off.

"I'm fine. Watch it with the dog."

Southern hospitality was evidently not something acquired by the simple expedient of moving south.

Taco was an exemplary patient till Anna unlocked the front door and Paul carried him inside. Being home didn't soothe his doggie nerves. Once indoors, he began to whine, then growl low in his throat. Feebly, he tried to struggle free as if, bandaged and crippled, he needed to give chase.

"Easy fella, easy boy," Davidson crooned

in a way Anna had heard half a hundred cow-boys croon to agitated horses.

"Hold him a minute," Anna said, and hurried down the dark hallway toward the back bedroom. The light switches in the Rocky Springs housing had been installed by a mischievous electrician. None were located where reasonable homeowners had been taught to expect them. The light to the hall was at the far end. Having traversed the hallway without incident, Anna didn't bother to locate it but stepped into an even darker bedroom and felt her way around the end of the bed to the far side to switch on the reading lamp.

With the sudden light, she felt relief and was surprised. She'd been strung tighter than she'd thought. Taco's growling didn't help. Either it carried a note of menace not accounted for by phantom pain in his severed leg or her imagination was working overtime. She sensed a wrongness about the house, or thought she did. But the lamp showed her bedroom just as she had left it, not terribly neat but comfortingly familiar even in its bleak just-moved-in persona.

Having gathered up the disreputable cushion that was the only keepsake Taco brought with him from his old life, Anna carried it back to the front room and arranged it by a stove she wouldn't need for six months.

Careful and conscientious as a practical nurse, Paul settled Taco on his bed. The growling continued, an alert and hostile sound that made Anna want to follow suit though she didn't know what demons the dog was seeing.

"Vets give them ketamine," the sheriff said. "Maybe they hallucinate just like people."

"Flashbacks?" Anna asked. Ketamine was a powerful hallucinogen that anesthetized animals without depressing the respiratory system.

"Who knows?" Davidson said philosophically.

Taco pulled his lips back and showed teeth ugly with intent. Scrabbling with his forepaws, whining against the pain, he tried to pull himself off the cushion and across the hardwood floor toward the hall. The fur on the back of his neck was standing on end. So was Anna's.

"Jesus, Taco," she said, then felt self-conscious, because Paul Davidson was a priest. "You're okay."

"Maybe he misses his kitty," Davidson offered.

When he said it, Anna remembered she had told the sheriff about Taco, about her cat. She'd told him about Molly and Zach, the husband she'd lost so many years back. Contrary to her usual practice, under the beneficent aura of the gun-toting man of God she'd talked a whole lot more than she'd listened. It had felt good at the time. Now it made her uncomfortable. Again the unwelcome feeling of exposure and vulnerability.

"Piedmont," Anna called to take her mind off her neurosis. "Here kitty, kitty, kitty." No cat. Perhaps that was the wrongness she and the dog sensed. Piedmont was a person-able feline. Unless occupied by nothing less irresistible than a mouse or lizard in another part of the house, the big orange tom never failed to meet Anna at the door.

"Piedmont," she called again, afraid that her bonding with, of all things, a *dog*, had forever alienated her friend.

Taco grumbled.

Despite the warmth of the night, Anna got a chill. "Check the empty bedrooms," she said. "I'll get the kitchen and the backyard."

"For the kitty?"

"For anything. Bad juju."

Davidson was on his feet. "Gut feeling?"

"Feminine intuition."

A floodlight declared the backyard empty of anything more sinister than two cottontail bunnies, neither bigger than the average soft-ball. Skittering roaches contaminated the kitchen, but though they made Anna queasy, they didn't frighten her.

"Bedrooms are clear," Davidson announced.

"Now we look for the cat."

Poking into the cramped spaces where a cat could secrete itself, Anna and Davidson worked from the living room down the hall to the study, to the room closed off for financial idiocy and finally to Anna's bedroom.

With Paul Davidson in her boudoir, Anna wished it was more hospitable: curtains on the windows, pictures on the wall, at the very least the bed made and her dirty underwear somewhere other than on the floor. Covertly, she watched him scan the room and was relieved to note he looked with the eyes of a policeman, not of a date.

"The window's open," he said.

"I leave it open."

"Without a screen?"

Anna crossed around him. He stood near the double-sized futon she'd slept on for nine years. The thought that it was time for a real bed, a queen-size, crossed her mind. Then she was at the window and the thought was forgotten.

"There was a screen this morning." She raised the sash and leaned out. The screen lay on the ground a couple of feet away. Wriggling around till her rump was on the sill, her feet inside and her upper body outside, Anna looked up at the fastenings: two flattened metal hooks, the kind designed to make the removal of screens easy.

Squirming back inside she banged her head again, just hard enough to make her mad.

"Oooh. Ouch," came a sympathetic voice and a warm hand touched her.

Anna flinched unbecomingly.

"Sorry. I didn't mean to startle you." He removed his hand, and Anna wanted her flinch back but it was too late. "Are you okay?"

"I'm fine," Anna said for the second time in twenty minutes. Fine. Her psychiatrist sister said when patients said they were fine too often it meant fucked-up, insecure, negative and evasive. One for the books, Anna thought sourly. "The screen's been taken off. Or it fell off," she amended.

Davidson leaned out to see for himself. Anna couldn't get away without squishing passed his behind or climbing over the bed so she remained trapped in the little space between the wall and the bed, wondering why she felt the need to escape.

"Was it latched?" he asked.

"I don't know. I hadn't gotten around to vacuuming the dead flies out of the sills yet."

Davidson laughed. Ducking, he managed to ease his bulk gracefully out the window and onto the grass. Looking lovely and man-about-the-house in moonlight and penny loafers, he picked up the screen and brought it back to rehang it. Anna didn't ask him if there were any signs of its being forced. Old house, old screens, the latch could be slipped easily by the blade of a jackknife or a bit of stiff wire.

While he rehung the screen, Anna looked at her room from a new perspective. If anyone had broken into the house, they'd apparently not found anything worth stealing. Illogically, she was offended. Her television was old and small, her computer a dinosaur her sister had forced upon her. A boom box served as a sound system, and she had no microwave. The would-be thief, if there was one, could probably take her to court and sue her for being hopelessly out of sync with modern criminal needs. A lot of money was tied up in her Navajo rugs, but only a specialist would recognize what they were worth.

Comfortably aware of her house being

secured from without by a man who used nice-smelling shampoo, her mind free-floated as her gaze moved slowly around the room. Was the clutter on the dresser rearranged? Maybe. Was her book, face down on the nightstand, at a different angle? Maybe. Had she left the lid of her trunk open? Maybe. Maybe not. Things looked as if they'd been moved ever so slightly, but in the scatter of unpacking, she could not be sure.

The sliding door to the closet was open about four inches. Odd. Open: not odd. Shut: not odd. Four inches, as though someone in a hurry had started to close it and left the job unfinished: odd. Naturally, Anna couldn't remember if that hurried distracted individual was her. She'd had a lot on her mind when she left to pick up her damaged dog.

Events that were out of the ordinary tended to stick in the brain. Things done every day, done without thought were virtually impossible to remember. Hence questions like "Where were you at eight-thirteen P.M. the night of January 7, 1999?" were more or less unanswerable. Except by the evildoer in question. One could always hope, even to criminals, a truly heinous crime was sufficiently out of the ordinary to stick in memory.

As she crossed the room, visions of bogeymen danced in Anna's head. By the time she'd traveled the couple of yards to the closet door, she was scared to open it. Norman Bates might've left the motel business and moved south to go into ladies clothing.

The front door opened and closed. Realizing she was waiting for Paul to return before she opened the closet, Anna was disgusted with herself. Since the age of four, she'd been checking under her own bed for tigers and witches. She wasn't going to ask for help now. In one sweeping move, she slid open the closet door, moving with it so when the butcher knife slashed down, it would miss her.

Bates wasn't on duty. An array of uniforms in various stages of decay hung undisturbed. Paul came into the room, and all at once Anna was aware of how few pretty things hung amid the green and gray.

"There he is," the sheriff said softly.

Anna's fears rushed back with such force that for an instant she could neither move nor speak. Cowardice saved her from the more egregious sin of foolishness. Paul crouched down and reached in among the piles of cordovan dress boots, shoes and hiking boots.

"The definition of a scaredy cat," he said as he lifted Piedmont from his hiding place.

"Somebody's been in the house," Anna said with conviction. "That's the only time Piedmont hides in the closet. He's done it since he was a kitten." She took the cat from Davidson's arms and hugged him, pushing her nose into the fur on the back of his neck as much to comfort herself as the cat.

Paul did not try to convince her that her house had not been invaded, and for that she was grateful. A screen off its hooks and a cat in the closet did not constitute much in the way of hard evidence.

Instead, while she brought Piedmont out to visit with a much calmed Taco, Davidson checked the windows, outdoors and in and, after asking Anna's permission, closed and locked them.

With far less awkwardness than she would have anticipated, She managed to offer him bread and wine and slip a CD in the boom box. She chose the soundtrack from *Leap of Faith*, feeling the mix of great gospel singers and Meat Loaf would set the proper tone for this makeshift communion.

Davidson seated himself cross-legged on the floor near Taco. Piedmont was rubbing against him shamelessly. The St. Francis of Assisi pose suited the priest, Anna admitted, as she joined them on the floor. Davidson broke a Triscuit in two, popped half in his mouth and gave the other half to the dog.

"Who'd want to search your house?" he asked.

Anna didn't know. Unlike the alligator incident, this wasn't meant to scare her off. The intention had been to go undetected. Nothing appeared to be disturbed or missing. Had the intruder believed she had any information on the Posey murder, her study would have been the obvious place to look if he was too stupid to break into her office in Port Gibson.

They belabored vague possibilities: kids looking for loose cash, campers intent on borrowing a cup of sugar, perverts who'd never outgrown panty raids. Finally they had to give it up.

Anna poured herself a second glass of Merlot. Davidson was still working on his first. Silence settled between them. Anna thought the awkwardness she had narrowly avoided earlier would creep in, but it didn't. Davidson had sprawled out. Lying on his right side. Head propped on his hand, he dragged for Piedmont's entertainment a bit of weed one of them had tracked in.

After a time he said: "This wasn't purely a social call." He looked up and added, "Though it was mostly." She wondered if he'd amended his statement because he glimpsed the flicker of disappointment she'd felt. "Leo Fullerton killed himself."

Anna took a swallow of wine to aid in processing this. Alcoholics Anonymous was a distant memory only slightly tinged with guilt. Some vices had to be accepted that one's virtues, as the playwright of *The Matchmaker* said, could spring up modestly around them.

"He took his bass boat out on the Big Black river, tied the transmission of an old VW bus to his ankles, and jumped overboard. My deputies found his boat half a mile downstream caught up in the roots of a drowned tree. The body hasn't been recovered yet."

Anna was having trouble making sense of the story. She'd talked to the re-enactors that morning. They'd never said anything about Leo being dead. Maybe AA wasn't such a bad idea after all. "Downstream? How do you know where Fullerton went in?"

"Found his truck parked on the riverbank. One of the pastor's favorite fishing spots."

The pastor. Anna remembered that Fullerton and the sheriff had been friends—or at least knew one another. "I'm sorry to hear that," she said.

"A lot of people will be. Leo was well liked. He helped his flock in more than just spiritual ways. Leo looked after kids when people needed to go on job interviews. Reroofed houses. Dug new cesspools. He was trying to get one old lady's book published before she died. It was her dream. A black woman telling her story of the slaves butchered in Port Gibson during the war. This will hit everybody pretty hard."

Anna let his words trickle down with another mouthful of red wine. "They haven't found the body?"

"We will. The Big Black's not a deep or fast river."

"How did you know about the VW transmission?"

"Leo called Jimmy Williams and told him what he was planning. Williams got hold of Ian McIntire, and they drove down from Jackson to stop him. When they got to his house, Leo was gone. They found his truck where he said it would be and called us."

"Why didn't they call you right off? It's nearly an hour's drive from Jackson to Port Gibson."

"They said they didn't think he'd do it. That he was just feeling down—he got that way sometimes, I can attest to that—and it would have embarrassed him if they'd called anybody."

"Was there a note?"

"We didn't find one."

"Is it possible it wasn't suicide?"

"Anything's possible, but Ian and Jimmy wouldn't have hurt him. The three of them have been friends since they were little kids. Their mothers were friends. The two living—Mrs. Williams and Mrs. McIntire—still are. I'm betting on suicide. Leo had an ongoing fight with depression. He never talked about it, and odds are it never even crossed his mind to get treatment. That's a danger with being a man of God, so to speak. If you don't watch it, you can start to take things personal. Shouldering crosses when there are perfectly good God-given forklifts sitting around to take some of the burden."

Davidson continued dragging the weed around in enticing patterns, but he was only amusing himself. Piedmont had lost interest. Taco slept, his breathing even and regular. "Stone's Throw from Hurtin' " played on the boom box. Its usually pleasant strains grated on Anna's ears. Air-conditioned drafts fell clammily across her neck and shoulders, and she longed to shut the damn thing off and open the windows to the healing fragrance of the night. Out of deference to Fullerton's death and Paul Davidson's mood, she remained still.

Finally stiff with cold or memories, Paul struggled into a sitting position. For the first time since Anna'd met him, he looked his age.

"I guess this was purely a social call, after all," he admitted. "Leo's got nothing to do with anything except you'd met him and I needed to talk about him."

"Anytime." Impulsively, Anna put her hand on his knee. Before she could feel silly or snatch it back, he'd taken it in both his own. She couldn't tell if the warmth she felt was from his skin or within her own. Slowly, as if it were an object of great value, he turned it palm up and traced what felt like an A on her palm. The phantom letter tingled in various portions of Anna's anatomy.

Davidson laughed. "Now I'm feeling guilty because I used poor Leo's death to pay you a visit. If it hadn't been for the celibacy thing, I'd have made a heck of a Catholic priest. Do you want me to stay?"

Startled by the abrupt change in the weather, Anna said nothing for a bit. The South. Nothing was as simple as it seemed. Beneath everything were seventeen more layers of everything else. "Do you mean am I scared to stay here by myself?" she asked carefully.

Davidson laughed again. Anna was growing to like the sound. "That's what I did mean. Freud would sure have a field day with me. But yes, after the break-in, if you wanted me to, I could sleep on your couch."

"No you couldn't," Anna said. The couch

was Victorian, designed to ensure no one ever lost their virginity or even enjoyed a moment's comfort in its uptight embrace.

She walked the sheriff to his car. The driver's door between them, solid as a bundling board, he leaned over the top and kissed her. The kiss was quick, light and not in the least brotherly. Though Anna stood her ground in true John Wayne fashion, she noted a wateriness in the vicinity of her knees and a faint humming in her ears different from the drone of the insects.

14

Anna was having fantasies. She wanted to buy a summer dress, new underwear, perfume, lipstick. The glossy magazines she routinely ignored in airport newsstands and hair salons had had a cumulative subliminal impact. If the phenomenon was progressive, she'd soon begin to worry about cellulite or invest in a Wonderbra.

It wasn't that Anna eschewed the feminine artifices on ethical, moral, religious or political grounds. They had simply been non-productive in her chosen profession. Used injudiciously, they became counterproductive. When arresting a drunk, one didn't want one's come-hither scent or kiss-me red lips to distract him from the respectful business of being cuffed and booked.

What Anna often forgot was there was such a thing as "off duty." The night before, with Paul, she had been genuinely off duty for a few moments. She had every intention of being seriously off duty again in the not-so-distant future. For the next eight hours, however, she had to drag her mind out of the lingerie department.

Turning off the Trace into the Port Gibson Ranger Station Anna noted several cars, one a patrol car. She hoped it was Barth. Randy Thigpen would be continuing his black-cloud persona, and Anna wasn't in the mood to have her psychological parade rained on. Then she remembered Randy was on four to midnight, and it was just noon. She was off the hook for a few hours.

George Wentworth was tucked in his office, his broad shoulders bowed over papers piled neatly on his desk.

Anna poked her head in his office. "Hey," she said, bubbling over with good cheer. "Any new offers for the next Air McWhatsis?"

George raised his head in the slow and unhappy way a bull might when it was deciding whether or not to charge. The whites of his eyes, usually a cool, almost minty white, were yellowed, the tiny blood vessels ruptured from stress, lack of sleep or booze. For an instant Anna thought he hadn't heard her or, at any rate, was not going to answer her. She was deciding whether to repeat the question or slink away to savor the better part of valor, when he spoke.

"Lockley's dropped out of college." His voice rolled the words flat, squeezing everything from them but the dull residue of disappointment.

"Shit," Anna said sympathetically. "That sucks."

"His mom's all tore up."

Anna capped off her good cheer and came into his office to lean companionably against the bookcase in the event he wanted to talk. "What happened?"

"We don't know. He won't talk to us. Won't talk to *me*." George's throat closed on him, and he stared out the window till he'd mastered it. "Everything seemed to be going along just fine, then he changed."

"Drugs, you think?"

"That's the first guess everybody makes. But Lock's never done drugs. He's too smart for that."

Anna said nothing. Even smart kids got duped into drugs. The really smart ones figured they could handle it, as if intellect could rule chemical dependence. George leaned back, stared out the window at the buggy grill on Anna's patrol car. His left hand twitched among the papers as if it continued working on its own.

"We thought maybe steroids," George said finally. "You know, the mood swings and all. We asked Lock about it and he said no." He looked up at Anna. "You'd have believed him. He didn't say it like he even cared we'd thought it. Just this quiet 'no' like it didn't matter."

Clinical depression. Anna'd been there. Too deep to care, too sick to pray. An ugly thought wormed through the layers of her mind.

"How long?" she asked.

"A week. Maybe less. It just doesn't make sense."

It did to Anna. Danni Posey had gone to Alcorn with Heather and Shandra Lea to a football game, and after the game they'd gone to a college football party. Heather and Shandra Lea thought Danni had met a boy there. Danni's brother, Mike, thought she had a black sweetheart. Lockley Wentworth, a handsome, charming, black football hero, goes into an emotional tailspin immediately after Danni Posey is found beaten to death.

If George Wentworth's son was not Danni Posey's lover, that was way too many coincidences for such a sparsely populated state.

"Did he get any bad news? Football teams or grades or a health problem?" Anna asked.

"That's just it," George said, and the frustration loaded his voice till it broke in anger. "Nothing like that. Nothing. He would have told us. His mother and I've been over it and over it. There's nothing he couldn't tell us. Even if he'd got a girl in trouble, something like that, he'd of told us."

Unless the girl was underage, white and dead.

Anna wanted to talk with the Wentworth boy in the worst way—without his parents' permission. George struck her as the kind of man who would lay down his life for his son. Admirable in a father. A pain in the butt in a murder investigation.

"How old is Lock?" Anna asked, suppressing the knowledge she was being opportunistic and hard-hearted.

"Just twenty. Hardly more than a boy. Too young to throw his life away."

Not a juvenile. Fair game. To assuage her conscience, Anna said: "My sister's a psychiatrist, and from what she's told me over the years, I'd guess Lock's suffering from severe depression. He's treatable. Don't let him cut off his options yet. When he comes out of it, he can pick up where he left off." Unless he was in the state penitentiary on a murder charge.

George accepted her crumb of hope for the crumb it was and returned doggedly to his paperwork.

Barth was likewise employed, head down over a pile of speeding citations, the top one so dimpled and smeared from rainwater as to be almost illegible. Either he'd decided to snub Anna or was distracted by his work. He didn't look up or acknowledge her greeting. Anna was happy to shut herself in her office and think.

Accepting the theory that Lock Wentworth was Danni's secret lover did not mean accepting him as the murderer. His sudden and acute depression indicated intense emotion. It was possible he'd killed the girl in a fit of rage or jealousy and was eaten up by guilt. It was equally possible he was doing Romeo to her

Juliet. In which case his life was at grave risk. Depression could be deadly. He could be suffering guilt because he wasn't with her, couldn't protect her. Shame because the relationship had been clandestine. The Poseys weren't going to be the only parents outraged. Anna doubted George Wentworth would be pleased to see his son risk his hopes and ambitions by bringing upon himself the kind of trouble a sixteen-year-old white girl carried with her. Lockley Wentworth might be scared out of his wits: his girlfriend was murdered, her brother frothing at the mouth to pin it on the black boyfriend, the body draped in a sheet reminiscent of the KKK, a symbol designed to frighten and intimidate. And who could he tell? His girlfriend was dead, and he couldn't even cry about it. At least not where he'd have to explain it to anybody. If he had killed her, it was a reasonable assumption that it wasn't premeditated. If he hadn't, he was bottling a poisonous mix of emotions and stoppering it with terrible anger at whoever had destroyed Danni and at himself for not being there to save her.

Anna flipped through her Rolodex till she found the number for the Claiborne County Sheriff's Office. The kiss she'd enjoyed so much the night before turned sour on her lips. Business with pleasure, like wine with whiskey, was bound to leave one with a hangover. This hangover took the form of second guesses. Was she calling him because she needed to share the new theory—it was not yet

evidence or even information, merely an equation she thought she'd seen in the welter of a
wounded father's words—or was she using it
as an excuse to call? If so, was it transparent?
This second adolescence rattling between
her ears, she knew when Davidson answered
she'd be all icy business. Then he'd wonder
what he did wrong. Would he shy away? Just
never—

"Oh, *shut up,*" Anna growled and punched
the numbers. To her relief, the sheriff was out.
She would have a chance to go through the
mental gyrations of a schoolgirl with a crush
all over again at around three-thirty when he
was due back.

"Have him call me," she snapped, then, to
make amends to the innocent deputy who'd
answered the phone, she said the first thing
that popped into her head. "Sorry. I just
dropped the dictionary on my foot." Whether
or not it made any more sense to him than it
did to her, he sounded placated.

For half a minute she stood where she was,
staring down at the smooth wood of the built-
in desk and absently pushing the antique belt
buckle around the way a tot might push a
Matchbox car. Colliding worlds of lust and law
enforcement, personal and professional,
pubescent and menopausal had left her mind
a blank, wiped clean.

"Ah," Anna said as time, place and task
flooded back into her reality. "Barth!"

The ranger did not appear and, rather than
shout again as her grandmother assured her

only fishwives were allowed to do with impunity, Anna stepped out of her office into the long dingy room that housed the coffeepot and the desks of her field rangers.

Barth sat as he had before. Back to her office, head sunk between thick shoulders, he gazed down at the same pile of traffic citations. Assuming he'd not heard her call, Anna started to repeat his name, then she noticed he sat in front of *exactly* the same pile of citations. The ticket defaced with rainwater was on top of the pile, partly hidden by the edge of Barth's meaty hand, right where it had been when Anna'd first come in. Between his thumb and forefinger, as before, was a government issue pen. Either the man was dead, asleep or caught in a time warp.

"Barth!"

He didn't start like a man caught napping. He began to stir slowly, as if her voice reached him through a fog faintly.

With the ponderous movement of the very old or those in pain, he turned his head to look at her. Evidently, there had been a time warp. Anna resisted the urge to check the wall calendar to see if years instead of minutes had elapsed from when she'd first stepped into her office to call Paul till she'd stepped out again to talk with Barth.

Bartholomew Dinkin was close to forty but retained a certain youthfulness. The years had touched him only lightly till today. This noon it looked as if Father Time had clogdanced on his face. His cheeks were dragged down, and red rimmed his lower lids. An ashen hue dulled the skin around his mouth. Alarming as these symptoms might be, the most disturbing lay on the desk in front of him: an untouched bag of Cheetos.

"What's with this office today?" Anna said, tired of other people's problems. "George is in a funk. You've gone catatonic. Is it the water around here? What?"

His baleful gaze rested heavily on her face. In the bleak depths of Barth's translucent eyes, Anna saw no accusation, no attempt to punish or inflict blame—the customary manipulations of the publicly bereft—but sadness so dead it looked like hatred turned inward. Anna had seen it once before, at Carlsbad Caverns, in the eyes of a woman who'd accidentally killed her sister in a climbing accident.

"I guess there is something in the water," she said more kindly. Uninvited, she crossed the small space to lean a hip against the end of his desk. "Do you need to take the rest of the day off or anything? You're looking a little under the weather."

"I don't want time off," he said too quickly, and Anna knew he was fighting some bitter memory. Saying nothing, she leaned, swung her foot. Then a partial answer came to her.

"You were friends with Leo Fullerton," she said. "I was sorry to hear."

Barth looked away but not before Anna saw what she could have sworn was shame in his face. Shame or guilt. Sadness was there, the sorrow of losing a friend, but the emotion wasn't pure. An energy underlay it that belied mere sorrow.

"What?" she demanded.

"He was my pastor," Barth replied. Anger flashed, making his eyes suddenly dangerous. Something wasn't jibing, but Anna chose not to pursue it.

"What are you messing with?" Barth asked, heading off a line of inquiry she'd already abandoned.

Without realizing it, Anna'd carried the Civil War relic she'd been playing with out of the office and continued to fiddle with it while they talked.

"I found it on the Old Trace," she said, and handed him the buckle.

Placed on his wide palm it looked no bigger than a doll accessory. Barth took a magnifying glass out of his desk and studied the brass rectangle carefully. "It's in good condition," he said. "Hardly even scratched. Union. Issued near the end of the war." Flipping it over delicately with the tip of a finger, he scrutinized the back. "Here's an interesting thing. Look here." He handed the buckle and the glass to Anna. She looked where he pointed. The inscription "G.G.35th" had been scratched on neatly with a sharp instrument. "My guess could be General Grant's army thirty-fifth division. Either the supply sergeant scratched it on or the soldier himself did it." Anna was impressed. "Are you a collector?"

Barth shook his head. "When I worked in Tupelo, I did a little curatorial stuff. Went to some training and the like."

"Is it worth anything?" Anna asked.

"It won't be if you keep on messing around with it. You'll scratch it all up. Besides, it's not yours."

"I know that," Anna said, slightly miffed.

Barth took it back and studied it again. "Historically, it would have been of some interest, but since you moved it that's pretty well shot."

Anna took the hit quietly. Barth was right. A relic, out of context, lost much of the information it might have been able to impart to archeologists and historians.

"These aren't that uncommon. I'm not up on my artifacts, but this might get you five, six hundred dollars or thereabouts."

Less than a third of what Jimmy Williams, in his persona of Captain Williams of the Avengers, had offered for it. She told Barth.

"Lemme look." Barth bent over the object. "This on the front is a state seal, the state where the soldier was from. That may make this a more important find. Who's this Jimmy Williams?"

"He's the guy with the mustache who makes that Civil War camp where Pastor Fullerton used to go." Now that the man was dead, it seemed callous to call him just Fullerton or Leo, so Anna accorded him his title.

The pastor's name brought the burden of guilt back to Barth's countenance and Anna was sorry she'd reminded him of whatever it

324

was she'd reminded him of. Maybe he'd missed one too many Sundays in the front pew.

Barth put the magnifying glass back in his desk drawer and set the buckle to one side where Anna couldn't further defile it with her oily little fingers.

"I'll catalog this and pony it up to Tupelo," he said. "Pony" was a term Anna'd only just learned. Road patrol rangers would carry packages to the next district and hand them off to a ranger there, a four-hundred-fifty-mile relay race.

"Re-enactors are usually serious about their hobby. It's funny this Williams would offer to buy a historical artifact off a district ranger."

"Maybe he thought I was crooked," Anna said.

"Or stupid."

"That too."

George Wentworth emerged from his office, nodded to them in lieu of good-bye, and left. His appearance reminded Anna she was in a bit of a hurry.

"I want you to come with me to talk to George's son," she told Barth. "I think he'll be more comfortable with a man, and someone he knows."

This time Anna drove. She needed the distraction and the control that driving afforded. As she told Barth what she had put together and why she wanted to talk to Lockley Wentworth, he grew more silent.

Disapproval radiated off of him in waves, thick and noxious. Anna stood it as long as she could.

"Barth, we're not going down to lynch the kid. I just want to talk to him," she finally said in exasperation.

"Got to talk to him," Barth agreed. "No good way outta that." The oozing morass of disapproval thickened.

Anna wasn't going to give in to it again. She switched the radio to 103 FM, the local station for the newest in boot-scooting and shit-kicking tunes. Lowering her window, she let in the sweet spring air. She took pleasure in the flower-dressed hills and marveled at the towering green graveyards where kudzu had suffocated parts of the forest, covering every inch with a thick, dank carpet of green leaves, a green so dark and voracious as to seem nearly evil.

Several miles north of Hermanville, where George Wentworth lived with his family, Barth broke his self-imposed silence.

"If what you say is true, they're going to pin that girl's murder on him."

"That girl," not Danielle Posey. Humanity had to be expunged before the political battles could be fought.

Anna turned off the radio, rolled up the window. "Who's 'they'? " she asked mildly. "Sheriff Davidson? Me? Chief Ranger Brown?"

"They is *they*," Barth said stubbornly and Anna remembered an exchange from the play *Lenny Bruce* that her husband had acted in.

"*They* is very paranoid, Lenny," Bruce's mother had said.

"They is very powerful, Mama," the comic had replied.

"You don't live in the same world we do," Barth broke into her thoughts. "Maybe it's not better, not worse. I'm not saying that. What I'm saying is, it's not the same. Sure, you hear stories about some middle-class black couple pulled over for nothing and some white cop throwing his weight around, calling 'em nigger or boy or whatever. Maybe you're a nice enough person. You think that's bad news. But it's not your news and you can tuck it away. 'Oh that was a long time ago' or 'there's bad apples in every barrel.'

"Our news is it wasn't a long time ago. And no, it doesn't happen often, just often enough you know it's still out there.

"Something like this comes up and they *want* Lock to be guilty. They *need* Lock to be guilty. The ninety-nine percent of good white folks'll maybe go 'Tsk, tsk.' Come Sunday, there'll be sermons about it. But nobody'll interrupt their day. And *they,* that stinking Posey one percent, that white boy who couldn't keep a job if he stapled it to his shirttail and wants somebody to blame, they'll push till it's a done deal. The truth'll get lost."

"A black jury won't buy it," Anna said.

"By the time it's been to trial, George is broke and Lock's lost what chance he's got to play ball."

Anna had no answer for that. Win or lose, a court trial was devastating to everyone but the lawyers, who in an underpopulated, poor state like Mississippi had to eke out a meager living charging only a hundred dollars an hour instead of the three-seventy-five their big city counterparts commanded. Feeling stung from the lecture, she said: "Life isn't over because you can't play football."

Barth looked at her as if she were from another planet. Football and hunting, not autumn and winter, marked the seasons in the South. Basketball and baseball were just something to pass the other six months till they came around again.

Anna switched back to her own brand of logic. If Danni had been "in love" with Lock, why had she gone to the prom with Brandon? Was it as cold as it seemed? Heather said Danni had taunted the DeForest boy, said she just used him to get to the dance. It could be true. At sixteen, one didn't realize that playing with the feelings of others could have very real and sometimes deadly consequences. Was Danni just toying with the boys? Was Lock Wentworth her "black experience"? Experimentation? A way to get even with her parents, her boyfriend or her brother Mike?

"I think children should go to same-sex convent schools," she said.

Barth said nothing.

Hermanville was east of the Trace and twelve miles south of Rocky Springs. Though Anna's mailing address was Hermanville—the town of Rocky Springs having been defunct for more than a century—she'd never been there. The town, if such a humble scatter of buildings around a crossroads and a single-room post office could be called a town, embodied the Northerner's view of the "real" Mississippi. The gracious homes of Natchez were not in evidence, nor was the classic architecture Anna'd seen in Port Gibson and the city of Clinton. Trailer houses and shacks sat at odd angles to the two-lane road as if they had fallen haphazardly from a passing cargo plane. A juke joint, Mississippi's homegrown version of the local pub—an antiquated building that looked as if it had started out as a beauty salon, passed a chunk of its long life as a storefront church, and finally settled into its dotage as a liquor-purveying establishment— had four cars parked in front of it. Catty-corner from the juke joint was a convenience store, windows blanked with a decade's accumulation of ads and flyers. On the broken concrete steps three young men, appropriately down-and-out, obligingly passed a bottle in a brown paper bag among them to complete the cliché.

If Hermanville could be said to have outskirts, the Wentworth home was on them. George's house was of brick with a tidy yard ringed by majestic pecan trees that predated the house by a hundred years. A kitchen garden, the corn already knee-high, had been planted adjacent to the two-car garage. Wentworth was evidently not one of those men who gives his all only in the workplace. The house, the yard, the garden, the gravel drive were all maintained with scrupulous care.

From what the maintenance head had told her on the tour he'd given her her first day in

Mississippi, Mrs. Wentworth was a bank manager in Jackson. She'd be at work. Knowing depression as she did, Anna figured Lockley would be home. Probably with the shades drawn and the television on.

She was right on both counts.

Lockley Wentworth answered the door clad only in a pair of sweatpants that looked to be in danger of losing the war with gravity. He blinked against the sunlight like an owl dragged out at noon. When he saw who it was, he snatched an old T-shirt from the back of a chair and put it on before coming out onto the porch.

The kid probably wasn't eating right, wasn't sleeping well—hadn't been for days—yet health and strength positively shimmered around him. He was an athlete in the peak of his form and the best of his youth. Muscles moved like wind on a wheat field, rippling his silky skin.

Sleepy, depressed, blinded, Lock moved with grace and precision. Maybe he was destined to be one of the greats: Michael Jordan, Nolan Ryan, Babe Didrikson, Tiger Woods. Before the beauty of his physicality could sway her, Anna brought to mind another roster of athletes. This list started with Mike Tyson, O. J. Simpson, and Mark Gastineau.

"Dad's not here," Lock said, pulling the shirt down to cover a stomach so flat Anna couldn't imagine such venal necessities as liver, pancreas or intestines could be packed within.

On a hunch, she decided to go in quick and

fast. "We're here to see you," she said flatly. "We know you and Danni Posey were lovers." Anna hadn't known, not for sure, but when her words hit Lock and the years dropped away till he looked like a little boy close to tears, she knew it was true. "We know you were with her the night she died." That fact she based on the semen found in the autopsy. If it wasn't DeForest's, Lock was the next likely candidate.

Anna left it at those two statements. She didn't want him to be officially a suspect, and she hadn't enough to arrest anybody at this point. But he didn't know that.

Lock looked from Anna to Barth. Barth kept his face like stone, betraying nothing, not a shard of compassion or pity, though it must have cost him.

Without warning Lock toppled, the movement so sudden, Anna's hand twitched toward her Sig-Sauer. With a groan reminiscent of a tree breaking in a high wind, he fell against the ironwork of ivy leaves and pineapples that supported the porch roof. The framing shook under his weight. He slid down till his butt rested on the flooring. "God, oh God, oh God," he mumbled into his hands.

Anna stepped away and nodded at Barth. Moving ponderously, as if to accentuate his age and nonthreatening qualities, the ranger moved to the steps and sat down several feet from Lockley.

"Talk to me, son," Barth said quietly.

"Dad'll kill me," the young athlete managed. "This'll kill Mom."

Too much death in the sentence for Anna. Maybe the stakes were that high.

"Nobody's killing anybody," Barth said reasonably if not accurately. "Just tell us what happened."

"I killed Danni," Lock said. He didn't uncover his face; the words were forced out past the heels of his hands. "I killed her."

A heaviness came over Anna, a weight so intense she didn't want to go on standing. Duty and common sense wouldn't let her crumple on the welcome mat, so she forced air into her lungs and held her post.

Barth was feeling it too. Anna could see it in the slump of his shoulders and the way his head hung, like the weight of it was too much for his neck.

"What did you hit her with, son? A tire iron?" Barth asked gently.

Lock lowered his hands. He looked hard at Barth and something like anger enlivened his eyes. "I'd never hurt Danni," he said. "Never."

Barth waited and Anna waited.

Lock looked around at the shaded yard, the ancient pecan trees, the mailbox with the sunflower painted on it, as if he'd never seen them before. Or wouldn't be seeing them again for a long time.

"I loved Danni," he said. To Anna it sounded more like he was trying to convince himself than them. For a long time, he didn't say anything else. Anna grew impatient. The misery of children was pushing hard on her mind. She wanted to move, talk, handcuff somebody. Anything to ease that pressure. Shifting her weight to the balls of her feet and resisting the temptation to crack her knuckles, she waited for Barth to handle the situation.

Barth never looked at her. He kept his eyes on the sidewalk between his feet. "It'd be easy to love a girl like Danni Posey," he said after a minute. "She was as pretty as they come."

"I loved her." Lock was beginning to sound obstinate.

"You better tell me about killing her, son. You're going to have to tell somebody sometime. May as well be me now. Here, where we're comfortable."

Lock eased out from the post he'd slid down and scooted his butt over till he sat beside Barth, unconsciously mirroring the older man's pose. After a time had passed to sanctify the new position, he started to talk. Two men on a porch stoop in the spring sunshine. It was as if Anna didn't exist.

Catlike, she crept closer to bear witness but didn't call attention to herself.

"Danni and me met after a game," Lock said. "We'd played Jackson State. Whipped some ass big-time."

"Fifty-three to seven. I remember."

"I was hot that game. I mean I could do no wrong. That ball was *mine.*" Both men rested on that, reliving the glories of the game—or so Anna surmised.

"Girls were all over me afterward. I mean all *over* me. I could have lifted my little finger and had half a dozen hot bitches begging me to do 'em."

Barth just nodded. Anna was glad he was point man. The weight of sorrow was beginning to lift. Having to arrest young Wentworth was looking less odious every minute.

"Then Danni comes in. I didn't know she was no sixteen. She was looking *fine*. Cool as ice. Smilin' and talking like she owned the place. This white girl never been there before. She wasn't tarted up, just cool, you know, in a little yellow dress, linen or nice cotton or something. Kind of stiff and ironed. She doesn't give me a glance." Lock laughed, remembering the courting dance, forgetting the last dance.

"We got to talking after a while and Danni's no rich bitch slumming with the nigger football star. Away from people she was this sweet thing. Almost shy sometimes. Then she goes and does something makes *me* blush, man. One minute she's like a little kid, never been to the big city before. Next minute it's like she grew up in Paris or something. I'd never met anybody like Danni. She just lit me up and smoked me like a good cigar."

Quiet settled again, the men were enjoying the glories of a different game. Anna'd put aside her fantasies of busting Wentworth. When he'd begun talking about Danni, his voice had changed. A note of what sounded like affection and respect wove between the dissonance of the language he used to express himself.

"We got tight pretty fast. Danni liked playing

the mystery woman—wouldn't tell me her last name, where she lived or anything. Said she worked at Victoria's Secret in the Metro Mall."

Barth blew air out through his nostrils, the sort of whuffing noise Taco made when Anna or the cat was particularly stupid. The message must've been the same between men as between species.

"Oh yeah, I could of found out. But it was the *game,* man. I didn't want to know."

Barth nodded again. He could understand that. So could Anna. Mystery, romance, the unseen, the unknown and, most intoxicating, the imagined. While it lasted, it must have been a heady affair for two very young people who'd never been any place more exotic than the watermelon festival in Mize.

A cardinal flitted into the pecans, blood-red and jewel-like. Leaves swallowed him from sight. Anna shifted her weight to keep her feet from going to sleep, not wanting to risk a move that might break the mood.

"Then comes this fucking prom. Danni wants me to take her, so she's got to tell me who she is, right? I find out she's sixteen. Sixteen! A high school kid and she wants to go to the prom and show me off to her girlfriends. 'One of 'em's black,' she tells me. Jesus. Now I'm gonna feel right at home? Shit. And she's *sixteen.* I been boinking a sixteen-year-old! No way I'm going to some fucking high school prom."

That should have been the end of the story: lovers part, hearts are broken, life goes on.

But it wasn't.

"I break up with her, right?"

Lock looked at Barth, who said, "Right."

"Everything's cool. She's callin' me every night telling me about this Brandon guy. How he's Mr. High School Football—like this is going to rack my bones. I'm cool with that. Hey, let her go to her prom. Then she calls me that day. She's gotta see me. So I go pick her up at her house. She's screaming at this shit-for-brains white guy, then up and runs and jumps in my car. It's her brother, and he's jumping around like he's got his dick in a grinder. Danni and me leave. We get it on. She starts in on the prom thing. I tell her I'm not going. She's crying and shit. I take her home."

Not the best love story Anna'd ever heard, but probably one that was a lot more common than the happily-ever-after kind that Danni— like every other American girl—was raised to believe was her God-given right.

Barth looked at Anna and nodded once. Despite their differences, black, white, big, little, male, female, Southerner, Yankee, she'd seldom worked with anybody as seamlessly as she worked with Bartholomew Dinkin. She knew instantly what he meant. In a smooth leap, the dramatic effect only slightly lessened by the fact her legs had grown stiff from standing so long, Anna was over the porch rail and standing on the sidewalk in front of Lock Wentworth.

"So you met her at Rocky Springs and bashed her brains out," Anna said.

Lock jerked as if she were an evil djinn who'd materialized from the center of the Earth.

"No!" he cried out, and she saw the bravado drain from his face. "No!" he said again, and his features began to blur. Tears filled his eyes, spilled down his face. "If I'd gone to the fucking prom, she'd still be alive. I loved Danni," he whispered.

This time Anna almost believed him, but she pressed on: "She called you. You met her. You killed her."

Lock was so deep in his own private hell, he didn't even hear. Or if he did, he was an actor of such a high caliber that he was wasted on football.

"Tell us what happened on prom night," Barth said gently. Anna stepped back and to the side. If Lock suddenly dropped the tears and innocence and made a run for it, she didn't want to be in his way. The beefy young quarterback would go through her as if she were made of straw.

"She begged me to go," he mumbled. "*Begged* me, and I just blew her off. She told me she was going to go with her old boyfriend. I said fine. I mean, who cares? She wants to go to the fucking prom that bad, she can go. Then next day she turns up killed. Sometimes Danni was downright stupid, I mean a fucking idiot. She probably blabbed about her and me and he killed her. He fucking *killed* her."

Tears were still flowing. Maybe they'd

337

started out as grief or guilt, but they'd heated up. Now they were tears of anger. Wentworth was clenching and unclenching his hands. Anna could see the strength in them as the muscles bunched in his forearms.

"Danni said she was coming to see you," she said coldly. "She met you and you smashed her skull so she wouldn't interfere with your journey to the Football Hall of Fame. Like a cracker like you would ever make it in the pros." Anna had no idea whether "cracker" was color specific. Maybe only whites could be crackers. Her aim was to rattle him. She succeeded.

In a lightning move that must have wowed them on the field, he swung a roundhouse left and smashed his fist into the cast-iron railing with such force that the entire porch rang with the reverberations. He was on his feet, glaring down at Anna. Tears were gone. Anger turned cold and aged his face. Under the threat of his bulk and youth, Anna's neck felt as fragile as a flower stalk, her arms like matchsticks. Loosening her locked muscles, she prepared to move quickly.

"You're dying to pin this on me, aren't you? Let that lily-white bastard waltz on up to Ole Miss and pretend to play football so his daddy can brag at the Rotary. I didn't kill Danni. If she said she was meeting me, she was lying. I never went nowhere that night. Never met nobody."

Barth was standing too, though Anna'd not seen him get up. "Easy, Lock," he said. "Nobody's pinning anything on anybody.

Just tell us where you were that night. That's all you gotta do."

"I was in my dorm room at Alcorn," he said. The fire went out of him as quickly as it had flared up. He let Barth put a hand on his shoulder and ease him back down till he sat again on the step.

"You got a roommate?" Barth asked.

"Oh shit." Stark terror flitted across the football player's face, chased by what looked to be despair. "He wasn't there," he said dully. "He went home that weekend to go to his cousin's wedding."

Stillness, deeper and richer for the agitated racket that had preceded it, settled around the three of them. Overhead, in the boughs of the pecans, squirrels scuffled. A car passed, bound for the metropolis of Hermanville.

"You going to arrest me or what?" Lock was looking at Anna.

Halfway through this interview, she'd been convinced Lockley committed the murder. Now she was more or less of the opinion that he didn't. What had changed her mind wasn't the tears, the anger or the protestations of love. It was the fear she'd seen when he realized his roommate hadn't been there, that there was no one to vouch for the fact that he'd been tucked up in his dorm room all night like he claimed. If Lock had murdered Danni, he would have known no one could alibi him, he would have been prepared for the question. The possibility that he was acting still existed, but Anna doubted this volatile young man was the Laurence Olivier of the gridiron.

"We didn't come here to arrest you," she said, as if she hadn't just accused him of murder half a dozen times. "We just wanted to talk with you. You said Danni's ex-boyfriend killed her. Tell us about that."

Wentworth made a few stabs at it, but it rapidly became clear that he had nothing to add to what they already knew. He just figured DeForest for the killer because he'd been Danni's date and because, though he wouldn't admit to it, the other boy was a rival.

Anna asked if he knew anything against DeForest, the kind of cheating or violence that might be known in high school or sports circles but that wouldn't necessarily come to the attention of authority. Lock wanted to say something against DeForest, but the only thing he could dredge up was that Danni'd said DeForest was a practical joker and the jokes weren't always all that funny to the victims.

Anna was impressed Lock didn't succumb to the temptation to make something up about the other boy.

After the usual mutterings that boiled down to "Thanks for your time" and "Don't leave town anytime soon," Anna went back to the patrol car. Barth stayed behind, said he wanted a private word with young Wentworth.

Anna'd almost given up on finding anything on the radio to listen to besides country or Christian when Barth rejoined her. "What was that about?" she asked as he buckled his large person into the passenger seat.

"Nothing official. I just told him to clean

up that mouth of his. There's no call for that kind of language in front of a lady. Or even a female ranger. And I told him if he doesn't get off the pity-pot and get back in school, then you're going to be right; he doesn't have what it takes to make it in the pros and he might as well just move on up into the Delta and get himself a job gutting catfish at the factory for all the good he is."

Anna started the car and cranked up the air-conditioning. Summer was breathing down April's neck. "That kid's a briar patch of emotions," she said. "Guilt, fear, insecurity, pride, anger. I don't suppose you suggested he see a psychologist for a while?"

"He doesn't need therapy," Barth said succinctly. "He needs to play ball."

"Guilt is a cunning and powerful adversary," Anna said. "Maybe more powerful than pigskin."

Barth, who'd been dragged out of whatever doldrums he'd sailed into by working with Lockley Wentworth, went into relapse. Anna could see him change as clearly as if the word "guilt" had opened a stopcock and the juice was draining out of him. In the few minutes it took to regain the Trace, he was looking lumpy, partially deflated, his hands between his knees and his strange gray-green eyes focused about ten inches in front of the windshield.

Anna pushed her mind back to what they'd been talking about before the Wentworth interview. It seemed a very long time ago, though less than two hours had passed by the clock. Mississippi, with her soft air and scented breezes, unraveled time at night and melted it during the days. Had she been living among the magnolias, egrets, kudzu and possums, Anna felt she could have synchronized her body clock to that of Mother Nature. But since she'd rolled into Claiborne County, her time was divided between cars and talk, neither of which was conducive to getting in touch with the Earth's rhythms.

Leo Fullerton, the Baptist preacher who'd suicided by VW engine, was Barth's pastor. That was the news that had knocked the stuffing out of her ranger. Guilt had come to Anna's mind before. It was back now. *What the hell,* she thought. *He doesn't much like me anyway.*

"Why are you feeling guilty over Pastor Fullerton's suicide?" she asked bluntly.

Barth looked at her, a new energy in his face. Dared she hope it was a spark of respect? Before he answered her—and she could have sworn he was going to—the spark was doused with distrust. Maybe he'd suddenly remembered she wasn't from around there. "You don't know what you're talking about," he said, and Anna knew she'd get nothing more out of him. At least not by being straightforward and aboveboard.

Thigpen's patrol car was parked in front of the ranger station. Anna felt her shoulders tensing and forced herself to relax. If he was going to wage a war of nerves, then she would be nerveless. Maybe she was overreacting. He had, after all, done nothing overt. And he'd responded quickly when she called regarding the alligator. It was possible the conspiracy to leave her in the lurch over the Posey/Doolittle car stop was a one-time thing.

Unaware she did so, Anna snorted. Thigpen gave her that cringing, sly feeling incompetents in denial always engendered. In government service, she'd felt it enough times to trust her instincts.

Randy was at his desk. The air was redolent with cigarette smoke. He was of immoderate good cheer. It made Anna wonder what he'd been up to. "Hey," he said, a grin growing out from beneath his brush of a mustache. "It's the Bobbsey Twins. You two are getting pretty cozy."

"Hey, Randy," Anna said. Sexual innuendo was the cheapest—and unfortunately the most effective—weapon in the malcontent arsenal. Barth could field this one. He was the man with the wife and family. Anna glanced covertly his way as she passed his desk, but he was still lumpy and deflated and had no interest in his officemate's chatter.

Anna cut between Thigpen and the coffee machine to visit the ladies' room. Never before had a female worked in Port Gibson, not in maintenance, not as a ranger. There were no facilities. In deference to Anna's gender, half the men's room had been partitioned off. She had two sinks, three stalls and four urinals all to herself. She enjoyed the privacy of the ladies' room so much that though she'd sworn, in her exalted position as a GS-11 district ranger, she would maintain an open-door policy, when she slithered from the privacy of the loo to the privacy of her office, she shut the door. A moment was dedicated to thanking the Trace architect who'd deemed a private office for the Port Gibson ranger a necessity. Guadalupe Mountains and Mesa Verde had left the district ranger plunked down among the hoi polloi.

Breathing deeply of the serenity of her eight-foot-square solitude, she punched the button on the answering machine to see what the rest of the afternoon held in the way of entertainment.

Sheriff Davidson called, said he'd had an interesting talk with Mike and Fred Posey. He'd fill her in later. Chief Ranger John Brown left a message asking her to call. His voice was clipped, empty, the sort of voice Sister Vionney used when she said: "Anna, Sister Mary Corine would like to see you in her office." Never a good omen. Anna had been on the Trace only a few days. She wondered what she could possibly have screwed up in so short a time.

Putting off both calls for entirely different reasons, she radioed Frank, the maintenance man at Rocky. He'd agreed to check on Taco, and Anna'd left her door unlocked. If her hunch was right, the place had already been weighed and found wanting by local criminals. She doubted they would break in a second time.

Unless it had been her they'd come looking for.

Taco was depressed, Frank said, the censure heavy in his voice. A woman's place was in the home, caring for her children, furred or unfurred.

Anna thanked him and promised she'd be back to Rocky soon.

"That cat's looking after him," Frank said, not letting her off so easily. "Cat can't look after a dog." Anna signed off, feeling as if she'd left her three-year-old to take care of a heart patient and now everybody with a radio knew what a rotten mom she was.

Fatigue settled like dust and with it an overwhelming urge to talk to her sister. It was five-thirty New York time. Maybe she would still catch her at the clinic. With a guilty glance at the door, she made a personal call on government time.

Nancy, the woman who had been Molly's receptionist for thirteen years and still treated Anna like a stranger, put her on hold. Half a minute later, Molly picked up.

Anna didn't even bother to ask any polite questions about the wedding, the weather or work. She wanted to talk. And she did. The sheriff, the football player, the suicide, the pornography at Clinton pullout, Barth's weirdness, Randy's hatefulness, Taco's gimpiness. It all poured out. She ended by telling how glad she'd been when Barth seemed to be coming around, how disappointed she felt over the big man's withdrawal.

"I wasn't just glad he was maybe going to be my friend, I was pathetically glad. It's so warm here, so moist, so scented. I think my backbone has begun to soften, grow fungi."

Molly said nothing for a moment, and Anna noted with satisfaction that the telltale shush of air—Molly sucking in a lungful of smoke—wasn't there. Maybe her near-death experience the previous summer would really keep her off cigarettes.

"Not enough estrogen," the psychiatrist said at last. "Without it bones get brittle, tissues shrivel, thinking processes grow sluggish."

Anna let the diagnosis sink in. "Perimenopause?" she said, confused. "Surely I've got a few years left."

"Not estrogen in your body, estrogen in your life. Where are the women down there? Barefoot and pregnant? No women rangers, maintenance, no secretaries, nurses, receptionists? The Trace sounds like a boys' club."

"There are women," Anna said. "But they're all in Tupelo. In administration."

"Where are they in—what's it? Port Gimlet?"

"Gibson. Probably in church."

"You'd better find yourself a place in the pew," Molly laughed. "Without women to talk to, the mind begins to play tricks."

Molly had to go. She was meeting Frederick at La Guardia. The FBI agent had established a regular commute between Chicago and New York to be with Anna's sister. Though Anna was unreservedly in favor of the relationship, she hung up feeling worse than when she'd called.

Lonely. That was it. In the twelve-step meetings she'd long since abandoned, they preached HALT: Never let yourself become too Hungry, Angry, Lonely or Tired. Anna was all of the above, and sure as hell, she wanted a drink.

Paul Davidson's message gave her the perfect excuse for calling him.

Lonely.

She was vulnerable. It would be akin to grocery shopping when she was starving. She dialed the chief ranger's number instead.

"Hi, it's Anna, what's up?" she said when he came on the line.

"I'm glad you called, Anna. I need to talk with you," Brown said in the measured tones of a man restating the obvious, not to buy time, but to lay the groundwork for some unpleasant revelation. Anna felt that clench in the pit of her stomach that is learned in childhood and never quite goes away.

"Shoot," she said.

"I got a complaint about you today. It was faxed to my office. One of your rangers is saying you are showing favoritism based on race and age."

"It's either Barth or Randy," Anna said. "I've only got two rangers."

"You know I can't divulge the name of the complainant in a whistle-blowing situation," Brown said, and he sounded as tired as Anna felt.

"Race and age?"

"Race and age."

"I've only been here a week, I must have been busier than I thought." Anna was being flippant. She knew it was juvenile and counterproductive. Humor had no place in bureaucracy, especially not when the terrifying specter of a lawsuit was raised. Brown breathed heavily into the phone, undoubtedly willing her not to make this any harder than it had to be. Momentarily she was tempted to apologize and treat the matter with the sincere concern it damn well did not deserve. This was Randy making a preemptive strike. Or just being a pain in the ass because he had too much time on his hands, his wife had left him or his hemorrhoids had flared up.

"How is this racism and ageism said to manifest?" she asked. She made a modest effort to alter her tone so it wouldn't sound snippy or snotty, but the attempt failed.

Brown, bless his mature and experienced heart, ignored it. "There's a few, but the major complaint is preferential scheduling. This individual claims that you have scheduled him to work less desirable shifts and that you have done this in a prejudicial manner because of this individual's age and skin color."

Anna had seen the destruction lawsuits caused, the loss of health and money and jobs and promotions, not because the accused was guilty, but because the legal process was punitive. Innocence, even if proved, didn't change the lawyers' fees and the stain that was left on the minds of those who heard only the accusations, who believed where there was smoke there was fire. But Randy had chosen to attack her on the basis of scheduling.

Relief softened her voice and she responded to the chief ranger like a grown-up. "I've been remiss on the scheduling," she said. "The murder has taken up so much of my time, I never got around to redoing the schedule. Both of my rangers are still working the schedule that Steve Stilwell had them on when he was acting district ranger."

"Can you prove that?" Brown asked hopefully.

Anna was relieved that he seemed to be on her side.

"I can ask Steve," she said.

"Do that. Document everything. This individual—and you've got a good idea who I'm talking about—has been a—"

Anna thought he was going to say "pain" or "headache" or "thorn," but Brown was too well trained. "A problem in several areas. He wants an early retirement. He's tried to get a medical retirement, and this isn't the first complaint he's made. He's threatened suit seven times and sued twice over one thing and another."

Anna felt as if she'd just been given an adder for a bedmate. "Nightmare," she said.

"Velvet gloves," Brown warned. "Velvet gloves and document everything."

After hanging up, Anna went through the schedule. The only bit of time Randy had put in that wasn't Steve's doing was a wildlife disturbance call that dispatch had sent him out on. He'd gone on duty two hours before he was scheduled. The assisting agency listed was Fisheries and Wildlife. Anna was on solid ground. Much good that would do her in a lawsuit.

Fifteen minutes till quitting time. She decided to sit it out doing nothing, staring at the clock. It was all she felt up to. At five of five the phone rang. For three rings she watched it suspiciously. On the fourth, she answered.

"Hey, it's Stilwell," came a light and breezy voice. The district ranger in Ridgeland: a nontoxic soul with good hair and kind eyes.

"Just the man I needed to talk to," she said.

"Want to do it over dinner? I can meet you in Clinton. I hear there's a four-star Taco Bell on the corner of I-20 and Springridge Road."

An errant thought, one that had been nagging at the edges of her mind, surfaced. "How about meeting me at the Clinton pullout," she countered. "Business before gorditas."

"In uniform or out?"

"Out."

"With Scotch or without?"

"With."

Anna hung up. The sexy sheriff would have to wait till her hormone level returned to that befitting a professional woman in her middling years.

At Rocky Springs Anna changed into Levi's and, in honor of her first dinner date in Mississippi, a teal blue silk shirt that was not only clean but ironed. She cared for Taco and Piedmont then, guilt as heavy upon her heart as the crippled dog's brown eyes were on the back of her neck, abandoned them once again.

Day had slipped into evening. A clogging heat mellowed to liquid breezes that didn't so much blow as saunter through the tops of the cornfields, running loving fingers through leaves too green to be of this world. Red clover on the banks of the road turned from carmine to blood in the angled light, and the wisteria glowed as if lit from within. Only in nature could the red and yellow and lavender coexist in such harmony. On a scarf or a dress, the colors would have clashed. Alive, they enhanced one another's beauty.

To either side of the road, tucked between acres of forest land, were cleared fields. Cattle and horses, hides iridescent with sunlight and high living, were scattered about as if placed by a talented photographer creating a postcard of pastoral peace.

Beauty soothed Anna as always. After years of being a law enforcement ranger, anonymity soothed her as well. She was just a middle-aged lady in a Rambler. Speeders were none of her concern. Lost tourists wouldn't flag her down. Bored visitors wouldn't buttonhole her with tedious stories. Malcontents wouldn't pour complaints into her ears.

By the time she rolled into the Clinton pullout, she had lost her taste for park business, but such was the force of habit, it never crossed her mind to simply laugh, drink Stilwell's Scotch and let unanswered questions lie.

Two vehicles were already there, a white 1997 Honda Accord with Hinds County tags and a mint-condition cherry-red 1949 Dodge pickup truck with chrome bumpers. In each of them sat a lone man stalwartly not looking at anything but the blank wall of trees beyond the picnic table. As Anna was parking next to the pickup, the Honda backed out and left. Through the Rambler's open window, Anna could see Steve lounging behind the wheel of the truck. He didn't look at her till she was standing on the passenger side of his vehicle, her hands on the door.

"Hey. It's you," he said. "I was afraid to look. If you'd been much later, I'd've been in grave danger of losing my manly virtue. Hop in."

Anna did, and he passed her the Scotch bottle. She took a swig. The stuff was foul-tasting, but the activity was comradely.

"How so your manly virtue?" she asked, admiring the exquisite detail in which the interior of the vintage truck had been restored. No street rod for Stilwell. Anna was willing to bet the engine in the old truck was, if not the original, at least manufactured in 1949.

"That guy in the Honda made two trips to the woods," Steve said, as if that explained things. "It was all I could do to stay behind the wheel."

Anna was mystified but not sufficiently intrigued to play along with Stilwell's riddles. "Come on," she said. "I want to show you something."

Steve got out of the truck, the Scotch bottle held by the neck, swinging loose in his right hand.

"When you do it, you look raffish and collegiate," Anna remarked. "If I did it, I'd look like a skid row drunk."

"It's a talent," he admitted modestly. "Openly enjoying wickedness is sufficiently rare these days as to pass for a brand of innocence."

At that moment, Anna liked Stilwell so much she nearly told him. "This way," she said and followed one of the social trails into the tangled woods.

"If you're planning a picnic, let's go to the city dump," Stilwell said from behind her. "This place is AIDS Central."

Anna had stopped in the midst of the tissue and condom bushes. "This is it. What the hell is it? There was a pornographic picture stuck up on that tree with a note: 'Follow Me.' "

"Yuck. What a mess," Stilwell looked around, both arms held high, keeping his hands—or more likely his Scotch—above the level of the contamination. "This has gotten bad. Tell George, and he'll send his guys in to clean it out. They'll bitch and moan but... yuck!"

"You knew this was here?" Anna asked.

"Can we talk about it somewhere else? Microbes are crawling up my pantleg. I just felt one go over the top of my sock."

353

Back in the pristine cab of Steve's truck, fortified by another swallow of the communal Scotch that Anna could tell wouldn't taste half bad in another shot or two, she realized what Steve had meant with his cryptic comments about his manly virtue and the threatened compromise thereof. It made sense when taken with the local cars, parked here after work, each empty or containing a lone male occupant.

"This is a homosexual trysting place," she said.

"Yes and no." Steve sipped his booze, said "single malt" and went on. "There's several hot spots on the Trace. Here, some north. I've busted a few. You know, the usual charge: disturbing the peace. Though, the way I look at it, I'm the one doing the disturbing of the piece. There's strong feeling against it in these parts. Had a guy up in Tennessee at one of the pull-outs come on to two good old boys. They beat the poor bastard to death. The verdict was accidental death. Seems they accidentally hit him about twenty-eight times. *Strong* feeling against it. We've run some sting operations. Tupelo wanted to run one down here with me as the bait."

Anna raised an eyebrow.

"What? You don't think I'm cute enough?" He cocked his head. Salt and pepper locks fell over his forehead. Stilwell was definitely cute enough.

"I declined. Not my bag. Out of sight, consenting adults. Let the chiggers get 'em is my motto."

"A benevolent soul," Anna said.

"I like to think so. But back to homosexuals. These guys don't think of themselves as gay or homosexual. They're upstanding pillars of the community with wives and families who stop off—and every man of 'em claims it's the first time they've ever done it, naturally—for stress relief. That's how they see themselves."

"I wish they wouldn't litter," Anna said, and Stilwell laughed.

"Tell George. That's his area."

Warmed by the Scotch and the good humor, Anna trotted out the day's slings and arrows.

"I'll back you on the schedule issue," he promised. "But Randy's trouble. The proverbial bad apple. He's on a lot of people's bad sides. He never gave me any problem."

"Why? Because you're white and male?"

"Careful," Stilwell cautioned. "Paranoia is the single most contagious of all the mental illnesses. Did you know that? Nope, he didn't give me any trouble because I was just acting district ranger, just passing through. There was nothing to get out of me, so he opted for asskissing. Never know whose ass is suddenly going to appear right above your lips on the ladder to success." The Scotch was beginning to kick in. Anna didn't mind. She took another swallow to catch up.

"I'll be careful," she promised. She told him about the suicide of Leo Fullerton, and he voiced the niggling suspicions that had been dancing in her head like poisonous sugar plums.

"Fullerton. He was one of the guys in the campground the night of your murder, wasn't he?"

Anna mildly resented Danni Posey being labeled her murder, but she said yes.

"Fishy?" Stilwell thought aloud. "A man's there. A girl's killed. A man commits suicide. Coincidences do happen but... fishy."

"One does wonder, don't one?" Anna said. "We've got no proof it was suicide. Fullerton, Pastor Fullerton, is presumably on the bottom of the Big Black river with a Volkswagen bus transmission shackled around his ankles—"

"What year?"

"I don't know what year."

"Could be worth something."

"Anyway, no suicide note. Just the word of his two buddies, also at Rocky Springs the night of the Posey murder."

"You think he might be tied into the girl's death?"

"Makes me nervous is all." They pondered over another round of Scotch. Drinking from the bottle, passing it back and forth in the cab of an antique pickup truck, created a mood of timelessness, of grassroots, round-the-campfire humanity. Anna felt utterly at home, a sensation she'd been missing since she'd accepted the promotion to the district ranger position in Mississippi.

"Was Pastor Fullerton connected in anyway to the Poseys?" Steve asked. Dusk had crept out of the woods and was caressing the truck. He turned the key and switched on the radio, his only concession to modern automotive luxury. The station featured oldies, very oldies, Fats Domino singing "Blueberry Hill" in a voice as rich as Mississippi mud.

"No connection I know of," Anna said. "Sheriff Davidson left me a report a day or two ago. He'd talked with the Poseys. No church connection. No schools, hunting camp, social club that jumped out at me. I'll ask again, given the new developments. I was thinking maybe Fullerton knew something. Saw something he shouldn't have, and his comrades-in-arms shut him up, but Paul said—" Anna hesitated a moment, feeling the odd and pleasurable sensation of saying the "boyfriend's" name out loud. The Scotch was kicking in in her brainpan as well. "Paul said the three of them were near and dear, boyhood pals."

"We mostly get offed by family and friends," Steve said philosophically. "Murder's like Christmas, people seem to want to be with their loved ones when it comes around."

"Williams—one of the two pals in question—said he'd gotten a call from Fullerton saying he was going swimming with the VW engine and rushed to the pastor's aid too late to save him. If it was murder, my money's on Williams. Who else?"

"Hey. Do alligators eat carrion?" Stilwell asked suddenly. "I wonder if the pastor will be munched."

Anna didn't know much about the culinary habits of alligators. "They like dogs," she offered.

"Maybe they taste like chicken." Their conversation was sliding gently into the Scotch bottle. That was okay by Anna.

"If Fullerton was murdered because he saw something and he was murdered by Williams—always go with the obvious is my motto—then did Williams have any connection to the Posey girl?" she asked.

"Can't help you there. Getting hungry?"

"I could eat," Anna said. "Taco Bell?"

"Better than that," Steve said as if better than Taco Bell was pretty doggone hard to imagine. "I am a man of many talents." Bending his wiry frame into intriguing shapes, he reached over the back of the seat and fished around. Finally he emerged with a paper sack, the top rolled to keep the contents from escaping.

"You cooked?" Anna was impressed.

"I constructed," Stilwell corrected her. "Cooking is a modest art compared to that of engineering the perfect sandwich."

By the light of the April moon they dined on peanut-butter-and-jelly sandwiches and Scotch and listened to the rising chorus of frogs and golden hits from the thirties, forties and fifties on 93.9 FM. Afterward they drank coffee from a thermos Steve had under the seat. Coffee, lacking the insouciance of alcohol, was dispensed in separate but equal cups.

Business was laid to rest. They didn't so much talk as swap stories, funny stories. As often as not, stories in which the teller was the butt of the joke. Anna could not have planned a more perfect evening. When the disk jockey announced it was ten of ten, she was amazed. Surely time had stopped the moment the truck door closed. The rude interjection of the clock reminded Stilwell he had to be up at four-thirty to get to Tupelo in time for a seven-thirty class he was taking on agricultural methods.

He waited till Anna was safe in her Rambler, then drove off, the guttural roar of the pickup's engine recalling a time when power was new and raw and had moving parts.

Not ready yet to start the forty-minute drive to Rocky, Anna sat behind the wheel of her car and closed her eyes, letting the rau-cous celebration of night sounds swirl in her head. On the mesas of southern Colorado, night was a time of stillness. Predators moved with stealthy grace, quiet as shadows. Birds ceased singing. Cicadas hushed their clatter. Com-pared with that, Mississippi could have been the template for Maurice Sendak's *In the Night Kitchen*. It sounded as if all manner of strange things had come out to play.

In this fecund matrix of mating frogs, pol-linating bats, creeping kudzu, things procre-ating, eating and being eaten, growing and dying, where even the stars lost their distant and pristine coldness to hang close to the Earth, as integrated into the frenzy as the fireflies that blinked their need in the cloaking scrub, Anna's mind turned on the men that, in their need, risked family, position and dis-ease to relieve themselves with strangers in her woods. And litter during the process.

What pressures built in them that brought

them here? Did they sit at their desks in offices, feeling dull and lonely? Did they worry about mortgages and braces for the kids, then, feeling overwhelmed and afraid, turn their thoughts to the end of the day, to excitement with a stranger, a sense of freedom and physical comfort for a moment? Did it matter what the strangers looked like, or just that they were strangers? Did they talk? What if it turned out to be someone they knew? Was there shame or a secret shared?

The phenomenon had to be emotionally costly. Secret lives, though they paid dividends in thrills, had a nasty habit of growing as burdensome as the life they had been constructed to escape from. To keep the payoff coming, stakes had to be constantly raised, new risks taken.

It was an area where Anna's knowledge was, at best, secondhand. To arrest an addict did not require an understanding of the mechanics of addiction. That was Molly's stomping grounds.

Her mind drifted, taking her back to when she'd first had an inkling of the humble pullout's kinkier aspects. Barth had been driving. He'd turned in. He'd said... what? Anna searched for his exact words. "Clinton pullout's kind of a problem area."

When he said that, Anna had assumed an explanation would be forthcoming, but that hadn't been the case. Barth suddenly shut down, told her the cars belonged to nonexistent joggers and sped away as if pursued. The next day he'd been distracted, depressed and, unless her instincts failed her, acting guilty as sin. Was Barth gay? Or whatever these guys who littered the public's little patch of woods were? Barth had a wife and children, but that was meaningless. According to Steve, this particular brand of park visitor lived the rest of his life as a practicing heterosexual right down to procreation and probably homophobia.

Barth as a frequenter of homosexual trysting grounds didn't fit. For one thing, in his own district, he would be far too recognizable. Besides, he hadn't gotten weird till after they'd driven into the parking lot in front of the picnic table. That's when he'd changed. And stayed changed.

Anna sat up straight, rubbed the encroaching sleep from her face and scrubbed her fingernails through her cropped hair to stimulate thought.

It was the truck. There'd been three cars and a truck at the pullout when she and Barth had driven through. The truck had a rebel flag on the bumper with the words HERITAGE, NOT HATE stenciled across the bottom.

"Oh shit," Anna whispered. She knew why Fullerton was dead. And she knew why Barth Dinkin had donned a hair shirt.

15

Guilt decreed that Anna stretch out on the Navajo rug in front of the cold stove and spend some quality time with Taco, the crippled wonder dog. Scotch and the sandman ambushed her there. She awoke just before dawn aching in most places a body can ache. There had been a time she'd been able to spring up mightily from a night on a hard floor—or a time creative memory insisted she had—but during the intervening years her bones had become cantankerous.

She made coffee and drank it in the shower, trusting the heat within and the heat without to melt the precocious rigor mortis and restore a semblance of life.

The precarious optimism lent by hot water and coffee was threatened when, on leaving, she found a paper sack on the top of her patrol vehicle. Inside were the dismembered parts of some small animal, probably a squirrel. Grim and chilling images of *The Godfather* and waking up with the severed head of a horse in one's bed were stirring her hackles to the vertical when she discovered the note. "Went squirrel hunting. Nothing like good red meat for a sick dog. Frank."

On her way out, Anna thanked the maintenance man for the thoughtful gift, then surreptitiously dumped it in the garbage can in the tiny visitor's center, careful to bury it beneath a layer of other refuse so Frank wouldn't inadvertently see it and get his feelings hurt when he collected the trash.

Barth was already at the ranger station by the time Anna arrived. Randy wasn't due on duty till four P.M. That suited Anna just fine. It galled her to feel driven from her space by one of her own rangers, but she'd lived with wormwood and gall off and on since joining the park service. Unlike some, she'd never developed a taste for the bitterness. Long ago she'd promised herself, should she burn out, begin to grow bitter, she'd quit and get a job waiting tables or welding.

Sitting at his desk, Barth had the look of a man who needed a good night's sleep, but when he looked up at her, his eyes were clear and his face animated. Either he'd recovered his equilibrium in the aftermath of Fullerton's death or he'd found something to distract himself with.

It turned out to be the latter.

Books and magazines were spread over his desk. On a scrap of clean folded cotton was the buckle Anna had picked up on the Old Trace.

"Looks like you might of stumbled on an important find," Barth said with the excitement of a born curator watching history materialize as a hologram trapped in a fragment from another time.

Anna had much on her mind and none of it had to do with the accoutrements of dead

363

soldiers, but as she knew the topic she would introduce was going to be painful, she gave Barth her attention. Pinching the brass buckle delicately between thumb and forefinger, he held it up for her to look at but not to touch.

"See the engraving there, that round etching?"

Anna peered dutifully at the artifact, but though she was still in denial about it, her ability to see tiny things was nowhere near what it once had been. "Uh-huh," she said.

"Here." Impatiently Barth plucked the magnifying glasses off his nose and pushed them into her hands.

Anna put them on. "Yes. Right. An eagle-y thing and OVI. Cool." She had no idea what it meant but didn't want to be a wet blanket.

"Some of the regiments stamped or engraved identifying marks on their equipment. Sort of a precursor to today's dog tags. That way they could tell what regiment or squad a man had belonged to even if his face was unrecognizable—as in the case of damage from the war itself or because the body was either not found or not recovered before the animals got at it. There was a detachment sent out by General Grant to Port Gibson. Five men, handpicked. It was in Vicksburg just before Grant pulled out. The whole detachment vanished. Nobody knew if Grant changed his orders, they got lost in the confusion of the next campaign, they went AWOL or what, but they never reported back to Vicksburg."

"I heard that story," Anna said. "Bits of it anyway."

"I think this buckle belonged to one of the men from the lost squadron. They were all from Ohio. They'd been together since the start of the war. Three of them were brothers. That was what some thought, they got fed up and headed home to Ohio early. This here's an Ohio state seal: OVI, Ohio Volunteer Infantry. There's a lot of boys from Ohio fought down here, but this may be something."

This time when Anna said "cool," she meant it.

Barth damped her enthusiasm by adding: "When you moved it, much of its historical value was lost of course, but it's still the first concrete piece of evidence that those soldiers passed this way on their road to wherever."

"I can show you exactly where I found it," Anna defended herself.

"It's not the same." Barth replaced the buckle on the cotton cloth and redeemed his reading glasses from Anna.

She remembered what she'd come to talk about and settled herself in Randy Thigpen's chair, facing Barth over the littered expanse of the old wooden desks.

"That night you and I went to the Clinton pullout," Anna said without preamble. "A truck was parked there, a new Dodge with a rebel flag on the bumper. I saw the truck before in Rocky Springs campground. The truck belonged to Leo Fullerton, didn't it?"

Barth looked up from his catalogs of war paraphernalia. He took the reading glasses off and placed them neatly to one side. After a pause so long Anna thought he wasn't going to answer her, he said: "Pastor Fullerton is dead. Why don't we let him rest in peace?"

It was not in Anna's plan to wantonly besmirch the memory of the beloved pastor. "The man's personal life is only of importance to me insofar as it has an impact on the park," Anna said. "I couldn't care less if the guy was gay. But he was at Rocky the night Danni Posey was murdered. Then he shows up dead, a suicide without a suicide note, reported by his two buddies who also happen to have been camped at Rocky Springs on prom night. The good pastor has a convenient history of depression. It crossed my mind that his late-night swim with a piston engine was not by choice, that he didn't kill himself but was hustled off to greener pastures by Williams and McIntire for reasons that would be of interest to me. So if Leo Fullerton had a reason to kill himself, a reason he might very well not want to explain in a note, I need to know it."

Barth picked up the glasses again and studied them as if they might have acquired a hidden historical nuance since their days on the rack at Wal-Mart.

Finally he quit fiddling and looked at Anna. "It was the pastor's truck," he said.

"Could he have been there for some other reason?" Anna asked.

"I've seen it there before once or twice," Barth admitted. "Those times I recognized it before turning in and just went on by. I didn't want him to know I knew."

"You think this time maybe he saw us?"

Barth nodded. His luminous eyes clouded. He stared over Anna's shoulder, his eyes wide, knowing if he blinked the tears would fall and she would see them. To give him time, Anna rose, turned her back and poured herself a cup of coffee she didn't want. By the time she reclaimed Thigpen's seat, Barth was again dry-eyed, a man among men.

"You think Fullerton would kill himself because you knew he frequented a homosexual trysting place?"

"I'm a member of his flock," Barth replied simply.

"Seems like overkill," Anna said and instantly regretted the literal application of the cliché.

"You haven't any way of knowing what that kind of gossip would do down here. It'd be like his good work never happened. He must've figured if he just took himself out then the church he'd built would go on, not be torn apart while he was being torn apart."

"You wouldn't have told anyone," Anna said. "Not only would it be generally ratty but, given your position, unethical."

"He couldn't have known that," Barth said.

"And you've been feeling guilty, thinking us stumbling on the pastor in his moment of weakness drove him to suicide."

Barth said nothing. He was getting that drippy, fogged look again. "Well that's a crock," Anna said sharply. "Maybe we were the straw that broke the camel's back, but that camel must have already been carrying quite a load. If it hadn't been us day before yesterday, it would have been somebody else—something else—tomorrow. Quit worrying about it."

Barth blinked. "That's it? Quit worrying about it?"

"That's it."

For a moment he stared at her, then he laughed. "I thought us having a lady DR we were going to have our feelings validated, get us a more interactive management style."

Glad to see he hadn't shut her words out entirely, Anna smiled. "Group hugs tomorrow at oh-eight-hundred," she said and pushed back from Randy's desk. "Could you talk to George today? Tell him about us meeting with Lock, so he won't think we're sneaking behind his back. And see if he knows anything."

Two more messages from Sheriff Davidson were waiting on the machine in her office. Anna dialed the sheriff's office, chagrined to realize her wayward thought processes had already committed the man's work number to memory. The sheriff was in and, to Anna's relief, apparently felt no awkwardness engendered by the kiss. He was warm, sounded pleased to hear from her and went straight to business as it was business hours.

Leo Fullerton's body had been recovered. Both ankles were tied together and then tethered to the VW bus transmission. Anna hadn't been the only one to wax suspicious. Fullerton had been treated as a homicide till it became clear there was no basis for it. The knot around the pastor's ankles had been a simple slip knot, one he could easily have loosed himself from, even under the water. No signs of struggle marked the body. There was no indication he'd been struck on the head or in any other way rendered unconscious and put in the water. A quick and dirty screening had been run on a blood sample, and no obvious drugs were found.

The recovered bass boat showed scratching on the inside and left gunwale that matched what could be expected if a lone man wrestled a heavy object overboard. Fullerton's fingerprints were on the starter pull of the engine and on the rudder. Other than the normal smudging, there was nothing to indicate another person had manipulated the controls, gloved or ungloved.

Anna weighed the pros and cons of telling Paul about the Clinton pullout scenario. In the end, she told him. Unless she'd read him wrong, he would not indulge in idle gossip and it might be of some comfort to him to know the reason why this gifted and depressive man had come to believe his life was intolerable, a risk to the bridge between the races he had worked so long and hard to build.

They took a moment, the telephonic equivalent of snatching their hats off out of respect for the dead, then went on. Anna was reminded of her grandmother's telling her that if she thought she was important she should just stick her finger in a bucket of water and pull it out to see how big a hole it left. No person, no matter how important when living, left much of a hole in the great scheme of things when he died.

Brandon DeForest remained to be talked to. Again. Heather had folded. Lock had appeared on the scene playing a part in the tragedy. Given the new information, it was time to squeeze the recalcitrant Mr. DeForest. Needing to pretend she was in control of some small aspect of life, Anna took her car; Sheriff Davidson rode in the passenger seat. Once again they would be pulling Brandon out of class, questioning him on school property. This time there would be two of them. Juvenile cases were tricky, each twist and turn in the investigative process fraught with rules, written and unwritten. But DeForest had turned eighteen on January twelfth. Anna'd gotten that bit of information from his driving record. In his junior year, he'd gotten a speeding ticket, fifty-five in a forty-mile-an-hour zone on Northside Drive in Jackson. The moment he'd run afoul of the law, even in this mundane and fleeting fashion, his information had gone into the computers. There was no such thing as a private citizen anymore. Anybody with a PC and a modem was welcome to drive down the information highway. Unless an individual kept a profile so low earthworms had to bend over to see it, he was bound to show up.

The high school shimmered in the heat, looking new and awkward with its complement of saplings not yet rooted deep enough to grow tall.

Adele Mack, the vice principal, was again the person the secretary steered them to. The door to the principal's office remained firmly shut, and Anna wondered if there really was such a person or if Ms. Mack had done away with him or her at some point and continued to efficiently run the school, the real force behind the paper tiger.

The growing heat was taking its toll on Ms. Mack's face. Her eye makeup had melted slightly when she'd been out-of-doors, then resolidified in a blurrier configuration when exposed to the air-conditioning. Other than that, she was impeccable: hair, hose, high heels in perfect order.

"Come in," she said, neither pleased nor displeased at Anna's return but clearly concerned. Anna had intended to sit quietly and let Sheriff Davidson do the talking for two reasons. One, she thought both he and VP Mack would be more comfortable with the traditional lines of male authority in place. Two, she was feeling lazy. But once they were all in Ms. Mack's office with the door closed, both the sheriff and the vice principal stared expectantly at her, and she was forced to give up yet another preconceived notion about Southerners.

Unable to think of any reason to withhold information, Anna told Ms. Mack what they knew of DeForest. That Danni had taken his car. That he and his cronies had pursued Heather and Danni to Rocky Springs after the prom. Keeping Lockley Wentworth out of the equation, she said that apparently there was another boy involved, that DeForest had known about him and that DeForest and his buddies, Lyle and Thad, had lied to Anna and the police about their memory of what had occurred that night. The boys all claimed they'd been too drunk to remember, but with new information, Anna thought they might be more forthcoming. Ms. Mack asked a few questions. Anna and Paul answered them the best they could. DeForest, Mack confirmed, was eighteen, an adult by legal standards. As was Lyle Sanders. Thad Meyerhoff was still seventeen and, as a minor, had a right to her protection.

Meyerhoff, they assured her, was not a suspect.

"But if he committed perjury—" Ms. Mack began.

"It's not perjury unless you're under oath," the sheriff said and by the look of annoyance that flickered across the VP's well-manicured face, Anna guessed she knew that and was embarrassed at having forgotten momentarily.

"Lying to the police then," she said.

Though law enforcement officers hated admitting it, there was no law against lying to the police. They might try and frighten Thad Meyerhoff with obstruction of justice but would be hard-pressed to make it stick.

Ms. Mack left to fetch the boys.

"We weren't entirely honest," Anna said after she'd gone. "If those boys were with Brandon when he killed Danni, they are both potentially accessories to murder. The way Danni was draped and roped and carried and dragged, it looks to me like it could have been the work of more than one person."

Davidson nodded. "There's no law against lying to vice principals either," he said, and Anna glimpsed a colder part of the man than she'd seen before.

By prior agreement, Anna and the sheriff kept the three boys separated, questioning them one at a time, Thad and Lyle first. They told neither boy of Heather's revelations but questioned them closely on details: the time they'd left the prom, where they'd gone drinking and a dozen other things. From the quick pat answers, it was clear they'd spent time rehearsing. Sanders was cocky, but Meyerhoff was nervous enough. Anna guessed they could crack him if they kept him away from the support of his peers and turned up the pressure.

Questioning concluded for the present, they tucked Sanders away in the absent principal's office and incarcerated Thad Meyerhoff in a small conference room to steep in their lies.

At a quarter of three, Ms. Mack showed Brandon DeForest into the little office she'd relinquished for the cause. He still grinned and strutted but Anna could see the wait while his friends had been questioned had worn him down a bit. His blue-denim eyes moved from object to object on Adele Mack's desk, and when he sat, his left leg continued to bounce.

Anna leaned back and looked intentionally smug. Paul leaned forward, elbows on knees, and ran his fingers through his hair, the picture of a tired, disappointed, but determined man.

"So," he said and scrubbed his face with both hands as if to rub away the knowledge of evil. "You argued about Danni's new boyfriend. Danni stole your car. You and Thad and Lyle chased her down the Trace and cornered her at Rocky Springs. You better talk to me, boy, and tell me why I shouldn't book you for the murder of Danielle Posey. You'll be playing football at Parchment Penitentiary for the rest of your life."

DeForest stopped jiggling his leg, stunned as if Davidson had hit him with a bucket of ice water. "Those shits," he said, and the red blood of righteous anger boiled into his face. Anna and the sheriff just watched, he with tired compassion, she with a look she hoped came across as gloating.

The boy's anger couldn't hold through the silent watching. Blood drained away as quickly as it had risen, leaving him pale and looking younger than his eighteen years.

"I just wanted my car back," he said sullenly. "We took Thad's car, followed Danni and Heather to Rocky. When they got out, I got in my car and drove home. I don't care what Thad and Lyle told you. That's the truth."

Anna allowed herself a small audible sniff that as much as said: "Hah!" Paul merely looked terribly sad. Neither one of them said anything. The second hand on the big round wall clock behind Brandon's head jerked its way around twice.

Silence having failed, Paul said: "Son, you're lying to me." Brandon started to protest, but the sheriff forestalled him with a raised hand. "We've got enough to arrest you on suspicion of murder. When you go to trial and we got two witnesses saying one thing and you saying another, it'll go bad with you. You get caught in one lie, and the jury will figure you're lying every time you open your mouth. I've had a long day, and I'm not fixin' to sit in this office and screw around with you for much longer."

The second hand continued on its appointed rounds. Anna watched a kaleidoscope of emotions flicker over DeForest's face. Nothing telling, just fragments, ill-fitting and out of context.

"Danni'd been going on about having this other boyfriend, and it was pissing me off. Then she steals my car and goes off to see this guy. Me and Thad and Lyle chased them to Rocky Springs like I said. We were just screwing with Danni, giving her some of her own back. We dogged 'em—you know, yelling and stuff—around that loop there at the campground. Then Danni tears out and we follow 'em around the back way to the old church up at the graveyard."

Brandon stopped. Anna guessed he was

mentally editing the next chapter in his story, deciding what would be damning and what would not, what he could get away with and what was already known.

"Danni and Heather got out and ran up through the graveyard. We followed for a while. Just giving them a bad time. Then we left. That's all that happened, no big deal."

"Then why did you lie to us?" Paul asked.

"Because it might've looked bad. You know, with that happening to Danni and all."

Anna never broke her laid-back pose of smug self-assurance. "Makes sense to me," she said reasonably. "Lying because the truth might look bad."

"That's all it was, ma'am," DeForest said earnestly.

"What I want to know is why you're lying now," Anna said.

Brandon turned up the sincerity and, wide-eyed, hurt, he said: "Lying? How? I don't know what you mean."

"You said you chased Danni and Heather, right? The two girls were together."

"That's right."

"You and Thad and Lyle, all together all the time."

"That's right."

Anna sat up straight and dropped the easy attitude. "Lyle and Thad returned to the graveyard without you. Heather and Danni were already separated when the boys came. Where the hell were you? Murdering your girlfriend because she dumped you for another boy? A black boy who's a better football player and a better lover than you could ever hope to be?"

"That fucking bitch..." He had lost it and knew he had. He pulled himself together, put his good-boy face back on. "No, ma'am," he said. "I never hurt Danni. Maybe I got separated from Thad and Lyle for a minute or two, but that's all."

"Two against one, Brandon," Anna said. "Lyle and Thad against you. Ugly isn't it? No honor among thieves."

"It could've been longer," Brandon admitted. "But I didn't kill anybody, and no way you can prove I did."

They'd gotten all they were going to get out of him on that subject for the moment. Anna switched gears. "Your cohorts tell me you've got a picture of Heather Barnes baring her chest, that you used it to get her to lie. That's blackmail and suborning perjury. Both felonies. You're young, and you're scared. You give me that picture and the negative, and I'll see to it those charges are not brought against you."

"Shit," Brandon said and, "Yes, ma'am."

Paul picked up his hat from where he'd placed it beneath his chair. "If you remember anything else, you call me or Ranger Pigeon," he said.

"I'm free to go?" Brandon looked both surprised and relieved.

"For the moment, son," the sheriff said gently. His kindness frightened the boy more than anything either he or Anna had done to date.

Anna let Brandon get to the door, his hand on the knob, the scent of freedom in his nostrils, before she stopped him. "By the way, why did you put that alligator in my carport?"

Convinced Anna knew way too much about him to risk another lie—at least on a lesser crime—DeForest said: "A man called and told us where the gator was. Said if we wanted you to quit poking in our business, asking stupid questions, we could go get it. Scare you off."

"What man?"

"Some man doesn't want you around these parts. Could be anybody."

Though Anna would have shot herself before she let it show, the last barb hurt. "That alligator bit the leg off my dog," she said.

"Yes, ma'am. We were real sorry to hear about that," he said with what sounded like genuine regret in his voice. If it had been her leg that had been bitten off, she doubted Brandon DeForest would have been half as sorry.

The door closed. Slumped elbow to elbow in padded industrial-strength arm chairs, Anna and Paul said nothing. The quiet deepened until Anna could hear the faint tick of the spastic second hand on the wall clock. Sunlight came thought the blinds of the west-facing window, painting yellow stripes across the top of Adele Mack's desk. Dust motes moved through the light in a lazy dance, then vanished the moment they were touched by the shadows.

"Lord, but I hate bullying children," Paul said. Another moment passed. The tension they'd maintained while questioning DeForest melted away like the dust in the shadow.

"I don't know," Anna said thoughtfully. "I think I'm beginning to develop a taste for it."

The sheriff shot her a sidelong look to see if she was joking. Anna chose not to let him know one way or another.

Ms. Mack reclaimed her office. It seemed to Anna as if they'd been camped out there several days, but just over three-quarters of an hour in real time had elapsed. They were given the small conference room, and it was made clear they were on borrowed time. Ms. Mack was tiring of having her institution of learning sullied by the less exalted realities of life. Anna didn't blame her. She'd been blessed to attend high school before police and teachers were forced to work together so closely. Wearing skirts too short, getting pregnant and smoking dope had been the crimes that plagued Anna's alma mater. Not murder and blackmail.

Armed with information, Anna and Paul mixed bluff and bluster and were quickly finished with Thad Meyerhoff and Lyle Sanders.

From Thad they learned that events had transpired pretty much as DeForest said until the five kids left their cars and took to the graveyard. There Heather, too drunk to run, had hidden from them, probably where Anna later found her in the walled plot near the edge of the forest. Thad and Lyle had stopped to look for her. DeForest had pursued Danni Posey out of the graveyard and into the woods, toward the Old Trace Trail that ended near the campground half a mile east.

The booze wore off a little. Sanders and Meyerhoff got scared. Without flashlights or much in the way of cognitive thought processes, they'd tried to find Brandon and Danni. The search had quickly been abandoned, and they headed back to the car. That's when Anna had talked with them. Neither one of them had seen or heard from Brandon till the following day. Thad had lied about remembering, because Brandon said he'd lost sight of Danni and gotten lost in the woods but thought nobody would believe him because they'd been fighting and he'd chased her.

Sanders, they got nothing from. He'd been abused and bullied by adults most of his life. Now he sat through the worst they could do locked in a private world he'd undoubtedly begun constructing the first time his dad got drunk and started beating on him.

With Thad's information, they didn't need much from Lyle Sanders and cut him loose after a quarter of an hour.

"Well," Anna said apropos of nothing.

"Right. Well," the sheriff replied.

For their afternoon's combined efforts, they'd learned a great deal and nothing at all. Brandon DeForest was the prime suspect with the big three: means, motive and opportunity. The means of the murder could be anything—Anna took an educated guess that it would be some item from the same trunk that harbored the sheet and rope that mocked Danielle's corpse, common things anyone could come by. Motive was the age-old, tried and true lover's triangle. But Danielle Posey had accrued a surprising number of reasons to be done to death for a girl of her tender years: the lure of forty thousand dollars in insurance money, the racist rage of her brother Mike, the insanity of her mother, the threat she could have posed to Lockley Wentworth's chances at the pros. Even, at a stretch, George Wentworth's wrath because, in endangering Lock's chances, she threatened George's dreams.

Opportunity was the factor that tightened the noose around DeForest's neck. Though it was possible, it was not probable that anyone, with the possible exception of Lock Wentworth, could have known of Danni and Heather's impromptu decision to steal a car and run with it down the Trace.

"We're going to have to arrest the boy," Anna said as she turned the key of the ignition and, like a true Southerner, reached immediately for the air-conditioning vent as if some minute adjustment would speed the cooling process.

"Looks like," Paul said absently. He slouched in his seat, the natty crease on his shirtfront crumpling under the shoulder belt. "Brandon's not going anywhere. I doubt he's a danger to himself or society. Let's hold off a bit."

"Why?" Anna asked, curious. She didn't care one way or another. If DeForest had killed his

girlfriend because his pride had been outraged, she sincerely hoped he was punished
to the full extent of the law. But she was in no
hurry to do it.

"I don't know," Davidson said. "It just
doesn't seem the time is ripe yet. Chances are
if we nail him and all we've got is circumstantial
evidence, he's going to get away with it."

"Do we have enough for a search warrant?
Search his car, match fibers from the sheet.
Hope to get lucky and lay hands on whatever
was used as a bludgeon?" Anna was afraid her
ignorance was readily apparent. It wasn't that
she was totally in the dark regarding probable
cause and the legalities surrounding the application
for a search warrant, it was just not a job that
often fell into a ranger's daily tasks. In all her
years with the park service, she'd only done it
half a dozen times and not for many years.

"We might could," the sheriff said wearily.
"I'll look into it."

It was in Anna's mind to ask him to dinner,
but something stopped her. They rode the forty
minutes to Port Gibson lost in a world of
their own thoughts.

16

Just before the turnoff to Port Gibson, on
impulse, Anna finally asked Paul to dinner.
To her excitement and dismay, he accepted.

382

Because she'd been tormented by motives of an ulterior stamp, she was awkward in his presence even as he'd tried to ease the evening by helping with the cooking and telling self-effacing anecdotes. It worked to a certain extent, but both spent a goodly amount of time talking to Taco and Piedmont, a sure sign of conversational strain.

In an attempt to recapture the comfort she'd felt with him during his first, unannounced visit the night of Leo Fullerton's suicide, Anna drank, three, maybe four glasses of Pinot Grigio, guzzling an expensive wine in an attempt to be out of her own skin, if only briefly.

Paul had been warm and Paul had been sweet and Paul had been funny. When he left her at just before seven-thirty, Paul had been believable in his excuse. Mrs. Ruby Tangeman, the old lady whom Leo Fullerton was trying to get published, had called. Her great-niece "did" for the pastor. Using the housekeeper's key, Mrs. Tangeman had visited Leo's home to discover her precious manuscript had gone missing. The good sheriff had promised to drop by to hold her hand and help her look.

Paul kissed Anna on the front step. Had he not turned and walked purposefully away, she suspected she would have tumbled into bed with him.

Grateful for being saved that premature act of idiocy, she promised herself—as she had done since her first cold beer after emerging from the bowels of Lechuguilla Cave two years before—she'd quit drinking or at least cut down. Even as the words formed in her mind, she knew they'd be meaningless come five o'clock the following day—the witching hour when one longs to drop a veil over the harsh glare of the day's events.

Customarily, Anna wasn't the least uncomfortable around men. She worked for them, alongside them and, most recently, as their manager. She'd always gotten on well with the brawnier gender. Nor had she led the life of a monastic. Some she slept with, some she dated and some she flirted with.

The hideous self-consciousness this time around was engendered by the fact that not only did she want to run barefoot, metaphorically speaking, through the sheriff's thick blond hair, but she liked him on a deeper level. One that made her want him to like her.

Too much time around teenagers, she thought acidly. Apparently, adolescent angst was a contagious disease.

Now all she wanted was to sober up. She'd been drinking long enough that three—or was it four—glasses of wine didn't disable her. That perhaps Paul hadn't even known she was knocking the stuff back too fast comforted her somewhat.

She longed to leave the leafy, suffocating confines of Rocky, but she hadn't descended the slippery slope far enough that she'd drive drunk. Not yet. Not unless she got a callout. Would she have the courage to tell dispatch she'd had too much to drink and to call someone else?

Shaking the thought from her, she left the house, not even the dog for company, and began walking toward the campground just to be moving. Daylight saving—or wasting, she could never remember the point of moving the clock an hour twice a year—was upon the South, and though the sun had set, the sky still glowed with a rich and lingering twilight. To the southwest, a storm was brewing. Deep purple clouds piled into the stratosphere, and Anna could hear distant thunder. Until it arrived, even when night fell, there would be no true darkness. A fat moon already hung above the trees.

Stealth mosquitoes, robbed of their whine, bored itchy snouts into her back and shoulders but she ignored them, too distracted to return to the house and spray herself with insect repellent.

As she reached the intersection where the spur of road to the employee housing met with the main road into the campground and picnic areas, the headlights of a northbound car strobed through the trees, giving her a momentary sense of vertigo.

The car turned into Rocky and drove slowly past the visitor center. When its high beams raked across her, it stopped, backed up half a dozen yards and parked in one of the handful of slots in front of the unprepossessing brick structure. The door of the Chrysler Sebring opened, and a woman dressed in a suit, as if she just had come from a vestry meeting or working late at the office, stepped out.

Anna had no wish to engage with anyone, but the woman had seen her and appeared to be waiting so she walked in that direction, prepared to answer whatever visitor-in-need questions the woman had brought with her. As Anna approached, the woman came toward her, hand outstretched, big smile, like a politician canvassing for votes.

"You must be the new ranger here. Anna Pigeon, isn't it?" she said, as Anna allowed her hand to be grasped and pumped. The woman's fingers were a good thirty degrees colder than the ambient air temperature. Either she had no blood in her veins or she'd been driving with the air conditioner on max.

"I am," Anna admitted. The visitor was about Anna's age and attractive in an anorexic, iron-coiffed kind of way. Her voice was high and melodic, made pleasant by a genteel drawl. Ladies' Garden Club material without a doubt.

"I was just coming back from Jackson and stopped in to use the facilities," she said with an easy laugh. "I don't like driving the Trace after dark. Everybody hears the stories. But the trucks on Highway 61 have gotten so bad it's more than your life's worth to go that way."

"What stories?" Anna asked feeling the dullness of the wine and her preoccupation.

"You know. They look for a white woman driving alone. And if you ever get run off the road... I think I'd drive straight into a tree before I let that happen."

The story smacked of an apocryphal tale handed down from one anonymous paranoid source to the next. "It happen to somebody you know?" Something was irritating Anna. Maybe the insinuating "they."

"No. But it happens." Clearly the woman didn't like her fears challenged. "You be careful," she said, and Anna guessed it was more to ratify her own neurosis than any real feeling for a sister. "Anyway, I'm glad I ran into y'all. I've heard so much about you."

Sensing a trap, though what kind, she couldn't fathom, Anna waited.

"You work with my husband, Sheriff Paul Davidson."

Snap: the steel jaws closed. Anna felt the pain in her gut as if the words had razor sharp edges. Like the Spartan boy with his stolen fox, Anna let the pain eat up her insides, never showing any of it on her face.

"How do you do, Mrs. Davidson. Paul's told me so much about you. I'm glad to make your acquaintance." In that instant, Anna's desire to be sober vanished. If anything, she wished to be a whole lot drunker before long.

What Mrs. Davidson had expected, Anna didn't know and didn't care. The woman lied. She'd come from the south, not north from Jackson, and she left without using the john. Not that it mattered. The message she carried had been delivered and received. Anna had no quarrel with her and wasn't in a mood to pass judgment on the techniques employed to protect what she deemed hers.

As the Sebring's taillights disappeared, winking like bloody stars dragged through the darkening woods, Anna felt the pain beneath her sternum wink out. The desire to numb herself with more booze was gone too. What she felt was a gaping emptiness, a bankruptcy of body, mind and spirit.

Such was the depth of the hole, Anna couldn't even tell what emotions would come to fill it. Disappointment? Cynicism? Bitterness? Sadness? Understanding? As long as it wasn't bitterness, she would cope. Buried so deep she only guessed at it and resolutely remained in denial about the possibility of its existence, a part of her suspected the hollow place was lined with loneliness. She'd come from a long line of lonely women. Women who'd come to take pride in it, overlay it with competence, independence and hard work. And despise any woman so weak she gave in to it.

Too tired to drag up the traditional defenses, Anna took her solace where she always did, in the natural world. The smell of the earth, the touch of the sky held for her a special alchemy able to turn loneliness into aloneness and, so, make it, if not sacred, at least bearable.

Careful not to think, careful just to be, feeling the roll of her feet as they met the asphalt, the silk of the storm-charged air sliding in and out of her lungs, she walked through the gathering darkness onto the loop road that corralled the campsites.

Fires glowed comfortingly from behind the broken wall of vehicles marking the perimeter. Children, wild with the night, sped by her on small-wheeled bicycles, screeching like birds of prey as they passed. Overhead, bats echoed their movement, albeit with less racket.

Anna was aware, but not a part. She watched the human species as a tree or a cloud might: with little interest and no judgment. And no kinship.

Drifting thus with the darkness, she reached the top of the loop, where the trail led into the woods. Over her shoulder, the moon poured light enough to see by if she stayed to the improved pathways. Weary of the noise and light and smoke people poured into the atmosphere, she left the asphalt and followed graveled steps, carved into the clay and stabilized with six-by-six beams, down toward the creek.

Breathing, five counts in, seven counts out, she felt her feet touching the gravel, noted the grating sound as her weight shifted the fractured stone. Clogging strands of spiderwebs or the fine silk the small green worms hung from the trees tickled her face and bare shoulders. Anna noted their touch but did not wipe them away.

Frog and cricket song swelled from the woods on every side, her quiet passing not distracting the minute musicians. The childhood smell of grape Nehi floated around her like purple gauze. She was in the kudzu.

The path she followed turned sharply to the left, running along the south side of Little Sand Creek. The moon began a flirtation with the clouds and its light, moving and uncertain, threw handfuls of silver coins on the rippling water.

For a long moment, Anna stood on the bank of Little Sand, watching the play of shallow water and moonlight so different from what she was accustomed to. Here the chorus of night creatures sang so loudly that the water seemed to run in silence, no murmur of liquid over stones. No stones. The creek bed was of soft, smooth, golden silt. By the willow-wisp light of the moon, it shone cold as pewter.

Clouds boiled up from the southwest. Rain clouds, towering cumulus filled with lightning and winds. Yet here, beneath and amidst the verdant cloak of life, Anna could not smell the coming rain, could not feel the gusts that would herald it.

The hollowness left in the wake of Mrs. Davidson's visit was edged with a new fear: had she run so far in search of a promotion that she left behind the tie with nature that had been her mainstay? Would moonlight, wind and wild things no longer bring her comfort?

From behind her, over the sound of the frogs, she heard a woman shouting at her children, then the jarring blare of an automobile's horn.

REPENT. That was what the sign said when she'd first driven into this part of the country. REPENT. The second sign read: FINAL WARNING.

Dredging little-used information from the archives stowed in her brain during sophomore religion class at Mercy High School, Anna remembered "repent" meant to turn away from, turn back.

And she'd thought God worked in mysterious ways. Evidently in Mississippi, he just scribbled out his warnings on plywood and nailed them to roadside trees. Anna wished she'd paid more heed.

The irate mother shrieked again, and Anna walked farther into the darkness to escape the brawl of humanity.

The moon was gone to a shroud woven by the coming rain. Anna carried no flashlight, yet she pushed on, taking pleasure in the concentration it took to move along the wooded path in near-total darkness. Her progress was creeping, one toe nuzzled ahead at a time probing, blind as a mole's snout, for roots or undergrowth lying in wait to trip her.

Hands loose at her sides, she continued to breathe five counts in, seven counts out, aware of each unevenness underfoot, every nuance of the frog concert. She was unafraid. She'd walked the path in daylight and knew there were no overhanging branches to bang her head into. Other visitors, out for an evening's stroll, would have sense enough to carry a flashlight so head-on collisions were pretty much ruled out. Coyotes were the largest predator in this part of the world, and as she was neither a cat nor a lamb, there was no danger from them. The only real risk was wading into the middle of a myopic and cowardly cottonmouth, but that thought never got past the booze and pseudo Zen that Anna was using to anesthetize herself. As she inched along, absorbed in her blind traverse, the emptiness within, if not healed, was filled with the richness of the night's sensory offerings.

Anna came finally to the three-cornered clearing where the path forked, one branch to the Old Trace, the other to peter out in the woods a quarter of a mile after crossing Little Sand Creek. Without the trees between her and the sky, enough light trickled around the edges of the storm that she could see. Being so long in the dark had made her night vision acute.

The Old Trace, wide and clear, would allow her freedom of movement. Tired of the sightless pastime she'd so recently taken refuge in, she took the left-hand path and felt the joy of stretching her legs, covering ground.

In less than a minute, the Old Trace opened before her. She slowed to absorb the picture it presented. Wind she knew must be escorting the clouds had arrived. Through the frog's chirring, she could not hear it, and down in the earth and foliage, though she longed to, she could not feel it. But the wide gully of the ancient highway cut a clear view to the tops of the trees on either bank and the clean ribbon of sky between.

Boughs tossed, leaves, black and ragged,

swept a cloud-strewn sky only slightly lighter than they. Silver-edged by the hiding moon, clouds raced by at a speed usually only obtained by filmmakers fast-forwarding. Viewed in this narrow scope, the clouds seemed to be passing at the rate of geese flying south for the winter: winging, shapes changing, shadows racing over the brief canvas of cleared ground allotted.

Surreal.

Anna liked it. The real had been pretty piss-poor of late, and she was glad to step away from it.

Letting wind she could neither hear nor feel blow her on, she entered a canyon beaten so deep in the soil that finally even the ravening vegetation had had to retreat to the top of the world's skin, leaving a trail easy on the feet of travelers.

Perhaps if she hadn't had three glasses of wine, or been intent on hiding from her feelings, Anna would have sensed the restless spirit of the murdered girl or the malevolent spirit of her killer, but she felt neither and moved down the sunken Trace as one caught up in a wild dream.

An eighth of a mile in, she began to feel raindrops and welcomed them. By the time she reached the great oak that marked where they had carried Danni Posey's body from the woods, the rain had settled into a steady downpour. The frogs had hushed, their symphony replaced by low growls of thunder. The shifting light of the moon was lost in sharp flashes of lightning still too distant to be seen in anything but sudden glows, like the fire from bombs exploding far away.

In one such unexpected revelation of light, Anna noted the earth had been disturbed beneath the tree and along the bank of the Trace, digging too deep to be accounted for by the mere rootings of armadillos in search of grubs. The disturbance stretched along the side of the Trace for thirty or forty feet. But for one, gaping like an open grave at the far end, there were no holes, just turned earth, as if the digger had prepared the soil for planting or, having dug up what was sought, filled the excavations in again.

Given the soft and melting nature of loess, the soil of the area, one good rain would dissolve the evidence of the dig.

The call of her profession, or the curiosity that kills cats, did for Anna what nature and wine could not. She was pulled out of her self-pity and her attempts at hiding from self-pity. Wiping the rain out of her eyes and wishing she had a flashlight, she walked along the freshly turned earth till she reached the hole at the end. Crouching, she waited for the next flash of lightning to tell her what was going on.

The rain on her shoulders wasn't cold; it didn't refresh, but fell in warm drops the size of nickels to trickle into her armpits and run down the small of her back into her shorts.

Lightning flashed and the hole before her was ignited. Harsh-cut edges made not by snouts or claws, but with the blade of a shovel. A shovel, edged but not necessarily sharp, long-handled enough to swing with tremendous force. Not knowing how she knew, Anna was sure Danni had been struck down by a shovel. Struck down here. In her dulled brain sparked the nonsensical idea that this grave had been opened to receive, to hide the girl's corpse.

Again a flash of lightning and Anna saw the bones. Washed clean by the downpour, they appeared in stark relief, like a Halloween skeleton under black lights, then were gone again in the darkness.

The lightning was followed by a crack of thunder so loud that it struck Anna down, a blow that landed her face in the mud.

Her ear was ringing from the impact and her mind struggling to right itself, form a cohesive thought, when the second blow landed.

Not thunder.

Reflexively throwing her hands up to protect her head, she felt rough canvas and fought, in panic, to pull it from her head and face. Hard hands batted her arms away. She dropped her fists to the mud, pushed, tried to rise, to roll. She was cuffed down again. Bare knuckles pounded: neck, back, shoulders. Weight dropped on her spine and her face slammed into the ground. She could feel water seeping through the canvas, puddling around her mouth and nose, threatening to drown her. Knees smashed down on the backs of her upper arms.

A big man, heavy.

Anna would not fight free of this one. A blow crashed into the side of her skull above her right ear. Her brain skidded away from the force, dragging consciousness in its wake.

Anna could not draw breath, could not move, could not see. Another blow landed on the back of her head. Her jaw smacked against the wet canvas. Muddy water, or her own blood, flooded her mouth and throat. She began to choke.

With a jerk, her head was pulled upward; then, as suddenly, it dropped again and she felt rough and uniform pressure around her throat. A noose. A noose like they'd found around Danni's neck had been put around hers. She too would be found in the woods, rotting down to feed the fungi and the creepers.

The rope pulled tight. Another blow landed, and Anna knew she was going to die. She'd dropped her guard, wandered tipsy and brain-dead in the night, trusting to a God who had never shown her much in the way of personal attention to watch her back.

Anna fought, but it was a lost cause. Like a rattlesnake with a gravel truck parked on its spine, she writhed, tried to unseat her attacker. Her arms were under his knees, pinned to the ground as surely as if he'd driv-en railroad spikes through them. Feeling from the elbows down was draining away, starved for blood. She tried to kick him with her heels but he sat too far forward, straddling the small of her back. Her struggle only won her more blows. If he'd had anything but his bare hands, she would already be dead. When he'd jumped her, he must have left his shovel behind. Once she lost consciousness, he'd go back for it.

Not long now. Anna couldn't think. Every thought was shattered by a blow. Strength had been spent, a sixty-second bid for freedom, all given, nothing held back, could not be repeated.

Possum. Play possum. Pushing her face into the mud, pulling her shoulders up to protect her ears the best she could, Anna forced her body to go limp. No longer even willing the beating to stop. Merely wishing without prayer.

It didn't. She blacked out, a moment, maybe more. A sharp rap over her left ear, piercing the eardrum, dragged her back. The bastard wasn't just going to kill her; he was going to beat her to death with his fists.

Anger, till now muffled by pain and shock and fear, sparked deep inside, a tiny spark not even so big as a firefly, but white-hot and located somewhere between her heart and her spine.

Not knowing if it was a false light, the one those surviving near-death experiences report having tried to lead them out of this world, Anna began shutting down, focusing on that spark, following it inside. Her mind was gone, reacting from the blows that fell as regularly now as men with sledgehammers battering through a wall.

The man on her back had raised up, weight on his knees, cracking the humerus bones above her elbows, the better to put his weight behind his work.

The spark moved through the blackness of Anna's hell, hotter than anger, colder than hatred. This light would not lead her to glory but into the arms of the devil. She didn't care.

The spark moved, with no will of hers, into her right hand. Slowly, dragging an inch at time, her arm, feeling no more alive than a bit of broken lumber, bent at the elbow, and her hand, palm up, moved over her hip, up onto her kidneys until her knuckles rested on her spine as if she waited compliantly to be cuffed.

The spark flared, a star of ugly strength, and Anna forced that hand into her assailant's crotch. His trousers were loose and soft—thin wool. He wore no underwear. Her fingers closed around his testicles, and the star flamed, welding her bones shut in a grip so tight she could feel her nails dig into her palms and a mute crushing as if she flattened clay.

The rain of blows was cut short by a shriek so high and wild it could have been the wind tearing sheets of tin off a barn roof. A desperate swing landed a fist against her neck. Had she been alive, the force of it might have paralyzed her, opened her hand. But Anna was just that spark now, just that hand closed over the man's testicles. Rigor would set in, connecting her fingers around their prize. She would never let go. With the odd, detached sensation of tightening a metal vise, she felt her hand crank down, the fingers close fractionally.

The weight on her back began to shift.

Knees left her numbed arms, booted heels drummed bruisingly at her legs. Anna felt only a deeper sinking in the mud as if the thrashing of the man on her back were but the lashing of the storm and she bedrock.

Bit by bit, the shrieking above her resolved into words as life began to reassert itself in her bludgeoned brain. Half words, through a tunnel. She was deaf in one ear.

"You're killing me. You're killing me," the wind shrieked, and the storm raged over her buttocks and thighs.

The words gave her strength. She pushed up, face free of the mud.

"Off," she croaked. Then louder: "Off." And the talons that her fingers had become clawed deeper. "Off."

The weight left her. All that remained was whatever was attached to the balls in her right hand. The thrashing ceased.

Feebly, Anna clawed at the rope securing the canvas over her head, but the slip knot had pulled tight and she couldn't get it free or drag the stiff canvas from under it.

She rolled to her side and pulled her knees up, never once loosing the grip she had on her assailant. Movement brought searing pain, so sharp and cruel she felt blackness come back to her brain, and for a moment, her world shrank down again to the spark, the hand.

If she let go, she would die. Maybe she was going to die anyway. Ribs were broken. Kidneys screamed. Her head was loose on her neck and felt broken inside and out.

"Move and I'll rip them off," she heard someone say and wondered if it was her.

Using her free hand, she pushed until she'd rolled herself up, knees tucked under her, face inches from the ground. The acid stench of vomit cut away a tiny bit of the fog from her rapidly swelling brain. She must have thrown up.

For what seemed like a long time, she stayed there, turtle-like, knowing the rain pelted down on her back but unable to feel it through the pain. There was no beginning to it, no end. She was made of pain. Muscle was gone to it and blood and bone and will, and she could not move.

And she could not hold on forever. And she would die. Beaten to death. The spark was dimming. Soon the pain would reach her fingers, and they would open. She had to get away. Blind, deaf and crippled, she had to get away.

Slowly, she breathed in through her nose, hearing the air hiss and bubble through the blood. With the breath, she pushed the pain down through her neck, her lungs, into her belly and held it there as long as she could. Then she let it out in a yell that grated the broken bones of her rib cage. On that yell, she summoned the power left of her rage and hammered the fingers of her right hand closed, then ripped with all her might.

The light wool probably kept her from dismembering her assailant, but she knew the joy of feeling his flesh tear and hearing him hiss out agony too deep for sound. Knowing she'd bought herself all the time she could afford, not knowing how much that was, she began to claw blindly up the slick and dissolving bank.

A hand grabbed her ankle, and she kicked out. The movement sent a racketing pain through her skeleton to explode in her neck, but she felt the hand slide free.

No thought. Just survival. She pushed on. Hands struck wood, the smell of grass seeped through her soiled death mask. Like a mortally wounded animal, Anna crawled an erratic path, trusting the storm to cover her noise. Rotting bark shredded beneath her knees. Broken branches gouged the skin from her chest. Thorns clawed at her arms. Head down, draped and noosed for the killing, Anna pushed on till she could move no more. Her arms and legs would not obey her and her mind was lost.

Curling up as small as she could, she raked the litter of the forest floor over herself and entrusted her keeping to the gods of darkness.

17

Anna slid in and out of consciousness, a sign that she was badly hurt. Brain damage. That sent a stab of fear through her so sharp her feet twitched with it. Her ankle. She had to protect it, not touch it, not rub it, keep it dry. Why that was so was lost, but she knew it needed to be done.

Noise came and went. Whether real or imagined, whether she was conscious or unconscious, she didn't know. In dream or mind's eye, she saw a form bent double, scouring the woods on a stream of invective hunting to kill.

A wounded rabbit, she lay still as death in her burrow, fear singing through nerve fibers till she could hear the hum in the broken places.

How to battle fear? She'd been told once. With faith, she remembered. Faith in what? Faith in herself had been battered out of her as the strength was battered from her body. Faith in her fellow men had proven a bad gamble. Mother Nature could only be trusted to do what was best for Mother. Father Time could be trusted to heal with annihilation.

Faith was not going to save her. Stubbornness might. Too stubborn to move, though it hurt to lie still. Too stubborn to cry out, though knives in her skull tried to saw voice from her. Too stubborn to stop breathing, though each intake of air pushed ragged rib-ends into her chest wall.

Time passed. Minutes or days or months. Consciousness rolled around again. The world had grown quieter. The storm had passed. The evil crashing of men had left the woods. Or waited in silence for her to give herself away.

Evil crashing. Anna's memory was cut into pieces. She remembered to be afraid, remembered she must hide, remembered her left ankle was somehow important. What she could not remember was why.

She decided to open her eyes and felt a creaking pain as she pushed swollen lids into bruised sockets but sight didn't come. Revealed as if in a flash of lightning, she saw herself kneeling in the rain staring down into an open grave.

She had been buried alive. Suffocating.

Forgetting the need to be still, she clawed at the dirt clogging her mouth and nose. Not dirt, cloth, canvas. And around her neck, a rope. That memory came back too. Not in a vision but in total recall of how the noose had felt tightening around her throat, forcing the stiff canvas folds into her flesh.

Feebly, she fumbled at the executioner's hood with fingers that felt made of rotting wood. So much pain accompanied each tiny movement she mewed like a kitten.

Pain cut through the panic and a thought surfaced—not because her brain worked, but because this had always been so, ever since she was a little girl. There was a jackknife in her pocket, the last in a long line of Swiss Army knives that served, were lost or broken, and replaced.

It took a long time to remember how to remove an item from her pocket, an inquisition of pain to execute the task, another eternity to pry open the small blade, and the briefest of minutes to saw through the binding rope.

Spent, Anna hadn't the strength to pull the canvas from her face, but lay panting shallowly, reveling in the seep of sweet air that came up under the edges now the rope was loosed.

Maybe she browned out again. Time was proving itself as relative as old what's-his-name insisted it was. Anna knew she should remember the name, it felt important, as if it would prove she'd not lost too much gray matter, that her brain would not swell and squash personality against the unforgiving confines of her skull. Thoughts were falling apart, leaking away through cracks.

With an effort that left her dizzy and nauseated, she lifted her hand and dragged the canvas off. Air, misted with minute warm droplets, touched her face like the end of a fever. Afraid of the pain in her ribs, she sipped at it, savoring it like a fine delicacy, while wanting to wolf it down as a starving woman might.

Faint gray touched the sky somewhere, Anna could just make out a tracery of branches overhead. "Thankyoubabyjesus," she whispered and laughed, a bark cut short by injured ribs. She was not blind. The beating her skull had taken had not robbed her of sight. Broken, covered in mud and blood and vomit, Anna was jubilant. Soon she was going to sit up. It would be easier to think then. She would sit up and wait for the light. That was all she needed to concern herself with. With the light would come knowledge of what the next right thing was and she would do that.

Sitting up took an excessive amount of time and brought such pain that bile she hadn't the breath to spit out trickled from the corner of her mouth. *I'm drooling,* she thought, but that was the least of her worries. Her head felt as big and heavy as a medicine ball, and she was afraid. If her cervical vertebrae had been cracked, its weight would tear them apart, paralyze her from the neck down. *Christopher Reeve, pray for me,* tinkled through her troubled mind.

As from a distance, through gun slits, she watched her hands pull her knee up and bind the canvas that had been her hood around her left ankle with fumbling care. She wondered why they did this. Her ankle, it seemed, was the only uninjured part of her entire body. Maybe her hands sought to preserve it for posterity.

Darkness came again. Not the void she'd fallen into before but a troubled dream state, the shadow world the comatose could recall only in pieces.

She'd been kneeling by a grave looking at bones, human bones. Why she'd been there was knocked from memory. A gold-colored belt buckle, her house searched, an old black woman complaining her book had been stolen.

These things came and went on flashcards held up by a teacher patient with her stupidity. Mrs. White from second grade? Sister Mary Patricia? No matter. Teacher and cards were gone, replaced by a squad of Union soldiers, ghost riders, vanishing into thin air, followed by a three-legged dog.

Anna could not lose consciousness again. The ebbing and flowing of the life of the mind bespoke head injury. If she could stay awake, she believed she could hold on to her mind by the sheer power of her thoughts, thoughts in a stream like the drizzle from the faucet left running on viciously cold nights: movement to keep the pipes from freezing.

Keep the pipes from freezing, she told herself. The flashcards, the ghost riders, the dog. Again and again she played them through her mind, a trickle, a flow. At some point they began to match up, one from column A and one from column B. Her brain wrote them on its damaged walls and drew lines between the matches as Anna had on countless tests throughout her life.

The ghost riders; the buckle.

The buckle; the search of her house.

The old black woman's book; the ghost riders. Leo Fullerton; the missing book; Civil War soldiers; the buckle. Barth with his books; Civil War soldiers. Danni's popliteal artery; Anna's bound ankle.

More lines and more till the map in her cranium was crisscrossed as a cat's cradle, and Anna knew all these things were part of a whole.

"Got to move." She tried to speak aloud and felt her lips moving but heard no sound. A blow to the ear. Deafness. She remembered that. Fear rose and fell. She could hear morning birds. One ear. That was enough. "Help," she said and heard what was meant as a cry come out a tiny whisper.

"Opening my eyes," she announced to her

brain in hopes of greater cooperation. After a while, the message was delivered and her eyes opened. There was sunshine now, shadows on the ground. Time had passed since last she'd managed this feat. Thirst troubled her. Peeing wasn't an issue. She was too dehydrated. "Not good," she whispered. And: "Moving my hand." Seconds later, a puppet's arm under the guidance of a drunken puppetmaster floated up before her eyes.

The arm was out of focus. A thing of green and brown, grass stains and mud. "Other arm," she commanded. Seconds passed, but pain disallowed compliance. The humerus was broken or cracked. *Knelt on me,* Anna remembered. *Somebody knelt on me.* A sensation flashed through her of being facedown in the dirt, a terrible weight on her arms.

Voices wove through the woods, and Anna stopped breathing to listen. Under this sea of green, she was utterly lost. Though she knew she was probably no more than fifty feet from an improved trail, she could not guess fifty feet in which direction. She would not let the thought form, but her body knew she could not crawl much farther than that. Her mind knew she would not be found where she was, not for many days.

One chance. Fifty feet. Toward fading voices. Anna listened with every fiber of her being. Aware of an ominous creaking of neck bones, she tried to turn her face in the direction whence the sound had come, but muscles were frozen.

Moving her upper body, she rolled to hands and knees and pointed her head in the direction she wanted to go. Spinning, pain, vomiting, Anna waited it out. Standing up was not in the realm of possibility. There was no way she could force the injured muscles to so much as lift her head so she could look where she was going.

For a minute, ten, maybe half an hour, she stared at the ground a foot from the tip of her bloodied nose. Even here at the bottom of the world, there were shadows, tiny, tangled, green, but shadows. If she focused, she could see they stretched ever so slightly to her left. Sure as compass needles, they would keep her on course.

Whispering orders to her body, she crept along. Fallen logs she would have stepped over without thought the previous day loomed as formidable obstacles requiring great presence of mind, and more physical courage to surmount than she'd realized she had.

Sweat poured off of her, then stopped, her body out of fluid. Winston Churchill: "Never, never, never give up." General George Patton: "Success is measured by how high you bounce when you hit bottom."

And Anna kept on, knowing now, first-hand, that Christopher Reeve really *was* Superman.

Watching the shadows, pushing ahead an inch at a time, she finally came to a place where the forest floor dropped away in a cliff of brown. She'd reached the Old Trace. She could lie down now and figure out why it was she was here.

The sound of voices came to her, and she remembered.

"Help me," she croaked. A woman screamed, and Anna knew why Danielle Posey had died.

Robbed of dignity, clothing and memories, Anna woke. A kindly black woman in the trim white authority of an RN uniform told her she was at the Baptist Hospital, then asked her gently if she knew her name, who was president of the United States, what day it was and what state Jackson was in. The first two Anna got right. The last two she failed. A C– in sanity.

Her brain took another holiday. When next it returned, and she opened her eyes, she remembered she was in Mississippi. If it hadn't hurt so much to reach the call button, she would have summoned the nurse and asked if she could get her grade raised.

"Hey," a voice said softly. "Welcome to the world of the living."

Only a slot of vision was allowed Anna, and she searched the small room till she found the source of the voice. Sheriff Paul Davidson, smiling, was seated to the right of the bed, his chair thoughtfully moved so she didn't have to turn her head to see him. A window was behind him, blinds lowered.

Distrust, so strong it threatened to become panic, engulfed her at the sight of him. Why, she couldn't remember. All she remembered was that they'd been friends. She didn't feel in the least friendly. She was scared. For a moment, she tried to ignite her fear, turn it to anger, but she hadn't the strength.

Ignoring the fear and the sheriff, she tried to raise her left hand. The arm was immobilized. She had better luck with the right. Sensing it would be most unwise to move her head, she let the hand make its discoveries. Her face was swollen. One eye was closed beneath a tender and jellied mass that had once been an eyelid. The other was better. It would open. Her nose wasn't broken. Several teeth were loose, but running her tongue over the familiar mouthscape, she detected no gaps. Her skin had survived intact; no cuts or gashes that she could find.

A woman is never too old for vanity, and Anna was relieved. For a few weeks, she might sport a visage that would give the kiddies nightmares, but she should heal.

"What happened?" the sheriff asked, and once again Anna was filled with alarm.

Had he been the one? Was that why she distrusted him? Bits of memory were floating up like the words in the window of the Magic 8-Ball she'd owned as a child. She would share none of it with Davidson till she knew why the little hairs on the back of her neck were crawling.

"You tell me," she managed. Her voice was cracked and whisper-thin.

"Would you like some water?" he asked

solicitously. He put a plastic cup with a straw in it in her good hand.

Anna's throat was so dry that she was surprised dust devils hadn't whirled out on her words, but she didn't feel thirsty. An odd sensation. As she wet her mouth and throat, she noticed she was on an IV. Probably normal saline for dehydration. That would explain it.

Paul Davidson took the cup from her and set it back on a rolling bed table, adjusting both so they would be near at hand when next she wanted a drink.

Anna was unimpressed. Sleazeballs and dirtbags occasionally had excellent manners. It proved nothing. "Tell me what you know," she said and was pleased her voice sounded stronger. "I can't remember much." With that half-truth, she realized she'd joined Lyle, Brandon, Thad and Heather in the epidemic of amnesia that was sweeping the southland.

"Some campers from Knoxville found you a little before ten this morning."

"What time is it now?" she interrupted.

Davidson looked at his watch. "Five-thirty-seven."

Anna nodded. She was reassured. It wouldn't have surprised her if she'd been unconscious for six months. Half a day. Not bad. Not so frightening.

"Keep going," she said. Then, because she was helpless and not because she was feeling polite, she added: "Please."

"You scared them about half to death. You were up top the bank about a dozen feet from

411

where we carried out the Posey girl. When you stuck your head out, the woman thought you were a bear."

"I must look pretty bad," Anna said. It wasn't a question, and he didn't contradict her.

"Her husband was a city fireman in Tennessee and knew first aid. He stayed with you while she ran back to the campground and found Frank. Frank got hold of Barth, and he radioed me. I called the ambulance out of Utica. You were dehydrated and not clear in the head, but you were a handful. You caught hold of the door frame and kept them from putting the stretcher in the ambulance. I got another call and didn't get to Rocky till you'd been taken away, but I heard an earful when the boys got back. They said you wouldn't let them load you till you'd talked with Barth. That you screamed 'my ankle, my ankle.' "

Her ankle. Wrapping it with canvas. The memory clattered through her head like a video on fast forward, leaving an ache behind. To her astonishment and relief, she also knew why she'd protected the ankle. Surreptitiously, she moved her cup of water behind the carafe out of Davidson's line of sight.

"They said you fought like a wounded cat till they got scared you would hurt yourself more than a delay would and let you have your own way. They got ordered out of their own ambulance while you had a private ranger meeting. After that, they said you were the ideal patient."

"Unconscious," Anna said, and he laughed.

"I strong-armed the doctor here into telling me how you were. Actually, it wasn't too tough; the doctor is my deputy's brother-in-law."

Anna tried to roll her eyes, but it hurt too much. There was something unsettling about having Sheriff Davidson know more about her than she knew herself, to have him talk to a doctor she couldn't remember about her medical condition. Anger wriggled wormlike under her breastbone. She was too weary to feed it.

"You've got a great-granddaddy of a concussion, moderate to severe soft-tissue injuries to your neck and shoulders. Four cracked ribs, one broken. The humerus bone in your left arm is cracked, and your left eardrum was traumatized but not ruptured. The hearing should return in a day or two. Abrasions and contusions, two black eyes, loose teeth. But for the soft-tissue injuries, you should be pretty much up to snuff in a month or so."

Soft-tissue injuries would haunt her for a while. She knew that. She'd injured her neck and back a couple times before. Muscles had long memories and did not forgive as completely as bone.

Paul was done talking. Anna had nothing to say and no energy to say it. Silence filled the room till small sounds from the hall crept into her awareness: a PA, wheels on linoleum, voices.

At length Paul said: "What was all that with Barth about?" His voice was oh-so-conversational, but Anna continued to be infected with distrust.

413

"I'll have to ask him," she replied.

"He was pretty closemouthed about it to me," Davidson said. A note of professional irritation colored his voice. "If it has anything to do with the Posey murder or the attack on you, I'd appreciate being let in on it."

They were on more formal ground now, down to the business of criminal investigation.

Anna dutifully related nearly everything she could remember. If he was there, she wasn't telling him anything new; if he wasn't, he needed to know. She'd been out walking. Rain had started. She'd stopped on the Old Trace. The grave, the bones, she didn't mention for a couple reasons: the fear she felt and the sensation she'd imagined it. Before she went out on that limb, she wanted to talk to Barth.

Somebody had bagged her from behind, sat on her, slipped a noose around her neck and tried to beat her to death.

"The canvas he put over your head probably saved you from deafness. You were lucky."

"A veritable leprechaun," Anna said dryly.

Paul had the good manners to apologize for his choice of words.

"I got away and ran for it. Crawled for it," she finished.

"My Lord!" Davidson had lost color under his tan, leaving his skin a pale muddy tone and his face looking old. "My Lord," he said again, then breathed slowly through his nostrils as if fighting a tidal wave of emotion. He looked like he was going to be sick, and some of Anna's distrust wavered and melted. Some. Not all.

"So you have no idea who attacked you? None at all?"

"None," Anna lied.

The sheriff's hands clenched on the wooden arms of the chair where he sat, the skin drawn and bloodless.

And unmarked. Anna's assailant had been bare-handed; she'd felt the heat from his skin when he'd grabbed her leg. The man who'd attacked her would have scraped knuckles. Her fear of Davidson didn't stem from the assault. Had Anna's ribs not been causing her so much pain, she would have breathed more easily. She took another sip of water, careless of the cup. She no longer needed to check out Davidson's fingerprints.

"How did you get loose of this guy?" the sheriff asked.

Anna didn't know. She closed her one good eye. The effort of remembering sunk her back into a nightmare so vivid sweat stood out on her forehead, salt stinging in the abrasions made by fist and canvas. The fingers of her right hand tingled and ached. She was so afraid she jerked, spiking pain in to her fragile cranium.

Anna opened her eye and told Paul how she had gotten away.

"I hope the bastard never walks upright again," he said with unpriest-like vicious-ness, and Anna was pleased. "I'll put the word out to area hospitals to report any man seeking treatment for groin injuries."

"Good," Anna said wearily. "I think I ruptured one of his testicles. That's got to be debilitating."

"Gee, you think?" Davidson said. Anna thought she heard a smile in his voice but hadn't the energy to open her eye and see. She wondered why she had a bad feeling about him. He seemed like a nice enough man.

"Tell Barth I need to see him first thing," Anna said. She hoped she'd said it aloud because she hadn't the strength to repeat herself.

18

At eight-thirty the following morning Barth Dinkin presented himself. Anna's mind had cleared somewhat. More chunks of memory were returned. Nothing from an hour or so before the attack, but much of what happened afterward had been restored. Other than that, she felt worse than ever, her muscles stiffened and her knitting bones angry.

"You look..." Barth was at a loss for words. He stood at the foot of her bed, his Stetson in his hands, his strange light eyes full of pain and awkwardness.

"Like shit. I know," Anna said. "Did you get the print off my ankle?"

"A partial. The mud was pretty bad smeared. I got a comparison with the one was lifted from

Miss Posey's neck. They matched on seven points. 'Bout a sixty-percent chance they came from the same person. I sent 'em off to run 'em against FBI files. Told them the case and they got right on it, but we got no matches."

"I didn't think you would. Worth a shot."

"I thought that print on the girl's neck was yours," Barth said.

"So did I. Sheriff Davidson said a print was on the pulse point. It never occurred to me to ask which one. I never touched the carotid. It was under the noose. I checked at wrist and knee. I should have made the connection earlier, but I didn't—not till my own head was in a sack." Anna rested for a minute, thinking. Her brain was not yet sufficiently recovered that she could think and talk at the same time.

When she opened her eyes—both now, though the left was merely a gummy slit—Barth was standing as she'd left him. "Get me some clothes," she said. "My house isn't locked. Ask Frank if he'll look after the animals. He probably already is, but check for me if you would. Get hold of Steve Stilwell. Tell him to meet us at the Honda dealer's in Pearl. If there's more than one, start with the first in the phone book. What time is it?"

"Eight-thirty-seven, but—"

"Tell him to meet us there at eleven. Will that give you enough time to get to Rocky and back?"

Barth looked both miserable and obstinate. His gaze wandered around the room looking for his courage. When he found it, he met Anna's eye.

"Might could," he said. "But you're beat up bad. You don't need to be getting up and running around about now. You'll bust something loose."

"That's my problem," she replied coldly.

"Not just. I been here a long time. You're the first lady ranger we've had. It's not going to look good if you get yourself killed because I was dragging you around when you were supposed to be in the hospital."

"It didn't seem to bother you much when you and Randy decided to hang me out to dry on that car stop." Low blow. Anna felt momentary regret as she saw it smash into Barth's face.

"That was before. I apologized for that," he said simply.

It wasn't the reminder of the apology that shamed Anna out of her peevish hatefulness, it was the word "before." Before Barth knew her, before he liked her, before he cared if she lived or died.

"Sorry," she said. "Blood under the bridge. I'm not my usual sunny self this morning."

Barth cleared his throat, an aborted laugh.

"I'll okay it with the doctor. If he says not to check out, then I'll stay," she promised virtuously.

Barth nodded, looking as if he pitied Dr. Munroe. "Anything in particular you want from your house?"

"Boots, socks, underwear. You'll find it. My uniform. Skip the duty belt. I couldn't buckle it, much less draw my weapon."

"That's the point I was making," Barth tried again. "Not fit for duty." A look must have crossed Anna's bruised face that alarmed him. "Be back in an hour and a half, maybe two," he said.

Dr. Munroe, seemingly the kindest of men, became huffy the instant his authority was questioned. When Anna asked if she could be released, he told her she needed to remain in the hospital for observation another day at least, preferably two. If she left, he would not be responsible for her health. Of course, no one would hold a gun to her head. If she wanted to leave, she could.

Anna took that as a yes.

When Barth returned, she wasn't a hundred percent sure she could do the things she'd planned but had no intention of admitting it to anyone, least of all herself.

The IV had been unhooked the previous night when she began ingesting liquids on her own. She didn't have to resort to anything as theatrical as pulling bloody needles from her arm, but moving had proved a struggle.

By dint of will, and the kind auspices of a hydraulic bed, she sat up straight, then worked her legs over the side. The pain in her neck, shoulders, head—basically all points north of her navel—was bad, but there'd been only token dizziness. As long as she didn't shake her head or stand quickly, it was controllable. Since she could scarcely move her head and could barely stand at all, she didn't think it would be a problem.

Till Barth returned, she tormented her tortured body with small yogic stretches. Though she'd undoubtedly pay for this extravagance later, the movement restored enough range to her neck muscles that she could twist her head ten degrees off center without actually screaming out loud. Her right arm was an even more unqualified success. The upper arm was badly bruised but bone had not been broken, muscle traumatized or tendons torn. Anna felt particularly good about her right arm. Maybe she should have told Barth to bring her duty belt after all.

The hard-won sense of accomplishment was snatched away by the interruption of the phone. John Brown, the chief ranger, was on the other end of the line. Beneath his probably heartfelt condolences, she heard a second message, one that comes to most women in law enforcement whether they deserve it or not.

Maybe she'd been hurt, not because she was careless, not because there were risks inherent to the profession, but because she was female.

Little. Weak.

The effort of sitting up was nothing compared to that of making light of her injuries to her boss. When she was finally able to get off the phone, her head was pounding and she was drenched with sweat that reeked of sickness.

True to his word, if not overly enthusiastic in the execution of it, Barth returned at eleven o'clock bearing a clean uniform and boots. Looking far more grim than Anna thought her condition warranted, he left her clothes on the chair and told her he'd wait outside.

Till she lost it, Anna'd not realized the agility required to dress oneself. By lying on the bed and wriggling, she managed to get on socks, panties, and trousers. During the process she heard her boots fall to the floor. Retrieving and donning them seemed impossible in her diminished state.

The shirt was beyond her capabilities. Her left arm was not quite useless but very nearly so. Shoulder and neck muscles she might have used to circumvent it were in full rebellion.

"Barth," she called through the door.

"I'm here."

"I'm having trouble with my top."

Silence followed. Anna was about to holler again when he replied.

"I couldn't find your, um. It. I went through drawers—I mean I didn't go through them, like, just looked in them and didn't find nothing."

For a moment Anna was baffled. Then she laughed. A big mistake. The pain brought on coughing that racked her broken ribs. For a while she shut down, concentrating on pain management and oxygen. When she'd regained control, she said: "No, I burned those in 1971. I meant my shirt. Give me a hand."

Another silence followed by: "Why don't you ring for the nurse?"

"I'd rather not."

Barth knocked politely then opened the door, his eyes carefully downcast. "They didn't release you, not properly, did they?" he asked accusingly.

"The doctor said I could go," Anna insisted stubbornly.

"You lied."

"Okay, I lied." The fact he was right sharpened her voice more than she liked. "Are you going to help me or not?" She couldn't do it without him and waited, torn between irritation and hope, while he considered.

"Don't blame me if you get yourself permanently crippled up doing this," he warned.

"I won't. Here."

Barth looked up at last. Out of deference to his sensibilities, Anna clutched her pillow modestly over her chest.

The big ranger pinched up the proffered shirt. In his hands, it looked like doll clothes. "This isn't in my job description," he said woodenly. Having learned her lesson, Anna did not laugh. A very nearly irresistible urge to flash him seized her. Dr. Munroe's painkillers, they lowered the inhibitions.

"Just hold it up," she said, careful not to think any wicked thoughts she might suddenly implement. "I'll do the rest."

Dressed, Anna survived the baleful stares of the nurses and Barth's unspoken disapproval, and made it unaided to his patrol car. The dizziness she was so pleased to have escaped found her halfway to the parking lot, but, like a practiced drunk, she trod carefully and managed without weaving or stumbling.

Wretched as she felt, she was not sorry to

have left the hospital. Sun on her face, the smell of hot asphalt and honeysuckle melted the stale food and antiseptic odors from her skin; she felt more like a living thing. Still and all, she allowed Barth to open the door for her and eased into the familiar contours of the Crown Vic's seat with relief.

Barth took his place behind the wheel, cranked the ignition and turned the air-conditioning up. Anna preferred the healing heat of spring, but considering what she'd put the man through, she stoically withstood the cold, soulless air.

Barth didn't put the car in gear. There was an ultimatum brewing; Anna could feel it. To pass the time, she cranked the rearview mirror around to survey the damage to her face. *Gross,* the childish word sprang to mind. Her unshampooed hair was flat and spiky by turns. Bed-head moussed in place with remnants of mud. Her left eye was in the enraged reds and purples of early bruising. The sides of her neck were black with it, and raw contusions striped her left cheek.

She thought she'd expected it, thought she knew how bad it would be, but it shook her.

"Wherever we go, whatever we do, you stay in the car or the deal's off." Barth came out with his terms.

"Of course," Anna said.

"With you there don't seem to be any 'of course' about anything. I'd make you promise, but your promises don't seem to mean diddly-squat when you want your own way. So I'm just telling you. This is how it is, and I got no problem with just stuffing you in the back and locking the doors."

"I'll stay in the car," Anna said. She would too. Not only was her strength of ten men seriously depleted, but one look at her face and she'd realized it would be highly unprofessional to appear in public, in uniform. The taxpayers do not like to see their servers and protectors looking like dog food.

Barth was placated. The car began to move.

The city of Pearl bumped up against the east side of Jackson just across the Pearl River. So named, Barth told her as they crossed the bridge, because of the freshwater oysters once found there. Whether the oysters were extinct and whether they had ever produced a single pearl, Barth didn't know.

Pearl didn't live up to its name. Possibly some fine old Southern architecture existed, but not on the street where the Honda sales lot was located. The town was indistinguishable from a thousand towns Anna'd been through: strip malls, fast food, stoplights and billboards.

Two blocks before they reached Bob Deckert's Hondas, Barth said, "Steve's here."

Anna hadn't been aware that she had closed her eyes until she had to open them to see what he was talking about. Stilwell, very sensibly, had parked in front of Payless Shoes, where he could watch traffic and wait for them. A lesser man would have plopped himself down in Deckert's showroom giving everybody too much time to wonder what he was doing there.

"Dozing?" Barth asked.

The note of concern in his voice annoyed Anna. She didn't answer him. In truth, she barely heard him. He was talking at her deaf ear. Anna sincerely hoped she'd been dozing. If she'd lost consciousness for another reason, she was in serious trouble. *It felt like a nap,* she reassured herself.

Barth pulled the Crown Vic into the Payless lot beside Stilwell. The other district ranger obligingly left his own vehicle to sit in the backseat behind the heavy wire grid protecting Barth and Anna.

"Howdy, howdy," he said amiably.

Anna could turn neither head nor body to look at him. Before she could muster a response, Barth betrayed her. With the swipe of one meaty paw, he cranked the mirror around so Stilwell could see her reflection.

"She oughtn't be here," Barth said stubbornly. "I told her that. You see now what I was getting at?"

"Whoa," Stilwell said. Then, as if needing stronger language, added: "Yikes."

"She's not fit to do anything." Sensing an ally, Barth grew more confident.

"I'm not going to do anything," Anna said placatingly. "You guys are."

"Then why didn't you just tell us what needed doing and stay put in the hospital like you was s'posed to?" Barth asked reasonably.

She had no answer to that. She trusted Barth and Steve. There wasn't much she could do but direct and ask questions at best, get in the way and distract at worst. She'd just had to get out of the hospital. Since she could remember, they'd given her the willies. After Molly's long stint in Columbia-Presbyterian, the willies had escalated to the pre-phobic warmups.

"There was nothing good on TV," she said.

Amazingly, both Steve and Barth knew what she meant, and though their voices were obnoxiously gentle when they addressed her, there was no more argument. Anna was relieved. She needed her strength to tell them what she thought had happened and what she wanted them to do.

"Doesn't make sense," Barth said when she finished. "That buckle wasn't worth much. Shoot, the paraphernalia from the whole Union army detachment wouldn't be worth this kind of stuff. You think Williams searched your house for the buckle?"

"He knew Taco wouldn't be there. I told him that morning he was at the vet. The search was like a lawyer search: no indication anybody'd really done anything."

"And he committed murder and attempted murder for what to him's gotta be a little bitty thing? It doesn't make a whole lot of sense."

"Do you think he was the one put the boys up to alligatoring your garage?" Stilwell asked. "Another attempt on your life."

Anna didn't. She was thinking about the over-time slip of Randy's with Fisheries and Wildlife

426

listed as the assisting agency. She was willing to bet a couple of calls to William and Pete would prove it was a pesky gator and had been left in the care of Ranger Thigpen.

"There's more to it than artifacts," she insisted. "Just what, I don't know. But right now we have exactly nothing: no confession, no witness, no evidence, not even probable cause to get a search warrant. If you two don't scare something up for me, odds are good this will be pinned on one of those boys: Brandon because we can prove he was there or Lockley because he can't prove he wasn't."

True to her promise and because her muscles, apparently not realizing she wasn't dead, had gone into rigor mortis, Anna remained in the patrol car when they reached the Honda sales lot. In an attempt to be kind, Barth left the radio and the air-conditioning on. As soon as he disappeared through the gleaming showroom doors, she struggled up far enough to turn the AC to low and switch radio stations. Gospel, old- time gospel, she'd developed a taste for. Contemporary Christian jangled her nerves.

The radio cooperated, and the next station the needle found played Perry Como's "Catch a Falling Star." Anna could live with that.

Steve and Barth were back in less than half an hour. They said nothing till the car was back on Highway 80 in the flow of traffic. Then Barth told the story.

"Ian McIntire's uneasy about something.

Couldn't tell what, but he's not a fella that can not show. He was upset. He looked to be healthy enough. Not like he'd look if he'd had—if you'd—if he'd suffered the kind of injury you said happened to the man assaulted you. And his hands and knuckles were clean: no bruises, no broken skin."

Stilwell had his elbows on the seat back, sitting forward, his face near the cage. Anna could see his floppy bangs and one of his eyes in the mirror. "Anna, he was real, *real* concerned about you," he said. "Genuinely concerned, seemed to me. The kind of concerned people are when they're scared because of another's injury. Are you and he special pals?"

"Not that I know of."

"Then he wasn't so much scared of what happened to you as scared of what might happen to him because of what happened to you, if you get my drift. Are you sure you had only one attacker?"

"Only one," Anna said. "As I live and breathe. Let's visit our lawyer."

Jimmy Williams wasn't at his office. Home sick, his secretary told Barth. Anna'd stayed in the car, Steve with her. She'd only thought she was in pain earlier. Now that the painkillers were wearing off, she found it hard to keep up appearances and not degenerate into whining and whimpering. Stilwell read the piece of paper a disapproving nurse had thrust upon her when she insisted on checking herself out of the hospital: persistent headaches, nausea, vomiting, loss of consciousness, unusual drowsiness. But for the headache, Anna was clear of alarming symptoms.

"I'll live," she told Steve. "But right now that's not a whole hell of a lot of comfort."

Because it was Mississippi, the last holdout in America against total paranoia, Williams' secretary gave Barth his home address and phone number.

They opted for arriving unannounced, and after they'd wandered around Ridgeland lost for twenty minutes, Barth got them to Dinsmor Estates, a posh community on the northern edge of Jackson.

Oversized homes on undersized lots, all looking more or less alike, formed a backdrop to the BMWs and assorted sport utility vehicles that would never see any off-road use, probably never even be shifted into four-wheel-drive. Stilwell summed up neatly: "*Très chic* track shacks."

The Williams residence was set on a manicured lot just a hair bigger than a house that looked, from the outside, to have given more than half its square footage to an impressive two-story foyer. Barth and Steve went to the door. Anna watched through a haze of pain as one of the double doors opened a crack and they were let inside.

By the time they returned, she had slipped into a lethargy that left her barely enough energy to worry what, precisely, constituted "unusual drowsiness."

Slamming doors and the jolt of Barth's considerable self plopping down on the bench seat roused her.

"Something's screwy," Barth said succinctly.

Stilwell leaned on the seat back, his mouth close to Anna's left ear. When he spoke, she realized she could hear a bit in that ear and was reassured. "Mrs. W. said hubby was on a business trip. Left day before yesterday. Out of town when you were assaulted."

"Allegedly out of town," Anna corrected him.

"We asked why his secretary said he was out sick and she fumbled around a bit, then said it was personal family business. Then said she didn't know where. Not a practiced liar."

"I take it, then, the Mrs. is not also a lawyer," Anna said.

"We got nothing." There was a mix of annoyance and finality in Barth's voice that indicated he was not committed to Anna's theory. "Without more to go on, we can't play hardball. No search. Can't make her tell us where Mr. Williams is."

"You can bet she'll be on the phone to him in a heartbeat," Anna said. "By the time we get a handle on him, any evidence will be gone."

The three of them sat without speaking. Anna could hear Stilwell wriggling around. Hands on the wheel in the ten and two position, Barth stared straight ahead. They'd come because Anna had asked them, but the spark of faith her surmisings had ignited in them was pretty much dead. They were tired of chasing wild geese and wanted to go home.

She was tempted to do the same. Pain, fatigue and the tail end of the painkillers had left her muzzy-headed. She was beginning to wonder if the answers that had burned so bright in her concussed cranium were just figments of a bruised imagination.

Maybe if the lives of children hadn't been in the balance, she'd have given up.

"She seem like a nice lady?" Anna asked.

"Real nice," Barth said. "Got two little kids just as cute as the dickens."

"Did she know why you were asking after her husband?"

"I don't think so. She seemed more confused and scared than protective."

"Time to play the sympathy card," Anna said. "Let's go show her my face."

"It'll scare the kids," Barth said.

He wasn't kidding.

"The little buggers'll just have to get over it," she replied, and turned her attention to the painful business of getting out of the vehicle. Going up the walk, she leaned on Steve's arm. She pretended it was just for effect, and he pretended to believe her. Barth remained in the car. Three rangers, even if one was small and looking the worse for wear, would be too intimidating for Anna's purposes. Stilwell rang the bell, and they waited. The sun was high and hot. In the shade of the porch, mosquitoes pooled, pleased at having lunch delivered. Anna suffered a couple bites on her neck and face. With the wearing off of whatever Dr. Munroe had given her to ease the hurt, her upper torso had seized up. She could barely raise her elbows. The blows to her neck had traumatized the muscles controlling shoulders and arms.

"Maybe she slipped out the back," Steve suggested. He sounded hopeful.

"No. She's here." Anna hadn't the energy to explain why she was so sure. The house just felt occupied, a faint tension generated by those hiding within. "Ring again."

The second bell brought Mrs. Williams to the door. She wore that harassed angry look nice women get just before they go ballistic. Anna was familiar with the phenomenon. Anger, real red-hot anger, was not okay for females. Most learned to repress it so successfully that they didn't even know it was there till it erupted full-blown. It was one of the many things that made dealing with women more challenging than dealing with men. Women's anger went from zero to sixty in sixty seconds—no warning signs, no time to get out of the way.

The sight of Anna disarmed her before she went off on them. "Oh my goodness!" she exclaimed. Her hand flew to her cheek in a cliché of feminine concern that was as genuine as the shock in her eyes.

"Do I look that bad?" Anna asked and smiled lopsidedly to keep Mrs. Williams' sympathy.

"No. No. You look... I'm so sorry. Come in. Sit down. Can I get you anything? Goodness."

From the kind flusterment of Mrs. James Williams, it was clear she had no inkling that Anna was the woman who'd tried to rip her husband's balls off. "We can't stay, but thank you," Anna said and didn't have to feign the weak and weary tone. "I was just hoping you could help me."

"Of course," Mrs. Williams said promptly, then a look of fear scuttled across her even features. "If I can," she added cautiously. Anna guessed she worried about the lies her husband had asked her to tell.

"A friend of mine," Anna said, "an elderly lady, has written a book. She's got no money and hopes this'll pay for her funeral when the time comes. Your husband said he'd take a look at it—you know, tell her what to do. Well, she's gotten to fussing and wants it back. Do you know if Mr. Williams has it here or at his office?"

Such was Mrs. Williams's relief at not being asked again where her husband was or why, she fell all over herself to be of assistance. While Anna and Steve stood inside the front door, she bustled through the foyer twice and eventually returned with a brown lidless box that had once held canned goods but now contained a sheaf of handwritten pages tied in a neat bundle by two bits of kitchen string.

"Is this it? Mrs. Ruby Tangeman?" She proffered the manuscript. Anna forced her arms up far enough to receive the box, holding it carefully by the edges.

"That's it," Anna said. "Thanks a million. Ruby will be so glad to get it back."

Anna insisted on carrying her prize herself. Steve hovered half a step behind her, one hand on her elbow as if she were a tottery old woman. It was annoying, but since falling over was a real possibility, she accepted Stilwell's kindness as the lesser of two evils. He opened the door for her. In order to regain her seat, she had to relinquish her prize. "Careful," she cautioned Barth as he reached across the seat to take it. "Edges only. Fingertip and thumb."

"What's in it? Goldfish?" he grumbled, but did as she requested.

"Are you going to tell us what we risked life and limb facing down a housewife and two toddlers for or are you going to torture us indefinitely?" Steve asked after they'd driven in silence for several miles.

"If I'm not mistaken, this manuscript belongs to a lady in Leo Fullerton's congregation. It's the book she wrote that he was trying to help her get published," Anna said. "I think it's why Danni was killed. Why I got beat up."

No great revelatory congratulations followed this assertion. Anna'd dropped down another notch on the credibility scale. Not only was she new, female and a Yankee; now she was an invalid as well. Head injury no less. Only slightly more believable than a raving lunatic. A couple more miles rolled by, then Steve said from the backseat: "Let me get this straight. You think Williams figured this was going to be a bestseller so he steals it? Going to be the next Southern lawyer to make it big in the world of publishing? My limited experience would suggest even copyrights are a waste of time. Not only does nobody want to steal your work, you can't *give* the stuff away."

"Besides, why not just kill Ruby?" Barth put in. "The Posey girl's got nothing to do with the book."

"Not the book itself," Anna said. "What's in it. You said that buckle I found was from Grant's vanished unit. I found it where Danni was killed, where they'd been digging all this time."

"It's still not worth enough money to murder somebody over," Barth said.

"What about *all* the stuff from that unit: swords, guns, buttons? What if he knew what happened to the soldiers?" Anna asked. "The entire unit?"

Barth thought for a while. "Still not that much. Not for a man like Williams. I'm betting he makes good money."

"There's something more to it besides buckles and swords," Anna said. "There's got to be. And it's in here." She tapped the papers tied up with string.

Nobody argued with her. Not because they thought she was right but because they felt sorry for her. Shoot, she felt sorry for herself.

"Maybe some hard evidence," Anna said when her mind focused again. That perked the boys up.

"How so?" Barth asked cautiously.

"Fingerprints. The box and the first and

last page of Mrs. Tangeman's manuscript. We'll check the prints against those lifted from Danni's throat and my ankle. We get a match, we at least got Williams for assault."

Steve Stilwell was left at his vehicle in Pearl. Anna and Barth threaded their way through Jackson's simple freeway system.

At Barth's insistence, they stopped at Kroger and got her prescription filled. Too tired to put it away, she set it on the seat beside her and was increasingly glad to know it was there as the last vestiges of Dr. Munroe's drugs wore off and a blinding, thought-consuming ache settled into the bones of her skull.

Ruby Tangeman's manuscript was still cradled on her lap. It weighed very little. Anna thumbed through it. Eighty-six pages. Not a short story, not a book. Not even the right length for a novella. Leo Fullerton's dreams of publishing on Ruby's behalf had been doomed from the outset.

The manuscript was handwritten. Anna's head throbbed at the thought of reading it.

"You want to go home or what?" Barth intruded into her thoughts.

Anna was afoot, she remembered, newly rescued from the soul-searing embrace of modern medicine.

"What time is it?"

"Two-forty," Barth read off the dashboard clock.

Home sounded good. Lying down. Quiet.

"No, pull into a gas station, Wal-Mart,

anywhere we can park awhile. I want you to read this with me. My Civil War history is confined to what I remember from *Gone With the Wind*."

Barth snorted in pointed agreement that her education had been severely lacking.

"Randy's coming on at four. You want me to get him up here early?" Barth asked.

Anna realized she was scared of Randy Thigpen. Not afraid he'd hurt her either personally or professionally. Just afraid of the unpleasantness of being in the same life with a sexist asshole.

Next week he'd be off the four-to-midnight shift. She'd be seeing a whole lot more of him. Probably to the good. Proximity would end the sense of hiding and avoiding that had grown up around her the past few days.

"No," she gave Barth the short answer.

He pulled the patrol car into a Conoco off Interstate 20, parked in the shade of the minimart and left the engine running. The air-conditioning was stiffening Anna's muscles. Not wanting a mutiny, she suffered in silence. "Here, you take the first forty-three and give me the last half." She set the manuscript on the seat between them. "Skim for content. Leo had access to this. Jimmy Williams took enough interest in it to spirit it out of the preacher's house."

"Think Mrs. Tangeman has your answers?" Barth asked. "An old black woman, no teeth, no money, no education?" Barth was tired. His voice had taken on an edge.

"History. Memories. Isn't that what glues y'all together? Ruby's got those. Start."

Ruby's story was not easily pieced together. The crabbed writing waxed hieroglyphic in places and the narrative wandered much as Anna suspected an old woman's mind, too full of stories, memories and dreams, might. She found she could not "skim for content" as she'd bade Barth do, but had to creep through one word at a time. From the huffing and resettling of haunches across the seat, Barth was doing the same.

As the sense of it began to leak through the stilted prose, Anna lost her impatience and was drawn in. Half an hour passed before she reached the end. Then she looked up as if coming out of a trance. Barth was staring at her, his reading glasses squatting on the broad flat nose.

"Give me the beginning," she said as he was saying: "Lemme see the end." They swapped halves and silence reclaimed them.

Another thirty minutes and Anna put down the manuscript, rubbed her eyes. "Wow," she said. "Can I buy you a Coke?"

Barth accepted. She creaked inside, pumped coins into the machine in the gas station and returned to the car with their drinks. It was an effort to hold the bottles, two in one hand, her left arm in its sling, and it was an effort to lift them up to place them on the seat. So much so, Anna grunted.

"You okay?" Barth said as he rescued his Coke.

"Right as rain. Tell me what you got out of that." She nodded at the manuscript.

"It's quite some story," Barth said. "Gonna undo a lot of myths and goodwill if you push it."

"Keep digging, you mean?"

"Find the letters or what's got to be letters."

"I don't need letters," Anna said. "And I've no taste for spoiling two sets of pretty stories. All I want's motive."

Barth nudged his reading glasses into place and thumbed through the pages once again. "Here's what sounds like happened. Ruby Tangeman's great-grandmother was born a slave on a plantation in Natchez. When Grant's army came through here, she was around eight, maybe ten years old—old enough to remember."

"Opal Tangeman."

"Just Opal. House slave. 'The head Yankee gentleman and his angels of the Lord took to Miss Alyssum,' " Barth read aloud.

"Head Yankee gentleman? General Grant?" Anna ventured.

"Angels of the Lord: his Union army come to free the slaves. Who else?"

"Beats me. What about Alyssum? Not a slave, I'm thinking."

"No." Barth read on. " 'There was comings and goings and everybody scared and polite but Miss Alyssum. She happy like a girl and her husband, Opal said when I was little, like a storm cloud fixin' to rain on everybody.' Then pages of cousins and whatever." Barth went through the loose sheaf. "Here she mentions it again. 'Great-grandma Opal liked smelling letters Miss Alyssum wrote to the Northern gentleman.' "

"Perfumed," Anna said. "Love letters."

"And here." Barth had filtered through more of Ruby's memories. " 'Great-grandma told of the Angels of the Lord meaning the Yankee soldiers maybe down from Vicksburg and how they rode down and Miss Alyssum giving them a bunch of papers tied in blue and green ribbons. Afterward going all to tears and the master kicking in the door.' "

"What do you figure?" Anna asked. "Miss Alyssum returning letters—let's guess love letters since she tied them up in ribbon and cried to be parted from them—to General Grant?"

"Could be. Husband gets wind of it and starts kicking in doors."

"Read that next part," Anna said. "I dog-eared the page."

Barth turned the pages carefully till he found the place she referred to. " 'Great-grandma said that night seven of the field slaves run off except one boy what was shot in the head and lived but didn't talk no more. That also was the night Miss Alyssum was dressed and killed and her husband killed, too.' "

"It makes sense," Anna said. "You said that buckle I found was from a Union soldier, one of the squad that vanished. That, put together with Ruby's story, explains it. Port Gibson wasn't 'too pretty to burn.' Grant had a mistress there. I got to thinking about the vanished squad, the plantation owner who shot his slaves."

"This says 'run off.' " Barth tapped the manuscript with his glasses.

"What would you tell a little girl when six grown-ups she knew were shot?" Anna asked.

"I'd tell her they run off," Barth admitted. "Caught the freedom train."

"So that same night he dressed his wife as a Yankee soldier and killed her, then killed himself. The wife was Great-grandma Opal's Alyssum. Her husband killed her for infidelity, then got his slaves to kill Grant's men and bury them where they fell along the Trace at Rocky Springs," Anna finished.

"Then he killed the slaves to keep them quiet. Or because they knew he'd been shamed."

"You can check, can't you? Find out the name of that Port Gibson alderman's slain wife."

"Should be easy enough," Barth said.

"Jimmy Williams must have added it up the same way we did. He and his buddies were mining those dead soldiers."

"For artifacts? Hardly worth killing for."

"For handwritten letters from Ulysses S. Grant to a Southern wife not his own. Worth a fortune," Anna said.

"If they exist."

"If they exist. If they ever existed. If an enraged cuckold didn't find and burn them.

Let's get that search warrant for Williams's place. Push it. See if we can get it for this afternoon. We'll look for shovels, Civil War clothes, and papers. Any copies of notes, research, et cetera. Artifacts from the vanished squadron. Let's do it before Williams gets home."

Barth looked as if he would protest the hour, the effort, the haste, but in the end, he didn't.

"I'll call Sheriff Davidson, see if he can expedite this thing," Anna said.

It was after six by the time they got the warrant. Anna was so tired she was sick and the aches had penetrated to the bone, yet she dared not veil her mind with painkillers.

Once the group was armed with the warrant, things moved quickly. Mrs. Williams had left town suddenly to be with her husband. The baby-sitter cooperated with a relish that didn't speak well of loyalty to the family.

Jimmy had left without the chance to cover his tracks. The artifacts from Union soldiers in Grant's detachment were found meticulously cataloged and stored along with a photocopy of Ruby Tangeman's manuscript and copious notes speculating on the letters from General Grant to Alyssum.

The coup de grâce was in an unlocked desk drawer in the captain's study: Leo Fullerton's suicide note.

Anna found Barth at Jimmy Williams' desk holding a single sheet of paper and looking stricken. "Pastor Fullerton killed the girl," he said in a voice so devoid of emotion it rang hollow.

"Let me see." Anna crossed the uncarpeted floor. Williams' home had been a dream to search. Furnishings were sparse and classy. Very few tchotchkes cluttered the shelves. A military orderliness was maintained despite the existence of small children.

Barth handed Anna the note, Leo's last communiqué on this side of the River Jordan. Though the light was good and the type of the usual size, letters blurred and Anna waited while a wave of dizziness passed and her vision cleared.

Pastor Fullerton began with a plea for forgiveness: forgiveness from his flock for abandoning them, from his god for the sin of despair, and from his friends for betraying their part in the death of Danielle Posey.

He told of how he'd struck her down in fear when she suddenly thrust herself out of the bushes above where he dug. He pleaded that whoever read this should know that in the dark and the fear he'd thought her a bear or a bobcat, not a girl. He wrote of how, when he and Ian had been sent back to camp for the rope and sheeting, he knew he could not live with what he had done and could not live with a deceit that would cause racial strife.

"Danni Posey didn't die of the blow to the head," Anna said. "She died of a broken neck. Fullerton didn't kill her, Williams did. While Ian and Leo went back for the sheet, Williams checked her carotid. We found his prints. She was alive and he snapped her neck."

"That just makes them both murderers," Barth said sadly. "The fact Leo's blow didn't kill her doesn't mean it couldn't've."

Anna could see the moral logic in that. "Bag it," she said and handed Barth the suicide note.

"The DeForest boy was telling the truth," Barth remarked.

"Eventually," Anna conceded. "He and the other boys terrified and chased Danni, but she stumbled on death from another quarter."

"That makes them murderers in a way," Barth said.

"We are all murderers in a way. It doesn't do to track the threads of death too far from their end."

"Why do you suppose they dropped the body where they did?"

"My best guess?" Anna thought a moment. "I'd bet Williams instigated the half-assed KKK red herring. Ian and Leo couldn't stomach it and backed out partway through. Williams couldn't engineer it alone, so Danni was left where they dropped her."

"Sad for everybody," Barth said. "Even the doers."

Ian McIntire was arrested as an accessory. Anna left as soon as he called for a lawyer, which was about the same instant he opened his door. Williams would be arrested when found and that wouldn't be long. The babysitter kindly gave them a number Mrs. Williams had left where she could be reached in case of an emergency with the children. Two calls established that Williams was in Birmingham at the Methodist Hospital. He had undergone surgery for the removal of his left testicle. Barth winced at the news, but Anna was unmoved.

It was nearly midnight when all was said and done. Anna was no longer able to hide either her pain or her fatigue and waited in the car while Barth finished up at the Madison County Sheriff's Office, where they had taken McIntire.

On the Crown Vic's radio, she heard Randy Thigpen make a traffic stop. When he got wind of the fact that they'd had all the fun without him, he was going to be about as easy to get along with as a badger with a sore paw.

When the time came, Anna would exhibit fairness and genuine concern for his issues. Faking that shouldn't be a problem and it would give her the distance she needed to keep from challenging him to a duel.

She'd fallen into a loose and miserable doze by the time Barth returned to the car, sleep full of dreams of spiders, rocks and things that gave the body disease.

Thoughtfully, he refrained from asking her if she was okay. Adjusting the radio to a station playing the gentlest strains of Ravel, he curled into his own thoughts and left her to hers.

Moving through the darkness of the Natchez

Trace, headlights cutting swatches of color to the sides of the road, fear nagged at Anna from the utter night of woods that pressed too close, felt too full of life.

She was glad when the ride was over.

"You gonna call Sheriff Davidson?" Barth asked. Davidson had assisted by phone, but an ugly domestic situation erupting in violence had kept him in Port Gibson. "He's gonna want to know the details."

Anna pried herself painfully out of the Crown Vic. She still suffered from a vague feeling that Paul Davidson was a shit. Though she couldn't remember why, she had no desire to talk to the man. "You do it," she said. "If anybody wants me, tell them I died and went to a hot bath."

Clutching her painkillers to her bosom like an old drunk with his bottle of rotgut, she shuffled toward the sanctuary of home and Taco and Piedmont.

19

Barth backed out of her drive and left. Soft clouds, gray in the moonlight, had materialized, wet and close to the treetops. There wasn't a breath of air, and in this strange time between late night and dawn, even the forest was still.

Anna slowed as she approached the now

familiar red door that was to open on home. It didn't feel like home. She heard the hum of Barth's tires change in tone as he turned right on the Trace, headed south. When the sound was gone, she was still standing on her front step.

She was scared. Craven, soul-sucking fear made her want to whimper and hide. She'd been beaten; blinded and beaten into the ground. An unseen man had tried to take her life with the brutal pounding of his fists. She was scared to stay out on her front walk, exposed, knowing another blow would undo her. And she was scared to go in her own house, scared of the shadows under the eaves and the dark places behind the door. She wanted to cry but was afraid a sound, even the smallest breath of a sigh, would call down some evil.

Anna had been afraid before—many times. Fear was good, heightening the senses, adding fleetness to the feet. But never like this. Not the knowledge that she could be shattered into so many pieces that all the king's horses and all the king's men couldn't put her back together again.

The longer she stood in the waspish moonlight the more frightened she became, unable to go in, unwilling to stay out. Fleetingly, she had a picture of Frank finding her in the morning, cowering on the stoop, her mind gone. The image should have been absurd, but it wasn't. It felt prophetic and loosed another bowel-jangling wave of terror.

From within, Taco starting barking. The

sudden staccato stab of sound hit her like a cattle prod, and she flinched. The animals. Even in the face of a paralyzing terror she'd not felt since childhood nightmares, she would take care of her animals.

"It's me, Taco," she said and pushed open the unlocked door. Her vocal cords had seized up along with the sphincters of her body and the words emerged as a high-pitched whisper. Despite the Minnie Mouse voice and Raging Bull face, Taco recognized her. She was greeted with a whine, a whapping of his tail against his bedding and the stink of an uncleaned kennel.

Taco was a cripple. Frank went off duty at three-thirty. The poor animal hadn't been out since breakfast. Guilt was added to the stew of emotions in Anna's soul. Taco didn't help any by taking the blame on himself, looking at her with shame in his dark eyes, his bedding stretched out where he'd pulled his bandage-swathed body as far from the scene of the crime as health and strength permitted. Shoulders and head were pushed up against the metal where the furnace had stopped his progress. Atop the heater, belly spread on the summer-cool tin, Piedmont had risen above the offal, but Anna noted with a second wave of guilt, the cat had not abandoned his friend.

"Poor old guy," she said to the dog, shamed by how joyfully he greeted her worthless self, grinning and trying to wriggle close enough to slather her with canine caresses. "It's not

448

your fault; it's mine. Let's not talk about it."
She knelt with great care, trying to keep her
head balanced on its precarious perch at the
apex of her spine. "Let's get you outside.
Your poor bladder must be the size of a
weather balloon. What a guy. Superdog."
Anna crooned compliments to Taco for holding
his water in hopes he'd forget he'd slipped in
other areas as she worked her hands gently
under his seventy-five pounds. Or was it now
seventy? What did a dog's leg weigh?

Whatever it was it was too much. The blows
to her shoulders and the side of her neck,
the hairline fracture of her humerus combined to drain the strength from her arms. She
could not lift Taco, and she started to cry.

Kneeling on the hardwood, she rested her
forehead against the lab's side and wept
because she was a terrible ranger, a damn
Yankee, a woman, a cripple and a lousy pet
owner, useless to man and beast. Had there
been worms nearby she couldn't even have eaten
them; she was not worthy.

Knocking at the door scared her so badly that
her wretched sobs were jerked up in a violent
hiccup and she froze as a rabbit freezes in the
shadow of a hawk. The knocking came again.
She flinched at each rap as if the knuckles
banged on her skull and not the hardwood of
the door.

"Anna? It's Paul."

The announcement of the sheriff's name did
not comfort. Perhaps he would go away if
she played dead. Hugging the dog, Piedmont

butting worriedly against her ribs, Anna tried to make herself invisible. Behind her, she heard the door pushed open. Taco began to bark, high alarm barks that cut into her bruised brain with the delicate touch of a double-bladed axe.

"Oh Lord! Are you all right? Anna…"

Footsteps sounded on hardwood followed by the muffled tread of shoes on the Navajo rug. Then warm arms were around both Anna and the dog. Taco stopped barking. Piedmont fled the crush, leaping back to the top of the heater.

"Did you fall? What's happening? Talk to me, Anna. Do you know your name? Where you are?" Paul Davidson's hands were running over her head, her neck, down her arms, as he deftly sought injuries in the way of those accustomed to field medicine. His skin was warm, his hair fragrant, his breath sweet, his touch gentle. For the first time in more years than she could remember, Anna wanted help, wanted a man to lift her burdens just for an hour or so, wanted to be held, told everything was going to be all right, tucked into bed. A piecemeal fragment of an old play her husband, Zach, had starred in at dinner theater in New Jersey the year they'd been married flashed to mind. *Harvey*. The psychiatrist sharing his greatest fantasy: to lie and rest, a beautiful woman holding his hand saying "there, there…"

That's what Anna wanted. She wanted it from Paul Davidson. Yet she could not unbend, not even to speak. There was an iron band around her heart—or her brain—made of two parts suspicion and one part self-preservation. Anna didn't trust him, and she couldn't remember why. Tears came again, weak and womanly.

Lest he see them and judge her as she judged herself, she buried her face in Taco's side. He licked her elbow, the only part of her he could reach. Prickles of affectionate angst scraped her scalp: Piedmont reaching down from his perch to claw concernedly at her hair. Anna knew she did not deserve such loyalty and the tears came thicker, hotter, drenching the foul-smelling fur she hid her face in.

Paul's warm hands left off their search for wounds. Whether he deemed her structurally sound or beyond saving, he walked away. Feeling both safer and abandoned, Anna pulled her face out of Taco's side and disentangled the cat's claws from her hair. In a minute, when she heard the front door close behind the retreating sheriff, she would stand up. Sit up. Something.

Instead of the slamming of a door, footsteps returned. Anna stifled an impulse to dive back into the dog and another to hide her face in her hands. She couldn't bring herself to open her eyes.

All that is required is that I look sane for a minute or so, she told herself. *Say something like "I'm fine" or "It looks worse that it is."* She opened her eyes a slit. Looked to Taco for courage, to Piedmont for attitude, but still she didn't speak.

"Come on," Paul said. "Upsa-daisy. I'm running you a bath. While you're soaking, me and the critters will get squared away. Take our evening constitutional."

Anna allowed herself to be led, coaxed, managed. It was sufficiently uncharacteristic that she wondered at herself even as she watched, a disinterested third party. Maybe it was the painkillers. Maybe it was the pain. Whatever had robbed her of her will, it was consistent. She said nothing till she was standing by the tub, the sheriff unbuttoning her shirt. Then she managed: "I can undress myself." Had he argued, she wouldn't have protested.

Her clothes dropped where she stood. Unlacing boots was a exercise in pain and enfeebled frustration, but it never crossed her mind to call him back. When she finally attained it, the hot bath was heaven.

Paul tapped on the door twice. Once he offered to bring her wine. She refused and knew she'd quit drinking. Again. Maybe for good this time. Mississippi was bound to have AA meetings. Tomorrow—the day after—she'd think about that. The second knock was to bring her dry, clean pajamas and tell her dinner was ready. Piedmont slipped in with the pj's and took his accustomed place on the edge of the tub, snaky orange tail swishing in the water. Idly, she wondered if he did that intentionally to take her mind off her troubles.

Dried, pajamaed and ensconced in the Morris chair, Anna sat while Paul brought her dinner of tomato soup and half a tuna fish sandwich. It was the meal her mother had served whenever she was sick, and Anna felt herself tearing up again as he set the tray across her knees.

"You don't have to do this," she said to ward off the untoward emotion.

"Yes, I do." He pulled up a footstool and folded himself down at her feet. A newly washed Taco dragged himself over to be near Davidson.

Traitor, Anna thought unkindly as she spooned soup into her mouth.

"I filed for divorce today," the sheriff said.

Anna forced the soup down through a suddenly constricted esophagus. That was it; that was why she'd not trusted him. The memory returned and with it a burning flush of shame. Mrs. Davidson had called to pay her respects shortly before Anna was attacked. The ensuing madness—or her own need to forget it—had driven the scene from her mind.

"We were married for eight years," Davidson said. "We've been separated for three. I filed for divorce today," he repeated.

"Why did you wait three years?" Anna asked.

"I never needed a divorce till now."

Tears came and Anna was helpless to stop them. Truth be told, she didn't try. They washed away the rusted iron she'd felt clamped around her chest.

"Do you want to go to bed?" he asked kindly.

Anna laughed and didn't mind that it hurt. "Yes. Now I want you to take me to bed."